J M Krause
Nov/12

High Orbit Hero

*A Blackmailed Teen's Struggle
to Protect His Sister*

Blackmailed Secrets Book One

J.M. Krause

iUniverse, Inc.
Bloomington

High Orbit Hero
A Blackmailed Teen's Struggle to Protect His Sister
Blackmailed Secrets Book One

This is a work of fiction. All of the characters, names, incidents, organizations, and dialogue in this novel are either the products of the author's imagination or are used fictitiously.

iUniverse books may be ordered through booksellers or by contacting:
iUniverse
1663 Liberty Drive
Bloomington, IN 47403
www.iuniverse.com
1-800-Authors (1-800-288-4677)

Because of the dynamic nature of the Internet, any web addresses or links contained in this book may have changed since publication and may no longer be valid. The views expressed in this work are solely those of the author and do not necessarily reflect the views of the publisher, and the publisher hereby disclaims any responsibility for them.

Any people depicted in stock imagery provided by Thinkstock are models, and such images are being used for illustrative purposes only. Certain stock imagery © Thinkstock.

ISBN: 978-1-4759-4529-4 (sc)
ISBN: 978-1-4759-4530-0 (hc)
ISBN: 978-1-4759-4531-7 (e)

Library of Congress Control Number: 2012917381

Printed in the United States of America

iUniverse rev. date: 9/20/2012

Chapter 1

"We picked our next little whore." Chin Hon pointed to the group of chatting schoolgirls in the holoview's two-meter cube. "Thought you might be interested." He bared his teeth in a fierce smile and adjusted the holoview.

Geoff Anders watched anxiously as the picture zoomed in on a girl with wavy chestnut hair, wide coffee-brown eyes, and a dimple in her right cheek. Barbara, his little sister! Geoff crossed his arms and clenched his fists underneath his elbows. Letting Chin and Lui see his anger and fear at them targeting his sister would not help his situation.

"What the hell do you want with her?" asked Geoff. "She's just a kid."

"Young is fun," Lui Ko said from the love seat on the other side of the holoview.

Chin smiled again, but his obsidian eyes burned into Geoff with no trace of humor. He stood up. Shorter than average, he still looked down at Geoff.

"She's got something I want," Chin said. His straight black hair brushed the shoulders of his embroidered magenta shirt. Prominent cheekbones made his black eyes appear small.

"What's that?" Even as he asked, Geoff realized Chin was only interested in Barbara as a means to control Geoff.

"There's a Taurid who's mouthing off and making waves," said Chin. "She's my way to get him back in line."

"You could try talking to the guy," Geoff said.

"I gave instructions. You ignored them. Now you pay."

"What?" asked Geoff. Ion-blasted, mutant hell! They were going to order him to lift something from a place with real security, so he would end up in youth rehabilitation or jail. His parents would blow orbit.

Lui tossed his long braid behind his shoulder and chuckled. His melonlike cheeks bunched up, nearly hiding his milk-chocolate eyes. His soft bulk jiggled beneath his navy shirt and pants that looked like silk pajamas.

Ice trickled down Geoff's spine. How many things worse than rehab were there?

"You know what the Simba is?" asked Chin.

"Yeah," replied Geoff. Chin made a come-on gesture, so Geoff added, "It's a dance." It was a competition dance, like Latino and ballroom dancing. He knew that because Barbara and their mother watched the dance shows on the holoview.

"At least you didn't say gay guy's dance," said Chin. "Lui and I used to dance. When he was skinny, we won our share of trophy money."

Lui made a rude gesture in Chin's direction.

Ignoring him, Chin continued, "There's a team in a rival family polishing their boots for the October competition. I want to beat them again, but since Lui'd die onstage, I need a new partner. You're it."

"Huh?" Geoff tried to think of a way out. "I can't dance."

Lui laughed and said, "That's the fun part."

"You have a pretty face and a feel for music," said Chin. "You'll have to learn the rest. That or—" He glanced at the image of Barbara frozen in the holoview and raised his eyebrows.

Geoff said, "Spell it out."

"You having trouble getting the message?" asked Lui.

Geoff kept his eyes on Chin's.

"Say it, and give your word," he insisted.

"Maybe you're smarter than you look," Chin said. "We won't touch your sister if you train with me and dance in the competition. You have my word."

"All right." Even as Geoff agreed, he wished he could take it back. He felt sick at the sight of Chin's grin.

"Can you touch your toes?" Lui asked.

"What?" asked Geoff.

"You gotta be flexible to dance," said Lui. "Can you touch your toes?"

"Yeah." Geoff had been in a gymnastics club until a few years ago. He had been very flexible then and still was.

"Here." Chin tossed a data card that was half the size of his palm and as thick as his fingernails across the room.

Geoff picked the strip of plastic out of the air.

"Do those exercises at least four times a day," Chin ordered. "Don't be stupid and pull a muscle, or I'll get the Mad Medic to fix you. It's quick, but it hurts a helluva lot worse than any injury."

"I got school and a job," Geoff said. "When do you expect me to exercise?"

"In the morning, at noon, after school, and at night," Chin listed. "Do it. I'll know if you don't."

"Yeah." Geoff pocketed the card. He hated mornings. He never got up until the last possible second.

"You don't work at the arcade 'til Friday this week," said Chin. "Tonight, tomorrow, and Thursday, meet us at the rec center on the heavy deck, entrance C, at 2055. Wear a snug T-shirt and bicycle shorts."

"Yeah." If they knew when he worked, they must have been planning this long enough to steal a schedule. Or else the families making up the Lung Organization owned the arcade.

"Don't tell anyone," Chin ordered. "If word gets out I'm dancing this fall—"

Chin did not complete the sentence, but Geoff nodded to indicate he got the message.

"Wait for Trevor out front." Chin pointed to the door.

Geoff left the apartment and stomped down the parquet floor, not that stomping was very effective in the two-thirds gravity of this deck. He was really deep-spaced without an air tank. Why did he have a blasted sister anyway?

By the time Geoff reached the front entrance and stepped out into the wide station corridor, he admitted the mess he was in had a lot more to do with himself than with Barbara. He plopped onto a bench and scowled at the flowering vines across the hall. Chin wouldn't call him pretty if he looked more rugged. His fine, almost delicate bone structure was his second worst curse in life. The first was his face. His wide-spaced, large brown eyes, straight little nose, and girlie mouth always gave him trouble. Being called pretty had landed him in more fights than he cared to count.

Maybe Dad could find a way out of this blackmail, but no one in Geoff's family even knew he belonged to the gang. How could he explain this? Besides, there obviously wasn't any way out.

Trevor's cheerful voice interrupted Geoff's gloomy thoughts.

"You look as happy as a politician named ambassador to Ur-anus," Trevor said. He sipped from a can of cola that Geoff suspected held some form of alcohol in addition to the soda pop.

"Blast off." Geoff got up and headed toward the transit stop.

Trevor walked with him. He stood a head taller than Geoff and was nearly twice as broad. Except for his light gray eyes, the features of his round face clearly showed his Chinese ancestry. A bright blue ring in the center of his left eyebrow matched the blue hoops dangling below the straight black hair covering his ears. The three earrings in each ear were a set with the chunky chain around his neck and one of his four finger-rings. Trevor was dressed in khaki jeans and a shirt with blue top-stitching that matched his jewelry; Geoff wore blue jeans and a purple-and-orange soccer jersey.

"I obviously had a better time there than you did," the larger boy said. "What'd they want?"

"You know better than to ask," replied Geoff.

Trevor shrugged and looked away.

Geoff scowled up at him and then stopped and planted his fists on his hips.

"They told you to ask, didn't they?" demanded Geoff. "To see if I'd say anything."

Trevor met his eyes and said, "I told them you wouldn't."

"What would you have done if I did?" asked Geoff.

Trevor shrugged again and said, "I dunno. I figured you wouldn't."

"What'd they tell you?" Geoff asked as he continued walking.

"You're working on a project that'll take some time. I should run interference if you need."

"I have to cut our game time short tonight," Geoff said. "And tomorrow...and the day after. The bastards aren't leaving me any free time. They're not happy unless everyone follows their orbit!"

"Black hole that kind of talk." Trevor's earrings chimed as he looked to see if someone was watching them.

"Why should it matter?" Geoff glanced down the hall lined with glowing and flashing hologram storefronts interspersed with a few potted shrubs. The twenty or so people around them were paying no attention to the two teens. "I'm not part of a Lung family. I'll never be more than a fringe runner."

They walked in silence for half a minute, and then Trevor said, "There." He pointed to a convenience store across the hall. "Let's get a snack."

"Okay." They were both hungry, and it wouldn't occur to Trevor to pay for snack food. At least Trevor chose places with weak security. How he knew he never said, and Geoff did not ask.

They walked in together. Trevor got the store attendant to open the display of sports-star collector holos. Each thumbnail-sized button held a holographic image of a sports figure frozen in action and would project ninety seconds of a great moment in that person's career.

Pretending boredom, Geoff circled until he could see the security monitors behind the counter. He checked what angle the cameras covering the snacks recorded from and strolled back to Trevor. After a moment, he wandered away.

Geoff went down one aisle and back up the next, tucking treats, including candies and chocolates only made on Terra, into his sleeves and pockets.

"Aren't you done yet?" Geoff asked when he returned to Trevor.

"Hold orbit," said Trevor. He moved his left forearm across the counter scanner so that it could read his implant, and then he leaned forward for the retina scan to authorize a bank transaction.

The clerk bagged Trevor's holo buttons and handed them to him.

"Have a good day, boys," he said.

"Thanks," Trevor replied. "Be seeing you." Outside the store, Trevor raised one hand to shoulder height, his palm outward, and grinned.

Not wanting his friend to know how much their visit to Chin and Lui had upset him, Geoff slapped Trevor's open hand and said, "Shadowhand and the evil genius, Trevor the Terrible, complete another successful mission to retrieve rations from the enemy stronghold."

Trevor laughed. As they headed toward the transit stop, he asked, "What'd you get me?"

Geoff handed him an apple.

"That's it?" Trevor exclaimed. "We hardly ever hit a store with Terran stuff, and I bought a pile of buttons!"

Geoff smiled and passed him two chocolate bars, a bag of candy, and a package of gum. He took a couple of pieces of the beef jerky, which had been made in the station's protein production lab, and gave Trevor the rest of the package.

"That all you want?" asked Trevor.

Geoff, his mouth full, nodded. Chin and Lui had ruined his appetite. Besides, stolen snacks didn't taste as good as they used to.

"Which ones are mine?" asked Geoff.

"Doesn't matter." Trevor tossed Geoff half a dozen of the colorful buttons. He lifted his ringed eyebrow and asked, "What?"

"What...what?"

"You've got that shove-the-station-out-of-orbit look," replied Trevor.

Geoff sighed and said, "I don't see what the big deal is if I don't always do things exactly like Lung wants. I don't have ancestors who worked with your ancestors. As long as I don't go against you all, it shouldn't matter what I do with my life."

"It's *us*," said Trevor. "You swore a blood oath to be one of us."

"I know." Geoff gave Trevor a troubled look. He had joined Trevor's gang, the Taurids, nearly three years ago, shortly before he had turned fourteen. "And I keep my word. I just don't want to be so...constricted. Under orders all the time."

"Hey, we all go through that," Trevor said. "Like rebelling against our parents. Just quit being so loud about it. Here's our car."

Geoff followed Trevor into the transit car. From the outside, all that could be seen were the wide double doors. Inside were two rows of ten seats, each of which could comfortably hold two adults. Bright light bars on the ceiling created good visibility for the security cameras at the front and back of the car.

It held a dozen other passengers. The two boys sat close to the exit and played their new sports buttons as the car silently rolled between the station walls.

They lived in Station One, the first station built for civilian habitation. It orbited Earth slightly behind and above the main transfer station where Terran cargo was offloaded from atmosphere planes and transferred to space-traveling freighters.

At eighty years old, Station One was far older than the development of artificial gravity. It had been started in the late 2060s and had been constructed as a giant spinning doughnut. The rate of spin was set to give the outer layer (or bottom deck) one Terran gravity. All but one school were on that heavy deck, so children would get the required hours in gravity for physical density and strength. Most business offices and residential apartments were on decks with lighter gravity.

Geoff and Trevor rode to a transit center farther down the line. Transit centers served as connector hubs for cars traveling across the deck and the rows of elevator cars that moved between decks.

"Let's have a game or two," said Trevor. "I figured out a way to get by you in Scout Ship." He took a couple of steps toward a cross-deck car.

"I got to meet Barbie," Geoff said. "Besides, it won't work. I'm too fast." Shadowhand was on the top-ten list of many different games throughout the station.

"What're you doing with your sister?"

"Babysitting."

Trevor snorted and said, "She's too old to need a sitter."

"We're going to the low-g market by the docks," said Geoff. It was a family rule that no one under sixteen went up there without being accompanied by someone older. Barbara was only thirteen. Geoff had had the freedom to visit the dockside markets by himself for less than a year.

"She's got you wound around her little finger," said Trevor, extending his pinky finger and making a circling motion with it. "Whyn't you tell her no?"

"'Cause I like the market," answered Geoff, knowing it was only partly true. "You should come with us. We could check out what's new in the weapons booths." He was going to look for a certain young salesgirl, too.

"I can do that standing here," said Trevor.

Geoff sniffed derisively. A computer-generated holo image, especially the little ones from personal links, couldn't compare to actually being there. Because the Lung organization's influence in the dock markets was limited to the section rumored to cater to black-market dealings, Geoff's friends did not have a lot of enthusiasm for visiting the market. Conversely, Geoff got a secret pleasure from going where Lung's influence was minimal.

They caught an elevator car. Like the cross-deck transit cars, it held two rows of seats. All were occupied by at least one person. Geoff and Trevor stood by the doors and lightly held the rail as gravity diminished.

"Show messages," Geoff whispered to his wrist com. It was his link to the station's net until he turned twenty-one and could get an uplink implant. Everyone below the age of majority only had their personal information—identification, medical records, and bank access—implanted.

Geoff had no mail, so he opened his school folder. He had math to finish, and sure as Sol was hot, he'd have something due in station systems, the class he had skipped. He did. Somehow, he would have to find time to get it done. If his grades fell, his parents would send him back to after-school tutoring. That had been bad enough in grade eight. He wasn't going there in grade eleven.

"See you tonight," Trevor said as he got off on the 0.7-gravity deck. Geoff rode up to the 0.6-gravity deck, wishing the trip was longer so he would have more time to come up with an excuse to be out late every night while he suffered with Chin.

Chapter 2

Geoff's family lived on deck thirty-four, section M, in apartment 133 on the corridor named Squamish Road. Each wedge-shaped section had its point at the center of the station and its wide base along the outer rim. He ambled down the hall, taking long steps with plenty of hang time. The walls were covered with leafy vines, flowers, and shrubs stretching up to the recessed lights above them. Bushy pecan trees guarded both sides of the Anders's door.

Inside the apartment, black shadows stretched across a living room made rosy by pink grow-lights. White-light ceiling bars brightened when Geoff entered. The dark blue living room rug showed wear spots by the entry and on the opposite side by the kitchen's navy-blue tile. Apartments were built long and narrow, with the bathroom, bedrooms, and storage areas beyond the kitchen.

Out of habit, Geoff went to the garden. The apartment's outer wall, which was divided in two by the door, held a closet on the left and a rack of hydroponic garden shelves on the right. These lined the walls behind the couches, curving around the corner and filling the next wall. Although all apartments were built with garden equipment so residents could offset station air charges, not all stationers used them. Both Geoff's parents liked to garden, so there was always something fresh to eat.

Geoff stole a few peapods from Barbara's little section of garden. As he crunched the tiny legumes, he checked the nutrient and temperature regulators. Then he picked a sweet turnip. He just had time to drop the empty peapods and turnip peel down the kitchen recycle chute when Barbara and Nadine arrived.

"He's here already!" Barbara yelled. "Let's go." She jumped and twirled and then landed facing Nadine and the door.

"I'm still eating," said Geoff. He bit into the sphere of crunchy vegetable as he walked toward the girls.

"You're always eating," Barbara teased, her dimple showing in her cheek and her wide brown eyes sparkling with fun.

Nadine looked from sister to brother and then said to Barbara, "You're right. You're taller than him now."

"You sure you want to come with us?" asked Geoff.

Nadine clapped her hands over her mouth and nodded. Her short, reddish-brown hair bounced around her face.

"Get lunch from the market," said Barbara.

"Let's go." Nadine opened the door and skipped out ahead of Barbara.

Geoff followed. The door slid closed and locked behind him. On its other side, the lights dimmed.

The three teenagers left the elevator car when gravity had all but disappeared. The market was near the center of the station, one deck below the inner hub. Centered inside the station's donut, the hub gave access to the hundreds of ships tethered to the giant metal parking frame orbiting beside the station.

Six times a day, at the beginning of every second odd-numbered hour, the hub disconnected from the station and stopped its rotation. While it slowed, the air was pumped from three-quarters of it and compressed into tanks. Once the hub was motionless, huge bulkheads opened, exposing the empty sections to space. Rovers, ship staff and passengers, outside staff, dock workers—everyone had two hours to move between ships and the station hub. Cargo went into the vacuum-exposed areas, and personnel air locks gave access to pressurized sections.

Mindful of the influx of people coming on station right after 1700, Geoff said, "We got an hour before the crowd. Let's go." He stepped forward, floating three meters down the hall before he put his foot down for another push. It carried him into the market proper, an open section so large the upward curves of the floor and ceiling were visible.

"Ummmm—" Barbara breathed deeply. "It always smells so exciting here."

"Yes," agreed Nadine. "Let's have some goodies before the spacers come. Then we can look at stuff."

"We're leaving before they get in," said Geoff. He led the way to the food booths. Many were identical to the ones in the food courts of the malls. Like the girls, he wanted to sample the ones that weren't.

A few minutes later, their hands filled with protein balls on sticks, assorted pastries, and crunchy, dehydrated sweets, they began to tour the market. Because it was a slack hour, they could stroll three abreast. The booths offered everything from handmade clothes to weapons to games.

Barbara and Nadine stopped to talk to a boy behind a table of Belter Pipes, little flutes made of the thin metal from beer cans.

Geoff paused long enough to decide that the young salesman was about the same age as Barbara and posed no threat, and then he went down the aisle to a table of wares handwoven out of stems, long leaves, and other dried plant material. It was presided over by a teenage girl.

"Hi, Dayle," said Geoff. "I came back." Her eyes were level with his, dark brown with a scalloped ring of lighter brown at the outside edges of the irises. He could stare into them for hours.

"And I'm still here." Dayle smiled and leaned forward. "Looking for something in particular?"

"Yeah." Geoff smiled back. "You." She was a Rover, someone who lived on a space ship. Her family had come to the inner system to get medical treatment for her grandmother, and they would soon be heading back to their usual routes. Normally, they traveled between the cities and small colonies of the asteroid belt. No one knew how many unofficial emigration rockets had taken off from Terra in the early days or how many people had crammed themselves into old shuttles and gone to the asteroids. Every now and then, explorers found little colonies of dead people, their DNA so badly mutated by radiation they could not procreate.

"How about this one?" Dayle picked up a cream-colored basket with a flat lid. It fit inside her hands. "It's a nice jewelry box."

"It is," agreed Geoff. He cupped his hands around hers. "Who would I give it to? My favorite girl already has one."

She giggled and answered, "Your mother?"

"Maybe." Geoff kept his hands on hers as they chatted. Part of his mind wondered what it must be like to live in a ship, safely distanced from bullies like Chin. It must be nice to break dock and move on when things got difficult.

After a few minutes, Dayle returned to the subject of the little basket.

"Maybe your sister would like it," she suggested.

Sister! Geoff had forgotten about Barbara and Nadine! He looked at the table where he had last seen them. They were gone.

Geoff spun slowly on his heel, searching the scattered shoppers for the two girls. He did not see them. Where the hell did they go? And why? Neither Barbara nor Nadine would hide just to annoy him. They liked coming here too much.

"I'll be right back," Geoff said. He jumped up, raising his hands over his head to keep from bumping the ceiling. As he rose, he twisted, rotating so he could view the entire market. No girls.

Wait. They were walking toward the far end of the food booths between two older boys...or young men.

Geoff reached the apex of his jump. He pushed against the ceiling to hasten his descent and hit the floor running—at least what passed for running in near-zero gravity. He bounded down

13

the aisle and jumped a table of crafts, making sure he went high enough to invert and kick the ceiling for added impetus. He landed halfway down the next aisle.

Then, strolling with apparent casualness but moving more quickly than his targets, Geoff approached Barbara and Nadine from behind. He stepped close to the girls and draped his arms across their shoulders.

Startled, they turned to look at him. Geoff halted, pulling them to a stop as well. The two older boys—Geoff guessed they were eighteen or nineteen—went one step farther before they stopped and turned.

"Get lost, kid," said the thin, black-haired one. He was taller than Trevor.

"No." Geoff turned his left wrist on Barbara's shoulder, making it obvious he was recording the two strangers. Calling 911 would bring market security, but they wouldn't arrive fast enough.

"We're talking with the young ladies," said the other stranger, a shorter, stockier fellow with brown skin and pale-blue eyes. "Go look at the market. They'll take you home in an hour or so."

"Uh-uh." Geoff inserted himself between Barbara and Nadine, moving forward so that he was in line with them instead of behind them. "I'm the *older* brother."

"And I'm Captain Galactica," said the tall boy. "Take a walk before we flatten your pretty face."

"Wouldn't be that easy," Geoff said. He glanced at the older boys' feet. Both wore boots with thick soles, probably containing magnets they could turn on at will. In a fight, that would give them a huge advantage. "You want to risk it for jailbait?"

Beneath Geoff's arms, Barbara and Nadine stiffened indignantly. He gently squeezed their shoulders to keep them from saying anything. As the two older boys considered what Geoff had said, he released the girls and stepped forward. He would need room to move if it came to a fight.

"Geoff," Barbara protested.

"We'll cross orbits some other time," the blue-eyed stranger said. "See you next time, girls." They walked away, taking two-meter steps that showed they had their boot magnets on low.

"What did you do that for?" demanded Barbara. "We were just talking!"

"What a rotten thing to call us," added Nadine.

"If they just wanted to talk, why'd they leave when they found out you aren't available for sex?" asked Geoff. Left over adrenaline sent shivers up his arms and legs. He was tempted to pick the girls up and carry them out. Instead, he shoved his hands into his pockets.

"They just didn't want to be around you," said Barbara. She turned away, her shoulders stiff with hurt and anger.

"That's 'cause they knew I knew what they were up to," Geoff said. "Let's go."

"We're not done yet," objected Nadine.

"How could you know?" demanded Barbara. "You don't know anything about them."

"I know what I think about when I meet a girl," said Geoff. He looked at his sister's angry posture and added, "Don't sweat it, Barbie. They weren't good enough for you anyway." He gestured for them to turn toward the exit by the food booths.

"Were you really going to fight for us?" asked Nadine. "Like a shining knight?"

"No." Geoff placed his hands between their shoulder blades and gently pushed. "Let's go." He still had to find out what he'd gotten into with Chin.

Barbara looked at Geoff, and her dimple flashed as she whispered, "Yes," to Nadine.

A few steps farther, Nadine asked, "How far did you get?"

"Huh?" responded Geoff, his mind on the Simba and Chin's data card of exercises.

"With the basket girl," Barbara said. "What's her name?"

"I forget," lied Geoff. "Doesn't matter. She'll be gone in a couple days."

"There'll be someone new," said Barbara. She linked her elbow in Geoff's and added, "Let's get some fresh buns for Mom."

They rode most of the way back together. The girls left the elevator to visit a friend two levels above the Anders's deck.

As Geoff rode the rest of the way home, he watched the computer's answer to his query about the Simba.

The demonstration dance that played in his com's little holoview was an athletic performance of swaying, steps, and turns during which the two men did not touch each other except to occasionally brush shoulders.

"This pattern of movements is repeated seven times during the dance," the audio recording said. "The first sequence is performed to a moderate beat. The speed increases in the second, third, and fourth sequences, then slows for the fifth, sixth, and seventh ones with the last round at the same tempo as the first." It looked complicated but not difficult for anyone in good physical condition.

Geoff scowled at the tiny figures dancing above his wrist. From what he recalled of the bits of competitions he had glimpsed on the holoview, there was more to it than that. He called up the last dance competition and ordered the winning performances from each of the three divisions to run.

The first was an athletic event much like the demonstration Geoff had just watched. The second was obviously a portrayal of lovers dancing. The partners danced much closer together and kept their hands on each other's torsos and legs almost continuously. The third competition class went a step further. Some of the gyrations in Geoff's holoview made him scowl at the thought of doing the same in public, especially with Chin!

"Blast me if I'm gonna do *that*," Geoff muttered. The third dance made the second look tolerable, but Geoff hoped with all his heart that what Chin had in mind was the athletic first category. He wished he had done his homework before he had looked at the Simba. How was he supposed to think about math now?

His mind on the dance, Geoff nearly missed his transit stop. Realizing the car was parked at his stop, he hurried out the exit and down the hall.

Back home, he put the leftover lasagna to warm and ordered chocolate milk from the kitchen lab. Their small lab was programmed with a dozen types of drinks, protein slices, cheeses, plus twenty flavors of ice cream and a variety of other foods.

Geoff took his snack to his room across from the bathroom. Barbara's was next to his, and their parents' was beside the bathroom. The end of the hall led to the storage area with its low ceiling to accommodate the maintenance and delivery tunnel above it.

Geoff's private space held a desk with a built-in console, a closet with a mirror on one of its sliding doors, and a single bed, unmade. It had drawers beneath it and cubbyholes in the wall beside it. The standard upper bunk was folded into the wall. In its place hung a long, narrow shelf loaded with treasures that included a plastic dinosaur-egg half shell heaped with sports holoview buttons, three small gymnastics trophies peeking out from beneath a tangle of sports medals on colorful ribbons, a blue plush bear with a torn ear hanging beside its face, and a carefully folded soccer jersey decorated with scrawling autographs.

While he was chewing, Geoff powered up his desk to find out what was on that card Chin gave him. A quick scan of it showed a half hour of exercises and stretches. No big deal, not like the dance. Geoff kicked his dirty laundry out of the way and restlessly paced the three steps his room allowed. What was he going to do if Chin ordered him to do a lover's dance? Tell him to take a walk without a suit? He couldn't. Pretend to be willing and do it so badly Chin would give up on him? That might work.

Now...homework. He'd better find out what went on in station systems before he did the math. Geoff ordered up his systems class lesson plan and assignment. He was in luck. Today's class had been recorded. If he deleted the time it took to get everyone settled down and skipped over all the stupid questions, he could be done in half an hour.

It took longer, but Geoff was already working on his math when Barbara came home. He resisted the temptation to yell at her to turn down her sappy music because that was sure to take fifteen minutes of arguing. Instead, he put in his ear buttons and played Twisted Gravity's newest release, bouncing to the beat as he worked.

By the time Geoff finished his homework, the noise outside his room had changed. The evening news provided background chatter to a three-way conversation between his sister and their parents. Geoff ran Chin's exercises at increased speed and halfheartedly copied them before he went for supper.

"Hi, Dad, Mom," he said as he entered the dining room side of the kitchen.

"Hey, Bubs," replied Tony from the couch. A small-framed man, he stood only three centimeters taller than his son. His angular face had a pointed chin, curly brown hair like Geoff's, a dimple like Barbara's, and dark brown eyes. "How'd school go?"

"All right."

"Well, look who's home," Barbara said. "When did you get here?"

"Before you did. What's for supper?"

"Stew and biscuits," Fallah said. She was as tall as Tony and looked like a mature version of Barbara—minus the dimple. Geoff was the shortest one in the family.

"What were you doing home so early?" asked Barbara. "*You* ate my peas!"

"Who? Me?" Geoff grinned.

"You did!" One bound took Barbara from the dining area into the living room. Tony ducked as Barbara jumped over him and landed beside her garden. When Geoff entered the living room, she launched herself at him in a waist-high tackle.

He laughed and jumped, pulling his knees up to his chest, so she would pass beneath him. She caught his ankles, and they tumbled onto the empty sofa and then the floor.

"Ow!" Geoff bumped his head and his right elbow, and he lost his breath as Barbara landed on top of him.

Geoff grabbed for Barbara's left foot; her ticklish feet were one of her few weak spots. She spidered her fingers along his ribs, and he quit his offensive in favor of defending his own ticklish area. He caught her wrists and tried to shove her off his chest, but she braced her legs against the sofa and held herself above him.

"Gotcha," Barbara laughed.

"Hmmmph." Geoff put his hands together. He changed his hold so that he held both her hands with one of his and used his free one to push himself up. Once he shifted enough so she had no leverage, it was easy to tip her over and sit on her.

"Not my feet!" Barbara's flailing legs shoved against the table.

Geoff slid back and pinned her shins.

"Say, 'I know you didn't steal my peas, but you can have them if you want,'" ordered Geoff.

"You did. You can't." She tried to squirm free. "Grow your own."

"That's enough," Tony said.

"Get the table set," ordered Fallah.

Geoff let go of Barbara and quickly jumped over the coffee table to get beyond her reach. He would set the table because he hated cleaning it off after the meal.

"That's why you hid in your room, thief," Barbara said.

"I wasn't hiding," said Geoff. "I got my homework done, even with your drippy music shaking the station. I'm going out tonight."

"You must be the reason some of those arcades stay in business," Tony said.

"I don't spend that much, Dad," Geoff said, though he knew his father was teasing. "I usually win more free games than I pay for."

Chapter 3

At the end of the meal as Fallah served cream pie smothered in sliced strawberries, Trevor arrived.

"Your timing is always perfect," chuckled Tony. "Pull up a chair."

"Thanks, Mr. Anders." Trevor sat in his usual spot beside Geoff. "It's 'cause I know when you have dessert."

Barbara reached over and tinkled the three blue hoops hanging from Trevor's left ear.

"New ones," she said.

"Yup." Trevor crammed half a biscuit in his mouth with one hand as he took a dish of pie from Fallah with the other. "Thank you."

"Quit spraying crumbs." Geoff elbowed Trevor in the ribs.

After dessert, Geoff and Trevor went to the arcade. Geoff enjoyed an hour of gaming and then went to the full-gravity recreation center. He exited the transit car on the far side of the soccer fields, a section he rarely went to. A park with winding paths through bushes and fruit trees separated the public area from the private gym.

Geoff did not want to be early and have Chin think he was eager, and he did not dare be late, so he timed his arrival for exactly 2055. As he walked up to the wide entrance, Chin stepped out of it.

"In here," Chin ordered. "You have to register."

Geoff nervously gave his name and identification to the woman at the desk. Outside of the doctor's office, he had never seen a staffed reception area. He was prepared to refuse to pay the membership fee, but she did not charge one.

Instead, she said, "Welcome to our club, Geoff. Your guest privileges are for one month."

Before Geoff could ask what guest privileges meant, Chin said, "Follow me."

Geoff bit the inside of his bottom lip as he went. He lagged behind Chin, his feet moving in small, reluctant jerks.

They passed a lounge, a weight room, and a small gym filled with overweight people hopping around and flapping their arms.

Beyond it, Lui waited in a well-lit room larger than a school classroom. A cushioned, rubbery black material covered the floor. The walls opposite the door and to the right were covered in mirrors from the floor to a meter below the ceiling. A waist-high rail ran the length of both walls. The third wall had doorways to two change rooms. To the left of the entrance were four chairs and a built-in wall console with music and holographic projection features.

Lui shifted the chairs, so three of them faced the far corner where the mirrored walls met. He set the fourth chair facing them and sat with his bulk spilling over on the three while his long braid hung behind them. He rested one foot on the single chair.

"Never mind him," Chin said. "Do what I do." He stripped off his shirt and slacks and tossed them on the floor by Lui. Chin wore skin-hugging exercise tights and an equally formfitting muscle shirt. Their bright orange matched the tie holding his hair in a braid down the back of his head.

It was a hairstyle Geoff had always associated with girls, but on Chin there was nothing feminine about it. With hard ridges of muscle rippling his tight clothes and the colorful tattoo inside his left forearm, he looked very intimidating.

Chin's tattoo was larger and much more complex than Geoff's. Although it had obviously begun the same, with a Lung dragon twined around a caricature of the station, his rank in the organization, family connections, and things Geoff knew nothing about all enhanced it. Another dragon marked the inside of Chin's right forearm. It looked like a scar from a dragon-shaped burn.

Chin kicked off his shiny boots and pulled little slippers with hard heels onto his feet.

"What are you waiting for?" he asked.

Geoff reluctantly removed his sweater and jeans, uncomfortable at half stripping in Chin and Lui's presence. He wore running shoes, dark purple bicycle shorts, and a green T-shirt. Not enough for warmth in the chilly dance hall. He shivered.

Chin strode to the center of the room and began to stretch. Geoff stood a couple of meters to his side and silently copied Chin's head rotations and shoulder shrugs. In the mirror, he watched Lui set a gym bag on the chair to his left. He pulled out a drink and snack.

Chin stepped closer to Geoff and knocked him off balance with a punch on his shoulder.

"Pay attention," he ordered. "We've got three weeks to work on technique. Watch."

They stood side by side, a meter apart, and facing a mirror. Chin rested his hands on his hips, bent his right knee slightly, and shifted his shoulders to the right and his hips to the left.

He held that position and said, "Do it slowly. Keep your back vertical."

Geoff did as instructed.

"Straighten up. Then shift the other direction," Chin said, suiting action to words.

Geoff copied him.

Chin turned, put one hand on Geoff's chest and the other on the small of his back, and pushed. "Vertical," he ordered.

Geoff pushed Chin away and said, "Keep your hands off me!"

"Get used to it. Do it again. Smooth, torso straight up and in a line with your extended leg. Glance in the mirror to check your position. Don't watch yourself." They practiced the first series of steps and then started at the beginning again.

Lui ordered on the music. It blared out of speakers in every wall, a heavy, throbbing sound that sped up Geoff's already fast heartbeat.

Chin smiled and said, "Start after the break... on my count... seven, eight. *One.*"

Chin swayed. Geoff attempted to but confused which leg to bend and ended up not knowing what he was doing.

Lui ordered the music off and laughed, "Kid's got two left feet."

"Get your brain working," growled Chin. "Again."

At the end of the lesson, Chin led Geoff through more stretches. Geoff dropped to the floor, happy to take his weight off his aching legs. Thank the stars he lived on a light deck and didn't have to stay in one gravity all night.

Five minutes later, as Geoff pulled on his sweater, Chin said, "You need hard-soled boots."

"I don't own any," said Geoff.

"Then buy a pair," Chin ordered. "Or steal 'em."

"Marley's has bad security," said Lui. "Don't lift from Omega."

"Right," Geoff muttered.

Chin patted Geoff's buttocks and said, "Be here same time tomorrow." He slid his hand forward over Geoff's hip and across his genitals.

Geoff knocked the hand away and strode to the exit.

Chin and Lui laughed.

Chapter 4

When Geoff's music came on the next morning at 0730, he was far from ready to begin the day. The dance lesson had left Geoff so sore that every time he moved in his sleep, knives of pain attacked his legs and he woke up. He groaned and pulled his pillow over his head. He had another three months of this? Tears of pain, frustration, and self-pity trickled into his pillow.

After a few minutes, Geoff told himself that Barbara would certainly feel worse after an evening with Chin and Lui and that every athlete suffered during the first part of a training regimen. He should have had the sense to put some painkiller, Lormal or Blissmaert, in his bedside wall niche.

Geoff clenched his teeth and gingerly sat up. His legs hurt so much that he lifted them with his hands to shift them sideways and get his feet on the floor. He hobbled to his closet and slowly dressed.

"Geoff, are you up?" called Fallah.

"Yeah." Why did mothers always ask? By the time Geoff finished dressing, some of his stiffness had eased. He went to the bathroom and found the Blissmaert. A warning about drowsiness covered half the package. For sure, he'd fall asleep in school. Lormal then, even though it wasn't as strong.

When Geoff went for breakfast, Barbara said, "What happened to you? You look like you broke something."

"I'm a little stiff," Geoff said. He put a breakfast pastry in the toaster and began to peel an orange.

"From what?" asked Fallah.

"Gymnastics." It was the best excuse Geoff could think of.

"Gymnastics?" echoed Fallah. "You haven't done that in a while. What made you go back?"

Geoff shrugged. "Felt like it. I kinda miss it, and Rob's always talking about his games. He made me remember it was fun." It used to be fun with old friends from before he met Trevor and the gang in the arcade.

"Well, I'm sure you'll have a good time," Fallah said. "Which club?"

"None." If he had a club, they'd want to see his routines. "Just the evening sessions at the rec center." He hadn't thought of it until just now, but besides an excuse for stiffness, going to the rec center or to drop-in gymnastics would give him a place to do Chin's exercises.

───────

Geoff hurt in gym class that morning. Even with another dose of Lormal, track and field in the recreation center beside the school was torture for the first fifteen minutes. After that, Geoff felt better. Maybe he'd look for boots after school.

He didn't. When school ended, the Taurids gathered at their usual exit.

"Let's go skating," drawled Rob. He had lived on Terra until he was ten and still stretched vowels when he spoke. Nearly as tall as Trevor but more slender, Rob had dark blue eyes and medium-brown hair.

"We should find a matinee of that new exploring Antares movie," Geoff said. He didn't care what movie he saw. He wasn't up to anything physical, and when Rob said skating, he meant the Rollerblade obstacle course.

Hans adjusted the headband over his long, toffee-colored hair and suggested volleyball.

"We haven't skated for a while," said Trevor. The oldest and largest Taurid, he was also the loudest in voice and appearance. Today, his eyebrow ring and earrings were the same dark red as his shirt.

"Why don't we just watch the girls at the mall?" asked Geoff. Maybe he could find a pair of hard-soled boots. It would only take a few minutes if he searched on his wrist link.

"We can do that after," Rob answered. "Let's go."

Unwilling to press the issue, Geoff said, "Only for a bit. I got stuff to do." They dressed in impact gear and in-line skates, rented a locker for their shoes and gym bags, and rolled two abreast down the wide path winding between trees and bushes.

This skating park—and the entire recreation area—was free to students. The membership fee paid by adults was considerably less than what Chin's private club charged. Still, it was a fine facility with high ceilings disguised by holograms of Terra's blue skies. Splashing fountains fed carefully routed streams. They gurgled under footbridges built into the walking paths and made a noisy distraction in parts of the bike and skating obstacle courses. Thanks to his classes at school, the stream always made Geoff think of hidden recycling systems and how the park streams and mall fountains served to oxygenate the water before it flowed into the purifier.

"Learned to handle those new wheels yet?" Rob asked Geoff. It was his way of reminding everyone that he had won the last Rollerblade competition the park had held.

"Yeah." Geoff's position and respect in the gang were for his talent as a "hand." He would lose no status by acknowledging Rob was a better skater. Geoff hit the curve and sped up for the first jump. He tripped on the landing and rolled off the ramp onto the grass-covered, dense sponge surrounding it. He definitely would be better off looking for boots. What would Chin do if Geoff didn't get any? Was he expected to have them for tonight?

"You okay?" called Hans as he sailed to the ramp, long hair streaming behind him.

"Yeah." Geoff waved him on. As Geoff rolled to his knees, Trevor coasted up the path, detouring the jump.

"Break anything?" he asked.

"My ego." Geoff rubbed at the newest scuff marks on his vest and elbow guard. He was so full of Lormal that he couldn't tell if he was hurt.

By the time they returned to the locker area, Geoff was not the only one sporting new bruises. It was too late to get boots. He would have to shop after supper.

"See you at the arcade tonight?" Trevor asked around a mouthful of peanuts as they rode the elevator car to their home decks.

"For a little while," answered Geoff. "I should be there by twenty." He had homework to do first.

⸻

The arcade, a three-level cavern with hundreds of play stations, held its usual evening crowd. Geoff put his name on the lineup for virtual sword fights before he went with Trevor to the Scout Ship game. Although Trevor had some new moves, Geoff easily outmaneuvered him. They attracted an audience, and Geoff flew against challengers until his turn with the sword.

"I don't know why you put your money there," Trevor said. "You never win. You never even get on the board."

"Maybe that's why," said Geoff. The game defeated him six times in two minutes.

"Ouch." Geoff laughed ruefully. "Cars?"

"Sure," said Trevor. They sat in simulators and drove a rally ride through an alien landscape of forests, deserts, and cities. Trevor had just taken the lead from Geoff when Geoff heard a boy say, "I gotta run, get home by twenty-one."

Twenty-one! Geoff glanced at the time and leapt from his seat. He ran toward the nearest cross-deck transit. This was the half-gravity deck. To go a third of the way around the station would be a shorter ride up here than down on the heavy deck.

Trevor followed him and yelled, "Where're you going?"

"Chin." Geoff wrinkled his face in disgust.

Nodding his understanding, Trevor turned back to the arcade.

Geoff took the transit to a bank of express elevators and then fidgeted in his seat as the car dropped. He sank into the cushions, mentally groaning at the return of his full weight.

A man presided over the desk at the entrance of the recreation club. He held Geoff up for an implant scan before he allowed him inside. When Geoff reached the training room, Chin and Lui were already there. Lui glanced at Geoff and continued arranging his chairs.

Chin said, "Don't ever be late. Get ready." He had on a green-and-yellow outfit similar to the orange one he had worn the day before. It revealed his imposing physique in just as much detail.

"I got a slow ride," Geoff said. He nervously peeled off his shirt and jeans.

Chin led Geoff to the center of the floor and ran through the warm-up.

"What's that from?" Chin asked, pointing to a blue welt above Geoff's knee.

"Rollerblading."

"Remember who pays if you break something and can't dance." Chin waited until Geoff looked at him and nodded, and then Chin added, "Put your boots on."

Uh-oh.

Geoff took a deep breath and said, "You never said I needed them *tonight*."

"You mean you don't have them," said Chin. "Your friends will pay for that. Bring boots tomorrow. Let's see if you remember anything." They faced each other, feet apart and hands on their hips.

The music began with the now familiar heavy beat. Worried about what Chin would do to Trevor or the others, Geoff hardly listened.

Chin counted mostly inaudibly but finished loud enough for Geoff to hear, "...seven, eight." Chin swayed to one side; Geoff belatedly copied him.

"Pay attention." Chin slapped Geoff on the side of his head. "Keep your back in a vertical line."

Geoff huffed a breath out his nose. He thought he had been straight and concentrated on staying vertical while shifting his hips and shoulders in opposite directions.

"Count," said Chin. "Stay with the beat. Center on *four*." Another beat, circle each other. Geoff remembered to act clumsy to get out of this chore. He stumbled as he pivoted through the turn.

"Smooth," Chin reminded him.

Geoff pretended to catch on slowly. When he did it correctly once, Chin moved on to the next steps.

"Again," Chin said after they finished the pattern. "Six-year-olds learn faster." They did it a dozen times and then ran through the whole routine from the beginning. Geoff made mistakes, some intentional, some not.

By the end of the first twenty minutes, despite Geoff's hesitations, they went through it without stopping. A two-heartbeat pause and they began the cycle again. It remained at the same tempo as the first two times had.

"Isn't it supposed to speed up?" asked Geoff.

"You ready to go any faster?" Chin asked for an answer.

"No." Geoff barely remembered all the steps. He turned to step out of the circle.

"Then thank me." Chin reached down and squeezed Geoff's left buttock. Chin moved back, so Geoff's punch just brushed his belly. Then he backhanded Geoff in the chest.

Geoff staggered back three steps before he fell.

Chin stood over him and said, "Never break the rhythm. You have to know this basic pattern so well you can do it in your sleep or while the station comes apart around you. Get up."

Geoff slowly got to his feet. He wanted to knock that smirk off Chin's face, but a physical confrontation would be less than useless. Chin had the longer reach and half again Geoff's mass. Chin was also a kung fu master.

"Keep your ion-blasted hands off me," Geoff said. "I just said I'd dance."

"Get used to it." Chin winked at Geoff and made a come-on gesture to Lui. The music began. "You might like it...seven, *eight*."

They danced the full seven rounds all at the speed of the first one. Geoff split his attention between the steps and where Chin was and how close he got and what he did with his hands.

Chin ordered a break. Geoff sat on the floor and leaned back against the wall. How would Geoff's friends have to pay for his not having boots? Should Geoff warn them? What could he say?

Closing his eyes did nothing to combat Geoff's dizziness from all the turns, so he watched in the mirror as Chin walked over to Lui and took a bottle of water from the bag. He drank, took out a second bottle, and tossed it across the room to Geoff.

Geoff caught it with one hand. He suspiciously inspected it before he cracked the seal. He would bring his own from now on.

Chin followed the brief rest with ten minutes of serious stretching. Geoff was surprised at how much more flexible he was after he had danced for a while.

Lui started the music as Geoff and Chin returned to the center of the floor. Geoff continued deliberately doing things wrong as they completed two more rounds. Then Lui called, "Shoulders back."

"That's for you," Chin said. "He'll say my name if he's talking to me."

Geoff adjusted his shoulders.

Lui had things for Geoff to correct throughout the pattern.

Those last ten minutes felt like an hour to Geoff. The music finally ended, and Chin sat on the floor for his finishing exercises. Instead of copying him, Geoff headed toward the exit.

"Stay," ordered Chin. "You're not crippling yourself by not cooling off properly. You can't get out of this that easy."

Chapter 5

Geoff's alarm went off too early again. At least this morning, Geoff had the Lormal within reach. Before he went for breakfast, he looked up Omega Boots.

"View stock," Geoff said. "Size six with hard soles." Brown and ivory boots appeared in the holoview.

"Solid color only." Geoff quickly found three pairs he liked. One he had just enough money to buy. The other two were beyond his bank account.

The inventory at Marley's did not look very different, but the prices were lower. Geoff found a few pairs he liked, one of which was just as costly as the better boots at Omega. He saved its stock number and then found a couple of cheaper pairs made by the same company. When he was at the store, he would decide if he was buying a cheap pair or stealing the expensive ones. He would need help for a heist.

Geoff rummaged among the data cards, styluses, and junk in his drawer and came up with a square gold ring that was really a tool to read inventory chips and overwrite them into an order. It was the illegal leftovers of a job he had done for Lung last month. He had not used it since; his conscience balked at ripping off really expensive stuff just for fun. Today was different. He had been ordered to get hard-soled boots, and he didn't want cheap ones that would hurt his feet.

Geoff tried to walk normally when he left his room.

"Still stiff?" asked Fallah. "Why don't you try some of that rub I bought at the beginning of bowling season?"

"What rub?"

"It's in the second drawer under the bathroom sink," answered Fallah. "Probably at the very back."

Geoff eagerly went to get it. Less than half the tube of Haynes Heet remained. He returned to his room and rubbed it on his legs and ribs.

"Ahhh!" He winced and rubbed less vigorously. Either the rubbing or the cream worked, because his soreness diminished.

When Geoff arrived at school, he anxiously looked for his friends.

Trevor and Hans waited a little apart from the stream of young people pouring into the school. Trevor had one gray eye swollen nearly shut, but he wore his usual quantity of colorful rings and earrings. Hans looked untouched. As Geoff walked up to them, Rob arrived from a different direction.

Geoff looked from Rob's black eye and fat lip to Trevor's misshapen face and swallowed bile.

"What happened to you?" asked Geoff in as natural a reaction as he could manage.

"Got blasted last night." Trevor gingerly touched his bruised cheek. "Just about blew us out of orbit."

"Over what?" asked Geoff. Maybe he was wrong. Maybe this wasn't Chin's doing.

"Don't know," replied Rob, his drawl sounding odder than usual through his swollen lips. "Four guys came out of nowhere, and we were into it."

"We should have been there to help," Hans said.

The five-minute bell sounded. The boys joined the now thinner crowd of students on their way to class. Geoff was glad they had to go. He couldn't look at Trevor or Rob.

The unfamiliar ache in Geoff's muscles lessened through the day, though it did not completely go away. Geoff felt close to his usual self when he and Trevor boarded the transit to go shopping…or shoplifting.

"Where'd you find boots?" Trevor asked.

"There are nice ones at Omega," said Geoff.

Trevor stiffened.

"No." Trevor leaned closer to Geoff and lowered his voice. "Not unless you're loaded and willing to spend it. We can't lift there."

Geoff said, "Found some almost as good in Marley's."

"That's okay." Trevor relaxed. "We going to eat first?"

"Sure." They bought burgers at a fast food restaurant, and then Geoff lifted drinks and candy bars from a nearby store. Internally fortified, they went for boots.

Marley's smelled of vinyl and polish. The storefront displays were, of course, all holographs. The wall behind the counter held tiny shelves, each supporting a left boot.

Geoff gave the clerk the four stock numbers he had chosen and asked if they had try-ons for any of them. She directed him toward the sales staff, a man and a woman who were assisting several other customers in various stages of choosing footwear. Geoff picked the courtesy stool farthest from them, where he could sit with a wall on one side and Trevor on the other. An attendant brought out two boxes.

"We don't have the exact ones you requested," he said. "But these are similar, made by the same company." He arranged them on the shelf beside Geoff's stool and then hovered nearby, watching Geoff and the lady he had been serving.

Geoff and Trevor chatted about last night's professional basketball game as Geoff slowly removed his runners. He needed another customer to provide a distraction.

"That's a nice, classic style," the attendant said when Geoff slid his right foot into a red boot. "It differs from the ones you picked only in color and decorative stitching."

Geoff did not care for the boot's fancy embellishments, but he was very interested in its stock tag. A tiny plastic bead hung from the top of the boot. His illegal tool should be able to read it.

After the huge settlements in privacy rights court cases, most manufacturers had quit using embedded computer chips and begun attaching small but visible inventory tags. They could be physically removed when the items were purchased, not masked or burnt out as the chips supposedly were.

"Let me try the other one," said Geoff.

Trevor handed him a black boot with a scale pattern. It was much more expensive than the first pair.

"Other foot." Geoff put it on his left foot and stood up in the mismatched footwear. He looked at them in the mirror and said, "I dunno." In fact, the black boot with its additional layers of more expensive cushioning felt far superior to the red one.

A man and boy came in. The woman went to the clerk at the counter, leaving the shoes she had tried on scattered on the floor. The attendant looked from that mess to the newcomers.

"I'm okay," said Geoff, eager to get the man's eyes off him.

"Let me know if you need anything." The man went to greet his latest customers.

Geoff glanced around the room and surreptitiously set the black boot's stock tag in his ring's crest to copy.

"That guy's coming back," warned Trevor.

"Done." Geoff pulled off the boots and stood up.

"Did you make a decision?" asked the salesman.

"Yes," Geoff said. "I'll go order." Before he put his runners on, he went to the back of the store and stood on the sensor plate, a smooth metal block a few centimeters higher than the floor. It would record the size of his feet, and his new boots would be made to fit.

Geoff ordered his boots at the self-serve counter against the far wall. He spoke the inventory number of the cheaper pair of boots. When the computer asked him to place his implant within range of the scanner, he held his breath and set the order thief there instead. It should give Geoff's identification while it snuck the inventory number of the expensive boots into the production order.

When no alarm went off, Geoff began breathing again. If the store used a standard program, it would be circumvented. The less expensive price would appear on the bill, but the better boots would be made. He would pick them up in half an hour because if he asked for them to be delivered, he wouldn't get them until tomorrow. He needed boots tonight.

"Let's eat," Trevor said. "We don't have time for anything else."

"Yeah." They bought a couple of Mall Dogs and milk shakes. Geoff nibbled with little appetite. If the theft program didn't work, he hoped it would at least go undetected.

The snack roiled behind Geoff's belly button as he and Trevor returned to Marley's.

"They're ready," said the friendly clerk. She reached beneath her counter and brought out a pair of shiny black boots. Boots with stitched patterns up the sides and around the top, with invisible seams running from the inside of the ankle to upper rim. The expensive boots. New symbols of his slavery to Chin.

"Thanks," said Geoff. "The bill?" It would be the proof of the effectiveness of the order thief.

As the clerk brought the invoice up on her screen, Trevor took his cue and said, "You should try them on first."

"Yeah," Geoff agreed. If the price was three hundred dollars, he would find something wrong with the boots. He glanced at the counter and held his breath. Maybe the computer couldn't decide which boots to bill! When the numbers finally appeared, Geoff inwardly smiled.

He walked over to the nearest customer service bench and kicked off his shoes. He pulled on the boots, walked in a circle around Trevor, and took them off.

"They're good," he said. "Let's go." He quickly put on his runners and returned to the clerk. She scanned his implant, and his bank account balance dropped by forty-nine dollars and ninety-five cents.

"Let's bike," Trevor said. They retrieved their bicycles from the storage facility beside the park and spent the next half hour riding.

Geoff got home early enough to have thirty minutes to himself before supper. He went to his room, put his chair on his bed, and did Chin's exercises. Even after he had used Haynes Heet and taken Lormal all day, the exercises hurt.

Chapter 6

The dance hall was empty.

"Down here," Lui said from the doorway across the hall and a few meters beyond Geoff. "This is where we'll be from now on."

"Why didn't we start there?" asked Geoff.

"'Cause it's too painful to listen to someone as clumsy as you learn to dance on a hard floor. Today's going to be bad enough."

"Then why do it?" asked Geoff as he walked toward Lui.

"If we wait, you'll never get the timing. In here." Lui turned and disappeared into the room faster than anyone would have expected from looking at his size.

Geoff followed him into a dance hall almost exactly like the one they had been in the previous two evenings, even to the coolness of the air. The exception was this room had a smooth, hard floor and different acoustics. Here, every sound ranging from Lui's shuffling steps to the hesitant thumps from Geoff's runners bounced clearly around the room.

Chin, in yellow-and-orange-patterned tights and muscle shirt, was stretching beside one of the rails along a mirrored wall.

"Hurry it up," Chin ordered. "Unless you want Trevor and Rob to get another lesson."

"No." Anger warmed Geoff's blood.

"You dance," said Chin. "No complaints. No acting clumsy. No pretending to forget the steps. Got it?"

"Yeah." Geoff kicked his runners against the wall beyond Lui's chairs. "I got it."

Chin impatiently worked his muscular arms and shoulders as Geoff took his gym bag to the wall by his runners. He removed his street clothes and took his new boots out of the bag.

"Put those on after warm-up," said Chin. "You can't stretch in boots. Fast, we don't have all night." Chin watched Geoff critically as they went through the starting exercises. When they finished, he said, "You haven't been stretching. I told you to do what's on that card four times a day."

"I've been doing it," Geoff said. He had, but only once or twice a day. "It's only been two days."

"Three." said Chin. "At four times a day for three days, I should see results."

"Maybe I'm not as flexible as you think," Geoff said. This was a good opportunity to work on getting Chin to decide he had made a mistake in expecting Geoff to dance.

"Don't give me that." Chin grabbed Geoff by the front of his T-shirt and gave him a shake. "I've been teaching since I was younger than you. I can tell right away what a student's capable of, so don't think you can get out of this by not working or pretending you can't do it. The deal was you'd train and dance in the competition. To get to the competition, you have to dance well enough to pass preliminaries."

"Preliminaries weren't in the bargain," Geoff said. Not that it mattered. Surely, Chin did not intend to actually compete. This was his way of punishing Geoff for speaking out of line.

"You won't be ready in time for them. As a previous champion, I can bypass the qualifying rounds. If I do that, I'm expected to show up with a partner who can dance. You're not going up there and embarrassing me." He pushed Geoff back a little and let go of him. "We're doing the same as yesterday. Put your boots on."

Geoff silently did as ordered.

At the same time, Chin removed his little slippers and pulled on a pair of worn boots.

Chin glanced at Lui. The room filled with music.

"Listen," Chin said. "Learn which beat we start on...seven, eight." They swayed, glaring into each other's eyes. Right, left, right, left, straighten, and step in a circle. Their boots clicked on the hard floor—toe and then heel—perfectly in time.

It surprised Geoff so much that he lost the beat.

"Pick it up at the next step," Chin ordered. "Turn in front of me, *step*." He moved forward and rested his hands on Geoff's shoulders. "Slow it down a little. Stay with the music." By the time the seven rounds were done, their footwork was synchronized more often than not.

Lui gave them a ten second break and started the music again.

Geoff concentrated on timing his steps to match Chin's.

He realized he wasn't paying enough attention to the rest of the dance when Chin thumped him between the shoulder blades and snapped, "Keep your back straight!"

Halfway through that song, Lui began calling corrections to Geoff. It felt endless, but as Geoff concentrated on carrying out Lui's directions, his remaining problem with his footwork disappeared.

"Two minutes," Chin finally said at the end of a song. He walked over to Lui for a drink of water.

Geoff sat on the floor beside his bag and drank his orange juice. With his weight off his feet, they began to throb. He wiped the sweat from his eyes and tried to shake off his dizziness.

"Told you he has a feel for music," Chin said.

Geoff heard him so clearly that he thought Chin had snuck up beside him. He defensively turned, but Chin, forearms on the back of the chair Lui used as a footrest, was hunched forward, speaking quietly. Geoff was not supposed to hear them. He had because of the room's incredible acoustics.

"Put it up to round two every second cycle and keep on his technique," Chin said to Lui.

Geoff groaned to himself when Chin ordered five minutes of stretching before they resumed practice of the dance. He was certain the mid-practice stretch was responsible for much of his pain.

"Reach!" Chin ordered. "There's no point in stretching if you're not stretching."

Geoff grimaced and extended his right arm. He was standing, feet shoulder width apart, left hand on left hip, bent at the waist to the left with his right arm up over his head and his hand pointed at the floor. For sure, he was going to hurt.

Back on the dance floor, Lui corrected Geoff's vertical alignment and turns most often. Geoff quickly figured out that Lui only called for other adjustments when Geoff had those two elements correct.

The continuous turns blurred the room. Geoff countered his dizziness by ignoring his surroundings and positioning himself in relation to Chin.

Chin usually stayed at arm's length. He made one exception during the front-to-back steps. Instead of resting his hands on Geoff's shoulders, Chin stepped closer, put both arms around Geoff, and blew in his ear.

Geoff braced himself and threw his right elbow at Chin's belly.

Chin let go of Geoff and continued dancing, swinging to the left and easily avoiding the blow. He punched Geoff in the back.

The air whooshed out of Geoff's lungs. He staggered forward but did not fall.

"Never break the rhythm," Chin said.

"Blast off," gasped Geoff. He skipped brushing shoulders and fell back into step for the side-by-side sway, staying a meter and a half away from Chin.

"Straighten your shoulders," called Lui.

Geoff kept his distance from Chin. He ached from neck to ankles. Below his ankles his new boots felt like they were pulsing two sizes smaller with every heartbeat. His feet dragged, his steps clicking a shade slower than Chin's.

"Look alive," Chin said.

"It's past my bedtime." Geoff sped up his turn and stepped into the front-to-back position on time and more than arm's length from Chin.

"Point your toes," said Lui.

Chin moved up behind Geoff and rested his hands on Geoff's shoulders. Geoff jumped a little, startled, but he did not lose the beat or interrupt his sideways swing.

The last half dozen rounds lasted an eternity. Geoff sighed with relief when the music stopped.

"Take your boots off," Chin ordered as he kicked his own toward Lui's chairs.

Geoff bit the inside of his lip to keep from groaning when he removed his boots. Thank the stars he had not gotten a cheap pair. Freed of the stiff footwear, his feet felt as if they were swelling with every thud of his heart.

That the slow movements and stretches of Chin's cool-down exercises actually felt good surprised Geoff. He still ached but not as intensely.

"I fixed it so tomorrow you come here during your last hour of work," Chin said. "They'll have you on record as being there because you're not officially here."

"Does that mean I get paid for the time?" asked Geoff.

"I'll think about it," replied Chin. "Saturday, be here at 0845. We'll train before you go to work. Next week—"

"I can't stay out this late every night," Geoff interrupted. "Three nights this week is pushing it." If he left the recreation center at 2200, it was 2220 by the time he made the transit connections and got home. His parents *might* let it go without comment. More likely, Dad or Mom would say something about responsible students making sure they were in at a reasonable hour. Besides, he did not want to be here every night. With any luck, Chin would quickly tire of this game.

"I got to schedule you around my classes," Chin said. "So days you don't work, Monday and Wednesday, be here for 2100, Tuesday and Thursday for 1900. Any time you work at the arcade,

I get you for the last hour unless I tell you different. If you have a Friday or weekend you don't work, I'll set a time."

"Yeah." Maybe by next weekend, Chin would have someone else to torture.

Chapter 7

Geoff's usual Friday shift at the arcade lasted from 1630 to 2200. He had time for a quick snack before he signed in. As Geoff brushed his left arm over the scanner so that it could read his implant, the manager came out of his office.

"I got the word," said Geoff's boss, a middle-aged man with a big nose and a bigger moustache. "You're gone the last hour of your Friday shift for the next while. You know how long a while is?"

"No, Mr. Manz." If Chin had not told Mr. Manz anything, Geoff would not either. With any luck, by next Friday he would be released from Chin's torture.

"Hell," grumbled Mr. Manz. "If they leave me shorthanded for more than a couple shifts, they're going to pay for the time."

Geoff blinked in surprise. He was really going to get paid when he wasn't here? Training with Chin fell under Lung business?

"Don't they tell you kids anything these days?" The permanent laugh lines around Mr. Manz's friendly brown eyes deepened. He lowered his voice and continued, "When the organization has you working on something and you're officially at work, being signed in and on the payroll is your alibi. I'll sign you out at 2200."

"Oh. Thanks."

"It's not too busy yet. Go drive a few rounds in car three of Indy 500. We had a couple complaints, but the system check didn't find anything."

When Geoff's alarm went off Saturday morning, he gave the Lormal a few minutes to work before he rubbed on the Haynes Heet.

Geoff dragged himself out of bed to stretch. If he didn't loosen up, he would really suffer trying to keep up to Chin. Besides, his parents would get suspicious if he poked his head out of his room too early. That chore completed, Geoff took out his new tube of skin regeneration gel. It was supposed to have anaesthetic in it. He slathered it on his feet before he pulled on his socks.

At 0818, Geoff made a dash to the washroom and then the kitchen.

"Morning, Dad," he said as he ran in.

Tony turned from cooking pancakes and asked, "What are you doing up so early? It's Saturday, you know."

"Yeah." Geoff smiled. His feet did feel a little numb! "I said I'd be at work early, and I can game first if I have time." Geoff popped the lid off a container of canned peaches. As he ate them, he stashed snacks in his gym bag.

Fallah entered the kitchen and said, "You could eat from a bowl, you know."

"This way doesn't dirty a dish," explained Geoff. "See you after work."

"We're going out for supper," Fallah said. "I'll leave you something in the fridge."

Geoff's Saturday shift went from 1000 to 1800. He usually came straight home, tired and hungry.

"Pizza?" asked Geoff.

Fallah smiled and nodded.

"Thanks, Mom. Bye, Dad." Geoff grabbed his bag and went to meet Chin.

He chewed on the inside of his lip as he went down the silent hall of the private club. He was as nervous this morning as he had been Tuesday night. Then he hadn't known what to expect. Now he dreaded the thought of showering here. He couldn't go to work dripping sweat, and it would take too long to go to the recreation center by the school to clean up.

Like before, Geoff's training session with Chin consisted of stretching and perfecting his technique of the basic steps. Before long, pain pulsed on Geoff's tortured feet inside his boots.

After the mid-lesson stretch, instead of holding Geoff's shoulders during the front-to-back steps, Chin cupped his hands over Geoff's buttocks.

Having learned through painful experience not to break off the dance, Geoff waited to retaliate until they were in the side-by-side position. He put his right hand over his left fist and rammed his left elbow into Chin's muscle-covered lower ribs.

Chin gasped and swore. His heel clicked on the floor a shade slower than Geoff's.

Geoff chuckled.

Lui laughed.

Chin stepped to the side, turned, and on the next beat, kicked Geoff in the upper chest. The sole of his boot landed perfectly centered, with the toe inside Geoff's left shoulder and the heel inside his right.

Geoff's eyes widened. He exhaled with a hiss and dropped to the floor.

Chin went to get his water bottle from the chair beside Lui.

"Dumb kid," Lui said through his chuckles. "He done for the day?"

"Ion-blasted little rock worm surprised me," Chin said. "He's not hurt." He glanced back at Geoff, who was sprawled out in the middle of the floor, motionless.

"And then he had the nerve to laugh." Lui grinned at Chin's scowl and added, "I don't think he's breathing."

"If he's not, it's not from that little tap," said Chin.

Geoff blinked away his tears as he listened to the two men. He would rather die than give Chin the satisfaction of seeing how much he hurt, but he was going to take as long as possible to get up. This more than made up for his not getting hit yesterday.

Chin lowered his voice, yet Geoff still heard him ask, "Has Do called? How'd the Oliver job go?"

"Haven't heard a thing," Lui said.

"Damn. It should be done already." Chin put his water down. "Get up, kid. We're not finished."

Geoff rolled onto his side. He would stay there and pretend he was hurt too badly to continue if he thought he could get away with it. There were two things wrong with that idea. Chin seemed to know the blow had hurt but not broken anything, and a stubborn streak of pride insisted Geoff get up and act as if he were not hurt at all.

"That was stupid," Chin said as they took the face-to-face starting position.

"Never said I was smart," responded Geoff.

As they danced, he nervously waited for Chin to touch him again other than on the shoulders. It came several rounds later. From holding Geoff's shoulders, Chin slid his hands down to hug Geoff's waist. He let go and swung aside, so Geoff's elbow missed. Neither of them missed a step.

When the lesson ended, Geoff took his bag and went to the change rooms at the other side of the dance floor. A low bench between rows of lockers stood between Geoff and a second exit. On his left below a wall of mirrors was a cream-colored counter holding a row of dark red sinks. At right angles to the sinks and facing the back row of lockers stood a line of shower stalls tiled in cream and red.

Geoff showered quickly, afraid that Chin or Lui would come in and harass him. Neither did.

Chapter 8

The other members of the Taurids gathered in the arcade shortly before Geoff finished work. They played a few games but were obviously waiting for Geoff.

Geoff was showing two young boys how the controls worked for virtual mountain biking. Only seven or eight years old, they had come to the arcade with an older sister or babysitter. She bought them one hour of game time and left.

"Everything working?" Mr. Manz asked when Geoff had the excited youngsters set up.

"They'll do all right," said Geoff. "I dropped the skill level for them." One of his jobs was to make sure new and inexperienced customers felt welcome and had a good time. That way, they would come back.

"Good job," Mr. Manz said. "You can start closing off anything you got going. Looks like you have something to do, so don't stay even if Jodi's a little late."

"Yeah." Geoff had no enthusiasm for going out with the gang. He was too tired and hungry and sore. He couldn't refuse to go, though, so he insisted everyone wait until he had something to eat before they even told him what was planned.

"I've been here all day, and I'm starved," Geoff said. "Why didn't you bring a pizza or something?"

"We'll hit a place on the way," responded Trevor. The fine gold chains hanging from his ears matched his eyebrow metal and the heavy chain around his neck.

"I still got to lift on an empty stomach," Geoff grumbled. "My touch might be off." He could not object more vigorously without arousing suspicions about his loyalty.

"We'll find an easy place," said Trevor. "Maybe the mall."

They rode the cross-deck transit to a high and wide mall hall lined with two levels of stores. As they bumped their way through the most crowded part of the food court, Geoff acquired supper.

"Excuse me," he said to a girl about his own age, holding her eyes with his as he took the French fries off her tray. Two steps farther, he snagged an Orange Julius off a tray a man had lifted up so a couple of kids could pass beneath it. Drinks were hard to get. They weighed so much they had to be filched from either the center of a loaded tray or else during a really good distraction.

Geoff passed the fries and drink to Trevor and pressed through the crowd in search of a burger. He bypassed young kids and everyone who looked like they couldn't afford to have their food stolen. It was something he had started doing nearly a year ago, when it had occurred to him that lifting free lunches for his friends created consequences for others. Being part of the gang had seemed like harmless fun a few years ago. Now he always wondered if someone suffered because of his actions.

He filched two burgers, gave them to Rob, and kept going. As he circled the food court, he picked up three more servings of fries, two of chicken nuggets, a fruit salad, a huge cinnamon bun with icing, and cherry cheesecake.

He met the other boys at their usual table in front of the ice-cream parlor. His haul was spread out and unwrapped but not eaten. As the hand, Geoff had first choice.

"Is one of those a chicken burger?" asked Geoff. As much as he would like to abstain from his illicit spoils, he was too hungry not to eat.

"Here." Trevor passed it to him. "What else?"

"Fries and the fruit and the Julius and a bit of that cinnamon bun."

Everyone else divided up the rest of the take. Then they all looked at Trevor.

"We got two jobs," their leader said. "First, we give a message to a store that isn't cooperating with the organization, and then we help distribute some product. Its usual route got slammed."

"I heard about that." Hans adjusted his headband to keep his toffee-colored hair out of his drink. "Things went bad at Oliver's, and they lost half the shipment."

The discussion flowed from Lung business to sports to girls. Geoff did the least talking, in part because he did the most eating. When he was done, he yawned and stretched.

"What're you doing yawning?" asked Rob, wrapping his drawled vowels around a mouthful of burger.

"We're just getting started," Trevor said. "Wake up."

"I already had a long day," said Geoff. "But I'm good for the job." He could not say anything else and keep his place with them.

"Let's go then," Trevor said. "We got to be ready for the deliveries by twenty."

Geoff's tiredness evaporated in the tense atmosphere of the transit ride to their first assignment.

"I'm not dressed for this." Geoff indicated the tight cuffs on his shirt. "Anybody got a sweater or jacket? How much are we taking?"

"Whatever we can, especially if it's expensive," Trevor answered. "The security's disabled 'cause there's a bunch of us visiting tonight. We're to turn the haul over to a senior."

Geoff nodded. Not being required to target a specific item made it easier.

Hans gave Geoff his light jacket. It was too big for Geoff; however, the elastic cuffs kept the sleeves off his hands, and with the zipper done up halfway, it fit snugly around Geoff's hips and made a baggy cavern around his torso, one perfect for stashing stolen goods.

"Ready," Geoff said. They switched cars and ended the ride on the second deck, a third of the way around the station from the arcade where Geoff worked.

"That one." Trevor pointed to a luxury goods import shop. "Rob, you're inside lookout. I'll pretend to order something. Don't break anything. This is a friendly persuasion visit."

The store owners stood shoulder to shoulder in front of the counter. Both were on the far side of middle age. The man was tall and broad, his wife nearly as large.

Geoff glanced at them, saw they recognized trouble when it came in, and looked away. He worked better if he only thought about the job, not the people.

Rob stayed at the door. Trevor went to the counter and asked about special orders. Geoff strolled down a display aisle, followed by Hans.

"Got some nice stuff here," Geoff said. "My mom might like that." As if he were really shopping, he pointed to a paper book.

"Or this." Hans tapped on the glass display case of jewelry.

Geoff continued pretending to shop for his mother as they both took everything they could hide on their persons. They walked out the door with odd lumps visible beneath their clothing. Trevor and Rob came out a moment later.

"This way." Trevor went to a store three doors from the one they had hit. "Leave everything here."

Geoff and Hans went to the back of the store and dropped off their take from the import shop. Most of it would be returned to the shop when the owners made a deal with the Lung families. Geoff fingered a smooth stone carving of a seal before he set it on the table with the rest of the loot.

The man collecting the items picked it up and rubbed it.

"Soapstone," he said. "Worth a fortune up here. You got some good stuff. That all of it?"

Geoff nodded.

"You guys making a delivery tonight?"

"Yeah."

"Head over there now."

"It's too early," objected Geoff. Trevor had said they were scheduled for 2000. It wasn't even 1930.

"Doesn't matter."

"Okay." Geoff left the store and told Trevor new orders were to do the delivery right away.

"Let's go then," said Trevor.

They arrived at the professional basketball court by 1940. It was game night. The noise of the fans in the packed stands could be heard out in the corridor.

"Entrance sixteen," Trevor said. He gave the man in the ticket booth his name.

"Four of you?" asked the man.

Trevor nodded.

"You're early," the man said as his small counter holoview filled with miniature images of the heads and shoulders of all four boys.

"The guy at our other job said come straight here," Trevor said.

"What the hell does he think the schedule's for?" The man held up his hand to prevent Trevor from answering and waved him inside. He carefully matched each gang member to an image in his holoview before he let them in.

"Washroom by E section," he said to Rob, the last one in.

They gathered around Trevor and strolled down the center of the walkway. It circled the stands surrounding the basketball court. Section E was nearly halfway around. As they approached the washrooms, another gang came from the opposite direction. Trevor swaggered, his gold chains clinking. Following his lead, the Taurids strutted as they arrived at the designated pick-up spot.

The burly man beside the maintenance cart blocking the washroom entrance looked from one gang to the other and said, "Get down the hall and sort out who's here first." He turned his back and pulled wrenches from the rack.

The two gangs of boys walked side by side, each group on one side of the corridor.

"We got to be quick about this," Trevor said. "Why don't you guys watch the game for a while?"

"This is our time," the other gang's leader said. "Take a walk." He copied Trevor's crossed arms and stared at him. On both sides of the hall, clothes rustled and shoes shuffled as the boys faced off.

"We can't rumble," Trevor said. "They'd de-orbit us for screwing up the delivery. Historian's challenge?" Most gangs had a member who specialized in learning the history of the Lung families. In a challenge, the historians tried to come up with a question the opposing historian could not answer. Long-haired, spacy-looking Hans prided himself on the volume of trivia he knew.

"Take too long," said the other. "Our hands can settle it." Everyone quickly agreed that was the thing to do.

Outwardly, Geoff did as well. Inside, he was not so sure. While a contest between hands was another accepted method of settling a dispute, with face saved for everyone but the losing hand, he was tired and sore and uncertain of maintaining his standing as the fastest hand. He could not refuse though.

The leaders cut a deck of cards. Trevor drew the low one.

"We'll slap," said the slender girl who was other hand.

Geoff handed his gym bag to Rob and stepped into the space between the groups, standing face-to-face with other hand. They held their closed fists in front of their bodies, the backs of their hands facing upward. Nervousness and fear heightened Geoff's perceptions, stretching the moment into a long wait.

"Ready," Trevor said.

Geoff and the other hand moved their fists toward each other until their knuckles touched. Geoff stared into the other's face, waiting for a sign she was about to act. He saw it in her squinted brown eyes as the knuckles pressed against his moved away.

Geoff jerked his hands toward his body. A gust of air pushed against his knuckles as the girl's hands swept through the space Geoff's had just occupied. Relief turned Geoff's legs to jelly. Leftover adrenaline made them tremble.

"How the hell?" the other hand asked.

"We'll go first," Trevor said. The other gang turned to stroll the circuit around the court and stands.

Trevor held up one hand, palm facing Geoff, and grinned. Geoff grinned back and slapped hands. He reveled in the congratulations of the rest of the gang during the short walk back to the washroom.

"Two at a time," ordered the man in the doorway. Rob and Hans went first. "Next," the man said a short time later.

Trevor and Geoff entered the bathroom in time to see Rob and Hans leave through the far exit. A man stood by the sinks with Trevor and Geoff's images floating in his wrist phone's tiny holoview.

He deleted them and said, "ID."

The boys pushed up their left sleeves. The man scrutinized their tattoos and then gestured toward the stalls and said, "Go get your load."

Two stalls had open doors revealing a fully clothed man seated on the toilet. Each held an open briefcase on his lap.

When Geoff stood in front of one, the man said, "Take your shirt off."

"I could just stash your stuff in my gym bag," said Geoff.

"No." From his briefcase, the man picked up a brown belt as wide as Geoff's forearm was long. It looked like it was stuffed with palm-sized pillows.

"This goes around your waist." As he helped Geoff wrap it around his torso, he growled, "You're too skinny. Hold still." He overlapped it in front of Geoff's belly and sealed the edge down.

Geoff shivered from the cool, slick feel of it. Covering him from below his waist to just under his armpits, the belt was invisible on casual glance. Geoff ran his hand over it. It even felt like skin.

"This is pretty tough, but don't abuse it," the man said. "You tear it, and we'll take the cost of what you lose out of your hide. Hold out your arms." He wrapped smaller bands around Geoff's upper arms, making it appear as if he suddenly had larger biceps.

The man pulled out two more bands and said, "These go around your lower legs. Pull your socks up over them."

Geoff stretched his socks around them and tucked his shirt back into his jeans. He had occasionally made drug deliveries before, but he had never carried so much at once. It felt heavy. The extra mass made his sore muscles ache.

"The other kid's got your instructions. Get it done, go home, and keep quiet."

"Okay."

Geoff and Trevor went directly out the closest exit before they stopped to play the delivery directions.

"We got eight stops," Trevor said.

Geoff groaned. This night was going to last forever.

"At least they're all on the same side of the station," said Trevor. "That makes it quicker."

"And they're on lighter decks." Geoff desperately wanted to get his weight and the extra he carried off his feet. Fortunately, the sports arena was surrounded by transit stops. He collapsed into a seat on the elevator car and sighed. Four decks up, he had to force himself to his feet again.

The first drop, Trevor's waistband, went to the night manager of a residential area fast food restaurant. Her face scowled briefly in Trevor's wrist phone holoview and then vanished. All the directions and the people designated to receive the deliveries were automatically erased after they played.

Trevor and Geoff spotted her as they entered the store. She gave a single nod and went to the office at the back. They followed.

As soon as the door closed behind them, she said, "Let's see it. How come it's so late?"

"We don't know," Trevor said as he pulled the band of drugs from under his shirt. "This is when they sent us."

"Well, tell them I got customers waiting. They don't like it when their stuff's late." She dropped the delivery in a desk drawer. "Get out."

Most of the other deliveries went as quickly and with as little courtesy, but they still took the better part of an hour.

"One left." Trevor poked at his wrist com to get the address for the last delivery. "Why the hell'd they send *us* to a bar?"

"It's probably the staff entrance," said Geoff. "If a cop stops us, we can say we're looking for your cousin."

"Who'd believe that?" Trevor led the way to the cross-deck transit stop. "We're better off telling them we're whores looking for customers."

"*You* say that." Geoff flopped onto the empty bench.

Trevor sat beside Geoff and said, "Be more believable from you." He laughed and ducked Geoff's swing. "You're slow."

"I'm tired." Geoff dragged himself to his feet at the sound of the approaching car.

Eight minutes later, they exited it onto a deck with negligible gravity. No shrubs or leafy vines lined this corridor. The walls were covered in flashing lights, three-dimensional signs, and holographic murals. Most advertised sex, alcohol, and recreational drugs. Some included illegal drugs and pornography.

"Been a while since we got thrown out of a place like this," Trevor said.

"We didn't even make it *into* that place," said Geoff. That had been almost a month ago. They had been with Rob and Hans, and a policeman had spotted them leaving the transit. He had ordered them all right back on it.

"Here it is." Trevor stopped at a metal door. He reached for the buzzer. The door slid open before he pressed it.

"Who's got my stuff?" asked the hairy man filling the doorway.

"Me," Trevor said.

"Get in here." The man let Trevor in but waved Geoff back. "You wait." The door slammed shut.

Geoff stepped to the side and leaned against the wall. It was early in the business day for this place, only 2100, so there were few other people around. The two who did drift past barely glanced at him.

Still, Geoff soon started to fidget. Trevor was taking a long time to come back out. The door opened. Geoff had his mouth open to demand an explanation for why he had to wait so long when he realized he faced trouble, not Trevor.

Chapter 9

Two men stood came out. The smaller one stayed in the doorway, arms crossed, bald head tilted slightly to the side as he stared at Geoff. His smooth face held dark, bottomless eyes. He wore black slacks and a scarlet silk shirt trimmed with lace. The shirt's collarless neckline began at his navel and revealed a smooth chest as white and hairless as his head.

The other man's broad front provided the background for a dozen gold chains. They sparkled against the gleaming finish of his dark brown, leatherlike shirt. Elongated golden teardrops hung from his earlobes, flashing among his chocolate-colored ringlets.

He waited until Geoff turned his involuntary half-step backward into a stiff stance and then said, "How'd you like to make some easy money?"

About to give a flat-out no, Geoff reconsidered on the chance they were with Lung and wanted something like a message delivered.

"Doing what?" asked Geoff.

A feminine giggle answered him. A young woman with artificially yellow hair joined the man in the doorway, making a show of attempting to pull her too-small bodice over her large breasts. She batted nearly pupilless blue eyes at Geoff.

"Whatever the customer wants," she said.

"Get back," snarled the large man. The woman ran inside. The man turned back to Geoff.

"Easy money," he repeated. "The pay's good, the fringe benefits even better." From his pocket, he pulled a small silver ball that was no larger than the tip of his thumb. When he twisted its halves in opposite directions, pink mist puffed up, spreading in a loose cloud between the three of them. The bald man leaned toward it and inhaled deeply.

Geoff pushed against the wall to move himself back. He didn't know what the mist was, but if the pimp used it for recruiting, it was probably highly addictive. Where the hell was Trevor? Friendship and one of the golden rules of the gang would not allow Geoff to leave without him. He might have to go in there and find him. He could now. All he had to do was get past the bald whore in the doorway.

"I have many resources," the pimp said. "And I'm always happy to do a favor for a pretty youngster. Call me for party supplies... or if you need a hand getting out of a tight spot. Just spread the word for Sammy to come help."

"Yeah?" Geoff backed farther away from the spreading pink mist. "I'll remember that." If he was going to charge past the guy in the doorway, he had to do it now. He'd have to hold his breath and dive. He was still close enough to the wall to brace against it to jump.

Before Geoff could move, Trevor stepped into view. The bald man got out of Trevor's way by moving into the dissipating pink cloud.

"Hold your breath," Geoff called in case Trevor did not realize the possible potency of the drug.

"No worry," Trevor said, but he did hold his breath as he skirted the pale fog.

"Don't forget," called the pimp as the two boys left.

Without turning, Geoff held up his right fist, middle finger extended.

"Forget what?" asked Trevor.

"What the hell took long? It doesn't take thirty seconds to make a drop."

"The guy showed me around," answered Trevor. "Gave me a drink, and we walked through the dancers' change room. Some of those girls—"

"You bother thinking why he did that?" Geoff stopped and waved back at the club they had just left. "While you got the royal treatment, *I* was stuck outside with a dirty pimp!"

"You take things too personal. What did he mean, don't forget?"

"To call him if I need anything," Geoff replied. He shivered, so tired the evening temperature drop felt more like ten degrees than four. Because he hadn't planned to be out this late, he wasn't dressed for it.

Trevor grinned and said, "That sounds friendly."

"Blast off."

"Let's go to the arcade 'round this deck," Trevor said as they boarded the cross-deck transit. "I heard they got a new asteroids game."

"I'm going home." Geoff dropped into a seat, rested his head against the wall, and closed his eyes. He ignored Trevor's spoilsport comments and let his mind drift into a gray place where his body did not hurt so badly.

"Wake up!" Trevor grabbed Geoff's shoulder and shook him. It hurt.

Geoff swung a fist at Trevor before he opened his eyes.

Trevor ducked.

"I'm not asleep," snarled Geoff.

"Sure you're not." Trevor let go of him. "What's with you? It's only 2120."

"Long day."

"Ten hours? Babies stay awake longer than that."

"Blast off. I was at Chin's project before I went to work."

"Mmmmm." Trevor did not comment further. Except for the time at the arcade when Geoff had run to the transit, in the four days since it had happened, neither of them had mentioned their visit with Chin and Lui.

Trevor woke Geoff up again to switch to an elevator car. Geoff sighed as the heavier gravity pulled him down into the seat cushions. It wasn't until Trevor transferred to the cross-deck car with him that he realized his friend had not continued down to his own home deck.

"Where are you going?" asked Geoff.

"Making sure you get off at your stop," Trevor answered. "Otherwise you're going to ride around till the vagrancy cops pick you up."

"Wouldn't," Geoff said, though he wasn't sure of that.

The walk from the transit to the apartment, which Geoff often did in less than two minutes, took nearly ten. He drifted down the hall with long, low steps that involved more hang time than walking time. When he opened the door, loud music blasted out of the apartment. Barbara and Nadine turned from the holoview.

"What are you doing here?" Barbara asked.

"I live here." Geoff shut the door and went to the kitchen for the pizza Fallah had promised.

"You're usually home late on Saturdays."

"I usually don't go out until twenty or 2100." Geoff found the pizza. There was only one slice left. "You ate my pizza!"

"I figured you'd have supper wherever you were," answered Barbara.

"That was *my* pizza. You know I always eat when I get home. What'm I going to have now?" If she knew what he was going through for her, she'd leave his pizza alone *and* bake cookies.

"The fridge is full of stuff," Barbara said.

Geoff finished off the pizza as he made a sandwich. He took it to his room so that he could check his messages in private as he ate. He was tempted to shove the clean laundry off his bed onto the floor; however, it would get mixed up with dirty laundry, and he'd never get it sorted. He piled it on his desk and then dressed in the shorts and oversized T-shirt he slept in.

As Geoff fell toward his mattress, he remembered he had to stretch. He had not done any of Chin's exercises since morning. Knowing he would not get up once he hit the mattress, he pushed himself to the side and landed on the floor. Even in half gravity, that hurt. Groaning, he rested his head on the warm clothes he had just taken off.

"Bubs," Barbara called from the other side of Geoff's door. "Are you all right?"

"Yeah."

"What happened?"

"I tripped on my chair." Geoff rolled onto his knees.

"Clumsy. You sure you're okay?"

As Geoff got to his feet, he said, "Come in already."

Barbara slid the door open and eyed Geoff.

"Well, you're not bleeding," she said.

"Told you I'm fine. Here, take this back." He held out the empty glass and plate.

"Take it yourself," Barbara said, but she entered the room and took them. "You going to watch the movie with us?"

"I'm going to bed."

She said good-night and left.

Geoff turned on some music, put his chair on his bed, and rushed through his required exercises as quietly as possible. When he was done, he ordered the music to shut off in five minutes and collapsed in his bed. He stayed awake just long enough to pull up the covers.

The next week went much the same. The fierce pain Geoff had suffered the first few days diminished to morning soreness. He advanced to dancing the third round at its proper speed.

The following Monday, the day that marked two full weeks since Geoff had begun to learn the Simba, was the day he refused to tolerate any more of Chin's groping. The first half of the training hour was spent perfecting moves Geoff thought he already did right. He even did them in his sleep and woke up sweaty and tangled in his sheets.

The music stopped. As usual, Chin walked over to Lui for a break without saying anything to Geoff.

That was fine with Geoff. He went to his bag with short steps, feet wide apart for balance against the dizziness. Geoff glared at Chin's smooth stride. How did *he* keep from being dizzy? Geoff sat by his bag, back against the wall, and sipped his juice.

"That special carton from Terra went bad," Lui said.

"All of it?" asked Chin.

Lui nodded.

"Found or dead?"

"Word is none alive," said Lui. "No one else knows. Let's hope they can keep it that way. The last thing we need is the cops in there."

In his quiet place against the wall, Geoff wondered what had died. Was Lung importing animals? Live pets in stations were very, very expensive and strictly controlled. Most stationers only saw living animals in the tiny "Touch Me" part of the zoo. The main part of the zoo was an empty chamber where feel 'n' smell holos were played of animals in their natural habitats.

Few people went through the trouble of filing an import request and proving they were wealthy enough to feed a pet and pay its station air and heat charges. If the organization found a way to smuggle animals on station, they could breed them. That would be a real moneymaker on the black market. Probably the only reason it had not yet happened were all the security checks travelers went through. Not even the minute amount of live material required to grow a clone could pass. Cargo that was not exposed to space was carefully screened and irradiated to prevent both smuggling and the inadvertent transport of pests.

Everyone in school learned about the Luna City rat infestation from 2044 to 2052. Students were also shown holos of stray and unwanted animals in Terran cities, but that didn't keep them from yearning for their own cuddly little cat or dog or hamster.

Because the really good android pets were as costly as they were cute, neither Geoff nor Barbara owned one. When they were very young, they had a robotic kitten. They loved it dearly, even after they grew older. It took a lot of convincing from Tony and Fallah before Geoff and Barbara agreed to give their kitty to a neighboring family with toddlers.

"Move it."

At Chin's call, Geoff pulled his wandering thoughts back to the present. He removed his boots and went back to the dance area to do the torturous stretches.

"Work on this one more," Chin said. He sat on the floor, legs spread in a sideways split, hands on his ankles, and chest on the floor.

Geoff nodded so Chin would think he was listening and would obey.

When Chin and Geoff had their boots back on and stood ready to dance, Chin said, "We start with the whole song now. Keep your turns sharp."

The music started, a basic rendering of the song that seemed to be one of Lui's favorites. The chubby observer watched silently at first, but by the third round, he apparently could not remain quiet any longer.

"Turn your leg out more," Lui said. "Pivot sharp to get in line."

Geoff did as ordered, spinning on the ball of his left foot to face Chin. The much anticipated round four, while considerably more rapid than rounds one and seven, was only marginally faster than rounds three and five. Geoff had been so thoroughly trained in correct technique that he easily completed the round without errors or falling behind.

"Again," Chin ordered as soon as the song ended.

Another version of the music played, and the routine of the last two weeks continued until Chin slid a hand down Geoff's back and buttocks.

Geoff retaliated with an elbow in Chin's ribs. The older man did not try to evade it but responded by hitting Geoff in the shoulder. The painful two-finger jab nearly knocked Geoff off balance. He struggled to complete the step and get his heel on the floor in time with Chin's.

They stopped face-to-face and swayed to the side as the sixth cycle of the song began. Chin smiled.

Geoff glared up at him.

As they turned, Chin leaned over and kissed Geoff's cheek.

Geoff promptly stomped on Chin's toes.

Chin delivered a stinging blow across Geoff's back.

They turned in opposite directions. When Geoff stepped into position for the front-to-back sway, he moved forward to be well in front of Chin.

Chin came closer, hugged Geoff to his chest, and nuzzled his neck.

Geoff jumped but did not break step.

Chin laughed.

Geoff straightened from the sideways swing and headbutted Chin in the face.

Chin swore and hit Geoff in the ribs.

Break apart and turn, Geoff got his breath back as they lined up to brush shoulders. He stepped forward and hooked a short punch to Chin's washboard belly. It hurt his hand and hardly drew a wheeze from Chin.

Turn again, step together in the side-by-side, Chin slammed the outside edge of his hand against Geoff's chest three times.

Geoff held on to his balance and finished the step before he felt the pain from the blows. It began at the points of impact and spread across his front. His ribs resisted breathing. Geoff refused to let Chin see his pain as they stood face-to-face to start the final round of the dance, but he winced in agony when he shifted his shoulders in the opening side-swing.

Chin smiled.

Geoff ended the stalk-and-circle closer to Chin than usual, and as they moved into the front-to-back sway, he stomped his heel on Chin's right foot again.

"Blast off," Chin growled. "Rock-headed little vacuum-brain." He pounded Geoff's back with eight quick blows, four from each hand in two rows from his shoulders to mid-back.

Geoff stepped forward to keep from falling on his face. He moved back and smashed his left heel onto Chin's left foot.

"Go to hell," Geoff said. He clicked his other boot, toe and then heel, onto the floor right with the beat. A quick spin on the ball of his foot moved him away from Chin and into the next step. Geoff clenched his teeth and glared up at Chin.

"Not bad." Chin smiled again. They brushed shoulders and pivoted, stepping into the side-by-side position.

As Geoff swung his weight back to center, Chin peppered his shoulder with a flurry of blows. Geoff let their force push him around and into the final face-to-face pose.

Chin turned and walked off the floor.

Not daring to leave the dance area before the session ended and unsure if he could even make it to his bag by the wall, Geoff dropped to the floor, sitting cross-legged. The places where Chin had hit him hurt more every second. Geoff leaned forward, laying his forearms on his legs and resting his head on his arms. The universe shrank to a tiny spot of cold, pain, and nausea.

Chapter 10

"Don't you look a sight." The cheery, unfamiliar voice seemed to come from the air above Geoff's right ear. He rolled his head to the side and opened his eyes. A young man knelt there, watching his handheld scanner. He wore shorts and a T-shirt and had a small towel hung around his neck.

"Who're you?" asked Geoff.

"Your doctor, at least for a few minutes." The man put his instrument into his small gym bag and pulled out a bottle of spray-on skin. "Chin calls me the Mad Medic. You're lucky I'm still here. You're even luckier he didn't want to really damage you. Take your shirt off."

"Huh?" Geoff couldn't process the information as fast as the Mad Medic talked.

The man grabbed the bottom of Geoff's T-shirt and pulled it up.

Geoff raised his arms so the shirt could come off, but the doctor only pulled it over Geoff's head and up to his elbows. He left it tangled around Geoff's forearms.

"Hold still," ordered the Mad Medic. "These are all superficial. Well, most of them, but you're shocky. Don't throw up on me." He began spritzing something on Geoff's bruises.

Geoff rested his arms in his lap again and blinked at the self-proclaimed doctor. He had the strangest bedside manner Geoff had ever encountered.

"I'm making bruise treatment patches," the doctor said. "Keep them on all night and shower in the morning. You'll be fine. Here." He dug in his bag again. "This is a Blissmaert III patch. He said I shouldn't give you one, but you might not make it home without it." He stuck it to Geoff's arm.

"I got Blisso," Geoff said, though he knew the Mad Medic's drug was stronger.

"Don't take yours for a few hours." The doctor moved to Geoff's other side and continued working. When he finished, he closed his bag and said, "Next time, pick on someone your own size. I don't want to see you again." He waved to Lui on his way out. As he crossed the hall to Chin's office, he called, "What do you mean...you think your toe's broken?"

Geoff put his T-shirt back on. Maybe he would stop shivering. He straightened his legs and rubbed at the twinges of cramps in them.

"Go home," Lui ordered.

Geoff pulled on his clothes, grabbed his bag, and left. Impatience ate at him as he waited for the transit. Once on it, he struggled to stay awake...or at least conscious. The station kept trying to fade away. Every movement hurt, so to stay aware enough to get off at the right stop, he kept shifting on his seat. He hoped he *had* broken Chin's toe.

By the time Geoff got home, the drug patch masked much of his pain with light-headedness, but he still felt nauseous.

"Look at this, Bubs," Tony said when Geoff entered the apartment. "The crazy fools are all dead."

Tony and Fallah were watching the news. A cargo container filled the holoview as the news anchor reported on a mysterious shipment. Geoff wondered if the shipment was the same one Lui and Chin had talked about.

The head and shoulders of the news announcer played in the back upper right corner of the holoview. Its center scene changed to a view of men carrying body bags out of the cargo container.

"...discovered at the transfer station earlier today," the newsman said. "The police advised the bodies will be identified so that officials can determine where they came from and what they were doing here."

Geoff took a few more steps and rested his hands on the back of the sofa between his parents. He squeezed the cushion to hide his trembling. The Lung Organization had tried to smuggle people, and they had all died.

A woman's image filled the holoview. She summarized Terran emigration laws, what people without specific specializations had to pay to move to Luna or a station orbiting Terra or Luna, and what standards in health and training they had to meet to qualify for free transportation and homestead rights on Mars or in the Asteroid Belt.

"It's pretty foolish for anyone to think they can sneak themselves into a closed society like this," Fallah said. "Without proper ID, they wouldn't be able to do anything."

"Maybe whoever's bringing them up here can put counterfeit ID into the system," said Tony. "Or maybe this is just a stopover, and they're going to the Belt. Everyone knows there are people out there with no IDs. Some of them aren't on any records. They're totally tax-free."

"Until they need something from the rest of civilization, anyway," said Fallah.

Geoff's stomach turned over, tangling his insides up. Lung wouldn't smuggle people unless there was money in it. How much could someone desperate enough to leave the planet in a cargo container possibly pay?

Tony said, "I don't suppose we'll know unless they find someone alive or figure out who's shipping them."

Geoff knew the answer to the second part. He swallowed to keep from throwing up and said, "I'm going to bed."

"There's blueberry pie in the fridge," said Fallah.

"I'm not hungry." As Geoff spoke, he realized how thirsty he felt. "Maybe I'll have something." He took a long, gliding step toward the kitchen.

"There's some sausage rolls, too," Fallah said.

Geoff got himself a glass of grape juice, drank it, and ordered another. He looked at the finger-sized sausages wrapped in flaky pastry. His mother was certain to notice if he did not eat. Ordinarily, he'd have half a dozen. Not tonight. He glanced back to make sure no one could see him and tossed two of the sausages into the recycle chute. He put a wedge of pie on a plate to take to his room. If he couldn't eat it later, he'd throw it away.

"Good night," Geoff said.

Barbara came out of the hall from the bedrooms and said, "I'm seeing things. It's only twenty-two. You're home and going to bed?"

"It's fifteen after," Geoff said. "And of course I'm home."

"I forgot. This is where the food is." Barbara went to kiss Fallah and Tony good-night.

Geoff set his plate on top of his glass and followed her back into the living room. He went to the garden and picked a peapod.

"I saw that!" Barbara threw a cushion at Geoff. He stepped forward so that it would not hit his plate. It brushed his left shoulder and back, leaving a burning trail of flame under his T-shirt. The dish of pie rocked and nearly fell.

"Take from the other part of the garden, Geoff," Fallah said.

"Yeah," said Barbara.

"Okay," Geoff said. He wasn't up to a tussle. He couldn't even manage their usual banter. Ignoring everyone's surprised looks, Geoff hid in his room. When he took off his T-shirt, he gasped in surprise. From his shoulders to the bottom of his ribs, he was covered in bruise patches. No wonder he hurt. Maybe now Chin had his mad out of his system, and he'd drop this ridiculous idea of Geoff dancing in a competition. The thought lifted Geoff's spirits. He dropped his clothes on the floor, put on his night shirt, and went to bed.

"Thank you, God, the Spirit of Space, and every other deity," he said, "for letting me live in light gravity." If he had lain down on a heavier deck, his bruises would have hurt too much to bear.

Geoff went right to sleep. His near unconsciousness gradually filled with dreams. He woke five hours later, lying on the floor and hurting. The hallway light came on and shone through the space under the door to his room.

"You okay, Bubs?" asked Tony. He slid the door half-open.

Geoff's bedroom lights began to brighten, making the red-and-blue plaid of his dad's pajama pants visible. Geoff ordered the lights off. He didn't want his father to see the tears in his eyes.

"You sounded like you were doing cartwheels in here," Tony said.

"Uh, maybe I was." Geoff pulled at a corner of the blanket that was tangled around him. He had not been dreaming of cartwheels. The beat of Simba music throbbed in his mind.

"You hurt?" Tony went to Geoff and held out one hand in a silent offer to lift him up.

"Just a bump." Geoff took his father's hand and carefully stood up. The muddle of sheet and blanket sank slowly to the floor. Geoff shivered. His bruises hurt.

"I'm all right." Geoff stood in front of his desk so his dad would not see the untouched pie and wilted peapod.

"I'll help you fix this." Tony picked the pillow off the floor and gave it a shake before he dropped it back on the bed. While he flapped the sheet so it spread out and drifted into place, Geoff put on his housecoat. He couldn't risk Dad noticing the bruise patches.

"I can do it," Geoff retrieved the blanket.

"I know." Tony took the warm cover and spread it over the sheet and then flipped back the corner by the pillow.

"Thanks, Dad." Geoff picked up his empty juice glass. He had to get a refill because he desperately needed a handful of Blissmaert.

"No more gymnastics in your sleep," Tony said. He ran his hand through Geoff's curls on his way out. "Night."

"Night." Geoff couldn't object to having his hair ruffled because the alternative was getting hugged. If his father did that, he might feel the bruise patches. It would also probably make Geoff scream.

Chapter 11

"Gonna run the course with us?" Trevor asked when school ended the next day. The Taurid leader was decked out in black with gold jewelry.

"Not today," Geoff answered. "I've got homework." Chin always said something when Geoff showed up with bruises from Rollerblading. After last night, Geoff did not want to do anything that might provoke his extortionist.

"Homework can wait till after supper," said Trevor.

"I got to meet Chin at nineteen," Geoff explained. He had to plan to go straight home after that because there was no predicting what condition he would be in.

"Well, let's watch the girls' volleyball team practice for a bit." Trevor grabbed Geoff's shoulder and steered him toward the recreation complex.

Geoff winced and pulled away.

"What?" asked Trevor, squinting his steel-colored eyes.

Geoff hesitated and then said, "I had a fight last night."

"With who? Why didn't you invite me?"

"Chin." Geoff strode toward the sports area.

"Are you out of your mind?" Trevor took a couple of long steps to catch up to Geoff. "Why aren't you in intensive care?"

"He needs me for his project."

"Keep arguing, and he might change his mind and pound you Jupiter flat." Trevor's round face crinkled with concern. "You could at least pick a fight with someone your own size...or someone who's not the station's kung fu champion."

Geoff shrugged and asked, "You got anything to eat?"

"Yeah." Trevor felt his pockets and came up with a bag of half-melted chocolate-covered raisins.

Geoff ate them with the required finger licking as they lounged in the bleachers and watched the girls play volleyball. He answered no when Rob came and asked if he was going Rollerblading, and then he headed home.

The empty apartment felt like the only safe place in the station. Geoff munched on a sandwich as he stretched in the living room. When Barbara came home, he picked up his plate and pretended to be on his way to the kitchen for a glass of milk.

"Eating again?" Barbara peered around the remains of Geoff's thick sandwich as if checking to see if he had any peas behind it. "Dad said the little oranges are ripe." They grew on a tree in the Anders's garden. Twice each year, it produced a few dozen oranges, each one slightly larger than a golf ball.

"I know," Geoff said. "I had one the other day." It had not been as sweet as he would have liked, but it had been the first ripe one.

"You're going to make yourself sick, always trying to get things first," Barbara said. "Let's go to the dock market."

"No."

"We've lots of time." Barbara's cheek dimpled as she smiled with the pleading expression that had gotten him to give her almost everything she had wanted since she had been a toddler. "I know your basket girl left, but I'm sure you could meet someone else."

"I've got homework." Geoff took his snack to his room. He finished his exercises in the little space between his bed and desk before he tackled his schoolwork.

Meteorites bombarded Geoff's insides as he went to the dance hall that evening. Although stubbornly determined to continue objecting to Chin's meandering hands—at least as well as he was able—Geoff was afraid another episode like last night would vanquish what remained of his courage. He had to force himself to walk into the training room with his usual stride rather than the tentative little steps his feet tried to take.

Chin knelt beside a boy wearing a white gi and practicing arm thrusts. As he had done on the other occasions when a dance or martial arts student was still present when Geoff arrived, Lui motioned for Geoff to stand behind him. Chin also shifted, blocking the mirrors so the youngster could not see Geoff's reflection.

Geoff waited silently, hoping Chin would say the punishment was over and there would be no more dancing.

Instead, when the boy left, Chin went to his office across the hall.

Geoff removed his outer clothes and began stretching.

Chin returned in tights and a muscle shirt covered with navy and red swirls that were impossible to focus on.

Geoff pretended to ignore him and continued stretching. Since Geoff had learned the warm-up routine, Chin often skipped it, presumably because he was warmed up from his class. He sat on one of Lui's chairs and criticized Geoff.

As Geoff prepared to put his boots on, Chin walked over and said, "No more funny business. We're good enough to go for trophy money, not just beat a has-been."

"Huh?" That did not sound like the release from torture Geoff had hoped for.

"I said we're dancing for prize money," Chin said. "Means a couple nights each week, we'll train on light decks so you learn real control."

Geoff crossed his arms and stared suspiciously at Chin. He didn't look like he was joking.

"You serious?" asked Geoff.

"Of course." Chin frowned down at Geoff. "I told you that."

"Yeah." Geoff shook his head. "Thought you dreamed this up as some skewed-orbit punishment." He had expected Chin to get tired of trying to teach him to dance and cancel the lessons after a week or two. The October competition was ten weeks away! If he'd known he'd be stuck doing this so long, he'd have talked Dayle into letting him leave on her ship. Would his family be safe then? Or would he come back here someday and discover Chin had tortured or murdered them all?

"It *is* discipline," said Chin. "You're too mouthy, but you're good enough on the floor for us to win prize money while you learn to keep your lips zipped."

Determined not to show he wanted to cry, Geoff stamped his feet into his boots. Maybe when Chin said no more funny business, he meant he was going to keep his hands to himself.

They went through the complete dance twice, with Lui calling out corrections to Geoff. There were even more than usual. Expecting to get hit, Geoff was nervous about being so close to Chin. Several times, as Chin swung his arms around, Geoff had to force himself not to flinch away.

"We're going to work on simple variations now," Chin said. "Copy what I do. I'll talk you through them, but you move back so you can see me. Watch in the mirror when you turn."

Geoff nodded. He stepped aside, distancing himself from Chin by a couple of meters. Geoff mimicked Chin through changes in arm positions, leg movements, and reversed turns. By the time the seven rounds ended, he was dizzier than he usually was after half an hour of their usual practice. Halfway through the second song, he lost his balance and fell. Images of Chin and Lui spun around the mirrors. Geoff closed his eyes.

"What the hell?" asked Chin.

"Dizzy," Geoff said.

"Should have taught him to spot," said Lui.

"Don't have time to cover everything," Chin said. He looked down at Geoff. "Why didn't you get dizzy any other time?"

"I don't watch in the mirrors," Geoff said. He cracked one eye partially open to see if Chin was keeping his distance. "You practically knocked my head off for that, remember?" Now that Geoff thought about it, he wasn't sure what he looked at while he danced. He kept his attention on Chin in order to know what he was up to.

"Wish I could do that with a few other students," Chin muttered. "Okay, a quick lesson in spotting. It takes a while to learn, so you're going to have to practice on your own. When you turn, focus on one spot on the wall. Keep your eyes there as your body turns and then whip your head around and get your eyes back on that spot." Chin demonstrated with a slow spin on the ball of one foot. "Try it."

Geoff got to his feet, standing with his feet wide apart for balance. He fixed his eyes on the console behind Lui and pivoted on his right foot, trying to copy what Chin had so smoothly demonstrated. It was an awkward attempt, and he nearly fell.

"Do it a few more times," Chin ordered. He watched as Geoff obediently did so. "We're not going to spend training time on that. Practice at home. Music." As they faced each other to begin, Chin added, "Forget the mirrors. See how you do without them."

Geoff nodded. The middle rounds went too fast for Geoff to pick up new variations, but if Chin demonstrated them at a slower round, Geoff could repeat them when the beat quickened.

During the break, while Geoff sat by his bag to get a drink and to mop the sweat from his face, Chin relaxed in a chair by Lui.

"I think you can forget about teaching him to spot," Lui said. "He spots perfectly...on you."

"That's not right," Chin said.

"Who's to care?' Lui's long braid bobbed when he shrugged his bulging shoulders. "As long as you're in the right place, he will be too."

"We'll lose marks if we don't both have stage and audience awareness."

"Make his focus look intentional."

Chin considered that a moment, lips pursed, and then nodded and said, "Don't tell him. He can still practice it on his own."

Over against the other wall, Geoff smiled behind his water bottle. He wasn't going to practice anything he didn't have to.

As the end of the training hour approached, Geoff increasingly expected Chin to physically harass him or say something about the previous evening. Neither happened. Chin continued to treat Geoff like a regular student.

When Geoff picked up his gym bag to leave, Chin said, "Go straight home after school tomorrow."

"Yeah," Geoff said. He walked to the transit with a ball of fear expanding inside him. Chin had not sounded threatening, but Geoff knew there would be some kind of message left in the apartment. Most likely a very obvious message in the form of something missing or broken.

That threat ate at him the rest of the evening, ruined his sleep that night, and haunted him through school the next day. He cut the last class and hurried home.

The apartment appeared untouched. The furniture was all in place and upright. The garden grew serenely under the pink lights. Geoff quickly looked in every room. Nothing. He flipped over the couch cushions and peered beneath all the furniture and appliances. Still no sign from Chin. Geoff turned on the holoview, checked the com stations, played with the air vents and delivery chute. No sign of sabotage. What could Chin be up to?

Geoff slowly straightened the mess he had made. Tension kept his heart rate up, but instead of the extra adrenaline making him fast, it caused him to be clumsy. It seemed to take a long time to set things back where they belonged, but he finished before school ended. Geoff eyed the little orange tree. Its fruit did not appeal to him. He was too upset to eat, so he paced around the apartment. The soft buzz of his wrist phone made him jump.

The call was from Trevor.

"Yeah," Geoff said

"What's up?" asked Trevor. "Where'd you go?"

"Nothing. Home."

"Well, something's off orbit. Hans and me—"

Geoff stopped listening as the apartment door banged into the wall.

Barbara ran in. She whirled around, slammed the door shut, and locked it.

Space-cold dread froze Geoff's chest. He knew what Chin was doing.

"Catch you later," Geoff said to Trevor. He shut off his phone. "What happened?" he asked Barbara.

"Some ion-blasted slimeworms followed me home." Barbara blinked tear-laden eyes. "And *your* creepy friends pointed me out to them! Trevor and that long-haired guy, Hans."

Geoff jumped over the sofa and ran to the door. He slid it open and looked down the hall. No one was in sight. He stifled an impulse to race to the transit to try to catch them. It would most likely be futile, so he turned back to Barbara.

"No, they didn't." Anger burnt off Geoff's fear from the last twenty hours. "Trev just called to find out what was wrong. I'll deal with those other guys."

"How? There's three of them, and they're all bigger than you."

"Doesn't matter. I know who sets their orbit. They won't bother you again." Geoff called Trevor as he strode down the corridor, each of his steps covering three meters.

"Where are you?" Geoff asked when Trevor answered his call.

"By the baseball park," replied Trevor. "What's going on?"

"Tell you when I get there." As Geoff rode down to the recreation center, he alternated between anger that his friends had betrayed him and hope that Barbara was wrong in thinking Trevor and Hans would send a strange gang after her.

Geoff barely noticed the distant ceiling of the ballpark. Four decks above the floor, it was the highest ceiling in the station, and until today, it had always filled him with awe. When he arrived at the bleachers beside third base, Trevor was sitting with Rob and Hans.

"Who were they?" demanded Geoff. "And what the hell business did you have sending them after Barbie?"

"We didn't." Trevor indignantly jumped to his feet. Standing on the first row of seats as he was, he towered over Geoff from the waist up. "Those guys were family!"

"They said they had a message for you," Hans said. "You weren't around, so they wanted to find her."

"You could've told them to blast off," said Geoff.

"You know we can't." Trevor was still angry. "*We* don't have a senior's protection!"

"Protection?" Geoff was too stunned to say anything else. He stared at Trevor in shock, amazed that he thought Chin was protecting Geoff.

"What protection?" asked Rob.

Geoff paled. He backed up against the fence between the stands and the diamond. He shook his head.

"He's working on a project," Trevor said. Understanding grew on the others' faces.

"We've all done it now and then," Geoff said. "And none of us ever talk about it. You trying to get me killed?"

"If you can survive a fight with Chin, you're not in any danger," said Trevor.

So that was it. Geoff scowled at his closest friend.

"You know if he figures I'm not worth the risk, I'll have an 'accident' and be replaced." Geoff pulled up the right side of his shirt to show the blue and green blotches decorating his lower ribs. The other boys' eyes widened. "Don't say anything to anyone."

"Yeah, we all know the rules," Trevor said. "Watch the game." He shifted slightly to make room. Geoff accepted the offered peace and the seat between Trevor and Hans.

"Here." Hans passed a bag of red licorice to Geoff.

"Thanks." Geoff took it. He really was hungry.

That ended the discussion of Geoff's project with Chin. The rest of the week flew past with the Taurids accepting Geoff's hour-long disappearances in the evenings as part of their normal routine.

Geoff had a short shift at the arcade that Friday evening. All was as usual except for Mr. Manz asking him not to react if the store security system rang a silent alarm on a particular customer.

"Don't say anything to him," Mr. Manz said as Geoff watched a short clip of an anxious-looking, black-haired young man. "Just let me know if he's here."

"Sure thing, Mr. Manz." The doorway cameras recorded everyone coming into the arcade. It would be easy for the system to pick out a specified person. Neither Geoff nor the computer spotted the mysterious man.

By 1830, Geoff was looking forward to some free time between finishing work at 1900 and meeting Chin at 2100. The part of his mind arguing in favor of going home for supper and then munching for an hour in front of the holoview was winning over the desire to hang out with Trevor and the guys when Mr. Manz came quickly out of his office.

"Geoff." He waved Geoff over. "Something's going down. I'll sign you out in half an hour."

"What's happening?" asked Geoff. "Did I do something wrong?" Mr. Manz seemed as angry as he was worried.

"No, kid." A brief smile flashed beneath Mr. Manz's bushy moustache. "The family just needs all her eyes and ears right now. I got to watch this place, though it's not likely he'll come this way. You're going with Wendy. She'll explain on the way."

Excitement at this unusual event could not completely take Geoff's mind off the fact that his short shift did not include a supper break. His stomach growled.

"Do I have time to eat?" Geoff asked.

"Dunno," answered Mr. Manz. "Close out and go to the office. She'll be here right away."

Sure enough, when Geoff entered Mr. Manz's office five minutes later, a tall, slender girl impatiently paced its tiny floor. Straight blue-black hair hung to the middle of her back. When she turned, dark eyes looked down at Geoff from between strands of her long bangs.

"I'm Wendy." She jerked up her left sleeve. On her forearm, right below the inside of her elbow, a Lung dragon spiraled around the delicate tracings of a tiny space station.

"Geoff." He pushed up his sweater sleeve to reveal his larger tattoo.

"Come on…we've got a traitor to catch," said Wendy. She spun around and strode out.

After a half second of insane fear that she had meant the traitor was him, Geoff hurried after her.

Chapter 12

"What do you mean?" Geoff asked as soon as he and Wendy were out of the arcade. The Lung Organization's usual response was to kill the traitor. "Where's the rest of the guys?" Any other time he had been called out on Lung business, at least one other member of his gang had been with him.

"They're looking already," Wendy answered without slowing her jog. "We got word a member's going to the cops. No one who knows what he does can do that."

"How'd we find out?"

"Dunno." Wendy impatiently jabbed the transit call button. "Doesn't matter. We gotta find him before he talks."

Geoff nodded as he tried to think of a way to get out of searching for the traitor. He did not want to finger anyone else for the likes of Chin to capture or shoot.

"How'd we end up partners?" asked Geoff.

"We're all working in boy-girl pairs." The car arrived.

"Oh." Geoff had another thought as he followed Wendy into the transit. If the guy they were looking for had the goods on Chin, his going to the cops would be a welcome reprieve for Geoff.

"Sit with me," Wendy ordered. She lowered her hand between her right knee and Geoff's left one. Her wrist phone's holoview filled with a picture of the same young man Mr. Manz had been watching for. Wendy even ran the identical recording Mr. Manz had shown Geoff.

"That's the guy," said Wendy. "Don't just look at his face. Study his shape and the way he walks. We might only see him from behind."

"Can't the organization tap into station security and look for him?" asked Geoff. The Lung families were powerful enough to do anything.

"I'm sure someone's doing that. We're insurance. Someone who knows how can avoid the cameras."

Geoff dutifully watched the short recording several times. Still, it would be hard to pick the traitor out of a crowd unless he looked nervous or otherwise acted suspicious. There was no better camouflage than to look like you belonged where you happened to be.

"How long will this take?" Maybe he could make supper last until it was time to meet Chin. "I haven't had supper."

"Until he's found. Eat later."

"What are we supposed do if we find him?"

"Call a senior and stay out of sight." The car slowed for another stop. "Get off."

Geoff stepped out of the transit and into the wide corridor of the shopping mall. Splashing fountains drained into a gurgling stream flowing down a green-tiled creek bed in the center of the hallway. Between it and the storefronts on both sides was room for shoppers to walk six abreast. Above them, wide openings in the ceiling showed glimpses of the upper level shops. Those fenced openings gave spaces for the trees, which were set in clusters of pots around the fountains, to grow close to the lights two decks up.

Escalators provided easy access to the double layer of stores. A Friday evening crowd filled the section with noise. Many purchases were made via holoview from home, but shopping remained a popular social event.

"We've got an upper-level search area." Wendy pointed up and to the left. "We'll stroll through and see if the traitor's anywhere around. In stores, one of us has to stay in sight of the door so we can see if he runs out." They rode the sliding stairs to the upper level.

"Pretend you're my brother or something," ordered Wendy before she entered a lingerie shop. "And we're looking for something for our mother."

Geoff dubiously eyed the holo displays of lacy underwear.

"You'd give your mother that?" he asked. Being here with Wendy felt very different than coming to a shop like this with the guys and discussing how the apparel would look on people they knew.

Wendy dropped back so she stood next to Geoff and whispered, "Forget the clothes. Look for the traitor."

"Like he's going to be in *here*," Geoff muttered as he looked around the store. There were several male customers. It was obvious the object of their search was not one of them.

Geoff turned and headed for the exit. Wendy followed slowly, her gaze on a slender young woman with long, dark brown hair. She turned away as Wendy and Geoff passed her.

Wendy abruptly changed direction, detouring a very wide woman to go where she could get a view of the long-haired woman's face. Wendy walked past her and met Geoff at the door.

"Well?" he asked.

Wendy shook her head and said, "Not him."

They strolled through two more shops before Geoff said, "Maybe he's in the food court. Let's go see."

"That's not in our search area."

"I'm starved." Geoff stopped beside a storefront filled with games and figurines and folded his arms on his chest. "And whoever's searching the food court could probably use help."

"We have to work through our area so we don't miss him. If we take off, he could move to where we already were, and we'd never know he got behind us."

"I need to eat." Geoff's stomach was an aching, empty cavern. "You can wait here and watch."

Wendy huffed out an exasperated breath and said, "Okay, but be quick."

She walked with him to the nearest escalator and then leaned against the rail beside it as Geoff ran down the moving stairs. In a few minutes, he dug into a large plate of supper, including half a dozen of the lab's latest version of chicken strips.

While in the food court, Geoff did not see the fugitive, but he did spot a pair of youngsters he guessed were part of the search. He returned to Wendy comfortably stuffed and wishing he could have a nap.

"Took you long enough," Wendy said. She straightened from her slouch against the rail and headed toward the game store.

"Will they let us know if someone else finds him?" asked Geoff.

"Of course." Wendy gestured for Geoff to walk around the displays while she remained near the entrance. He did not see the traitor but found a new game that looked interesting. He and Trevor would check it out later.

Geoff looked at Wendy and shook his head slightly before he left the store. They repeated that process with Wendy strolling through a clothing store.

"You really think we'll find him like this?" Geoff asked.

Wendy shrugged and said, "We're here as much to make sure he's not as to herd him into a corner if he spots us and tries to stay ahead of us."

They continued working their way through the shops. Geoff's mind wandered to the easy comfort of home, a soft couch, a movie, and something sweet to nibble on. He returned to the search in the mall with a mental jerk, knowing he had seen something that didn't belong but not certain what it had been.

The careful movements of a pair of younger boys gave them away again. Geoff relaxed as he realized that what had alerted him was not the traitor but novice shoplifters who didn't know the key to getting away was to act innocent.

"What?" asked Wendy when they met at the exit.

"Just them." Geoff tilted his head back to where the shoplifters were being intercepted by store security. "I knew they wouldn't make it."

Two stores later, as Geoff wandered around the virtual displays at the front of a women's clothing store, he saw the traitor. Something not quite right—perhaps a hint of furtiveness—caught his attention. He swung his gaze back to the cluster of five people on the far side of the service counter. Of the couple holding hands, the man was too large, the woman too small. He looked more closely at the three single women. The two younger ones wore snug sweaters and tight slacks, the older one a loose blouse and jeans.

One of the younger ones obviously was not the traitor. The other gave Geoff a friendly smile. He smiled back and nearly forgot to take a closer look at the older woman.

Examined more carefully, she was not that much older. It just seemed that way because of the bags under her eyes. They were deep brown eyes that stared from beneath a curly, dark red wig. Eyes that showed the same trapped feeling Geoff experienced every time he had to train with Chin and Lui.

Wendy returned to the front of the store.

Without conscious decision, Geoff stepped forward. He hooked his foot on a nearby lady's ankle and fell into Wendy. Geoff made certain he hit her hard enough to knock her down. The woman he tripped over staggered.

"Sorry, ma'am," Geoff said from the floor. "Are you okay?"

"Yes." She frowned down at him and added, "You should be more careful." As the woman walked away, Geoff shifted his leg off Wendy.

She jumped to her feet and glanced around the store before she glared down at him and demanded, "What d'you think you're doing?"

"I tripped." Geoff rolled slowly to his knees and stood up. The desperate young man—Geoff could no longer think of him as a traitor—had disappeared. The people who had stopped to stare returned to their shopping. Others detoured Geoff and Wendy, stepping briefly to the side and then resuming their chosen direction.

"Thought you were a hand," Wendy grumbled. "Who ever heard of a clumsy hand?"

"I was distracted." Geoff tried to sound defensive. What he really felt was an alarming mixture of relief and confusion and apprehension.

"By what?" Wendy flung her right arm out over the holographic models. "There's not even any underwear here."

Geoff spotted a good excuse by the try-on booth behind Wendy and said, "Her." He pointed at a voluptuous female turning in front of a holographic image of herself. She wore a green, low-cut dress; her image, dressed in an orange bikini, duplicated her moves. As they watched, she requested a change. The image blinked out and then reappeared wearing a blue swimsuit.

Wendy muttered something about testosterone as she stalked out of the store.

Geoff did not listen. He had more serious things to consider. Like what would happen if anyone ever learned he had let the man escape? And why had he done it? Did he feel sorry for the guy? Or was it because he was afraid that one day he would be the one branded traitor and running for his life?

Geoff hid his inner turmoil from Wendy as they walked through a dozen more stores.

"That's it for us," Wendy finally said. "Keep your eyes open for him. If you spot him, follow him and call a senior."

"Yeah," Geoff said. He checked the time. After 2000 already. Not enough time to do anything but have a snack and catch the transit down to meet Chin.

Geoff arrived at the private recreation center still feeling troubled. This evening's incident made him doubt the strength of his oath. And what if making that commitment to the organization had been a mistake?

Unwilling to face that question, Geoff pushed it from his thoughts. He entered the dance hall. Lui was not there. Chin stood at the wall console, facing the image of a young woman who looked enough like him to be his sister. She reported that the traitor had not yet been found. Chin waved Geoff to the center of the room to warm up.

By the time Geoff removed his shoes and outer clothes, Chin had ended his call. He stayed there, staring at the blank holoview and tapping his teeth with a stylus as Geoff silently began to stretch.

Geoff surreptitiously watched Chin for a few minutes. He had just decided Chin was too preoccupied to be his usual pain in the butt when Chin snapped, "Reach! There's no point in stretching if you don't work at it."

Correction. Chin was in a nasty mood. Geoff's hour with him would feel like an eternity.

Geoff's second assessment proved correct. Chin continued to find fault with Geoff's stretches.

"You have to work at it," Chin said. "Judges give points for flexibility." He planted his left foot against the wall above head height, put a hand on either side of his foot, and rested his face against his leg. "You've got to make splits look easy."

Chin's mood continued to worsen throughout the evening.

"We're starting training on light decks," he said, "so you're not a total disaster." He took a pile of dark blue material from a chair and threw it at Geoff. "Put that on so no one can ID you."

As Geoff shook out the long robe with a deep hood and put in on, Chin grumbled about wasting practice time traveling between decks.

"Keep this up." Chin jerked the hood forward. It was so long that it draped down over Geoff's face. All he could see was a small piece of floor in front of his feet.

"Follow me."

Geoff followed Chin's boot-covered feet—the only part of him visible from beneath the hood—down a hall and into a tiny elevator. It was so small he could have touched the sides by standing in the center and stretching out his arms. Instead, he tucked himself into a corner and held on to the vertical bar as gravity diminished to one-quarter of one *g*.

"This's private transport between rec clubs on different decks to save people like me a whole lot of time," Chin said. "You can't access it by yourself."

The elevator opened onto a hallway with an open arena for low-*g* sports on one side and a dance hall on the other. Chin said nothing more until he ordered the music to play.

Geoff was accustomed to adjusting to several different strengths of gravity each day, but he had never tried anything like dancing the Simba in one-quarter *g*. It required such careful control that he found it difficult to move quickly enough. His steps clicked after Chin's.

Chin glared and wordlessly growled. He gave Geoff one round to figure out how to keep the beat with minimal help from gravity and then began a litany of instructions.

"Lift your knees higher," ordered Chin as they circled each other. In the front-to-back sway, it was, "Keep your spine vertical. Extend that leg."

His perfectionist little corrections quickly irritated and then angered Geoff. Not wanting to get knocked across the room, he tried to make the adjustments. So focused was his concentration that he did not notice Lui enter the dance hall.

"Took you long enough," said Chin. "Well?"

"Huh?" Geoff replied.

"Not you, stupid. Turn your leg out more."

Lui said, "Nothing." He sat down and unwrapped a sandwich.

"Ion-blasted mutant-bait," growled Chin. "We've got a sieve on every damn camera in the station. He must have crawled into a vent and not moved in six hours."

Geoff caught himself on the verge of asking a question. He pressed his lips together and pivoted to get into position to begin round seven.

"What?" asked Chin. When Geoff did not answer right away, Chin said, "Well?"

"What's a sieve?"

"A program that picks a person out of visual records. Point your toes!" Chin hit Geoff in the ribs. The blow knocked him three meters sideways.

Geoff gasped to refill his lungs and hurried back into position. It was going to be a really, really long hour.

It was. Chin ordered Geoff to work on his cool-down stretches in the elevator back to the heavy deck. Geoff was so physically and mentally exhausted that he did not even worry about the desperate man until he boarded the transit home. The evening's search rode with him.

When Geoff got home, he inhaled the atmosphere of the apartment with a profound sense of relief. The aromas of hot roasted chestnuts and buttered popcorn mingled with the washed-plants smell from the garden. Barbara, Fallah, and Tony were all in their favorite places in the living room, watching a movie and munching on snacks. Home was a comfortable, safe haven.

"Hi." Geoff picked a lettuce leaf larger than his outspread hand and went to make a sandwich.

"Look who came home," Barbara said over their parents' greetings. "Where've you been?"

"Out." Geoff layered protein slices, cheese, and the lettuce into a large bun as the lab produced a glass of milk. He added a couple of dill pickles to his plate. There was a package of giant muffins on the counter, so he took one of them as well—a chocolate one packed with chocolate chips.

Geoff jumped over the back of the couch with a single, slow-motion step like running the hurdles in track.

Tony held out the chestnut bowl containing the last handful of buttered nuts and asked, "Want these?"

"Please, Dad." Geoff nodded. Instead of waiting to take the bowl after he put his lunch on the table, Geoff gently tossed his muffin toward the ceiling. While it made its slow arc up and began to descend, Geoff took the offered bowl, turned to face the coffee table, and set everything on it. He caught the muffin as it came down and asked, "What are we watching?"

Geoff sat between his father and sister, forcing her to pull her feet and blanket toward herself so he wouldn't sit on them.

"You stink," Barbara said. "Why don't you shower in the gym? Or at least before you sit here?"

"I'm too hungry." The show was an old race-across-the-solar-system-and-shoot-'em-up movie Geoff had seen several times. He was not interested in it but felt reluctant to leave the coziness of the couch for his nightmare-laden bed. After he ate, he curled up, rested his head on his father's shoulder, and fell asleep.

Geoff roused when Barbara nudged him with her toes and said, "He hasn't done that in a while."

"He used to fall asleep there a couple times a week," Fallah said. "I don't think he's sat still long enough lately."

"He's been acting funny," said Barbara.

"All teenagers act funny sometimes." Tony stood up and gently lowered Geoff onto a cushion. "Throw your blanket over him. He's too big to carry to bed."

"He's going to get it all smelly," Barbara grumbled as she spread it over Geoff.

Not fully awake, Geoff barely felt its soft warmth before he returned to deeper sleep.

Chapter 13

Geoff woke in midair. He suffered a split second of panic before he landed on the floor between the coffee table and the sofa.

Stretched out in the dark, Geoff looked up at the hazy pink reflections from the grow-lights. He tried to untangle himself from Barbara's blanket but only succeeded in bumping his elbow on the table edge. He bit his lip to keep from swearing. He had better not have woken up his parents. If they knew what kind of nightmares disturbed his sleep, they'd send him to a psych.

Geoff silently got to his knees and then carefully stood up. As he shook himself free of the blanket, he got a whiff of the odors beneath his shirt. Barbara was right. He needed a shower. Now she was probably going to give him a hard time about sweating on her favorite blanket.

Too bad. He dropped it on the floor and circled the couch. Halfway to his room, he stopped. Sweaty and smelly as he was, she *had* given him her blanket. He should at least put it in the laundry basket. He went back and picked it up.

As Geoff dropped the blanket in the hamper in the bathroom, the shiny tiles and clean scent of soap convinced him he needed to shower before he went to bed. He didn't mind if he woke anyone up with the sound of the shower. He wore a towel across the hall to his room but need not have bothered. No one else got up.

When Geoff's music blared on the next morning, he groaned and pulled his pillow over his head. It should be against the law for alarms to operate on Saturdays. Geoff peeked at the time—0750.

"Blast off!" Geoff had the late shift at the arcade from 1400 to 2200. Chin wasn't expecting him at the rec center until 1230.

"Bubblegum, off!" Geoff had changed his password to the computer system a few times but had always returned to his original one. When he wasn't fully awake, all he ever remembered was that old code name from years ago. "Bubblegum, for this morning only, set alarm to 1130." As soon as the computer repeated his instructions and confirmed they had been carried out, Geoff closed his eyes and went back to sleep.

Five minutes later, Fallah knocked on his door and called, "Geoff, do you work this morning?"

"Huh?" Geoff woke up, but not in time to hear what she had said. "Come in."

Fallah had already cracked the door open. She slid it aside and said, "I heard your alarm. Do you work this morning?"

"No." Geoff half sat up to look at her. "I forgot to reset it. I don't have to be up till noon." He flopped back down, thankful the terrible soreness of the previous three weeks had dulled to stiff aches and sharp twinges, and those were only where Chin had hit him.

Fallah closed the door and left. Geoff briefly considered extending the interruption in his sleep for breakfast and maybe some of Chin's cursed stretches, but it had been too long since he'd slept away a Saturday morning. He luxuriated in the freedom of having nothing urgent to get up for until sleep reclaimed him.

Geoff wandered into the kitchen a couple of minutes before noon. His parents were preparing to eat lunch as they watched the midday news.

"Morning, Bubs," Tony said.

"Sleep well?" asked Fallah.

"Morning," Geoff replied. "Yeah." He went in search of breakfast.

"I put some on for you," Fallah said.

Geoff checked the cooker. Sure enough, the timer was counting down the last seconds on a dozen thick strips of crinkly bacon. He smiled. They looked like the old bacon, the kind Mom had always gotten before the protein lab fooled around with the recipe.

When Geoff lifted the cover from the bowl on the counter, steam erupted from a mound of hash brown potatoes. He shook a package of yellow goo. It would turn into scrambled eggs when he popped the heat tab.

As Geoff finished piling his plate with food, Tony exclaimed, "Can you believe that? There's been another murder!" He set his mug on the table with a sharp click. "Used to be that sort of thing only happened on Terra and out on the docks. Now ordinary folks are getting it."

Geoff carried his brunch to the table and asked, "What happened?"

"Shhh," Fallah said.

Tony waved his hand toward the holoview.

The male news anchor said, "The victim, twenty-one-year-old Wilf Gnida, is believed to have been the target in a gang-related homicide." An image of the young man Geoff had let escape the previous evening replaced the newsman.

Geoff felt himself go white. He hadn't saved the desperate man. Cold sweat beaded his face and torso as his heart hammered against his ribs. He felt ashamed at his next thought: Now the man couldn't tell anyone Geoff had let him go.

"Gnida was found in his own apartment earlier this morning," continued the news anchor. "He is reported to have been hit with a stunner and then brutally slain by a blaster. His assailants didn't just kill him. They burned his face and his shoulders and arms, everywhere there might have been identifying marks or tattoos."

"Oh, how gruesome," murmured Fallah.

"Yeah," Geoff agreed. Good thing he was wearing a long-sleeved shirt. His parents wouldn't be reminded about his tattoo and begin to wonder if that little snaky dragon on the station was really something more.

"That's the problem with gangs," Tony said.

"It's all those kids whose parents don't take time to know what they're doing or who they're hanging around with," said Fallah.

Geoff felt sick, but he filled his mouth to keep from having to answer any questions. He had hidden his gang affiliation from his family for three years. His parents knew Trevor, Hans, and Rob but had no idea they were anything more than a group of friends. Tattoos were so common that few people took a second look at a kid with one on his arm.

"Speaking of which," Fallah continued, "what are you doing today?"

"I work at fourteen," Geoff replied around the bacon and potatoes. Work, which he loved, had become a synonym for dance, which he hated. His hands shook when he took a swig of milk and added, "I'm going blading with Trev first." Or maybe he was going to go throw up.

When Geoff arrived at the dance hall, the atmosphere was very different from the previous evening. Chin, with his hair loose and wearing an eye-searing orange-and-yellow outfit that looked painted onto his muscular physique, sat on the floor near Lui's chair. He had twisted himself into a seemingly impossible pretzel. Lui's thin braid jiggled behind his chair in time with his chuckles.

Chin unwound himself when Geoff dropped his gym bag on the floor.

"Get started," Chin ordered.

While Geoff did his warm-up, Chin continued, "This morning, they announced the competition requirements. We do a character in a quarter g and a traditional in one g, only one lift and one jump allowed."

Geoff asked, "What's a—"

"Stretch. A character dance is acting out a story," Chin lectured, "portraying a person or character as part of the dance." Chin was in his teacher mode, which, except for the previous evening, he had been since declaring that he and Geoff were going to dance for the prize money. Today, he also radiated enthusiasm. "It's like a drama play. Pull."

Geoff, his belly on the floor with his hands gripping his ankles and holding his heels against his buttocks, asked, "What kind of story?"

"A fun one. We'll use a flirty arrangement. I'll chase you, and you play hard to get."

Geoff gave Chin a surprised look. That did not sound too bad. He had expected Chin to choose something romantic that Geoff would hate. They finished warming up without talking beyond Chin's demands that Geoff continually extend his stretches. Geoff did not have to stretch in the elevator up to the one-quarter-g deck because with three of them in the tiny chamber, there was barely room for breathing.

After they put on their boots and got in the starting position in the center of the low-gravity dance floor, the room filled with an arrangement of the Simba already familiar to Geoff. It was a lighthearted version that began with flutes and violins.

"Okay," Chin said. "Body language is everything. You pretend to not see me, so no eye contact at the start. We'll get extra points for a difficult beginning." He stood facing Geoff but did not begin dancing when the preliminary music flowed into the dance sequence.

Geoff started to shift his shoulders on the beat, hesitated when Chin did not move.

"Keep going," ordered the older man. "Look to the left, left hand on your hip, back of your right hand against the back of your right hip. Don't turn your head so far."

Geoff got his left hand correct. It was easy because he had always kept his hands on his hips for this opening pattern.

"Like this," growled Chin. He turned his back to Geoff and demonstrated. "Copy me. Remember it. You have to do the steps exactly the same every time. Do it again." At Chin's order, the music cut off and began again at the beginning.

Startled, because that had not happened since the first few days, Geoff missed the initial beat and began his sideways swing late.

Chin thumped him sharply in the chest, knocking his breath out in a rasping cough and making him step back for balance.

"Pay attention," ordered Chin.

Lui restarted the music.

Geoff made sure he began to move on the beat.

Chin watched critically and then said, "Arch your ribs a little when you put your hand on your neck." He thrust his chest out slightly to demonstrate. "Keep going." He led Geoff through a different variation for the second sideways swing.

"Next step." Chin made small circle with his right hand, directing Geoff to continue the dance.

As Geoff pivoted and began to stalk in a circle, Chin stepped into it behind him. Without breaking the pattern, Geoff glanced downward and rolled his eyes to the side to sneak a look at Chin.

"Save that look for later," said Chin. "Right now pretend you don't see me. Toss your head a little during that last turn." He had the choreography for the entire first round prepared and pushed Geoff to learn it all in that hour.

By the time they finished, Geoff was as mentally tired as he was physically.

For the next two weeks, Geoff's dance lessons consisted of learning different variations of each step. It was hard work. More than that, he often found it embarrassing. Like the day they worked on round two. Geoff had to stop ignoring Chin, acknowledge he was there, and still pretend he was not interested in him.

"Flounce," Lui said. "And as you turn, toss your head so your hair flips up."

"Flounce?" Geoff ran a questioning hand over his short curls. How was he supposed to flip his hair?

"You know, like girls do when they think a boy they like is watching and they want to get his attention." Lui heaved his bulk off his chair—they were in the one-g dance hall—and rocking his shoulders and hips from side to side, he bounced across the floor with mincing steps. His long braid swayed as his rolls surged beneath his loose clothes, but he captured the essence of a girl wanting to be noticed.

Geoff couldn't help smiling at the incongruity. He said, "My hair doesn't do that."

"Not funny," said Chin. "Learn it."

"You'll have a long wig," Lui said.

Geoff tentatively flounced a few steps. It felt absurd. It probably looked hilarious. He felt his face redden.

"You've only got four steps to create that image," said Chin. "It's a *show*. Do it like you mean it, even exaggerate a little." He looked at Lui.

Lui moved back to his chair, repeating his imitation of the bouncy walk.

"Do it," Chin ordered.

Geoff did it. For Barbara's sake and his friends', he had to. Besides, if those two could act like that, he could, too. He would just think of it as a show nobody he knew would ever see. Geoff froze in mid-motion. Mom and Barbara watched dance competitions on the holoview.

"Now what?" Chin punctuated the question with a slap to the top of Geoff's head.

"People I know watch the competitions," said Geoff. "I need a mask."

"You'll be made up," Chin said. "Your own mother won't recognize you. Do it over."

The steps got worse as the dance progressed. Geoff's character went from ignoring Chin to shyly acknowledging his presence to flirting. One evening, he found himself sitting beside Lui, practicing batting his eyelashes in front of a mirror.

"Tilt your head down, so you're looking at the floor," instructed Lui. "Then keeping your head down, turn a little to the side and look up where Chin will be. No, *don't* lift your head. Roll your eyes. You'll have fake eyelashes to match your wig. Look up through them."

Geoff tried it again. How was he supposed to remember all those different dance steps and this stupid stuff as well?

"Good," Lui said. "Now bat your eyelashes a few times. Three times."

"Okay," Chin said from behind them. "Practice that."

Geoff got so caught up in performing his eye movements properly that he forgot the choreography for his feet.

"The *other* way!" Chin rabbit-punched Geoff in the chest. They were on the quarter-g deck, so the blow knocked Geoff across the room.

He twisted and landed lightly on his feet.

They did round three twice more and ran through the entire first part before they began round four's choreography.

Geoff learned the steps; however, he had a very hard time trying to make himself move naturally in such close proximity to Chin, and he simply couldn't portray the passion Chin insisted on.

Lui said, "I think you'd better stick with teaching him the steps and work on presentation later."

"We're running out of later," Chin muttered. "We should be working on the next one, too."

He brought that subject up again during the break. Across the room, Geoff listened as he rested and sipped his juice.

"Quit second-guessing yourself," Lui said. "You know he'd mix them up if you tried to teach him the next one before he knows this one."

"Yeah," agreed Chin. "And he probably won't do it if he doesn't get through this one first, but we're running out of time."

Chapter 14

"Hey, Geoff!" Earrings chiming, Trevor ran a few steps to catch Geoff at the school exit. "The girls' dive team has a meet. Let's watch before you go to work."

"Okay." Geoff enjoyed looking at all girls in swimsuits, but he guessed Trevor just wanted to watch Lori. Geoff stepped into the outer corridor and began strolling toward the recreation complex.

"What's with you?" asked Trevor as he fell into step with Geoff.

"Nothing." Nothing he could talk about, at least.

"You got no enthusiasm for nothing lately."

"Do so." The only thing Geoff had no enthusiasm for was dancing with Chin. Geoff shifted sideways and knocked Trevor into the ugly girl from science class. He smiled and kept walking as Trevor regained his balance and apologized.

Trevor ran after Geoff and said, "You skewed-orbit, brain-blasted mutant." He swung his fist at Geoff's shoulder. The shorter boy easily evaded the blow.

"You work tomorrow?" asked Trevor. "We could get the guys together and go blading."

"It's my weekend off—" Geoff left his sentence unfinished. He couldn't admit how much of his life was ruled by Chin's schedule and Chin's ideas of what he should and shouldn't do.

"Good. You've hardly used those new skates lately."

"Been busy." With the stretches Geoff had to do throughout the day, travel time, and the hour on the dance floor with Chin, training took up a huge amount of Geoff's day.

"Well, unbusy. The rest of us are free orbit, too. Let's all meet in the park after lunch. Afterward, we can go to a movie or something." They stepped onto the wide path between the row of trees marking the edge of the recreation section, and Trevor began to jog. "Come on."

Geoff followed him. The short run and having nothing to do and no place to be for at least half an hour woke up his sense of fun. He grinned as he found a seat in the bleachers surrounding the pool. Geoff dug out a package of beef jerky from the station's protein lab.

"Trade?" Trevor held out a bag of peanuts.

"Sure." They each took a handful of the other's snack.

Hans came and sat on the other side of Trevor. He helped himself to some peanuts, too.

"I think my parents are going to make me go up to Terra with them over break," he complained. "It's like being stuck in a big park full of dirt and bugs, and you can't even go up to a light deck when your feet hurt."

"That's better than what I got to do," said Trevor. "*I'm* spending the vacation working in my uncle's store."

"At least you'll get paid." Hans shoved his headband up off his eyebrows. "What are you doing, Geoff?"

"Working at the arcade most of the time. I got a couple days off in the middle of the week. I'm going to lie on the couch." He looked forward to that more every day. With his luck, Chin would probably plan the hour in the dance hall for the middle of the morning. Maybe he could talk him out of it.

He had as good a chance of knocking the station out of orbit. Geoff sighed, a drawn-out breath that seemed to come from his toes.

A small group of divers came out to take practice dives.

"There's Lori." Trevor pointed to a girl with dark brown hair. She was tall and heavily built, with plenty of curves beneath her one-piece swimsuit. She did not look up at the bleachers. Her attention remained firmly on the diving board and pool.

To Geoff's surprise, he could see elements in the complex dives he had never noticed before. His eyes picked out pointed toes and evenly aligned limbs and difficult extensions. It made the competition something more than a chance to watch girls. He did not mention his new skill.

After half an hour, Geoff stood up and said, "I got to get home and get ready for work. See you guys tomorrow."

The apartment did not provide the solitude Geoff sought. Barbara and a couple of girlfriends had piled the living room furniture against the walls. In the resulting open area, they jumped around, twirling and giggling as they talked.

"Why don't you go to the gym?" Geoff yelled over their music. "You're going to break something."

"No, we won't," Barbara said. She dropped gently to the floor.

"Aerobics are pointless on this level, anyway," said Geoff. He hopped over a pile of chairs to get to the kitchen.

"We're *dancing.*"

That ruined Geoff's appetite. He shut the fridge.

"Other people live here, too," Geoff said. "You could have a little consideration."

"Why don't you join us?" asked Nadine.

"Yeah." Barbara's grin engraved her dimple in her right cheek. "We used to have a lot of fun dancing like this."

"That was years ago." At least, it felt like years to Geoff.

"Uh-uhhh." Barbara wrinkled up her face as she thought. "Only a few months or so."

"Forget it." Geoff shot across the kitchen in two bounds.

"What's got into you?" demanded Barbara.

"Nothing." Geoff shut himself in his room. He didn't have time to go to the rec center by the school. Now he had to do Chin's blasted stretches in that tiny space, and he was sure to bump himself.

Geoff's sour mood lasted until he went to work. The noise and activity of the arcade always seemed to make the rest of life less important. His lift in spirits ended at 2045, when he boarded the transit to meet Chin. Walking into the private recreation center made him feel like a slave. He had no control over anything that happened there.

An unusual tone sounded when Geoff signed in at the club's automated client-service console.

The receptionist on the other side of the room turned from her desk and said, "Your guest privileges end today. Would you like to buy a membership?"

"No."

The woman looked surprised but said with her usual courtesy, "Then I'm sorry. This will be your last day with us."

Geoff wished he had that option. He said, "Charge my fees to Chin Hon."

"You realize I have to confirm that with him." Technically a statement, she made it sound like a question.

"Yeah." Geoff took his bag and headed down the corridor.

"You're almost late," Chin warned when Geoff entered the dance hall.

"The woman at the desk held me up," said Geoff. "I've run out of guest time. You have to buy a membership."

"Why didn't you buy it?"

"I don't have the money." Geoff had not asked how much the fees were. He had no intention of paying them.

"You're costing me more all the time," Chin grumbled. "Warm up. Let's get this choreography finished."

Geoff prudently refrained from telling Chin it wouldn't cost him anything if he dropped the idea of dancing.

At the end of the evening, Chin said, "Be here at 1230 tomorrow. That'll be our regular Saturday time. You have the fourteen shift at Manz's on weekends."

"Yeah." If Chin expected a thank you for setting a schedule that allowed Geoff to sleep late, he wasn't going to get it. Geoff was certain his own comfort had not been considered in Chin's choice of times.

As instructed, Geoff returned to the private recreation club shortly before 1230 the next day. He tensed as he walked inside, not sure what he would do if he was not allowed in until he paid for a membership.

"Good to see you," said the older man who usually sat at the reception desk on Saturdays. "You want to book some time in some of the other facilities, maybe the pool or hot tub?"

"No." Surprise made Geoff blunt. He remembered his manners and added, "Thanks."

"Well, if you change your mind and everything's full, just let one of us know. We'll fit you in."

Geoff eyed him suspiciously and asked, "Why?"

"Anything for a friend of Chin's." The man's even voice gave no indication of what he was thinking, but his little smile made Geoff wonder what kind of "friendship" he was supposed to have with Chin.

"Maybe later," Geoff mumbled. He escaped down the corridor.

Lui waited in the dance hall.

"Warm up," he said. "Chin'll be right here."

Before Geoff completed his warm-up routine, Chin arrived wearing black, mid-calf trousers. A sheen of perspiration dampened his face and bare chest.

"Work that stretch," he said. He left. A minute later, he returned dressed in blue tights. He pushed Geoff to the limits of his flexibility until the warm-up was done.

"Get your boots on." Chin kicked off his slippers and pulled on his own boots. "Next week, go to Rudy's. That's Rudy's Costumes and Dance Wear on deck five, and get sized for dance boots. I've already ordered what you need. They just have to measure your feet. Get fitted for contacts while you're there."

"Okay," Geoff said. Another new pair of boots? Why'd he have to buy the first pair? His feet ached at the thought of breaking in new boots.

"Let's see what you forgot." They ran through the first six rounds of the dance while Chin and Lui frequently corrected Geoff's performance.

"Do it over," Chin ordered. "Get it right."

Geoff only made a dozen errors that time.

"Okay for now," said Chin. "We've got to get the last round done. We'll skip the opening swing for now and start with the circle. You got eight beats." Chin met Geoff's eyes.

Geoff nodded. When Chin repeated something he expected Geoff to know, he always wanted confirmation that Geoff really did know it.

"Instead of four steps, we're going to take sixteen and turn as we go."

"Like in round five?" asked Geoff.

"No. Every round is different. This time, we both turn to the left." Chin faced Geoff with about one meter of space between them. "As you finish the swing, turn your left leg out ninety degrees." He demonstrated as he talked.

Geoff copied him. For the next twenty minutes, they turned endless circles. As soon as Geoff became adept at the footwork, Chin increased the speed of the steps and then added upper body movements. Geoff's head spun from the turns. Being unable to stretch his arms out for balance made the tricky steps twice as difficult. He eventually lost his balance and fell.

"That looked good," Chin said. "You've got the balance of a cat. Don't expect me to believe you lost it." His tone held no anger, though, and he calmly walked over to Lui and sat down.

Geoff glanced at the clock in the console behind Chin and Lui—1300. Time for a break. He would have liked to crawl to his usual rest spot, but pride wouldn't let him. Despite the burning in his legs and feet, he got up and walked over to the wall.

As Geoff tasted his grape juice, Chin said, "I'm a genius."

"How're you going to put that in your resume?" laughed Lui.

"Don't know yet." Obviously pleased with himself, Chin chuckled. "Twenty minutes. Kid doesn't know a pirouette from a schatze, and I got him doing a Shute in twenty minutes."

"What're we going to do if he doesn't get his feet lined up?"

Now totally serious, Chin said, "He'll do it. If I have to cut the tendons in his legs, he'll do it."

In his quiet spot beside his gym bag, Geoff shivered.

Chapter 15

Slumped in his seat in the transit car, Geoff thought about Chin's threat to cut the tendons in his legs. Technically, it was not a threat. Geoff was certain that Chin did not know Geoff could hear him and Lui talking. Still, could such a thing be done? Was such surgery to increase flexibility possible, or would that leave Geoff unable to even walk? He didn't want to know. He would make sure he learned to place his feet how Chin wanted them.

The gang waited at their usual table. Geoff saw they all had drinks, so he lifted a couple of burgers and a pack of fries on his way through the crowd. As he sat down, he traded one of the burgers for Rob's drink. Rob always got a strawberry-banana Orange Julius.

"It's Hans's turn," Rob protested. "Or Trevor's."

"Okay." Geoff pushed the drink back to Rob. "They can buy me one of these."

Hans went for the drink.

Trevor said, "There's a new *Jungles of Venus* movie playing."

"In the big theater?" asked Geoff. Those jungle safari movies were entertaining. Certainly more fun than Rollerblading when his legs already ached. "That'll be great."

"I thought we were going blading," Rob said.

"It's already almost 1430," Trevor said. "We don't have time for both. We'd miss the matinee."

"I'm for the show," said Hans.

"Blading," Rob voted.

"Blading," Trevor said. "We haven't all been in the park on a Saturday afternoon in ages. Let's put on a show."

Trevor's idea of putting on a show meant complicated follow-the-leader. Fortified by more Blissmaert, Geoff enjoyed it. His in-line skates hummed along smoothly and soundlessly. He rolled through the winding recreational paths in line and in step with the rest of the gang. Their steps became fancier as they switched leaders. When Rob took over at the head of the line, they moved onto the advanced trails and the challenge course.

Hans fell first. Trevor went next, a spectacular sideways flop off the swinging bridge.

Geoff, following a couple of meters behind him, tried to slow down to check on him. He hooked a wheel in the crack at the edge of the bridge and tumbled over the side. Geoff landed partly on the spongy floor and partly on Trevor's feet. Pain seared through his right arm. It felt so bad he couldn't tell exactly where he was hurt. If he had broken something, he'd better find a way to hide it from Chin.

"You trying to kill me?" asked Trevor.

"No, me—" Geoff cradled his right arm in his left hand and sat up, freeing Trevor's legs.

Trevor propped himself up on his elbows and frowned at Geoff.

"What?" he asked.

"I couldn't think of anything intelligent to say." Geoff had said it without thinking. Now he wondered if somewhere in the depths of his mind, he thought suicide was the only way to escape from Chin. He experimentally straightened his right arm. Pain pricked his shoulder and upper arm, but it was not broken. "You okay?"

"Yeah. Some vacuum-brain fell on my feet, but otherwise I'm fine."

"We should've gone to the show," Geoff said. He probably had a monstrous bruise above his elbow guard. He should see if the aid station could give him a bruise patch, so the mark would be mostly gone by Monday night. What Chin didn't know wouldn't hurt Geoff...or Barbara.

"I think I need a patch," Geoff said. "Your skates got me between the guards." He wanted to make a leisurely roll off the course. Unfortunately, that would make everyone ask questions. "Let's catch up."

Geoff avoided more bruises by detouring the hardest obstacles. After they finished skating, the medical staff in the first-aid booth stuck a bruise patch on Geoff's upper arm. They treated blue and purple lumps on Trevor and Hans as well.

When Geoff entered his family's apartment, he stepped into the multitude of mouth-watering aromas that meant his mother had been home most of the afternoon. That sweet smell of toasted coconut had to be the chewy cookies with rolled oats. Geoff could pick it out through the spicy tomato aroma of spaghetti sauce and the buttery scent of crusty garlic bread.

"What's wrong?" Fallah pointed to Geoff's right arm, which was tucked against his side.

"A bunch of us went blading. I fell on Trevor."

Fallah insisted on inspecting the bruise patches before she allowed Geoff to escape to his room. The sight of his chair on the bed, where he had put it that morning while he had stretched, reminded him to repeat Chin's exercises. And he had to add turning his feet so that he'd be able to do that latest stupid step.

The pain from that dulled Geoff's appetite. He ignored Barbara's call to come to the table and flopped on his bed, wondering if eating was worth the effort.

Monday after school, Geoff ducked out on his friends, left his com turned off, and caught the transit to deck five. Rudy's Costumes and Dance Wear was a large store. The holographic window displays on the left side of the entrance showed ballet performances and several other types of dances Geoff could not name. To the right, the display holocubes were filled with images from live theater shows.

Geoff stood and watched for a few minutes before he stepped into the store. The shoe department was at the back. He strolled past more holographic displays. *This place must spend a fortune powering them all,* he thought. *Then again, maybe what they pay for that balances out in saved inventory and shoplifting costs.*

The men's boots began with racks of lace-up jazz and tap boots. Behind them were pointed-toed boots with large, chunky heels and high, wide tops.

"Can I help you?" The store assistant was a skinny young woman wearing a long black sack with ragged sleeves.

"I need boots," replied Geoff.

"You've come to the right place." She gave him a friendly smile. "What kind?"

Geoff hesitated. He had not seen any boots that looked similar to Chin's.

"What dance are you in?" asked the clerk.

"The Simba," Geoff mumbled.

"You must be talented. That's not an easy one." She touched the side of the rack of pointy boots. They disappeared. A row of shiny, narrow-looking boots appeared. They had the same low heel and tight ankle coverings as Chin's.

"What style do you like?" she asked.

"I don't get to pick," answered Geoff. "My instructor already ordered them."

"Oh, are you Master Hon's student?"

Geoff nodded.

"We're expecting you." Her attitude underwent a subtle change from professionally polite to a real desire to please. "This way, please." She led Geoff to an open office at the back of the display area.

"Here's Master Hon's student for the fitting," she announced from the doorway. She smiled at Geoff and left.

He stepped inside the small room and looked around. An old man who had to be at least fifty sat behind a large console that took up half the room. The remaining area held two chairs, one facing the desk, the other beside a smooth metal square on the floor. It measured about half a meter per side and was five centimeters higher than the carpet.

"Have a seat and bare your feet," said the man at the desk. "We'll be done in no time." As Geoff removed his runners and socks, the man fiddled with his console.

"How do you know I'm the right person?" asked Geoff. No one had asked him to prove he was Chin's student.

"Chin sent your picture. What's your name?"

"Master Hon's Student." If Chin had not told anyone Geoff's name, Geoff certainly wasn't going to.

"Okay, Master Hon's Student. Stand on the plate."

Geoff stepped onto the shiny square. It felt warm and very smooth.

"Keep your weight even on both feet. So you're dancing this competition with him, eh?"

That was supposed to be a secret!

Geoff kept his voice casual as he asked, "What makes you think that?"

"Why else would he pay for solid-cast foam linings and then shell out for ceramic taps to match his? Stand on the balls of your feet."

Geoff shrugged and said, "Maybe he has sensitive ears." Now what? Should he tell Chin and risk getting knocked into the wall? Or should he just keep quiet about what the boot man had deduced?

"Ha. Stand on your right foot. Lift the left up. Flex it. Point your toe. Do the other one. That's it. Put your shoes on." The man kept talking as Geoff pulled on his socks and shoes.

"You got nice feet. Strong and flexible. I'd bet my job you never took ballet. I c'n always tell when I get a ballet dancer in here. Sit in the other chair."

Geoff moved to the chair in front of the desk and asked, "Why?"

"This's where we fit the contacts." The top of the desk split in front of Geoff. A section opened, and flat bars embedded with equipment rose as high as Geoff's forehead.

"Look straight ahead at the green light," instructed the man. "Keep your head straight and look left to the yellow light. Now roll your eyes to the purple on the right. That's it. You're done."

Geoff said good-bye and left. That hadn't taken long. Just long enough for the old man to figure out Chin was secretly planning to compete. Did Geoff dare tell Chin?

That evening Geoff shivered with more than cold as he began the warm-up exercises in the dance hall. He had decided to not raise the subject of what the man at Rudy's thought he knew. Apprehension that Chin would somehow discern Geoff was hiding something made him nervous. Geoff sighed and made a face at the floor. Chin for sure would see that he wasn't himself. Maybe he should just tell him. Geoff argued with himself as he hid in the blue hooded robe and rode up to the quarter-*g* deck with Lui.

When Chin came in wearing muscle-hugging green and turquoise, his hair flying loosely around his head, his presence seemed to fill the empty dance hall.

Geoff stood in front of Chin, ready to begin the dance.

Chin held one hand up toward Lui, his palm flat, and asked, "What?"

That hadn't taken long, Geoff thought.

Aloud, he said, "The man at the boot store knows you're dancing the competition. With me."

Chin raised his eyebrows.

"You tell him that?" he asked.

"No."

"So—" Chin crossed his arms and waited for Geoff to continue.

"He said it's the only reason you'd want the ceramic things on our boots to match."

"Yeah, he'd know that. What'd you say?"

"You got sensitive ears."

"Hmmmpf. Why'd you tell me?"

"So you'd know it wasn't me that talked if word gets out."

"He won't talk," Chin said. "He wouldn't have a customer left if he blabbed who's dancing with whom." He waved for Lui to begin the music.

Geoff looked away and counted the beats. Starting with no eye contact really was difficult.

When they had rehearsed the first part of the dance, Chin said, "We're going to get the rest of this done tonight."

Distracted by Chin's unwelcome physical closeness and overwhelmed by the volume of steps in the choreography, Geoff again forgot some of the elements of the steps.

"Turn your left foot out!" Chin ordered when Geoff pivoted incorrectly.

Frustrated, Geoff asked, "How do you expect me to remember all that?" It was beyond him how Chin remembered everything both of them were supposed to do.

"Huh? Only the first step takes remembering. Everything else follows." Chin linked his fingers together in front of his chest. "It all fits together."

Geoff looked doubtfully at Chin's joined hands.

"Picture it as you go," said Chin. "See it mentally. It flows."

Geoff glanced up at Chin. He did not speak.

"We spent hours writing this," Chin said. "It's the smoothest choreography, except for our second routine of course, you'll ever see. You just fall into each next step."

Geoff shook his head and said, "I don't." He waited for the blow he expected Chin to deliver.

Chin looked over at Lui and raised his palms in an "I don't know" gesture.

"Show him," Lui said.

Chin shrugged and then said, "At three-quarters. No sound." He tapped Geoff's shoulder and gestured for him to move aside.

A hologram of Geoff and Chin standing ready to begin the dance appeared in the center of the dance floor. It shrank until the images became chest high. They began to move, torsos swinging sideways. Embarrassed at seeing himself dancing with Chin, Geoff did not want to watch.

"Look at the elements of the steps," Chin said. He stepped into the images and pointed as he talked. "You finish the first swing with your hand coming up here behind your neck. It's only natural that you continue that motion as you start the next swing." He talked through the entire dance, pointing out how the end of each step served as the beginning of the next.

Geoff had known that, but he had never visualized it. Seeing it gave him a new perspective. It also brought home how very close to Chin he was during the dance. He had mentally distanced himself from that aspect of the performance. Geoff did not want to deal with that. He ignored the holographic Chin and thought of the dance as a series of Simon Says actions.

Lui turned off the hologram and started the music.

When this was over, Geoff was never going to listen to flutes again. He forgot to count and did not start on the beat.

Chin thumped him in the chest and growled, "Wake up."

The music began again. To Geoff's surprise, he discovered that Chin's impromptu lesson with the hologram really did make it easier to remember the finicky details of the choreography.

At the end of the hour, they returned to the heavy deck for a series of leg-torturing contortions. Geoff recognized that rubbery-legs feeling. He wouldn't be able to get out of bed tomorrow without painkillers.

Geoff was right. He woke up hurting, and he didn't have the energy or desire to fight through it and get up. He decided to skip the first class at school.

"Geoff!" Fallah knocked on Geoff's door. "Are you up?"

"Yeah." Geoff answered promptly, but he stayed in bed until everyone else left the apartment. Then, jaw clenched with pain, he hobbled to the bathroom. After a hot shower and a Lormal patch, he got to school only half an hour late.

"You just earned an extra assignment," Geoff's social studies teacher said when Geoff limped into the classroom. "I'll put it in your file."

"I got held up," Geoff said. He didn't have time for additional assignments, but if he did the extra work, the late would be erased from his record.

When the school day ended, Geoff walked to the transit with Trevor and Rob.

"We on for a game?" Rob asked.

"Not me," Geoff said. "I got to be somewhere this evening, so I got to do my homework now." Meeting Chin at 1900 on Tuesdays and Thursdays left Geoff no time for anything else.

"Me, too," said Trevor.

Rob boarded a different transit than Geoff and Trevor.

Geoff plopped onto the seat beside his friend and said, "Thanks." He knew Trevor did not have anything to do that evening except call Lori. He had passed on going to the arcade to make it easier for Geoff.

"I got your back," Trevor said. "You know it."

Chapter 16

That evening, Lui met Geoff outside the dance hall. Inside it, Chin was speaking with a couple of martial arts students and their parents.

"Warm up in here," Lui said. He crossed the hall and opened the door to Chin's office.

Geoff walked into the warm room. His shoes sank in the soft carpet. The office was as large as the kitchen and dining area in the Anders's apartment, with a solid-looking desk console to the right of the doorway. A padded chair filled the space between the desk and the wall unit behind it. Two hard plastic chairs faced the desk.

To the left of the door, the other half of the room was empty space surrounded by mirrors, half-open closet doors, and pictures. Holographic images of Chin doing kung fu and of Chin and Lui dancing covered the walls.

"Get to it," Lui said. "Don't touch anything." He closed the door when he left.

Geoff set his bag on a plastic chair and looked around as he removed his outer clothing. Some of the holograms were old. Chin looked thinner and younger, and Lui was only a third of his present size. Geoff stood in the center of the open area and began his exercises. The closet in front of him held hangers of clothes, everything from suits and shirts to joggers and dance wear.

The door slid open, and Chin said, "Out." He pointed across to the dance hall.

Geoff grabbed his bag and left. A minute later, Chin, now wearing scarlet dance tights, joined him on the dance floor.

"Let's get this last scene finished." Chin stepped close to Geoff and rested his right arm on Geoff's shoulders. "We should have got it done yesterday. End that last side-by-side here. Get in position."

Geoff checked that his left leg and hip were snug against Chin's as he put his left arm around Chin's back. Geoff's right hand rested above Chin's right hip. He placed the left side of his face against Chin's chest. For the thousandth time, he wished he could get away from this. After that competition in October, he would make certain he never saw Chin or Lui again.

"On the last beat of this step, start turning…toward me." They did it over…and over…and over until Geoff could consistently finish the maneuver in the proper position.

"We'll work on that some more later," said Chin. "Let's get going on the traditional dance."

New music filled the room. Drumbeats and heavy bass notes throbbed beneath low-toned strings. The sensual feel of the song quickened Geoff's pulse.

Chin grinned.

Geoff wished he were somewhere else. *Anywhere* else.

Chin stepped closer to Geoff. Geoff forced himself to not back up.

"We'll begin the first round the same as most of the others we've done," Chin said. "Only difference is we don't ever break contact for more than a split second." He stood so close his chest pushed against Geoff, upsetting his balance.

Geoff stepped back to keep from falling. Chin grabbed his shoulders and held him in place.

"Get your feet back in position," he said. "Hold on to my waist."

Geoff obediently repositioned himself. Chin radiated heat scented with cologne and coffee-tinged sweat. His hard bulges of muscle made him seem larger than life.

"Hold eye contact," ordered Chin.

Geoff tilted his head back, moving his line of sight from Chin's muscular shoulder to his black eyes.

The music cut off and began again with the final notes of the preliminary bars. Having no instructions to the contrary, Geoff followed the standard opening, shifting his shoulders right and hips left.

"Keep your face against my shoulder," Chin said. "You might have to shorten the sway a little. Make up for it by shifting your hips over more. Look like you're made of rubber."

Geoff's neck soon ached from looking up. By the time the hour was done, the ache had expanded into his shoulders and face. Continuously staring into Chin's eyes was as bad as always having to keep his hands on Chin, not to mention having Chin's on him. Geoff headed home with only one thought in his mind: *to scrub down in a hot shower.*

The cross-deck transit gave Geoff the solitude of anonymity in a crowd. He curled up in the back of the transit car, resting his heels on the seat and his forehead on his knees to relieve the pain in his neck and shoulders. He had to escape from Chin, find someplace to run where the Lung Organization could not control him. He should investigate moving to Luna...or Mars... or even the Asteroid Belt or Ganymede. Could he find a way to do it without leaving his family here where Chin could get at them? Geoff rubbed his face in frustration. Tonight, as always, he was too exhausted to think things through to find a way out.

Immersed in his thoughts, Geoff missed his exit. He got off two stops later and caught a car going back the other way.

When Geoff finally arrived at his residential corridor, his overworked neck muscles had stiffened, adding to his misery. Hoping the movement would make him feel better, he rotated his head as he walked.

From that sideways angle, he spotted something strange: a round silver object on the floor beside a shrub. About to walk past it, Geoff paused. The shape pulled at his memory, as if he should recognize it.

He slowed, letting the half dozen other people who had gotten off the transit with him get a few steps ahead. Geoff knelt beside the plant and slid the object out from behind the pot.

No wonder he thought he should know it. The round part he had seen was the base of a superhero figurine that was small enough to hide in his fist. Barbara collected them. She had a couple dozen of the silly little things. In fact, she might even have this one.

Geoff examined it as he slowly walked home. It was a white-skinned man wearing a long black cape and a helmet with pointed ears on its top and a mask that covered the upper half of his face.

"Batman." Geoff identified it from old cartoons. He stuck the little statue into a pocket. If it was Barbara's, she would eventually miss it. If she didn't, he could use it as a distraction if he needed one.

Geoff opened the apartment door, and all thoughts of the little superhero and his misery at dancing with Chin vanished.

Barbara sat on the couch, bawling into a crumpled wad of tissue. Tony sat beside her, a comforting arm around her shoulders.

Geoff's first thought was that Chin had done something to Barbara. An iceberg grew around his heart, squeezing his lungs and making him shiver.

"What?" Geoff's voice wouldn't work. He was afraid of the answer but cleared his throat and tried again. "What happened?"

"She lost one of her little heroes," Tony answered.

"Huh?" asked Geoff. Barbara's hysterics had made him certain something truly horrible had happened. His fear turned into anger at her for scaring him. "I thought you'd been raped or something. All that fuss over a toy?"

"Not just any one," wailed Barbara. "The original Batman Uncle Ron and Aunty Sue brought me from Terra!"

Shaky with relief that his sister's distress had nothing to do with Geoff's association with the Lung families, Geoff slid the door closed and wobbled into the living room. He dug into his pocket and pulled out the figurine he had found in the hall.

"Did it look like this?" Geoff asked.

"Yes!" Barbara's shriek made Geoff and Tony wince. She jumped up and grabbed it from Geoff. "Where'd you find it?"

"On the floor in the hall."

"We *looked* there."

"It was between the plants. I just noticed the silver base."

"Oh, thank you." Barbara engulfed Geoff in a flower-scented hug.

He didn't even mind when she pressed her wet face against his.

"You're welcome." Geoff squeezed her in a bear hug. It felt good to be appreciated, even for such a small thing.

"Go shower." Barbara released Geoff and gave him a little push toward the bathroom.

Geoff took his time cleaning up. On his way back to the living room, he stopped in the kitchen.

"Where's Mom?" Geoff asked. She would make him something if he asked her to.

"Community association meeting," Tony replied.

"Oh." Geoff found some leftover macaroni and cheese. Something was in the cooker. Not wanting to wait, he decided to eat his snack cold.

Geoff sat on the couch beside Tony. The holoview was playing a silly sitcom. Barbara, who was sitting on the floor and arranging her miniature superheroes, was more interesting to watch.

The cook unit in the kitchen buzzed. Barbara jumped over the chair and went to it. Geoff ate his macaroni and tried to figure out what sorting system she had used.

The heroes were not grouped according to any criteria he could fathom. Old Justice League characters stood beside the latest

Defenders of the Galaxy. Their colors, talents, and creators were just as jumbled. So was quality, as the limited-edition original Superman from their grandparents stood beside the cheap Star Rover he had bought.

"I made dip." Barbara placed a bowl of tortilla chips and a shallow casserole on the empty end of the table. It was Geoff's favorite, layers of sour cream, salsa, and cheese melted together and topped with bacon bits.

"Thanks," he said. That would fill up the empty spaces around his first snack.

"You don't get the whole thing," Tony said as he scooped dip with one of the triangular chips.

"That's okay." Geoff watched Barbara transfer another little figure from the floor to the table. "Barbie, what order are you putting those in?"

"From people I love best to," she paused, "the others." She set the last one farthest from the ones bought by Geoff and their grandparents.

"Who are the others?" asked Geoff.

"Well, that last one I got from someone I don't like anymore."

"Why keep it?"

"I like *it*," Barbara explained. "Just not who I got it from." She moved up onto the couch and said, "Put something good on."

They watched the last hour of a movie together.

Geoff did Chin's stretches, including the extra ones for the Shute, before he went to bed. He continued to work on that every chance he got for the rest of the week. He had to. Chin pushed him to do more every day. They always practiced the character dance on the light deck with Lui critiquing it. He did not criticize the second dance, always performed on the heavy deck, because Geoff was still learning the choreography.

Geoff learned a few other things, too, such as not laughing when tickled.

Thursday night's choreography had Geoff holding his left hand above and behind his head, resting it against Chin's face.

Chin ran the back of his fingers from Geoff's upraised elbow down to his lower ribs. Geoff chuckled.

"What?" asked Chin.

"Tickles."

"No," Chin said. "Dancing does *not* tickle. Do it over."

That time, as Chin's fingers trailed down his ribs, Geoff restrained himself to a grin and half giggle.

Chin slapped Goeff's ribs.

Geoff gasped. His eyes watered. When they repeated the step, the tickle barely made him smile.

Chin slapped his ribs again.

Geoff doubled over, holding his side.

"Start over," ordered Chin.

Geoff forced himself upright and began the round again. He felt no tickles through the burning on his side. He didn't even smile.

Chapter 17

Friday evening, Geoff whistled on the way to work. With school out for a week, he intended to make the most of his free time by catching up on his sleep. Lately, he had been really tired.

"Evening, Geoff," Mr. Manz said when Geoff signed in at the arcade. "Simon's gone, so I'm going to get you to take over some of his work."

"Where'd he go?" asked Geoff. Simon was a university student who had worked for Mr. Manz for four years.

"Got too busy with his classes," Mr. Manz said. "You're really good with youngsters, so I'm going to keep you on the floor part-time. Instead of the counter work you used to do, I'll teach you what he did back here."

"Okay. What about—" Geoff hesitated. He didn't want to seem reluctant to learn something new.

"Curt?" asked Mr. Manz.

Geoff nodded. Curt had seniority over him.

"He'll get the parts of Simon's work you don't. He's not Lung, and this's stuff you don't talk about. It's family business."

"Okay," Geoff repeated. Family again. Every way he turned, the Lung organization wanted something from him. He felt betrayed that it would intrude into his time at the arcade. This used to be his escape.

"You'll work here in my office," Mr. Manz said as he led the way there.

Geoff sat at the second workstation, which was set at right angles to Mr. Manz's desk. He leaned forward so the scanner would pick up his retina print. The console activated.

"You got to input two security passwords," Mr. Manz said. "Pick what you want, and I'll approve them." He shut down the system and had Geoff log on again.

"What you do here is look for possible new members," explained Mr. Manz. "We have a list of skills the family needs. You're the first step in recruitment. This system tracks the game cards and lists how the players do. Here's yours."

Geoff stared in horrified amazement as a list of all the games he played appeared. Beside the game and location—some were from other arcades—were his scores and the aliases he had used.

"We sort that into a picture of skills and recruit who we want," said Mr. Manz. "That's what you do now. When the computer flags someone as a possible match for what we're looking for, let me know. When I get the word to go after him...or her, you schmooze them a little, and we get him in our games room to meet the right people."

"Who are they?" asked Geoff.

"Who? The right people?"

Geoff nodded.

"Kids that'll draw him into a gang. Sometimes it's real easy, sometimes not. You, young man, were the toughest recruitment I ever did."

"Me? I wasn't recruited." Trevor and Rob and Hans were his friends!

"Yeah, you." Mr. Manz leaned back in his chair. He folded his hands on his belly and smiled beneath his moustache. "You've got the best hand-eye coordination and the fastest reflexes I ever seen. Can't imagine why you never picked up on those sword games. You maybe need a few lessons in technique."

"They're my friends!" Geoff shifted, leaning forward and clenching his fists between his knees.

"Of course they are. It wouldn't work elsewise. When we find a kid we want, we nudge some of our kids over to make friends, form a relationship. That didn't work with you."

"What do you mean?" Anger as well as betrayal colored Geoff's question.

"Easy, Geoff," said Mr. Manz. "Those boys *are* your friends. We pushed a dozen family kids at you over several months, and you didn't buddy up with any of them. You had your own friends, a good family. You didn't need us, but Lung needed you, still needs you. We were wondering what kind of new strategy we'd have to come up with when one of the boys here noticed you and Trevor played together a fair bit. So what we did was pull him out of his first gang for you. Your gang was built of people *you* accepted as friends. The family's got a lot invested in you."

"Oh." Geoff needed time to absorb all that. "And you want me to do that now?" Trevor was family and part of Lung whether he was Geoff's friend or not. But what about the others? Would Rob or Hans be tangled up in this if they weren't Geoff's friends? Had he done this to them?

"You're in charge of maintaining skills profiles: who's fast, who can remember stuff, who's good with numbers. You also keep track of who they game with and who we've tried to hook them up with. You'll do some of that recruiting, too."

"How?" Geoff really didn't want to know. He wanted to quit his job and never set foot in an arcade again.

"Most times it's just arranging for them to win free games together. Sometimes give a gang free games or stuff, if they invite a kid we're interested in to go with them."

"That doesn't sound too complicated." Geoff said it as a question. Simon had spent a relatively large amount of his time at this desk.

"Tracking people like that's illegal, against the privacy laws," Mr. Manz said. "You got to run the information through a couple different secure programs and then decode what you end up with."

Chapter 18

The dance hall echoed emptily when Geoff entered it. He stopped just inside the door, wondering if he had missed instructions to be somewhere else. The escalating music of his wrist phone made him jump. He was not surprised to see Chin's stern image when he answered the call.

"Get started," Chin ordered. He terminated the connection.

Geoff looked at his blank phone and muttered, "Shortest call in history."

He shuffled over to the far wall and dropped his bag in the usual spot. Uneasy in the empty room, he set his com to play music as he warmed up. Music he liked, not the throbbing Simba that he could not keep out of his dreams.

Five minutes later, Chin came in and ordered Geoff to turn off his music. Chin wore emerald-green tights with turquoise swirls. His hair hung in its usual tight braid.

He began warming up beside Geoff and said, "We're doing the jump today. Hard to keep it as fluid as the rest of this dance, but we can't put it in the character one because it has to be in one g."

By the time Chin and Geoff finished their preliminary routine, Lui had arrived and settled onto his chair.

Geoff followed Chin to the center of the dance area, not daring to ask what kind of jump he would be expected to do.

"We'll make the jump the second step of the sixth round," Chin said. "You mince in a tight circle. I'll do a couple of turning Russian splits around you. Make sure you follow your line exactly, or I'll knock your head off." He frowned and added, "Do you know what Russian splits are?"

Geoff shook his head no.

"Figures." Chin looked at Lui and jerked his head in a "come here" gesture.

As Lui ambled across the room, the music started.

"Get out of the way and watch." Chin pointed at Geoff and then to a spot beside the mirrors.

Geoff was surprised at how well Lui danced. Despite his size, his movements were graceful and on the beat. For the second step, instead of stalking in a circle, Lui turned with tiny steps. Beside him, Chin jumped up, spreading his legs into sideways splits and leaning forward to touch his toes. This placed his chest above Lui's head.

Geoff swallowed a gasp as he watched Chin hang in the air and complete a quarter turn. The power in that jump really would take off his head if he stood in the wrong place.

Chin landed with a thump in time to the center beat and immediately repeated the maneuver. He landed in position for the front-to-back sway.

"That's it," Lui said. "Dry run. Copy me."

Arms crossed in front of his chest, Chin watched critically as Geoff duplicated Lui's tight turns.

"Again," Chin said. "Be precise. I'm not taking an injury to compensate for you being in the wrong place."

Geoff got the first steps right. Nervousness tightened metal bands across his back as Chin's legs swept up alongside him. Geoff reflexively flinched away from Chin's muscled limbs.

"Never do that." Chin's lips brushed Geoff's left ear, making him flinch again. "Stay in the turn," ordered Chin as his feet hit the floor. He jumped again.

Geoff was not sure he stepped with the beat, but he held his position as Chin landed behind him.

"Do it over," Chin said.

The next day, Geoff dragged himself out of bed at 1130. As he groaned his way through his morning stretches, he consoled himself with the thought that school was out for a week. He could sleep in every morning. And because he did not work Wednesday and Thursday, for those two days, he only had to get up to eat and maybe go out with the guys—until his evening appointment with Chin, of course.

When Geoff arrived at the recreation center at noon, Lui waited in the dance hall. His feet rested on a chair; his plump, soft-looking hands kneaded and folded a black boot.

"Here." Lui tossed the boot to Geoff, who caught it with his free hand.

He dropped his gym bag beside the wall before he turned back to Lui. The fat man had picked up the matching boot and was bending it, first curving the toe up toward the boot top and then down toward the heel.

"Work that one some more," Lui said. "They never make them soft enough."

Geoff held the boot heel and toe and pushed. The boot sole folded in half and his knuckles bumped together. He grunted in surprise and examined the pliable footwear more closely. Except for the heel and a small ceramic plate at the toe, the sole was very supple. So was the vinyl top.

"These are your competition boots," said Lui. "Try them on."

Because they had been designed to mold to his feet rather than just be the correct size, their perfect fit did not surprise Geoff. That they were the most comfortable things he had ever had on shocked him. It was like standing in firm Jell-O. He hadn't expected Chin to give him anything that felt this wonderful.

"They're good," Geoff said.

Not satisfied with that declaration, Lui knelt beside Geoff and carefully felt his feet through the thin material.

"Okay." Lui heaved himself upright. "Try on the contacts."

Geoff's steps made sharp double clicks as he followed Lui back to the chairs. The sound made him very conscious of how he walked.

Lui handed him two small plastic boxes with the tops divided into two lids, one marked left, the other right.

"Here's the cleaner," said Lui, handing Geoff a white plastic bottle that sloshed. "You know how to take care of 'em?"

Geoff shook his head no.

Lui said, "These aren't like ones for vision. Those you change every few months. These you only wear for shows. I guess I have to show you how to put them in, too."

It was not a question, but Geoff nodded. He had not even known there was a particular method of doing that. He followed Lui over to the mirrors and received a quick lesson on how to look upward, set the contact on the white of his eye, and then slide it onto his cornea. Ten minutes later, he still did not have even one in.

Chin entered the room and said, "Aren't you ready?"

"He keeps blinking them out," said Lui.

"Well, you do it. You'll be doing his face anyway."

"True." Lui turned Geoff so they faced each other. "Look up."

"I'll get it," Geoff said. He did not trust Lui to safely put anything in his eyes.

"Take forever. I said look up." Lui did not wait for Geoff to acquiesce. He held Geoff's jaw with his left hand, and with his right, he deftly popped the contacts into Geoff's eyes.

Geoff blinked. The left contact fell out.

Lui replaced it and said, "Don't blink. Just close your eyes a second. If they're watering, dry them before you open them."

Geoff lifted the hem of his T-shirt and squeezed his tears onto it. He opened his eyes and looked in the mirror. Dark purple irises with light flecks stared back. The color in the contacts created a fuzzy, colored ring at the periphery of his vision. Geoff instinctively reached up to rub his eyes and remove the blurriness.

Lui slapped his hands.

"No touching," he ordered. "The other pair's silver with dark blue. You'll wear them on alternate days. Quit admiring yourself and stretch."

Geoff and Chin put on their new boots to dance. They sounded terrific when stepping to the beat together, but any extra steps or foot movements were incredibly loud.

"No shuffling," Chin said when Geoff inadvertently clicked his toe tap. "Clean steps."

During the break, Geoff stretched out his legs and tried to determine if he was getting blisters. He did not think so. His feet didn't even hurt.

As Geoff sat there, sipping water and staring at the ceiling, he listened to Lui and Chin discuss a raid on a family business. It sounded as if it must have been a night club or bar of some type. Apparently, the police had been foiled by illegal exits cut into the station walls and decks.

Geoff was so tired that the last half of the practice seemed to take forever. He sighed with relief when Chin ordered the boots off for the winding-down stretches. His relief changed to horror at his extortionist's next words.

"You have next week off, so we're going to take advantage of the extra time and get this choreography finished," said Chin. "We'll keep our regular evening schedule plus do an hour and a half every morning before you go to work. Those two days you're not at the arcade, I'll schedule us for the afternoon, too."

"What?" Geoff did not want to believe his ears. He was *so* looking forward to some time to himself.

"You objecting?" Chin filled the two words with menace.

"No." Geoff dropped his boots beside the chair holding his contacts and went to stretch.

As he often did, Chin stayed beside Geoff, doing the same routine and ordering minor corrections to Geoff's performance of the exercises.

When they finished, Geoff grabbed his bag and headed for the locker room. He did not want to go to work smelling of sweat; he couldn't stand spending the day smelling like Chin. They had danced so closely together that he needed to wash off Chin's sweat as much as his own.

"Don't forget your gear," Chin said.

Geoff looked from his contacts and boots to Chin and said, "What do you want me to say when my mother puts a snack in my bag and asks me what I'm doing with colored contacts and those funny boots?" It wouldn't happen. His mother believed anyone old enough to reach the cupboard was old enough to pack his own snacks. Geoff just did not want to possess those concrete reminders of his slavery.

"Tell her you're old enough to pack your own lunch," Chin said.

"She only hears what she wants to."

"Okay," said Chin. "Be back Monday at noon."

"Yeah." Geoff went to shower, only slightly concerned that either of the men might follow and harass him. They had been treating him relatively well since they had decided to compete for prize money.

By the time Geoff finished work that evening, he was so exhausted that for the first time in weeks, he skipped his evening exercises. He slept until noon on Sunday, and then he only got up because he needed to go to the bathroom. Once awake, Geoff realized he was hungry. *Starving.* The rumblings in his stomach echoed like the empty dance hall.

"You sure slept," Fallah said when Geoff wandered into the kitchen.

"I was tired," said Geoff.

"You've been tired a lot lately." Fallah frowned at Geoff. "Maybe you're run-down...or a little anaemic."

"I'm fine." Geoff looked in the refrigerator. Hungry as he was, nothing seemed appetizing. To prevent his mother from nagging, he took the little container of leftover scalloped potatoes.

"That's not much of a breakfast," Fallah said. "Are you not hungry, or do you just not feel like cooking?"

"A little of both." Geoff put his breakfast in the cooker.

"I'm about to make lunch," said Fallah. "It'll be ready in half an hour."

"Okay." Hoping to find something interesting to watch as he ate, Geoff took his snack into the living room. He found Tony and Barbara fussing over the garden while a golf game filled the holoview.

"You're not watching that, are you?" asked Geoff. There should have been a real sport on…or cartoons or a movie.

"Don't change it," Tony said. "I want to see who wins. It's almost over."

"That's as boring as watching chess." Geoff drifted over to the garden. "Why do they bother showing it?"

"I'm sure I'm not the only one in the system watching. Have a tomato." Tony pointed to a red globe half the size of his fist.

Geoff shook his head and said, "I'll take those tiny ones before they get too ripe." The little tomatoes, no larger than the end of his thumb, were his favorite.

"What little ones?" Tony looked back at his plants as if doubting his eyesight.

"We had them for supper last night," Barbara said.

"You what?" Geoff knew he was overreacting, but he couldn't stop himself. "You know I like them!"

"You fall off the wrong side of the bed or what?" asked Barbara. She looked at Geoff as if he had sprouted a third eye. "There'll be more, you know."

"Those were mine." Stomping as well as he could in the half gravity, Geoff headed for his room.

"You didn't grow them," Barbara called after him.

Geoff went back to bed. He pretended to be asleep when Fallah came to get him for lunch. Shortly afterward, he did fall asleep.

He woke in midafternoon. Silence filled the apartment. Where was everyone? Geoff checked the message circuit of the holoview.

"We're going to the water park," Tony's image said. "You can meet us there if you like, or we'll see you back here at sixteen. Lunch is in the fridge."

Geoff found the bowl of soup and two sandwiches. As he devoured them, he watched part of a basketball game and considered what to do. There really wasn't time for him to go swim with the rest of the family. What he ought to do was Chin's blue-ioned exercises. He had not worked through them since yesterday afternoon. Amazingly, he could feel he needed to stretch. His arms and legs felt crumpled.

In an effort to make up for skipping his stretching regimen, Geoff worked at it extra hard—not an easy job for some of the exercises in half gravity, but he had a system for holding himself in position. As he lay on his back, his left foot wedged under the corner of the couch and his right one kicked up to touch the floor over his head, a burning pain streaked down the back of his thigh.

"Oh, hell," Geoff groaned. He tentatively tried to repeat the leg movement. He couldn't. He must have torn a muscle. Great. Chin would really blast him for that. Maybe if he rested it for the remainder of the day and took a few Lormal before he went to the club tomorrow, Chin wouldn't notice.

And maybe the station would fall out of orbit.

Knowing Chin's expectations, Geoff carefully worked through as much of the rest of his routine as he could. No sense getting beat up if he could prevent it.

He followed the stretches with a hot shower and thorough rubdown with Haynes Heet. They did not help his injury. Damn. Maybe the first-aid techs at the sports fields could help him.

Geoff limped to the transit and rode to the recreation center by the school.

Hobbling in one gravity, he made his painful way to the nearest first-aid station. Its small front room was open on one side. Two of its three walls were lined with chairs. The third held a small desk console and a door to the treatment rooms. A woman wearing a dinosaur-print shirt sat at the desk.

Geoff limped up to her and said, "I think I pulled something."

"So I see," replied the woman. "Sign in. We'll have a look right away."

Geoff swiped his implant over her scanner and explained that he had been doing some stretches before going to gymnastics.

Less than ten minutes later, he limped out the exit at the back of the treatment room, having been instructed to stay off his leg for a few days, put cold packs on the injury, and take Blissmaert.

"Like I couldn't have figured that out for myself," Geoff grumbled as he rode home. He'd been hoping to get his leg fixed.

The apartment was still empty. Geoff settled onto the couch with a bag of popcorn. He was still munching on it when the rest of the family came home.

"It's alive," Barbara said.

"Feeling better?" asked Fallah. She briefly rested one hand on Geoff's forehead and then ran it through his dark curls.

"Yeah." He gently pushed her hand away.

Barbara grabbed her ever-present blanket off the chair and curled up beside Geoff. She smelled good. Her hair, damp and clean and scented with flowers, tickled his neck.

Geoff flicked it away and said, "You're wet."

"Can I have some?" She reached a hand toward his bag of popcorn.

"Yeah." He tilted it toward her. Maybe she wouldn't mention his blowing up at her earlier. "Who all was at the park?" He didn't care and hardly listened as she chatted about the friends she had met on the waterslides. He was content to have her talking so that no one would ask him anything.

Geoff's leg stiffened as he lolled on the sofa. Despite the half gravity, when he got up shortly before supper, he limped to his room.

"What happened to you?" asked Barbara.

"I think I tore a muscle." In the privacy of his own space, Geoff scrunched up his face with pain and slathered more Haynes Heet onto the back of his right thigh. How the hell was he going to hide this from Chin?

Chapter 19

That question worried him all night and the next morning. He did what exercises he could without further hurting his leg, but they only demonstrated how much the damaged muscle inhibited his movements. He dosed himself with Lormal before he went to the club.

Walking normally on the heavy deck proved impossible. Geoff limped until he approached the dance hall and then tried to stick to his usual gait.

Lui looked up when Geoff walked in.

"Hell," Lui said. "Blue ion-blasted mutant bait—"

Chin spun around. His eyes narrowed with anger.

"You blasted idiot!" he yelled. "What the hell did you do to yourself?"

"*Your* exercises." Geoff dropped his bag and forced himself to glare up at Chin.

"You should damn well know how to do them by now. Take your pants off."

Thankful he had decided to wear his bicycle shorts even though he had hoped to get sent home, Geoff dropped his jeans to his knees.

Chin knelt beside Geoff. He held Geoff's right knee with one hand and felt the back of his thigh with the other.

Geoff twitched but resisted trying to kick himself free.

"It's torn, all right." Chin pushed Geoff toward Lui. "Get your contacts in and go warm up. Don't extend that muscle."

Surprised at Chin's apparently calm acceptance of the injury, Geoff stood there and stared at him.

"Move," ordered Chin.

That was easier said than done. Lui put the silver-and-blue contacts in Geoff's eyes. Then Geoff struggled to get through the preliminary exercises. He ended up further hurting his leg.

"We're going to work as usual," Chin said. "Fudge the steps you can't do. Work on the upper body moves."

They spent the next twenty minutes on the low-g deck performing the character dance. As usual, Lui pointed out every minuscule error.

"You're flopping around like a rag doll," Chin said. "Get your arms under control."

Geoff clenched his teeth and tried. His leg hurt even without doing the steps. His concentration suffered. He had an even more difficult time when they returned to the heavy deck and reviewed the choreographed rounds of the traditional dance.

"Get your head around it," growled Chin. "Do it over and get it right. You're going to learn the rest of this one today." They did it again…and again.

Through his own pain, fatigue, and frustration, Geoff could feel Chin's fury at how slowly they were progressing. They stopped for a break without having begun any new choreography.

As Chin cracked the seal on his water bottle, he asked, "You called Doc?" Lui nodded.

Geoff clicked the top onto his juice. Lui had called the Mad Medic. At this point, Geoff was even willing to receive treatment from him.

"Let's go," Chin said. "Same sway as last time. Quit leaning on me," Chin said. "You're supposed to look like you're doing it yourself. Effortlessly."

They worked through next few steps, and then Lui shut off the music and shuffled across the floor to Chin and Geoff.

"Now," Chin said. "Instead of both of us swaying, I drop to one knee as I go right. You pivot and lie on your back across my shoulders." He knelt and placed his left hand at the back of Geoff's right leg just above his knee.

As Chin's large hand gripped his lower thigh, Geoff hesitantly leaned backward.

"Farther," Lui grabbed Geoff's shoulders and pulled him back. "Get your waist on the back of his neck and curve sideways so your shoulder blades rest on either side of his right shoulder." Lui arranged Geoff on Chin's shoulders.

"Like this," he said. "Now drop your right arm so he can hang onto you."

As Chin and Lui argued about positions, Geoff blinked at the upside-down wall across the room and wished they'd hurry and make up their minds. Chin's muscular shoulder felt bonier by the second. Geoff thought his back would break and stomach split open. Tears rolled down his forehead and into his hair. Roaring filled his ears. Chin's shoulders disappeared from beneath him, replaced by drifting grayness.

As Geoff wavered at the edge of consciousness, his arms and legs dangled around Chin like the limbs of an abandoned puppet.

"I like that," Lui exclaimed.

"Me, too." Chin pivoted 360 degrees, watching the centrifugal force lift Geoff's hands and feet. "Not with a spin, though."

"Complete the sway," said Lui. "It'll be perfect."

Chin shifted to one side and then the other. Geoff's hanging limbs swayed with him.

Chin turned his back to Lui and said, "Catch." He pushed Geoff off his shoulders.

Just aware enough to realize he was falling, Geoff did not have time for fear before he landed in Lui's arms. He lay against the fat man's cushiony chest as Lui carried him to the edge of the parquet dance area.

Lui knelt and, not roughly, laid Geoff on the floor.

Geoff promptly curled into a ball in a semiconscious attempt to relieve his tortured stomach muscles.

"Sleeping like a baby," Lui chuckled. "Shall I wake him up?"

Chin, who was counting to himself as he repeated the motions of the lift, shook his head.

"Just play the music," Chin said. "He'll wake up."

The heavy beat did rouse Geoff. He opened his eyes and saw three Chins, each one dancing with an invisible partner. They swayed, knelt, rose, and smoothly continued the sway, straightening at center before tilting their shoulders for unseen dancers to slide down into the curve of their left arms. Geoff shook his head and blinked. The trio separated into one real Chin and two images in the mirrored walls.

Chin looked at Geoff and said, "Get up here."

The music stopped. Geoff rolled to his feet and wobbled to the center of the dance floor. Lui returned as well.

"Dry run," Chin said. "When you lie on my shoulders, curve sideways around my neck so you can balance. Stay that way till you slide into the dismount."

They walked through the rest of the choreography for that round and the first two steps of the final one.

"We'll finish that off when you can use your leg," Chin said. "Cool off. Be back here at twenty-one."

Geoff went to shower. When he stepped out of it, a vaguely familiar man wearing a warm-up suit handed him his towel.

"Who are you?" Geoff asked as he wrapped it around his waist.

"You don't remember me?" asked the man. "I'm crushed." He didn't sound upset, though, and his cheerful voice did sound familiar to Geoff.

"I know your voice," Geoff said. He frowned, trying to remember where he had heard it.

"You should. I'm the doctor who patched you up when you picked a fight with Chin a month ago. Mop off that water and let me look at your leg."

Geoff nodded. This was Chin's Mad Medic. Geoff dried himself and stood in his towel while the doctor scanned and then felt the back of his right leg.

"That's torn, all right." The Mad Medic pointed to the bench between the rows of lockers. "Lie down on your stomach, and I'll fix you up."

Geoff obediently lay on the narrow platform. He'd do almost anything to get rid of the pain.

"Lucky for you I practice sports medicine," the doctor said as he dug in his bag. "Hold still." He stuck a small circle attached to a wire to the back of Geoff's neck.

It tingled. Geoff tried to reach it. His arms wouldn't move. Panicked, he attempted to roll off the bench. He couldn't move beyond turning his head slightly.

"Relax." The Mad Medic's firm hand pressed Geoff's face into the bench. "You have to lie absolutely still while I put regeneration fluid into that tear."

Chin and Lui entered the locker room.

"Well?" asked Chin.

"I'll give it a squirt." The Mad Medic opened a small case containing a holoview projector. "This is cold," he warned before he pushed the towel off Geoff's right leg and laid sensor strips on it.

Geoff tried to turn his head to watch.

"Quit trying to move. The sensors give me a picture of the damage inside." He unfolded a small pack. It held needles, syringes, and a coffee cup-sized insulated cold pack holding half a dozen tiny vials. After he readied a syringe with a small amount of clear, green-tinged fluid, the doctor scrubbed Geoff's leg with pink solution.

"That's a bit of local anaesthetic so you don't feel the needle," said the Mad Medic. "I can't put the inside to sleep. It interferes with regeneration. What that means is...it's going to hurt."

"He doesn't mind," Chin said.

"Do so," Geoff managed. The electrode on his neck did not allow him to control his breathing for speaking. He had to try and talk through an involuntary exhalation.

His eyes on his holoview, the doctor slowly inserted his needle into Geoff's thigh.

It hurt. Geoff clenched his teeth as his leg caught fire from the inside. He couldn't hold his breath, so he moaned with each exhalation.

"Sorry, kid." The Mad Medic did not sound sorry, and he repeated the process twice more. "That's it. Now—" He pulled bruise patches out of his bag and stuck them to the blue handprints on Geoff's upper right arm and above his right knee.

He peeled the sensors off Geoff's leg, looked at Chin, and asked, "While I'm here, you want me to put in a little joint juice? Fix all his flexibility problems."

Although he knew it was futile, Geoff tried to get up. Whatever "juice" that was, he didn't want anyone messing around with his joints. Fear made his heart hammer against the bench.

"Too risky," Chin said.

If he had been able to, Geoff would have sighed with relief. His surprise and touch of gratefulness disappeared when Chin added, "We don't have time to chance crippling him for a month."

Their social chatter as the doctor packed up his equipment bypassed Geoff's ears. Cold seeped through his pain.

Surprise widened his eyes when the Mad Medic knelt where Geoff could see him and said, "I put a pain patch on you, so don't take any Lormal or Blisso for four hours. You can walk with little steps and lie down. No running, stretching, or prolonged sitting for at least five hours. Then take it easy for another ten, or we'll be doing this all over again." He stood up and gestured for Lui and Chin to come closer. "Hold him down."

Lui straddled the bench and sat on Geoff's lower legs. Chin pressed one knee onto Geoff's back. The doctor removed the electrode from Geoff's neck.

Geoff jerked with a violent spasm. His arms flew out. One hand struck Chin's leg, the other flailed in the air. He would have fallen if Lui and Chin had held him less firmly. When Geoff relaxed, both men released him. As badly as Geoff wanted to curse them or better yet, give all three a solid punch in the face, he knew he couldn't. He quietly sat up and adjusted his towel. He shivered.

"Don't get shocky on me," the Mad Medic said. "Keep that leg straight." He picked up his bag and walked out. Chin grabbed Geoff under the arms and stood him up.

"No straining the injury," he said.

Geoff leaned against the lockers as Chin and Lui left. He shivered again. The places where Chin's warm hands had briefly held him were his only spots without goose bumps.

During Geoff's supper break, he met his friends at the restaurant near the arcade. Hans was already at a table when Geoff limped in.

"What happened to you?" asked Hans.

"He must have gone blading without us," Rob said from behind Geoff. "You look like you slid off the high one," he added.

"No," said Geoff. How was he going to explain this? "Just pulled something. Slide in." He gestured for Hans to move over. The long-haired historian obligingly shifted down the bench. The table had a padded bench along one side and chairs on the other.

Geoff held on to the edge of the table. Resting all his weight on his left foot, he kept his right leg straight as he awkwardly sat down.

The other two boys snickered.

"You're a sorry-looking hand," said Trevor as he walked up. "When'd you get so clumsy?"

"Didn't," said Geoff. He activated the menu screen set into the table. "One house-special medium pizza and two large chocolate milks," he said. "As soon as possible. Don't wait for the rest of the table." Geoff held his implant up to be read and then leaned forward for the retina scan.

"Now he doesn't even want to eat with us," said Rob.

"I got to get back to work," Geoff said. They knew that. Why did they have to rock his orbit about it?

"You know, when professional athletes pull a muscle or sprain something, they get it fixed," said Hans. "The trainers squirt in regeneration gel."

"Yeah, but you think the docs'll do anything for us ordinary folk?" asked Trevor.

"They would if you paid for it," Rob said. "It's supposed to hurt like hell, though. Why would anyone pay for that?"

"So they don't have to walk like gimpy," laughed Trevor. "And can sit without looking like they got a fork up their ass."

"Blast off," growled Geoff. He knew they meant it in fun. It just didn't feel funny.

"Oh-ho," said Rob. "Gimpy's sense of humor is sprained, too."

"'Cause my friends are acting like ion-blasted vacuum-brains," Geoff said. He couldn't even stomp out and leave them there. It was hard to make a statement with your exit when just standing up would take two minutes of clumsy maneuvering. Geoff slumped against the back of the bench. He didn't have energy for even a friendly argument. He felt like he was about to cry like a girl.

"I hurt, okay?" Geoff said. His painkillers were in his gym bag, which was in Mr. Manz's office. It had been about four hours since the Mad Medic had dispensed his treatments, and Geoff needed another dose of Blissmaert. He shifted uncomfortably and winced. What he really needed was to go to bed. Why hadn't he had the sense to ask Mr. Manz for the day off?

"Don't you have Blisso or something?" asked Hans.

Geoff shook his head and said, "Not here."

"I might." Rob checked his pockets and shook his head. "No Blisso, but I got Lormal." He pulled crinkled patches from his shirt pocket and passed one to Geoff.

"Thanks." Geoff pushed up his left sleeve and stuck the painkiller to the inside of his forearm. It was good to have friends, even if they were skewed-orbit mutant-brains sometimes.

Chapter 20

Tuesday morning Geoff's feet dragged. He had not felt this bad since the first few days of training. The pain in his leg had gone, but his abdomen muscles felt like they had all been torn.

"Look alive," Chin said. A light sheen of sweat glistened on his face and arms.

Geoff glanced at him but said nothing. Chin stood and watched Geoff remove his outer clothes.

"You're not limping," Chin said. "Does that mean Doc actually knew what he was doing?"

Geoff shrugged.

"Let me see that." Chin knelt.

Knowing objecting would be worse than useless, Geoff stopped beside him. Chin felt the back of Geoff's leg, his touch clinical and impersonal.

"I think that did it," he said. "We'll know right away."

He led Geoff through the warm-up, starting slowly but quickly turning it into an energetic aerobics routine. Geoff's stomach muscles shrieked at the movements. A rush of pain-induced tears washed out his right contact.

"What the hell?" demanded Chin. "What are you crying about?"

"I'm not." Geoff wiped his eyes with the backs of his hands as Lui waddled over.

"He strained his abdominal muscles yesterday," Lui said as he put the colored lens back in Geoff's eye. "He's moving like a hundred-year-old grandpa. Here." He pushed up Geoff's T-shirt sleeve and slapped a patch onto the inside of his upper arm.

Seeing the Lormal logo, Geoff did not take it off. He could use the double dose.

"You're supposed to be in half-decent shape by now," Chin muttered. He resumed the preliminary exercises. When they were finished, the three of them crammed themselves into the elevator and went to the light deck to practice the character dance.

"Get your shoulder out more," Lui called after the first few beats. He kept up a litany of instructions throughout the dance.

Geoff tried to do what he was told, but he couldn't remember things, and the music kept going too fast.

"Do it again," Chin ordered. "Get it right."

"I'm trying," said Geoff. He really was, but nothing worked.

"You did this for an hour last night," Chin growled as they rode back down to the one-g recreation center. "How could you have forgotten it all?"

"Don't know." It was a sullen, tired mumble.

"You are a vacuum-brained moron." Chin punctuated the words by poking Geoff in the chest four times.

Geoff rocked backward a little at each impact of what felt like a tristillian hammer, but he didn't have the energy to get angry.

In the one-gravity dance hall, Geoff shambled over to his bag and slumped down against the wall.

Chin sat on a chair beside Lui and asked, "What'd you patch him with?"

"Lormal. Why?"

"He must have taken something else, too."

"Hmmmmm." Lui stared thoughtfully at Geoff, who sat slouched against the wall, legs spread, feet flopped outward. He had not picked up his juice or water.

"I hit him in the chest, and he didn't react," Chin said. "Not one little flicker of mad. No fire in those baby browns at all."

Lui took a deep breath, as if startled.

"He's burnt out," he said.

"Blast off," said Chin. "We've only been at this a month and a half."

"Six weeks exactly," agreed Lui. "That's," he said and blinked twice before he continued, "a total of thirty-two and a half hours. If you figure an hour of individual instruction is equivalent to four hours of classroom time." He stared at the ceiling and blinked again, and then he said, "That's 130 classes. With two instructors, half again that amount is 195. There's twenty-nine classes in a year, so he's had 6.7 years of dance in six weeks." Lui looked at Chin and repeated, "He's burnt out."

"Blast off." Chin looked over at Geoff and shook his head. "Oh, hell." Resignation filled Chin's voice.

Geoff, staring at the ceiling and pretending he was not listening to them, wondered what would happen next. What under the stars would he do if Chin ordered him to not feel too hollow and weary and listless to do anything?

Chin finished his drink and walked over to Geoff. Augmented by the taps on his boot soles, his steps sounded like the drums of doom from an old horror movie.

"Get out of here," Chin said.

"Huh?" Chin's words were so far from what Geoff expected that he couldn't immediately understand them.

"Get out of here." Chin waved one arm toward the exit. "Go home. See a movie. Find Trevor and lift yourself some new toys. Go chase girls." Chin paused and looked consideringly down at Geoff.

"Okay." Geoff pulled his feet in and stood up before Chin could change his mind.

"I'll cancel your shift at the arcade today," added Chin. "That'll give you three days off. Make sure you do your stretches at least four times a day. Be back here ready to work on Friday at 1130."

"Friday," Geoff repeated. It was hard to believe. He nodded and headed for his bag, afraid Chin would see the tears in his eyes. Maybe Lui was right. Maybe he was burnt out…or stressed out… or had just been pushed as far as he could be.

Geoff dressed in record time. He strode quickly out of the dance hall. By the time he jogged through the front doors of the club, he wore a grin as wide as his face. Geoff jumped up and spun around. His gym bag narrowly missed hitting a couple of older women.

"Sorry," he said.

One frowned, but the other smiled and said, "You look like you're having a good time."

Geoff nodded and smiled back. He felt like the weight of the station had been lifted off his shoulders. The tiredness that had consumed him even on the light decks had vanished. He wanted to have some fun. Maybe he could talk Trevor into skipping work this afternoon.

He found his friend loading grocery orders into a station delivery truck. A long rack of shelves with a seat and steering wheel at each end, it traveled the maintenance tunnels between decks. Those meter-and-a-half-high hallways provided access both for product deliveries and maintenance of utilities, air, and recycling.

"Aren't you supposed to be at work?" asked Trevor.

"Got the day off." Geoff grinned. "Let's do something."

"I can't," Trevor said. "I got to deliver this stuff."

"You get to drive?" asked Geoff.

Trevor smiled and nodded.

"No wonder you don't want to go," said Geoff. The opportunity to drive a real vehicle was not to be passed up. "You want company?" He had been on a truck only once, two years ago when Trevor's uncle had given them both a short ride on an empty vehicle.

"Not allowed," said the middle-aged woman loading the other side of the racks. "You shouldn't even be back here."

"How about we meet at the arcade after supper?" asked Trevor. "Uhhhh, do you have time tonight?"

"Yes." Geoff couldn't contain his grin. "Got three days off."

On his way home, he detoured through the deck-four shopping mall. Just for fun, he lifted a handful of expensive jewelry. He walked out of the store and past a clerk with a friendly smile, a slightly lopsided smile like Dad's.

Geoff turned around and went back to the sales counter.

"You need to check your security," Geoff said to the man behind the display case. He retrieved five rings, three bracelets, and four necklaces from his clothing.

"Where did you get those?" asked the clerk. Geoff pointed to the displays he had strolled past a few moments earlier.

"So long." Geoff left before anyone detained him. That had been a dumb thing to do. He meandered down the mall hall. Without friends, the mall was boring. Besides, his excitement at having three free days was fading into tiredness. He went home.

Barbara and Nadine were there, talking and laughing and making a mess in the kitchen.

"What are you doing?" asked Geoff. They had stuff everywhere.

"Practicing," replied Barbara. She solemnly juggled two chocolate chips with one hand.

"We're making her birthday cake," Nadine said. She dipped a spatula in a container of frosting and then used it to snag one of Barbara's airborne chips.

"Your birthday's a week away," said Geoff. "And that woman down the hall always makes the cake."

"She's teaching us how to decorate it." Barbara's dimple appeared as she grinned. "We have to make a cake, though." She waved at the cake mix, pans, and clutter on the counter. A bucket of chocolate-chip cookie dough sat there as well. "We're making cookies, too."

"How'm I supposed to get lunch? You're taking up the whole kitchen."

"There's plenty of room," said Barbara. "Unless you're going to cook a whole meal."

"I'm not now." Geoff hadn't planned to cook. There should be leftovers or sandwich makings in the fridge. He tried to ignore the girls, but their cheerful silliness was infectious. As Geoff piled ham, cheese, lettuce, and tomato in a bun, he enjoyed the fun Barbara and Nadine were making out of baking.

"This is our sample one," said Nadine as she sculpted a fist-sized mound of cookie dough in the center of a pan.

"That's too big to bake properly," Geoff said. He remembered that from years ago when he had thought baking was fun. "I'll fix it for you."

Geoff sliced the blob of dough in half. He speared the nearer chunk with the tip of his knife and set it on the plate beside his sandwich. He broke off a lump and popped it into his mouth.

"Hey!" Nadine yelled. "Get your own. That's mine."

"Not anymore." Geoff picked up his dish and glass of milk.

Nadine threw a tiny ball of dough at him.

Geoff ducked and chuckled.

From his other side, Barbara tossed a dozen chocolate chips that hit him in the shoulder.

Unwilling to sacrifice any of his stolen cookie dough, Geoff balanced his plate on his glass and reached for ammunition with his left hand. He got two fingers in the frosting. A quick flick against his thumb and a spreading pattern of soft brown blobs flew toward Barbara.

She sidestepped some and caught some on her hand. The rest landed on her shirt, hair, and face.

"Oooohhhhh!" She shrieked and laughed and grabbed for more chips.

"I'll get him," Nadine yelled. She chucked the remains of her giant cookie at Geoff.

He spun aside, laughing as it sailed past him. A quick grab rescued his sandwich. He rebalanced it on his glass and reached for more frosting.

"Oh, no!" Barbara snatched it off the table. She dropped a fistful of chocolate chips into the frosting and then scooped them up and threw them at her brother.

Her aim was good. Laughing, Geoff tried to catch the gooey missile in his mouth. He got half of it. The remainder spread across the right side of his face and hair.

The girls screamed with laughter.

Geoff choked on his mouthful of frosting and chips. He coughed and sprayed sweet chocolate fluff and chunks across the kitchen floor. As soon as he caught his breath, he started laughing again.

As the three of them roared hysterically, Geoff felt his mood swing again. He hurried to his room before his sobs became audible. Plunking his snack on the desk, he picked up a dirty T-shirt and wiped his face. He folded it over and sobbed into it. What was the matter with him?

"Hey!" Barbara called. "You've got to help clean this up."

Geoff took a deep breath and tried to get his voice under control.

"I need a shower," he yelled. That was no lie. His hair was full of frosting and chips.

"We'll save some for you," Nadine said as Geoff crossed the hall to the bathroom.

"Some what?" asked Geoff.

"Mess."

Geoff showered and dressed. He decided to shop for Barbara's birthday present as he ate. It shouldn't take long. He had pretty well decided what to get.

A minute later, he knew there were now five stores on station that sold the little superhero figures Barbara collected.

"Don't show anything under twenty dollars," Geoff ordered. "Correction, show all stock priced at nineteen dollars and fifty cents and higher." That would include all the ones listed at just under twenty. He did not set an upper price limit because he had not decided on one. After all, how expensive could they get?

As Geoff watched the displays move slowly through the space above his desk, he poked his stylus into the figures he wanted a closer look at. When the inventories were done, he ordered his selections into the holoview. There were over twenty of them, each labeled with the name of the figure, the artist, which stores carried it, and its price.

In short order, he narrowed the field to five statues ranging in price from thirty to ninety dollars. He deleted the most expensive one. The remaining four were all in the same store, a little place across the station and up on the 0.3-gravity deck.

Geoff marked Sun Man, a hero from the Captain Galactica cartoons and the least expensive of the quartet. Before he bought it, he looked again at a statue twice Sun Man's price called Storm. She was a dark-skinned woman with silver hair and eyes. Geoff did not know what story she belonged to, but there was something in her expression that attracted him. Unable to choose between the two of them at that moment, Geoff put a one-week hold on both. His deposit would go toward whichever one he bought.

The aroma of freshly baked cookies seeped into Geoff's room. He ordered his console off, picked up his plate and glass, and licked his lips as he left his room.

The worst of the mess had been cleaned off the kitchen floor. Barbara and Nadine were pouring dark brown cake batter into two round pans.

"You owe me a cleanup," Barbara said. "Don't touch those."

"Wasn't going to." Geoff wanted a handful of the cooling cookies. Given the precariousness of his emotions, he did not want to get into an argument because he feared he would start crying again. He might have to shock his sister and ask her nicely.

Unwilling to take such a drastic step without careful consideration, he went to the other end of the kitchen and refilled his glass. Now he needed something to put on his plate so that it wouldn't look like he had kept it just for cookies. A chunk of cheese and a handful of crackers took care of that.

Geoff strolled back to the table.

"That edible?" he asked. He set his plate on his glass and dipped the tip of his finger into the cake dough stuck to the inside of the mixing bowl. He popped it into his mouth before it could drip. Sweet, runny chocolate spread across his tongue. "Mmmmm."

"Of course it is," Barbara said.

"*We* made it," added Nadine.

"Get away from our cookies," ordered Barbara. She carefully watched Geoff as he licked the last trace of chocolate from his finger.

"Okay." Geoff didn't move.

"We'll trade for some," offered Barbara.

"What?" If she wanted him to clean the kitchen, he'd steal a handful of cookies and run.

"Make milk shakes."

"For how many?" Everyone liked Geoff's milk shakes. They were a good negotiating item.

"Four," Barbara said.

"Eight," bargained Geoff. Four cookies weren't enough.

"You'll be sick," said Nadine.

"Too many," Barbara said at the same time. "Six."

"If they're the last ones out of the oven," agreed Geoff.

Geoff set three mugs in the freezer and then ordered a triple helping of ice cream. As the lab dropped the icy treat into a bowl, Geoff put berries, a package of protein drink powder, and a scoop of sugar into the blender. He ate his cheese and crackers by the time the drinks were finished, so he took his cookies and milk shake to the living room. A nature show about Terran mountain animals played in the holoview.

Before he could order it off, Nadine said, "We're watching that."

"You're cooking," said Geoff.

"It's almost over," Barbara said.

"I want to see the eagles hatch," said Nadine. "Then you can pick something."

As ugly, wet chicks struggled out of their shells, Geoff used the alternate viewer to look for something he felt like watching. He couldn't find anything. Afternoon programming was terrible. He closed his eyes and savored the chewy cookies and chunks of melted chocolate.

"Aren't they adorable?" Nadine leaned over the holoview and scrunched up her face at the now fluffy baby birds.

"It's over," Geoff said. They settled on a race-across-the-galaxy adventure movie. Geoff fell asleep halfway through it.

Chapter 21

When Geoff woke, the holoview was dark and silent, and the living room lights had been turned off. Shadows shifted across it from the kitchen where Barbara, Nadine, and the woman from down the hall worked at the table.

On his way to his room, Geoff paused to look at the girls' decorating. He took a cookie wearing a droopy icing flower.

"I'll get rid of this one for you," Geoff said to Barbara.

"Okay." She straightened and smiled at the flower she was making. "This one's much better."

"It just takes a little practice," the neighbor lady said.

In the quiet of his room, Geoff considered what to do with the remainder of his afternoon. He felt more relaxed than he had in a very long time and didn't want to lose that tranquility. He could go to an arcade, but how could he tell if Mr. Manz was tracking him?

Maybe he should just play a game in his desk holoview. He had some good strategy ones. No, he'd better do Chin's ion-blasted stretches. He could go down to the rec center by the school and work out on the gymnastics mats. He would do that again after supper before he met Trevor and the boys.

That set the pattern for Geoff's next two days. Apart from his required exercises, he did no work. He felt so good by Thursday afternoon that he completed his overdue science project and wrote the social report that was due the second day back at school. Feeling extremely pleased with himself, he left home early enough to spend half an hour in the gym before Trevor got off work.

"You're sure living the easy life," Trevor said when he saw Geoff waiting for him.

"We're going shopping, remember?" replied Geoff. "I got to get Barbie something for her birthday."

"Oh, yeah." Trevor's hoops and chains reflected light around the hall as he nodded. "How old's she now? Fifteen?"

"*Four*teen."

"Forgot." Trevor's gray eyes sparkled mischievously. "She's so tall now."

Geoff rabbit-punched Trevor in the ribs.

Trevor laughed and asked, "Why don't you just order it? Or are we going to lift something?"

"If they deliver it, she might see it," Geoff said. "Besides, I haven't decided which one." He had put the two little figurines in his holoview several times to look at them. He had almost decided to get the silver-eyed woman. He wanted to hold them in his hands to make sure.

"Which one what?" Trevor asked.

"You know those silly little superheroes she collects? One of them."

"Where do we have to go for that?"

"Up to the 0.3 deck." Before he had to dance in low *g*, drifting around the really light decks had been fun. "In that section of tourist shops below the dock market."

A short time later, the two boys bounced slowly into the souvenir shop. Geoff stopped just inside to look at a holographic display of the most expensive superhero figurines.

"You're joking," said Trevor. "You're going to *buy* one of those?"

"No, just looking." Geoff touched the control so the rows of images would rotate. "Do you suppose heroes would be heroes if nobody knew?"

"Huh? They all have secret identities. Nobody knows them."

"But everyone knows they're doing something good, even if no one knows who's under the mask," said Geoff. His own secret suffering with Chin and Lui was different. Nobody anywhere knew what he was going through to protect his sister and his friends.

"I think these days off gave you too much time on your hands," Trevor said. "You're right off orbit."

"Aren't." Feeling let down, Geoff went and asked the clerk to bring out the two statues he had reserved.

"What do you think?" Geoff asked when the two tiny heroes were placed on the counter's display pedestal. Even as he asked, he knew he would get Storm. There was something in her determined expression that appealed to him.

"Who is she?" Trevor lightly touched Storm's head. "She looks blind."

Geoff shrugged. He hadn't researched the character. He just liked how she looked.

"She's from our historical collection," said the man behind the counter. "One of a group of popular heroes over a hundred years ago. Her special ability was to control weather, especially lightning storms."

"I'll take her," Geoff said. He'd seen weather and storms in movies.

"Of course," said the clerk. "Would you like it delivered?"

"No, I'll take it now," answered Geoff. "It's a gift. If you deliver it, she might see it."

"I understand." He processed Geoff's payment and then put the little statue in a padded plastic box.

"What now?" asked Trevor when they left the store.

"The big mall," Geoff replied. "I'll get this wrapped, and we can get something to eat."

"Let's meet the guys there," said Trevor. "You can lift us supper."

"Sure." Geoff stuffed the little box into the calf pocket of his trousers and grinned. It would be just like old times, out with the gang and not having to take off early to meet Chin.

Friday morning, Lui met Geoff in the dance hall. He wore deep purple pajamas and held a bag that probably contained lunch.

"Hurry it up," Lui said. "Don't forget your contacts." He stood over Geoff as he warmed up, badgering him to extend every move as far as possible. Perspiration shone on Geoff's face and arms by the time he finished.

"Get your boots on," ordered Lui. He pulled on a battered pair of dance boots and waited for Geoff in the middle of the floor. "We'll run through both numbers here, make sure you haven't forgotten anything. There's a few minor changes. When Chin gets here, we'll teach you the rest of the choreography for the traditional dance."

Lui performed Chin's part of the dance correctly and gracefully with smoothness and expression. He only omitted the jump and the lift. Instead of the closeness the choreography called for, he kept a hand's width of space between himself and Geoff.

They had time to do the first dance twice and the choreographed portion of the second dance once before Chin came in. He wore an expensive, dark blue business suit. His hair floated in loose waves around his head.

"Ready?" he asked.

"He's getting there," answered Lui.

"Keep on it." Chin left. He returned in turquoise-and-orange dance tights, his hair bound into its usual tight braid down the back of his head.

"I have to warm up again," Chin said. "Do it with me so I can see if you've done your homework."

Suddenly thankful he had spoiled his brief holiday by going to the gym, Geoff kicked off his boots and silently joined Chin in his warm-up.

"Keep working on turning your legs in," Chin ordered when they finished.

Geoff nodded as he pulled his boots back on. He could not see any alternative but to agree.

"Okay," Chin said. "Let's get up to the light deck and spend a few minutes on that flirty number before we finish the other one."

They danced it over and over, getting shoulder extensions and angles of their torsos, arms, and legs perfectly matched. The dance had to be performed exactly the same every time—except when Chin or Lui decided some little thing had to be changed. Chin's few minutes lasted half an hour.

They returned to the heavy deck for their usual break. Geoff sat on the floor and sipped his water. He tilted his head against the wall and listened to Chin and Lui's whispered conversation.

"Take a month to get everything set up," Chin said. "Word is there'll be enough *volunteers*."

"Not valuable ones, I hope," said Lui. "In case they all end up in body bags again." He shot a sideways glance at Geoff.

Geoff blinked at the ceiling. It took all his control to not move. Practicing acting innocent was coming in useful for something besides getting away after a heist. He would be the victim of a very serious, if not fatal "accident" if Chin and Lui ever learned he could hear them. That had sounded like people smuggling. What could he do? Chin was sure to find out if Geoff called the cops or even walked within shouting distance of one.

"Let's go." Chin stalked to the center of the dance floor. Geoff got up to follow him. He was so upset about what he had overheard that he stumbled.

"Get it together," growled Chin. "You're not getting another holiday." They performed the traditional dance once, stopping near the end where Geoff did not know the choreography. Ten minutes later, he had learned the last of the steps.

"We end in a tableau like last time," Chin said. "Finish the side-by-side here, pivot to face-to-face." When they turned, they stood chest against chest.

"Sag," ordered Lui from where he stood at the side of the dance area.

Geoff leaned against Chin, loosening his posture so it looked like he had melted against the older man.

Chin put his left arm around Geoff's waist and said, "Set him up."

Lui stepped forward. He put Geoff's right hand in the small of Chin's back.

"Right makes a fist," Lui instructed. "Left hand open, fingers spread on his chest." Lui didn't like where Geoff put his left hand and pulled it a few centimeters lower. Then he turned Geoff's head and pushed the right side of his face into the hollow of Chin's left shoulder. "Remember that."

"Hold it five seconds," said Chin. "Don't move until after I do." He surrounded Geoff's shoulders with his right arm and dropped his head forward.

Geoff tried to not flinch as Chin's sweat-dampened cheek rested against his forehead.

"Hold *still*," Chin ordered.

They repeated that dance during the remaining hour of practice time. Geoff got so tired that he found himself thankful for the brief moments he lay across Chin's shoulders. He didn't even mind that his T-shirt slid up and got tangled when he dismounted. He ignored Chin's usual mutter about proper dance attire.

When Geoff collapsed onto the floor to cool off, he spread his legs and rested his head on the floor between his knees. He gripped his ankles to try to still the trembling in his legs. Ten minutes later, as Geoff shuffled slowly to the shower room, the muscle tremors had stopped, but he felt as if his bones were overcooked noodles.

"Be back here by 2100," ordered Chin.

Geoff nodded, too worn out to make the effort of giving an audible response. How was he going to make it through a whole day at work? Maybe he could catch a bit of a nap during his supper hour. Mr. Manz wouldn't mind, not like the morning manager. She never let Geoff stretch the rules.

In the transit on the way to the arcade, Geoff's stomach began audibly demanding lunch. All he had in his bag was a squashed energy bar. He devoured it and then hurried to the snack counter down the hall from the arcade. He'd rather be a few minutes late than suffer from hunger the entire afternoon.

The food improved Geoff's physical well-being and his mood. He worked on the floor, helping customers and checking equipment for the first couple of hours. Mr. Manz then directed him to the office to catch up on his other duties.

"I did some of it," the older man said. "Mostly, I left it for you." He handed Geoff a bag of peanuts and a soda and left.

Geoff reluctantly sat in the soft chair at his workstation. What if he was setting up some other kid to end up in a trap like he was in? Could he change things, make it so no one looked good enough to recruit? He wasn't sure how, and if he fouled things up, Mr. Manz was sure to ask questions.

Chapter 22

After two hours in the office, Geoff's overworked body was stiff and sore. Ready to go for supper, he stood up and rotated his shoulders, groaning at the painful protests from his muscles.

"You sound like you're my age," Mr. Manz said from the doorway.

"Just got a little stiff," said Geoff.

"Your buddies are here to take you for supper," said Mr. Manz. "Be back a little early."

"Okay, Mr. Manz." Geoff tried to stretch out his kinks as he left. Chances were his friends expected him to lift at least part of their meal.

"Where we going?" Geoff asked when he joined the gang waiting outside the arcade. They wore loose casual clothes, clothes that would not be noticed in a crowd and had room underneath for product being delivered. "I've got to be back early."

"Someplace close," Trevor replied. "We got a job tonight." He strolled down the corridor. Everyone else followed.

"You coming with us?" asked Rob.

"Not that I know of," answered Geoff. "No one called me to leave work."

"They said you're working on something else," Trevor said. "Didn't say what." They all looked at Geoff.

He said, "Yeah."

"Let's go eat," Trevor said.

"That thing you been working on for a while?" asked Hans.

"Yeah," Geoff repeated. "Let's have pizza."

"It's not that good here," Trevor said. "But it's close."

They crowded around a table, and as they ate, they watched girls and speculated on which basketball teams would make the play-offs.

Knowing he had to do Chin's stretches, Geoff made sure he got back to the arcade with time to spare. He did a few exercises in the office and then locked himself in the bathroom for five minutes and hurried through a few more.

When Geoff returned to the dance hall at 2100, Chin was dancing in front of the large mirrors. Instead of his usual muscle shirt and tights, he wore a long-sleeved, light orange bodysuit. The top could have been painted on. It fit so snugly that it revealed every bulge of his muscular arms and torso. The tightness continued to his hips.

The material loosened over his legs, snug enough to display the latent strength of flexing thighs but baggy around knees and calves. A narrow cuff held the ankle material tightly over the top of his boots. He watched himself perform a few steps of the flirty character dance, stopped, and did them over with slightly different hand and arm movements.

"Hustle," Lui said.

Geoff turned to him to get his dance boots and contacts. A folded pile of shiny lime-green material was on the chair with them. It was a singularly ugly color.

Lui picked it up and gave it a shake. It had looked no larger than a T-shirt, but it opened up into a full bodysuit, a smaller version of what Chin wore. Matching tights fell on the floor.

"Put these on," ordered Lui. "The tights and suit. No underwear. You come out here with lines showing under that suit, and we'll rip it off you. You'll dance naked."

Geoff believed him. He went to the locker room, stripped, and pulled on the tights—or tried to. They were so stretchy that he only got his foot halfway down them before the top part he held was up at his waist. He was still struggling with the first leg when Lui stepped into the change room and laughed.

He turned around and called to Chin, "I told you he'd need a lesson in dressing." He went to Geoff and grabbed the tights.

"I can do it." Geoff tried to knock Lui's bulky arms away. He might as well have tried to push the station out of orbit. He settled for snatching his T-shirt off the bench and covering his groin.

"Like this," Lui said. With quick grabbing motions, he bunched the material of the empty tights' leg into his hands, stopping when he had everything but the toe in his fists. "Stick your foot in."

Reluctantly, Geoff set the tip of his foot into the toe of the tights. As Lui drew his hands up, one on each side of Geoff's leg, he let the material slide through his fingers. In a second, he had the tights up above Geoff's knee. He let go and picked up the green dance outfit.

"Put your feet in from the neck," Lui instructed. He demonstrated the elasticity of the wide neckline with a tug. "Move it." He tossed the suit at Geoff and left.

Geoff sighed and clumsily gathered up the fabric of the tights for his right leg. He got them on and tugged at the upper part to center the lined pouch. He had never worn tights. It felt strange to have such snug clothing on his legs.

The locker-room door slammed open. Chin stood there.

"Hurry it up," he growled. He stayed there, feet apart and arms folded on his chest, as Geoff struggled into the suit.

Geoff did not have time to check how it looked. He followed Chin into the cool dance hall.

Chin said, "You're putting vertical splits in round six of the traditional dance."

Geoff looked at him, waiting for an explanation.

"Every dancer has do demonstrate that degree of flexibility to have a chance at the money," said Chin.

Geoff nodded, only then realizing that the choreography already called for Chin to do several standing splits.

"That means for the second step, I'll do the stalk in a circle, and you'll pivot on one foot with the other on my shoulder," said Chin.

One thing Geoff did like about the dance outfit was its lack of friction when he and Chin brushed against each other. The smooth, tight material slid easily without binding or bunching up.

This worked against Geoff when he lay across Chin's shoulders. He leaned back quickly, bending sideways at his waist and balancing his weight before letting his limbs dangle down around Chin. Although Chin's movements as he straightened and swayed to the side were as smooth as always, Geoff felt himself begin to slide down Chin's back.

Geoff quickly decided he would rather fall than grab Chin's braid, the only part of the older man he had a hope of keeping a grip on. He braced himself for a landing on the hard floor.

Chin spun around and caught Geoff.

"Balance better," he said.

They did it over…and over. Geoff discovered another disadvantage to the slick dance outfits: the material was useless for wiping off sweat. His sleeve smeared the moisture around instead of absorbing it. He was going to have to start keeping a towel with his water bottle.

When the hour ended, Geoff dropped his lime-green clothes on the floor beside his boots. He was not taking them home. Geoff took a quick shower. He reached for his towel while water still streamed over his eyes.

The thick, soft material his hand encountered was not the old towel he had in his gym bag. Geoff wiped his face and looked at what he held—a bright-pink bath sheet with a young woman holding the other end of it.

She smiled at him.

He jerked it out of her hands and wrapped it around himself.

"Who are you?" asked Geoff. "What are you doing here?"

"Cheri." She smiled again. Deep-red lips surrounded her perfect teeth. Wavy light brown hair framed her face. The cobalt blue of her eyes was too intense to be natural.

"I'm supposed to collect your stuff," Cheri pointed to the pile of sweaty green material, "and take care of anything else you need."

"I don't need anything." Geoff eyed her suspiciously. Her being here had to be some convoluted scheme of Chin's.

"No?" She turned away and picked up a pale pink gym bag with a rhinestone ballerina on its side.

Geoff silently watched as she bent over and put his boots in the bag. She wore a yellow dress with no back to the bodice. The front was held up by a strap around her neck. Beneath the short skirt, she wore nothing.

Next, she took a soft bag and stuffed Geoff's dance outfit into it. Her small hands were adorned with half a dozen rings and nail polish the same deep red as her lips. She picked up the contacts cases and looked at Geoff.

"These can be worn for weeks at a time, you know," she said.

"They're part of a costume," said Geoff. "It'd look stupid." Forgetting he had her towel clutched around himself, he waited for her to leave.

"I can't imagine you looking stupid." Cheri tucked the contacts into her gym bag and kicked off her sandals. She padded over to Geoff in her bare feet. "Be a shame to mess with your beautiful browns, anyway." Her impossibly blue eyes were level with his.

He stared into them. The blue contacts obscured the expression in her eyes, yet somehow he knew she wasn't leaving. His heartbeat tripled, his body responding to a thought his mind had not finished forming.

Silence filled the room. A drop of water fell from the showerhead and crashed on the tiled floor.

"I'll dry your back," Cheri breathed.

Geoff forgot his half-formed objection. If Chin wanted to bribe him with a whore instead of beating him up, why complain?

Chapter 23

Geoff caught the transit, feeling a little ashamed for letting Chin's prostitute so easily seduce him. He told himself that if she tried it again, he would send her out, but by the time he reached his home stop, he admitted that if a pretty, practically naked girl kissed him in the shower again, he would most likely repeat what he had just done.

"And is that so bad?" he rationalized as he strolled down the corridor. He had already taken Chin's punishments. Why shouldn't he help himself to whatever rewards were offered? The big question remained: *Why* had Chin sent Cheri to Geoff? Having her take care of his gear did not seem a good enough reason. Did Chin think she could keep Geoff from getting burned out again?

With no way to answer, Geoff put the question out of his mind. He tried to eliminate Cheri from his thoughts as well, but that did not work. The memory of their short time together stayed with him.

Saturday morning, when Geoff walked into the dance hall, Chin was performing the character dance. Lui, straddling a chair backward, watched from his usual place beside the console. Smirking at Geoff, he pointed to the change room.

A plain black bag sat at one end of the bench in the locker room. Inside it were Geoff's boots, contacts, red tights, and a red-and-purple dance outfit. Geoff made a face at it, but really, it wasn't any worse than the eye-searing blue and yellow Chin had on.

The music ended as Geoff changed. He went to warm up, careful to not slip in the slick material of the tights.

"Have a good evening?" Chin asked.

"Yeah." Geoff's face warmed. Chin never engaged in social chitchat with him. He had to be referring to Cheri.

Chin chuckled.

To Geoff's relief, Chin got busy with the exercises without saying anything else. Cheri was shoved to the back of Geoff's mind while he danced. Chin and Lui demanded perfection and kept Geoff busy trying to meet their exacting standards.

When those two hours ended, Geoff dragged himself to the locker room. He straddled the bench and leaned forward, rubbing his aching neck and shoulders. Sweat stung his eyes. He got up, wanting to shower before Cheri arrived. If she was coming.

Cheri waited with a smile and a towel when Geoff finished his shower. He ended up not having time to stop for lunch. On the transit going to work, he ate the apple and pepperoni sticks from his bag. Maybe Mr. Manz would let him take an early coffee break. He'd run out and get some real food.

Monday at school was the usual post-holiday crackdown as teachers tried to get their students' attention back on their studies. Feeling supremely pleased with himself for having his assignments all caught up, Geoff did not mind the get-to-work expectation of the teachers.

He and Trevor played tennis after school—a good excuse for Geoff to do some warm-up stretches—and then went to the mall with the gang.

"Let's catch a movie," Rob suggested.

"I got a date," said Trevor.

"I got to go home," Geoff said. "It's my sister's birthday. I'll really be in it if I'm not home for supper." While he made it sound as if he would rather not share in Barbara's birthday supper, he was actually anxious to be there. He wanted to see her face when she opened his present because he had spent more time selecting it than any other gift.

When Geoff entered the apartment, it was filled with balloons, streamers, and giggling girls. He turned down a few invitations to join their game and hid in his room. While he liked most of Barbara's friends, there were a couple who acted really silly.

Supper was a noisy affair. Geoff put his present for Barbara on a chair and dropped a towel over it. He stayed at the dining room table with Tony and Fallah. The girls sat in a circle in the living room.

"It's nuts in here," Geoff said to his parents. "I'm going out."

"Did you do your homework after school?" asked Fallah. Geoff shook his head. He had not even looked at it.

"Do it before you go play," Tony said.

"Okay, Dad." Geoff watched the mob of girls clear away their dishes and bring out a pile of presents. Maybe he'd stay and watch Barbara. It was certainly more entertaining than doing homework. The cluster of girls seemed to have as much fun seeing the gifts as Barbara had opening them. The table was soon covered in clothes, trinkets, and makeup. While the last one was being admired, Barbara looked inquiringly at Geoff.

"What?" he asked. He tried not to but couldn't help smiling.

"Where is it?" asked Barbara.

"What?" repeated Geoff.

"I know you got me something." Barbara stood up and held out her hands. "I can tell by you're grinning." She wiggled her fingers and smiled even wider.

Geoff took the present off the chair and tossed it to her. He had gotten it wrapped in a flat container that resembled a box of chocolates.

Barbara ripped it open.

"Oh!" She squealed with delight when she recognized the inner packaging. "Who did you get?"

"I forget," said Geoff.

"You didn't." She opened the tiny box. "Ahhhhh," she breathed. "Storm. She's so beautiful...and a *Rhimay*."

"What's a Rhimay?" asked Fallah.

Geoff shrugged.

"She's the artist," Barbara replied. "Her stuff's gorgeous." She hopped over her seated friends and kissed Geoff on the cheek. "Thanks, Bubs. I love her."

"You're welcome." Geoff smiled, pleased the little figure made Barbara so happy.

As Fallah and Tony began cleaning the kitchen, Geoff returned to his room. He had to meet Chin and Lui at 2100. If he could get his homework done in an hour, he would have time to stop at the arcade.

A message waited in his com's "in" file, but Geoff did not open it. It was probably one of the guys wanting him to go out. If he didn't view it until later, he could truthfully say he got the message too late.

Half an hour later, with most of his research completed and an outline for his social paper on the screen, Geoff decided to read his mail. He did not recognize the return address, so it wasn't one of the guys after all. He ordered it to play in his desk console.

Chin's head and shoulders appeared. He said, "Don't forget why you dance."

"Happy Birthday" began to play. Chin's image was replaced by that of a curvaceous young woman. She wore Barbara's head, but the replacement had been so poorly done it was obvious it *was* a replacement. Geoff watched in horror as four men attacked and raped the woman. The little movie ran at faster-than-normal speed. It lasted ten seconds, but to Geoff, it felt like an hour. The holoview went blank.

Numbly, because he was too stunned to verbally give the order, Geoff reached out to delete the message. The appalling piece of mail was not there. It had self-erased.

Geoff stared into the now empty place above his desk. Although his eyes saw nothing, the attack replayed in his mind.

He jumped from his chair and dashed across the hall to the bathroom to throw up. Even after his stomach emptied, his body kept heaving. It took forever for the retches to stop. Geoff splashed his face with cold water. With trembling hands, he held a towel against his face.

"Are you all right?" Fallah asked.

"Yeah." Geoff opened the bathroom door. "I must have had something bad at the mall."

"Hmmmm." Fallah gently touched Geoff's forehead. "You're not fevered."

"I'm okay." Geoff jammed his quivering hands into his pockets so she wouldn't see him shake.

Back in the seclusion of his room, Geoff could not bring himself to sit at his desk. He lay on his bed and listened to music. His upset gradually gave way to anger that still burned when he went to the dance hall.

"Still mad?" Chin asked as he joined Geoff to warm up.

Geoff glared at him.

"Good," said Chin. "Hang on to it." When they had their boots on, Chin added, "You know the steps. Now we work on presentation, putting feeling into the motions, body language, and facial expressions."

Geoff found it impossible to do what Chin and Lui asked. He simply did not feel the emotions they wanted him to portray, and he did not know how to act like he did. His frustration soon got the better of him, and as he pivoted, he stamped his heels with real anger.

"Perfect!" Lui exclaimed. "Only you're in the wrong part of the song for that much. Do it over…just like that, with that kind of expression but softer." He stood up and demonstrated.

They kept Geoff so busy he did not have time to think about Barbara or Cheri. When the hour was up, he wished he could just grab his bag and go home. He did not dare take the dance outfit there, though. The questions would be impossible to answer. Besides, he wanted to see Cheri. If he changed and showered here, she might show up.

She didn't. When Geoff stepped out of the shower, no one else was there. He dried quickly, angry with himself for being disappointed in Cheri's absence.

A middle-aged woman knocked on the locker-room door and walked in while Geoff was dressing.

"What are you doing here?" he asked.

"The little girl usually can't come this late," she said. "I'll take your things." She picked up Geoff's dance gear and left before he put his shirt on. He finished dressing slowly, wondering if Cheri couldn't come because she was busy entertaining someone else. He knew what she was, but that thought made him feel hurt and angry.

Geoff did not check his com until he was on the transit going home. He sighed with relief when he had no calls. Back in his room, he put his gym bag on the bed, looked at his desk console, shivered, and walked out. After he set a plate of leftovers to warm, he cut a piece of birthday cake and sat beside Tony to watch the evening sports.

Fallah looked at the huge chunk of cake and said, "Feeling better, I see."

Geoff nodded.

The sports program ended at 2300. Unwilling to go to his room, Geoff stayed up to watch the whole thing.

"You'd better hit the sack," Tony said. "School tomorrow."

"Yeah." Geoff exchanged good-nights and reluctantly headed for bed. It had been a few nights since he'd had a nightmare. He was probably in for big one.

Going to sleep proved impossible. The loathsome movie clip kept replaying in Geoff's mind. At midnight, he got up. He wanted a shower to wash away the sweat that made his T-shirt clammy, but he did not dare wake his parents. Instead, he changed his clothes and did his math.

Geoff went to sleep late, and his few hours of slumber were disrupted by bad dreams. The loud music of his alarm interrupted another. Geoff rolled out of his tangled bed, thankful he did not have to find out what further horrors his mind could make up. He did his stretches and went for breakfast.

"You look awful," Barbara said.

"I'm fine," said Geoff. The truth was that he felt as bad as he looked. He wasn't even hungry.

"Stomach still upset?" asked Fallah.

"A little," Geoff said. It was as good an excuse as any for his wretched appearance.

The school day crept by in a drone of meaningless instruction. Geoff dozed off in class in the middle of the afternoon. He used food poisoning as an excuse for being off orbit and managed to avoid detention. After school, he joined Trevor, Rob, and Hans in the recreation park.

"What skewed your orbit?" asked Trevor.

"You look half-dead," added Hans.

"I was up all night," said Geoff. "It must have been that coleslaw I lifted. Made me sick as a groundling."

"Let's grab a sandwich and go blading," Rob said.

The others liked the idea, but Geoff said, "I've got to get home." He desperately needed a few hours of sleep. If he went to the dance hall in this condition, Chin would throw him through the wall.

Geoff woke up in time for supper. Afterward, he packed a towel and water bottle and headed for the door.

Fallah looked at Geoff's gym bag and said, "Maybe you should stay home and take it easy tonight."

"I won't be long," Geoff said. What would he tell Chin if she insisted? "Twenty-one at the latest." It was Tuesday. He'd be done rehearsing by 2000.

His session on the dance floor was as grueling as always. Geoff hit the shower, thinking he was too tired to appreciate Cheri if she showed up. He was wrong. Her smile and the way she fussed over him when she wrapped him in a warm towel reenergized him.

Geoff knew Cheri had to be under orders to be nice to him, but her attentions made him feel good. He didn't want to spoil it by asking why she worked for Chin, what hold he had on her.

During the next two weeks, Cheri met Geoff after practice every Tuesday, Thursday, and Saturday. Once, she unexpectedly showed up on a Wednesday.

Geoff looked forward to seeing her, so much so that he started thinking of training with Chin less as torture and more as a means to be with Cheri. Her friendliness and apparent interest in Geoff encouraged him to talk about things he liked to do.

On one mid-September Saturday afternoon, Geoff stumbled into the locker room after two hours of trying to meet Chin's impossible demands. He dropped onto the bench, exhausted.

Cheri came in and said, "You poor dear. Here, let me help." As she pulled off his boots, she asked what he was doing that afternoon.

"I don't work till sixteen," Geoff said. "I'm taking my sister to the dockside market first."

Cheri sighed enviously. She quickly hid that expression behind a brilliant smile.

"Sounds like fun," she said. "I haven't ever been there."

"Why not?" asked Geoff. "It's great."

"I'm not allowed out." Bitterness colored her whisper. Her eyes widened. She looked terrified. "I'm sorry. I'm not complaining." Cheri glanced anxiously at the door. "Please don't tell anyone I said that. Please. I'll do anything you want." Her hands, which were resting on Geoff's knees, trembled.

Geoff pushed them off.

"What do you think I am?" He jumped to his feet. "You think I want to be here? I'm as much his slave as you are."

"Huh?" Cheri pulled Geoff into the shower. Under the noise of the water, she whispered, "What are you doing here?"

"I'm training," Geoff paused. He wasn't supposed to talk about the dance competition. Still, Cheri already knew he was dancing, didn't she? So what was she asking?

"I know," Cheri said. "We don't share Chin's secrets."

They never raised that subject again, but from then on, Geoff believed he was more than just another John to Cheri. He vowed not to let Chin know he cared for Cheri. Once Chin knew that, threatening Cheri would be one more way for Chin to manipulate Geoff.

Chapter 24

"We should walk our beat," Trevor said on Tuesday after school. "We haven't done that since last week. People'll forget we're the ones here." He buffed his rings on his khaki shirt and tossed his head so his blue hoop earrings chimed.

"You mean you want to scare off anyone who's at our table in the food court," Hans said, adjusting his cap over his long toffee-colored locks. "Okay."

"I got roller hockey," drawled Rob. "Won't be done till twenty-one."

"I can be there at 2030 or a little later," Geoff said. That would give him some time with Cheri when Chin and Lui were through with him.

"We should do a job while we're out," said Trevor. "Maybe hit the place that threw us out last week."

"What place?" asked Geoff. "You mean go make a ruckus there?" Trevor probably meant to wreck or steal something, but Geoff hoped to divert him with a less hurtful suggestion.

"Sports shop on the lower level of the big mall," Trevor replied. "Said if we weren't buying anything, we had to leave. Bring your burner."

"Why not just 'accidentally' knock something down and break it?" Geoff frowned at their presumption he was willing to steal for them. "It would accomplish the same thing." And it wouldn't be on his conscience.

"You know that's not how it's done." Trevor scowled down at Geoff.

"Yeah." Geoff did not argue. Arguing about stuff like that had led to his having to dance with Chin. He went home for a snack. On the way, he checked his mail. Fifteen days after Chin's message threatening an attack on Barbara, Geoff still sighed with relief when there was no message from his extortionist.

By 2040, Geoff had his hand's tools in his pockets and his gym bag stashed in a rental locker. He joined the rest of the Taurids at their usual mall entrance.

"You got a plan?" Geoff asked Trevor.

"We're going to the store," Trevor said. "They don't know you, so you go separate. While we distract them, you lift something valuable."

"Like what?" asked Geoff. There were a limited number of sports items that he could fit into a pocket. At least a big store like this wouldn't be hurt by the loss of one little item, and he could later tell Cheri about his successful escapade.

"One of those new antigravity air disks," Rob said. He made flying motions with one hand.

"I can't exactly shove that up my sleeve," said Geoff. Air disks operated like skateboards without wheels. They contained very expensive artificial gravity technology, and they were nearly a meter in diameter.

"Shove it inside your sweater, over your chest," said Rob.

"Get real," said Hans. "Some games or one of those new cameras."

"A camera," Trevor decided. "If you act serious about buying a camera, they'll bring them out for you try."

"We got security data?" asked Geoff.

"Yeah," Trevor said. "It looks pretty standard. I went in by myself and bought a tennis racket to check. Wouldn't hurt for me to nose around a little and give you a sign, though."

Trevor went into the store. Geoff waited a couple of minutes and followed him.

Because it was a Tuesday evening, the store held neither a large body of customers nor a full complement of staff. Geoff checked the floor plan and then strode directly to the accessories department. Holographic images of a variety of picture and movie-taking equipment slowly rotated in a display column. Geoff scrutinized them and stuck his head into the holoview to see some from a different angle.

"May I help you?" The clerk sounded as pleased at having a customer on such a boring evening as the prospect of making a sale.

"Yeah." Geoff stared at a miniature camera a moment longer before he turned to the salesman. He was young, maybe a few years older than Geoff, with an angular face decorated by acne that was not fully controlled.

"I want a camera," said Geoff. "A little one, but it's got to be good enough to take pictures of us on the obstacle course. And the girls' dive team." He grinned. Trevor would appreciate that.

"You want underwater capability?"

"No."

"Okay, these are out." The clerk deleted several images from the display. "If you want it for fast action, these are too slow." He removed a few more.

Geoff pointed to the two largest cameras left and said, "Those are too big."

Hans and Rob entered the store, talking loudly about the upcoming batta ball play-offs. They stopped just inside the store and began arguing about which department to go to first.

Geoff glanced at them—it would have looked suspicious if he hadn't—and then he returned his attention to the clerk. He asked for an explanation of the different features of the cameras as Rob and Hans went to the soccer department.

"This is one of the best," the clerk said, pointing to a camera smaller than Geoff's palm. "You'll get nice shots that'll stay sharp and solid up to two-thirds life-size. You can run them like a movie or freeze it to look at details. Just the thing if you want to perfect your technique on jumps."

"Can I try some?" asked Geoff. "That one and these two?" He touched the images with his forefinger.

"Certainly. If you'll come this way—" The clerk led Geoff to a counter a few steps away.

Trevor walked past. He met Geoff's eyes and shook his head.

Geoff nodded slightly. Security wise, nothing had changed from the last time Trevor was here.

Rob and Hans's argument got louder. Two of the three other customers left the store.

Trevor stood beside a display of pocketknives a little behind Geoff and in direct line of sight of the clerk serving Geoff. Trevor looked at the display and acted as if he were impatient to talk to the clerk.

"These all have standard upload capabilities, or you can use data cards," the clerk said to Geoff. He pulled a plastic strip half the length of his thumb from a drawer and inserted it into the first camera. "Try it."

Geoff took the camera and turned in a half circle, recording the displays around him while he tried the zoom and other features. He played the short clip back. The images, about as high as his forearm was long, showed above the counter.

"They'll play in any holoview, of course," said the clerk.

Geoff nodded. He shifted sideways, glancing at his noisy friends and pretending they were making him nervous. He removed the data card and set the camera down beside his left elbow and then pointed to another camera.

"How about that one?" he asked. He repeated his test.

The clerk watched Rob and Hans more than he watched Geoff. Geoff hoped his friends did not get carried away enough to have the cops called. That was the last thing he needed in the middle of a heist.

As Geoff tried out the third camera, he held it with his right hand only. With his left, he took a small tool from his pocket. Flicking it on with his thumbnail, he hid it in the palm of his hand and ran it over the first camera he had tested. The zapper would burn out all the security chips. He had it turned on full strength, so it could have burned out the camera too, but that didn't matter. The idea was to ding the store.

Geoff had his zapper back in his pocket before he played back the images from the final recording. He leaned forward on the counter, arms in front of the damaged camera, as he watched the little movie. Careful to shield the action from the clerk, he used his left elbow to nudge the camera to the edge of the counter, against his ribs.

"I kind of like this one." Geoff picked up the second camera.

Store security began escorting Hans and Rob, both of whom were now loudly complaining about the service, out of the store. Geoff and the clerk paused to watch them go.

Trevor stalked toward the exit. As he passed Geoff, he took the camera from between Geoff's elbow and ribs and tucked it into his own pocket.

At another profane outburst from Rob, Geoff said, "I'll come back later." He pushed the two cameras toward the clerk and stepped back.

"Where's the other one?" asked the clerk.

"Other what?" responded Geoff. He looked puzzled.

"Camera. I gave you three."

"No." Geoff shook his head. "Just those. I tried that one first, then the other one, then that one again." He shook out his sleeves, pulled up his sweater to show there was no camera stuck in his waistband and patted his pockets.

"I had a 900A model out," the clerk insisted. "I told you it was the best." He looked beneath the counter as if to check how many cameras were left.

Geoff took the opportunity to leave. A few fast strides, and then he sauntered as quickly as he could without looking like he was hurrying.

Geoff caught up to Trevor two stores down.

"Ace." Trevor held up his hand, and they slapped palms. "Let's go." They were to meet Rob and Hans in the food court.

Halfway there, two mall security men, both armed with holstered stunners, stepped in front of them.

"Just a minute, boys," the big one said. Huge, with a layer of fat over bulky muscle, he towered over Geoff and even made Trevor seem small. The other man, who was just as tall but less wide, circled to stand behind them.

"Sure," Geoff said agreeably. Inside, though, his guts turned to water.

"What is this?" asked Trevor. "We got just as much right to shop here as everyone else."

"Shop, yes," the fat security guard said. "Steal, no. Walk with us." One on each side of the teenagers, the men guided them toward the station corridor adjoining the wide mall hall.

Geoff and Trevor exchanged glances. Being taken out of the mall was bad news. Someone had evidence. The security men had not even checked what Geoff and Trevor were carrying.

"Wait," Trevor said. "I need to go to the bathroom."

"In a minute," the thinner man said. "We either search you first, or I stay with you while you go."

"You have no right to make me wait," objected Trevor.

"Shall I pat you down in the middle of the hall here or stand over you in the stall?"

"I'll wait." Geoff heard Trevor's sullen mumble, but the man appeared to not understand him.

"What was that?" he asked.

"I'll wait," Trevor repeated.

Geoff noticed Hans and Rob watching from across the hall. There was nothing they could do. He would have to help himself. Trevor had the camera. Geoff simply had to ditch the illegal burner.

How to do it was the problem. He could hide it in his hand and then throw it up over the second level railing. Problem was that the people up there wouldn't necessarily dispose of it. Too bad they hadn't arranged for Rob and Hans to spread out and be ready to catch something like that. They had not made contingency plans for getting caught. They weren't supposed to get caught!

Maybe something less obvious would work. If he used the tip of the burner to rip a hole in his pocket, he could push it down his pants leg and lose it. The security guys might not notice it slide out the bottom of his trousers.

Geoff shoved his hands into his front pockets. With his left, he began to turn his illegal tool.

"Hands out of your pockets, kid," the larger escort said. When Geoff did not immediately comply, the security officer stepped closer as if to grab Geoff's arms.

Geoff lifted his hands, empty and open, and briefly held them up in front of his shoulders. So much for that idea. He'd better come up with a way to keep his parents from finding out about this. They'd ground him for sure, and what would Chin do then? Fear made an aching black hole beneath Geoff's belt buckle.

The security men took Geoff and Trevor to an office at the end of the wide walkway. Its door was partially hidden behind a cluster of bushy trees growing in three round pots, each one a meter across and just as deep.

A female mall security member waited inside the office. She was young, maybe mid-twenties, and pretty. Trevor smiled at her. Geoff hardly noticed her.

One security man stayed between the boys and the door; the other directed them to four chairs along the wall. They sat on the center two.

"Got a couple thieves to process," the large man said. He motioned for Geoff to stand in a bare corner of the office. It was well lit, with pale-blue tiled floor and walls. A darker blue stripe at Geoff's eye level bisected the walls. "This will all be recorded," advised the large guard. "Face the corner and place your hands on the dark band."

Geoff went with slow, reluctant steps, unwilling to believe this was actually happening. He was too good a hand to have been picked up like a ten-year-old lifting candy. He flattened his palms against the navy tiles. They were smooth—slick and cold. He waited a moment. When nothing happened, he turned his head.

An outline image of Geoff stood, arms outstretched, above the woman's desk. Blinking red spots marked the image where Geoff carried his chip burner, pocketknife, and nail clippers. Orange indicators flagged the bag of jerky in his back pocket, data cards, belt buckle, implant, and wrist phone.

"Empty your pockets and take off your com." The security man held out a clear plastic bowl, shallow and large enough to hold everything Geoff had, including his clothes and shoes.

Slowly, Geoff removed his com. The band made a scraping sound as it slid down the curve of the bowl. The package of jerky crackled as it landed.

"Hurry it up," ordered the man.

Geoff dug into his right front pocket for his knife and clippers.

"There," he said.

"The other pocket, too."

Geoff glanced at the outline above the desk. Red still flashed from the left front pocket of his jeans.

"Oh, yeah," Geoff said. "The trimmer thing." He pulled it from his pocket and tossed it into the bowl.

"Trimmer?" asked the woman at the desk.

"It's for sideburns." Geoff rubbed the sparse hairs at the side of his face. "A guy gave it to me to try. I haven't used it yet."

The man with the bowl snorted and said, "Hands back on the blue."

"That's everything," Geoff objected.

"Occasionally, the scanner misses some materials." He handed the bowl of Geoff's possessions to the woman and gestured to the corner.

Geoff turned and flattened his palms against the navy tiles. He got them almost over the warm spots where he had put them the first time. The outside of his left hand rested on a cold place.

The man's large hands encircled Geoff's left wrist. They pushed his sleeve up to mid-forearm and then moved up his arm, briefly tightening at intervals.

To Geoff, it felt like a giant mouth was gradually swallowing his arm, biting a little higher each time it closed its teeth. After repeating the procedure on Geoff's right arm, the security guard quickly patted Geoff's chest, sides, and back. He then slid his hands down Geoff's legs.

"Sit down," ordered the man. He pointed at Trevor. "Your turn."

Trevor underwent the same procedure. Two city police officers arrived in time to watch the large guard finish searching Trevor and order him to a chair beside Geoff. The smaller male guard left.

Geoff pasted on his best innocent expression and looked at the new officers. The man looked like a squarely built block of muscle, the woman the same. They could have worn each other's uniforms.

The female security guard scanned the camera and said, "The antitheft chip's fried. So are half the camera components."

"A burner would do that," the mall security guard said.

"You got it?" asked the female police officer.

"Yes." The guard smiled, a wide baring of white teeth. "Got a copy of the store's security record, too. These two are a pretty slick team. Looks like they had a couple of their buddies in there to stir things up, too. You can take them. The store's pressing charges."

Struggling to maintain his innocent appearance, Geoff glanced sideways at Trevor.

"We didn't do anything," Trevor protested. He jumped to his feet. Before he could move, both police officers had stunners pointed at his belly.

"Sit," ordered the man. "Be quiet."

Trevor silently returned to his chair. Stunners did not cause permanent damage, but their after-effects were nausea, muscle cramps, and nerve fire, ghostly pain that swept along a person's nervous system.

Geoff and Trevor were not given an opportunity to speak as the police completed the forms to take over custody of the boys and their belongings. The woman watched them, holding her unholstered stunner as the man made the arrangements.

"Stand up. Hands behind your necks," ordered the female police officer. "Single file…walk slowly out to the hall."

Geoff clasped his hands behind his neck and followed Trevor out of the security station. A third police officer waited beside two narrow hall cars with blue and red lights. Thank the stars the lights were not turned on and attracting even more attention. Similar to groundling golf carts, the cars could hold four people sitting very close together. Each one had an enclosed and secure backseat with blacked-out windows.

Trevor was ordered into one, Geoff into the other. He sat in the little box, hands squeezed between his knees, and stared out the tinted plasglass. His heart beat in heavy, fearful thuds. How could he get out of this mess?

Chapter 25

Processing at the police station went quickly. The officers dealt with Geoff and Trevor at two separate desks. Geoff had a retina scan to confirm that his identity matched his implant. Then he was informed he could call his parents.

"I left home when I turned sixteen," Geoff said. He couldn't begin to explain this situation to his parents. He was afraid that once he started, his mother and father would question him until they found out everything he had gotten tangled up in. As good a liar as he was, they knew him too well to be completely fooled, and once they caught him out with one lie, they wouldn't let it rest until he confessed everything.

"Your address of record is the same as theirs," the clerk said.

"I never changed it," Geoff said sullenly.

"Where do you live?"

"I stay with friends, here and there." Geoff glanced up at the clerk and then looked back down at the countertop. He wasn't positive, but because he was over sixteen, he thought the cops couldn't call his parents if he had separated himself from them.

After he declined to make a statement without having a lawyer, Geoff was escorted to a small cell. A two-tiered bunk took up half the room. It was the only furniture. The floor, ceiling, and three walls were light gray. The fourth wall was clear. Set into it was a clear sliding door.

"This room's monitored, audio and visual." Geoff's escorting officer pointed to a camera mounted opposite the clear wall. He motioned for Geoff to go into the cell.

Feet dragging, Geoff reluctantly took two steps forward. The officer slid the door shut, checked that it locked, and left.

Geoff pivoted in a circle. He had nowhere to go, nothing to see, and no way out.

Loud footsteps heralded Trevor's arrival. The larger boy had two escorts, one of whom held Trevor's upper left arm. They advised him the cell was monitored and ordered him in with Geoff.

Trevor's entry forced Geoff to step farther into the tiny room.

Trevor waited until the two policemen left and then said, "He coming?"

"Who?" Geoff couldn't imagine who Trevor expected.

With his back to the camera, Trevor wrote four letters on his chest that spelled, "Chin."

"You called him, didn't you" Trevor pushed straight black hair away from his gray eyes. The police had taken his rings and chains, leaving his face looking naked.

Hoping he was quiet enough the recorder could not pick up his voice, Geoff breathed, "Why would I?" Telling Chin about this would be almost as disastrous as telling his parents.

"Because he's connected, you moron." Trevor pushed past Geoff and began pacing the length of the bunks. "Who did you call?"

"No one." Geoff stared at the side of the mattress on the top bunk. He stuffed his hands into his jean pockets and balled them into fists.

"Me either." Trevor frowned down at Geoff and whispered, "I figured for sure you'd get him to pull us out of here."

"Why would he do that?" asked Geoff.

Trevor stopped pacing.

He leaned close to Geoff again and murmured, "You're valuable to him."

"He'd beat me flat." Geoff threw himself onto the bottom bunk. He stretched out on his stomach and pulled the pillow over his head.

"I'm getting out of here." Trevor stood in front of the door and yelled for someone to let him make a call.

Still hiding under his pillow, Geoff considered his options. It was about 2130. He had less than an hour before his parents would try to call and remind him to get home.

Maybe he *should* see if Chin would get him out of here. Taking a beating from Chin would be easier than explaining things to Mom and Dad. Maybe he should get that drug-dealing pimp to rescue him. No, he wasn't that desperate. Not yet. Besides, he couldn't even remember the guy's name.

He'd have to call Chin. As soon as he decided that, Geoff reconsidered. The dance competition was only two and a half weeks away. What if Chin decided he didn't want Geoff too damaged to dance and took his anger out on Barbara instead? Would he do that? If Barbara was already hurt, Geoff could refuse to dance in the competition. Or could he? Chin might hurt Barbara just enough to punish Geoff.

He couldn't call Chin. There was no way out. What he had to do was buy himself some time. If he asked to make a call and told his parents he was spending the night at Trevor's—but how could he do that without the cops knowing who he called and without his parents wondering where he was calling from?

Trevor came back to the little cell.

Geoff peeked out from under his pillow to make sure the person entering his cell was his friend.

"That was quick," Geoff said.

"It took forever," said Trevor. "I didn't have the number and could only find Lui's. He's sore because I interrupted his evening snack—"

Geoff pushed himself upright. The pillow landed on the floor with a soft plooph.

"You called him? Tell me you didn't!"

"They'll have us out of here in no time." Trevor jumped triumphantly onto the upper bunk, his lower legs hanging down beside Geoff.

The smaller boy punched him in the calf.

Trevor jerked his feet up onto the bunk and yelled, "Blast off. Some thanks."

"Thanks?" Geoff got up and paced beside the bunks. "I told you *not* to."

"Oh, hold orbit," said Trevor. "He wasn't even mad. Thought it's funny."

"Lui acts like everything's funny, but he's as mean as Chin." Geoff aimed another punch at Trevor's leg and threw himself back on the bunk. He was really in for it now.

"So who'd you think I should call?" Trevor was getting angry, too. "Your folks? They'd off orbit. My dad? He wouldn't get you out, and he's just as likely to leave me here as punishment for getting caught."

Geoff remained silent for a few seconds and then said, "Yeah, I know. This wasn't supposed to happen."

"I can't believe it, either," Trevor said softly. "We're too good to be in here."

"Tell it to them."

Time dragged. Geoff lay on the bunk, the pillow over his head, and tried to keep his mind off what was likely to happen in the next couple of hours. Thinking about Cheri worked for a few minutes; however, she was connected to Chin, and that took Geoff right back to how Chin would vent his anger at Geoff. Geoff preferred Chin take it out on him instead of Barbara, but he hurt just thinking about it.

"How can you sleep?" asked Trevor. He jumped down and paced in the small space beside the bunk.

Geoff's muffled reply was, "I'm not."

"We should be out soon." Trevor sounded positive and cheerful. "I told him you'd be grounded if you were out late."

"What'd you do that for?" Geoff swung the pillow against the wall and sat up. He had told the cops he didn't live with his parents! Geoff kept his face toward the opposite wall and rolled his eyes in the direction of the camera outside the plasglass wall.

"'Cause you would be. What're you so mad about?"

"Being here." Geoff flopped back onto the hard mattress. Trevor didn't get it. He didn't understand Geoff's precarious relationship with Chin either, and Geoff couldn't explain it, especially in here with the cops listening. "I can't believe this."

"Me either." Trevor paused his pacing, leaned briefly against the clear wall, and then resumed walking.

Geoff watched him go back and forth, marking off the seconds with his footsteps.

It felt like half the night passed before the door unexpectedly slid open.

"Geoff Anders and Trevor Lee, return to the front," a disembodied voice said.

Trevor, who was only two steps from the opening, quickly left the cell and headed down the short hall to the administrative area. Not wanting to be stuck there if the door suddenly shut, Geoff scrambled off the bunk and hurried after him. He was so thankful to be out of the cell that for the moment, he didn't care who was responsible for his release.

The officer at the desk passed Geoff and Trevor their belongings and said, "The store dropped the charges. You're free to go." He spoke coldly, obviously angry. Silently, he watched the boys sign for their belongings.

The burner was not with Geoff's snacks and phone. He did not mention it.

"Thank you, Officer," Geoff said, wondering what strings Chin had pulled to make the store back off.

"We'll be seeing you," the policeman said.

Geoff followed Trevor out of the police complex.

In the familiar bustle of the public corridor, Geoff heaved a sigh of relief and said, "Let's go."

"Not so fast." The man leaning against the wall on the other side of the hall straightened and walked toward Geoff and Trevor. "Someone wants to see you."

"Who?" asked Geoff. He *had* to get home.

"Whose night did you just blast?" asked the stranger.

"Lui?" guessed Trevor.

"Ha." The man guided the boys onto a cross-deck transit and rode with them to the shopping mall the police had earlier escorted them from. "In there," he said and then pointed to an electronics store Geoff knew was owned by a Lung family. "Back room."

The clerk at the front of the store waved the boys toward the rear. Another store staff member pointed to an "employees only" door in the back wall.

Geoff hung back, not wanting to go through it. If Lui was there, chances were Chin was as well. And even if he wasn't, Lui was just as dangerous.

Trevor strode through the door. Geoff hesitantly followed.

Chin stood beside a counter piled with packaged stock. The family's kung fu master wore a burgundy suit. Its impeccable fit emphasized rather than hid his perfect physique. Bulging muscle filled his clothes. His long black hair floated up as he turned toward the two boys.

Geoff's steps slowed even more when he met Chin's black eyes. He couldn't read their expression, but could guess Chin's anger from the stiff solidness of his shoulders and the tight line of his jaw.

Trevor said, "Thanks—"

"Stow it," Chin said. "You and your gang owe the family the cost of the camera, the burner, and the payment to get the store to drop charges. You also owe me for getting dressed up and coming down here."

Trevor looked at Geoff and wiggled his eyebrows suggestively.

"Moron." Chin slapped the back of Trevor's head. "I was training. There's a masters' tournament this weekend. You'll pay for that, too. One more thing...everyone else has already been told. He—" Chin said as he looked at Trevor and pointed to Geoff, "is not to be mentioned in connection with this fiasco."

Chin directed his black glare to Geoff and said, "You keep a low profile. We spread the word Hans was arrested, not you. Go directly home. Do not go near that store again. Stay away from any place that's not entirely holos. Be early tomorrow."

Geoff nodded. Tomorrow was Wednesday. His lesson with Chin and Lui was scheduled for 2100.

Geoff and Trevor caught an elevator car at the nearest stop. Geoff boarded first, anxious to get on his way.

Trevor dropped into the seat beside Geoff and sighed with relief.

"Could'a been worse," he said.

"Worse is coming," predicted Geoff. He dreaded tomorrow evening. Maybe he could break his leg or something. That would put him out of commission for a few days.

Geoff's phone beeped. Predictably, it was his father.

"We're on the way," Geoff said. He turned his wrist to show Tony the elevator and Trevor in the next seat. "We had free games to use up."

"It's a school night," Tony said. "You're supposed to give them away."

"I know, Dad. It was our favorite. I will next time." Agreeing was easier than arguing. Besides, Geoff was so relieved to be safely on his way home that he did not want to fight with his parents. With any luck, they would never find out where he had been.

Tony and Fallah, both in pajamas and housecoats, occupied the couch when Geoff got home at 2240.

"I'm sorry," he said before either of them could speak. Geoff's evening had been so traumatic the two words came out loaded with feeling. He hoped his parents would read it as contrition. "I'll watch better. The time, I mean."

"Set an alarm," Fallah said. "Have a snack and get some sleep."

"Okay." Geoff's stomach no longer felt tied in knots, but it seemed to be flipping around inside his belly. Although he wasn't sure he could eat, he helped himself to a handful of barely filled peapods and went to the kitchen for a glass of milk and a sticky cinnamon bun.

Geoff exchanged good-nights with his parents as he headed for his room. Once inside, he set his snack on the desk. He was ready to shower and go to bed, but he knew he had better stretch first. Chin would know if he didn't, and Geoff was not going to give him any more reasons to be angry.

Chapter 26

The next morning, Trevor, decked out in black and gold, waited for Geoff at the school transit zone.

He watched his smaller friend walk up and then said, "You don't look like Chin worked you over."

Geoff shook his head and said, "Not yet."

They walked into the school together without further mention of the previous evening, but when Trevor spotted Hans and Rob, he swaggered over and said, "Well, we sure got out of there fast." He began an exaggerated recounting of their experience at the mall security office.

"We could'a saved you the trouble if you'd tossed us the evidence," drawled Rob. "I could'a grabbed it and ran."

"I looked for you," Geoff said, finally breaking his silence.

"We couldn't get there fast enough," said Hans. "They really hustled you away. Didn't give us half a chance."

"But we sure showed those store owners," Rob said. "They won't mess with us again."

"The family'll mess with you if you go near there," said Geoff.

"Huh?" Hans's hair flew around his shoulders as he whipped around to face Geoff. "What's that mean?"

"Oh, yeah," said Trevor. "We're banned from there. *Chin* told us when he bailed us out."

"Rescued by the heavyweights!" exclaimed Rob.

Hans began recounting Chin's impressive standing in the Lung Organization.

Everyone but Geoff seemed to think the arrest had been a grand adventure. He couldn't help thinking about being pounded by Chin or seeing him grab Barbara and turn her into one of his girl druggies. Still, he was not going to tell his friends he thought they had all done something dumb. He could caution them about celebrating, though.

"Don't forget the part about us all owing the family," said Geoff. "There's no telling what they'll want."

"We'll just do a few jobs," Trevor said. He waved his arm dismissively.

"Yeah," Geoff muttered. He knew it wouldn't be that easy. In phys ed, he played soccer with abandon, hoping that in the fast action of the game, someone would run over him so he'd get confined to the hospital. It didn't happen.

Hoping to slightly appease Chin's wrath, Geoff arrived at the recreation center a full fifteen minutes early.

Chin and Lui were in Chin's office. Chin, dressed in blue-and-black tights and a muscle shirt, lounged behind the desk. Lui's emerald-covered bulk overflowed the chair across from him.

A ragged woman cried on a chair in the corner of the office. Her hair hung to her shoulders in tangled clumps. She wore an old T-shirt; the edges of the sleeves hung in frayed tatters around her elbows, but her perfect nails were decorated with deep pink polish. Faded blue jeans covered her legs. Her feet were bare, the toenails painted to match her fingernails.

Geoff glanced at her and then looked away. He had the terrible feeling she was there as an example of what Chin could turn Barbara into.

"Well, look who's here," Chin said. "Your friend, Geoff."

The wretch in the corner obediently lifted her head and looked at Geoff with red-rimmed hazel eyes.

Surprised at being called the woman's friend, Geoff turned to see her better. He did not recognize her. She was older than him, with blotchy skin and purple circles around her eyes. Blue bruises marred the left side of her jaw. She smiled at Geoff and held her hand, palm up, toward Chin.

When he ignored her, she said, "I waited like you said. He's here now." She thrust her hand out demandingly.

"What do you say, Geoff?" asked Chin. He picked up a plastic-wrapped drug patch. "I figured it's too close to the competition to beat you, so I punished Cheri instead. Should she get her candy?"

Geoff stared blankly at Chin for three seconds, and then comprehension began to grow. He looked again at the woman. Could she really be the beautiful girl who joined him in the shower room after dance practice? She looked more like Cheri's mother!

"Yes, Geoff!" Cheri smiled and jumped up from her chair. She ran to Geoff and held out her hand beseechingly.

Geoff turned back to Chin. The older man laughed and tossed the drug patch to Geoff. He picked it out of the air.

"Hurry up and decide what you're going to do with it," Chin said. "Then get changed." He pointed to the corner of the desk. Only then did Geoff notice the gym bag with his practice gear was there. Chuckling, Chin and Lui left.

Geoff opened his right hand and gazed at the little square. What did Chin mean? Decide what to do with it? If he didn't give it to Cheri, what options did he have? Throw it away? Use it himself? Sell it? He didn't even know what it was.

Cheri knelt and hugged Geoff's knees.

"Please," she said. "I'll do *anything.*" New tears trickled down her cheeks. "Don't you take it. Once you do, you're their slave. Please, Geoff."

Horrified and a little disgusted, Geoff silently gave the drug to Cheri.

She sat at his feet, scrubbed the inside of her arm against the seam of her jeans, and expertly stuck the patch to the abraded place on her forearm. Oblivious to Geoff, she curled up and stared at the floor just beyond her pink toenails.

Geoff stepped around her to get the gym bag off the desk. Chin had orchestrated this scene to send Geoff a message about the perils of getting into trouble. More than one message. It was at least partly to show him what Chin could do to Barbara. It also told him Cheri had not been sent to him as a bribe.

Chin had probably ordered her to get Geoff to like her so that she became another means for Chin to control Geoff.

Geoff changed in the locker room as usual. He tugged the flashy green dance suit straight over his shoulders and took a deep breath. It did not help the sickness that roiled between his belly button and backbone. Knowing he couldn't make Chin wait, Geoff walked out of the locker room.

In the time it had taken Geoff to put on his Simba suit, Chin had changed as well. He sat on the floor, his legs wrapped around his shoulders.

"You'd better not be cold," Chin said from beneath his shins.

Geoff shook his head no. He warmed up before he arrived as often as he could because Chin's pre-dance exercises were so demanding. Not as much as the dance itself, though. As always, they spent the first half of the lesson up on the quarter-g deck, doing the lively character dance.

"Kick your heels higher," ordered Lui.

"Do it over," growled Chin. They did it half a dozen times, with Lui or Chin snarling a correction at Geoff every time he did not exactly follow the prescribed choreography.

Geoff knew the steps. He did them in his sleep every night. It was remembering the details like when to curl or straighten his fingers, when to pout and when to smile, and whether his eyes were supposed to be all the way open or half-closed that he had trouble with.

"Watch," said Chin.

Lui ordered a section of the dance they had just done to play. Chin stepped into the hologram and delivered a backhand slap through the image of Geoff's fist.

"Body language," Chin said. "You wanting to deck me is coming through. This is a show, a performance. *Think* like you're flirting. When you turn around to wink at a girl, you don't wave a fist at her."

Geoff nodded. The image vanished. Music started again.

By the time Lui called for the mid-practice break, Geoff dripped sweat. He wiped it onto his hooded robe as they rode the elevator back to the heavy deck.

Leaning his back against the wall, Geoff slid to the floor. He spread his legs, dropped the towel between his knees, and rested his forehead on it. He held his ankles and then slid his feet farther sideways into open splits. It made him feel like a cartoon character splayed against the front of a fast-moving scout ship. He lay there, listening to Lui and Chin's quiet conversation.

"Well?" Chin asked.

"Maybe if we get him here four hours a day for the next week," replied Lui.

"When does he work?" Chin drained half a water bottle as Lui consulted his reader.

"I arranged for the next four days," said the fat man. "He gets Monday and Tuesday off and then works another five-day stretch. Weekdays are four hour shifts."

"Get him out of the arcade," said Chin. "He has to make an appearance there, so have him here the first and last hour and a half of his full shifts, one hour of the short ones. I'll join you when I can."

"Same for the weekend?" asked Lui.

"Yeah. Don't know how the hell I'm going to manage."

Lui laughed and said, "It'll keep you loose between bouts."

His statement made no sense to Geoff for a moment. Then he remembered Chin had a kung fu masters' tournament. Geoff groaned to himself as he sat up to reposition his legs. He did not want to be here three hours a day. At least Chin would be gone some of the time.

"Sundays?" asked Lui.

"Yes," answered Chin. He immediately changed it to, "No. Last thing I need is to burn him out."

"Yeah." Lui pulled a candy bar from his bag. "Heard from Dom."

"And?" asked Chin.

"It's a go," Lui said. "Should arrive in three weeks."

"Let's hope some of the bastards get here alive this time."

Geoff shivered. Lung *was* smuggling people up to the station. And they'd be here the middle of October. He couldn't warn anyone, though. Not without ending up dead himself. It wouldn't take much for Chin to figure out who had talked.

As always, after the short rest, they practiced the traditional dance. Geoff had become accustomed to spending the entire dance with his head tilted back, looking into Chin's eyes, but he still was not comfortable with the close body contact. Even after they performed the first dance, which was just as physically close during the last half, it always took Geoff until after one performance of the traditional dance to stop thinking about Chin's nearness and concentrate on getting the moves correct.

"You're a disaster," Chin declared before they completed the first round. "Start over." For the next twenty-five minutes, they danced, stopped to view brief holomovies of themselves, and danced some more.

It left Geoff, as usual, physically and mentally fatigued. He stumbled wearily to the change room, hoping Cheri would be there so that he could make sure she was okay.

Cheri did not come. As Geoff left, the old woman arrived to collect his gear.

He said hello. She did not acknowledge him.

Chin waited in the dance hall.

"You're getting extra shifts at work," he said. "For the next two weeks, you're booked for four-hour shifts Tuesday to Thursday and your regular shifts Friday and Saturday. You get Sundays off.

Tell your parents Manz needs you to help catch up on stuff for an audit. You'll be here for the first and last part of each shift."

Geoff nodded obediently but asked, "What if they say no?"

"Convince them. It's only two weeks."

"Might not be that easy," Geoff said.

"Do it."

Despite what he told Chin, Geoff did not think his parents would object to extra shifts as long as it was for only two weeks. He was right.

Chapter 27

The next morning, Trevor looked at Geoff and said, "You don't look like Chin worked you over. Guess he wasn't that mad."

"He was," said Geoff. And Cheri had suffered for it. He hoped he would get a chance to tell her he was sorry.

"What?" asked Trevor.

"Nothing. We'd better get to class." Geoff turned and found himself facing Rob.

"Hans got jumped last night," Rob said. "Four guys. Punched him purple and broke his arm."

"Chin's making us pay," said Geoff.

"The family wouldn't do nothing like that," Trevor said. "We're going to deal with those guys. Today. Right after school."

"Hell, yes," said Rob.

"We'll skew their orbits," Trevor said.

"I'm working," said Geoff, glad of the excuse because he did not want to be part of an ongoing feud. He already had more than he could handle.

"Call and cancel," ordered Trevor. "We gotta fix these slime worms."

"I—" Geoff did not want to be seen as a traitor, but he could not tell his friends why he couldn't call in sick. "I'll try."

As soon as Geoff's last class ended, he dashed out a side door of the school and onto the transit. He made it home before his phone lit with a call from Trevor. Geoff stared at it, unwilling to respond when there was nothing he could say. The music stopped, indicating the call was forwarded to his mail.

Geoff grabbed a snack before he called Mr. Manz to say he would be late for work. He felt he had to, even though Lui had arranged for his time away.

"I got the message," the arcade owner said. "You'll have less floor time 'cause I need you to keep current on the office work."

That wasn't the only thing Geoff had to keep current on. His homework had to be mostly done before he left. If he didn't keep up on it, his parents would make him quit work.

Geoff put his science assignment in his desk holoview and tried to do it as he ate and stretched. In a hurry to get finished, he spilt some milk, dropped his orange, and nearly choked on the cookies. His homework and warm-up went just as badly.

Before he left for the recreation center, Geoff checked his mail. The message from Trevor was short.

"We're on standby for a job this evening," Trevor said. "Maybe we'll come by the arcade and visit you."

"Oh, hell," said Geoff. He scowled at his friend's image. If they came looking for him, they'd discover he wasn't working!

Maybe Mr. Manz would help. Hoping that was the case, Geoff called his employer.

"I got a problem," Geoff said when his boss answered.

"And you think I can fix it?" asked Mr. Manz.

"Yes," answered Geoff. "Well, maybe. My friends said they'd stop at the arcade to see me, and I won't be there."

"I'll just tell them you're working in the back and can't be interrupted," Mr. Manz said. "That work?"

"Yes." Geoff heaved a sigh of relief. "Thanks, Mr. Manz. I'll be there later." One problem solved. Now he had to deal with Chin and Lui for most of the evening, and he'd better hustle, or he'd be late.

Geoff grabbed his bag and ran out of his room.

"Hey!" Barbara yelled. She ducked toward the bathroom as Geoff grabbed his doorframe to help him stop. "Watch where you're going."

"Stay out of the way." Geoff started moving again as he answered her. "I don't want to be late for work."

"I live here, too," Barbara said. "And you don't start till seventeen anyway."

"I've got to go." It took a little longer to get to the recreation center than the arcade. On top of that, Chin was a lot less forgiving of a little lateness than Mr. Manz was.

"You just want to game before you sign in," accused Barbara.

"Don't." Geoff dashed through the kitchen in two long, low-gravity steps. He jumped the sofa and landed neatly in front of the door.

He arrived at the recreation center with scant seconds to spare. Lui waited in the hall. He tossed the bag with Geoff's dance clothes to him.

"Get changed quick," ordered Lui. He pointed to the open door to Chin's office.

Geoff dressed and then followed Lui to a small room. It looked like a meeting room with no table. A half of a dozen tall stools lined one wall.

"Chin's got a class," Lui said. "We'll work here for now."

He supervised Geoff through a grueling fifteen-minute warm-up.

"I got tired watching," Lui said.

"Humpf," responded Geoff through his sweat. Lui, in his navy silk pajamas, still looked cool and relaxed.

"So you dance solo," Lui continued. "Put your boots on and pretend you have a partner." He started the music, playing it off his wrist phone.

"In here?" Geoff looked around the small room. He was sure to bump into the walls if he tried to dance.

"Yes." Lui ordered the music to begin again.

Poised and ready in the center of the room, his eyes focused on the wall to his left, Geoff somehow missed the beat and started late.

"Wake up!" Lui swatted the back of Geoff's curly head.

As Geoff tried to blink the stars away from in front of his purple contacts, the music restarted. He got the beginning of the dance correct that time but little else. Lui demanded constant corrections.

"What the hell is the matter with you?" he finally asked.

"Nothing's working." Geoff waved an arm at the strange room. "It's all different."

"You gotta do it the same no matter where you are," said Lui. "Don't forget you'll be on a stage in front of judges and spectators and cameras."

"Uhh." Geoff tried very hard never to think about that.

"Start again." Lui stood in front of Geoff. "I'll be Chin."

As far as Geoff could tell, Lui performed Chin's part of the dance perfectly while he still was able to pick out all Geoff's errors, even without a mirror. His participation did little to help Geoff's performance, though.

"Bend that elbow," ordered Lui.

"Why don't you dance with him?" asked Geoff. "Then you wouldn't have to fix my mistakes." He got a blow to the ribs that knocked him out of step.

Lui canceled the music.

"You think I like being tortured like this?" he asked. He dragged a silk sleeve over the film of sweat on his face.

Geoff shook his head no, even though he had the impression Lui enjoyed the practices, especially when he got to demonstrate steps.

"Besides," added Lui. "Judges like to see physical perfection or skinny striplings. You never see a 150-kilo guy in a competition."

Geoff caught an undercurrent of bitterness in that statement. He did not dare say anything about it. He still hurt from Lui's last punch.

Chin arrived ten minutes later, with his hair tightly braided and his red-and-orange dance leotard painted onto his ridges of muscle.

"Well?" he asked.

"The hell and away off orbit," Lui replied. Lui and Geoff were still working on the first dance. Geoff had not improved much.

Chin pointed his forefinger at Geoff, the tip a few centimeters from his nose, and said, "Focus. It doesn't do any good to put in the extra time if you don't accomplish anything."

Afraid of the consequences if he didn't, Geoff put all his energy into getting his performance correct.

"Technically, you're getting there," Lui said. "But you got to remember to show the emotions, too."

Geoff's badgered spirits sagged. What would happen if he *couldn't* get as good as Chin and Lui wanted?

He worried about that during their short break. The fear of Chin drugging and raping Barbara was always present. So was the thought of more of Geoff's friends being set up on a bad job. Then there was Cheri, who had no defenses.

Geoff wished he didn't have a family...or friends. It would make his life a lot simpler if he didn't have to worry about anyone else.

At the aroma of hot food, Geoff's mouth watered. He straightened from his stretch and saw Chin and Lui each eating a roast beef pocket with gravy dripping onto paper napkins. Geoff blinked in surprise. He had not heard anyone deliver it.

His stomach rumbled. It was 1745. His insides expected supper.

"Have one," said Chin. "I don't want you fainting from hunger and if you have too much, you'll probably puke."

Geoff wanted to refuse, but the sight and smell of the stuffed little buns was too much. He took one from the half of dozen remaining. He was still crunching the last bit of crisp crust when Chin called him back to the center of the room.

They practiced the traditional dance. Before long, Lui's litany of "get your hand higher," "keep your eyes half-closed there," and "extend your leg" pushed Geoff too far.

He stopped in the middle of a round and demanded, "What makes you think I can do this?"

Lui laughed. His long braid bounced above his wide backside.

"You *are* doing it," said Chin. He checked the time and added, "I've got a class." Kicking off his boots, he pulled on his slippers and left.

Still chuckling, Lui tossed Chin's boots beneath the row of stools. He stood in front of Geoff and ordered the music on.

Geoff crossed his arms and refused to move.

"What?" asked Lui.

"I can't do this," Geoff said.

"Too late." Lui laughed again. "You showed you could two months ago."

"Huh?" Geoff did not remember doing anything to give that impression.

"Remember the time you stomped all over his feet and he beat you till you couldn't stand? Doc had to come patch you up."

Geoff nodded. It still hurt to think about.

"Well," Lui said through his chortles, "You stomped and elbowed right with the music. Never missed a beat."

"Like I had a choice," Geoff muttered. If he missed a beat for any reason, Chin hit him.

"Beautiful to watch."

Speechless, Geoff just stood there.

"So, we know you can do it. We considered staging a fight for the character show, but you're too small." Lui ordered on the music. "Dance."

Geoff still found dancing with Lui awkward. His shape was too different from Chin's.

Lui did not care. He insisted Geoff perform the dance as choreographed—every minute move.

207

At 1830, Geoff bought a sandwich and ate it as he hurried to the arcade. He slipped in through the employees' side entrance and went directly to the office. He only had a short time to compile and sift data. As always, the way he had been manipulated into joining Lung angered Geoff. The thought that he might be doing the same to some other kid turned his stomach. Maybe he should quit working at the arcade.

It seemed like a good idea. Then he wondered, "*Could* I quit? Would they let me leave, knowing what I know?" Maybe he had to stay there the rest of his life.

That question bothered Geoff the rest of the evening. It made him wonder again if he could mess with the data he was sorting for Mr. Manz. Was there a way to keep people like Chin from getting their claws into other unsuspecting kids? Geoff promised himself he would try to figure out a way to fudge the data so only kids belonging to the Lung families seemed to be the ones Chin and his ilk wanted to recruit.

The idea gave Geoff an uncomfortable feeling of double-crossing someone who trusted him. After all, Mr. Manz had always treated Geoff well, although now that, too, was in doubt. Geoff wondered if Mr. Manz really liked him or if he was nice to him only because the family ordered him to be.

No, Geoff decided. He had worked for Mr. Manz for over a year and known him a lot longer. Maybe Mr. Manz had started out just like Geoff. A shiver rippled down Geoff from neck to toes as he envisioned himself in Mr. Manz's position in forty years.

Geoff said good-night to Mr. Manz and returned to the recreation center.

After another hour of training with Lui and Chin, he was so tired he forgot to wonder where Cheri was. He stood under the hot shower, leaned against the wall, and let the steamy stream pound his shoulders and back.

A soft touch between his shoulder blades made him jump. He slipped and nearly fell.

"Careful," Cheri said.

Hurt and angry that she would disappear and then show up like nothing had happened, Geoff considered telling her to leave. He didn't. He did not even admit to himself whether it was because inside he knew Chin gave her no more choice than he gave Geoff or because he feared she would go and not come back.

"Are you okay?" Geoff finally asked.

"I'm fine." She did not look up.

"I mean, really." He shut off the shower and wrapped himself in his towel.

She smiled, a sad little quirk of her lips, and said, "Really. It's a long time since I tried to OD. I've learned to cope." She put her hand over his mouth, preventing him from speaking. "And having a friend like you makes all the difference."

Geoff's eyes teared. He couldn't offer to help her. He couldn't even help himself.

Friday morning, Geoff slept in, so when Fallah woke him up, he found himself short on time. To top it off, in as good condition as he was, last night's two hours of training had overworked his muscles. Geoff patched himself with Lormal and then groaned as he dug around the bottom of his gym bag.

"There," he muttered with relief when his hand closed around his tube of Haynes Heet. He rubbed it on his aches instead of doing Chin's wretched morning stretches.

Arriving at school, Geoff was surprised to see Trevor, Hans, and Rob waiting for him. They were lined up at the transit stop, standing straight, with their feet planted apart and their arms crossed on their chests. The other students detoured widely around them.

Geoff hitched the strap of his bag on his shoulder and stopped. Facing them, he folded his arms and copied their judgmental stance.

"What?" asked Geoff.

"Where were you last night?" demanded Trevor.

"Working." Geoff looked from Trevor to the other boys. "You knew that. What're you so burnt about?"

"We had a job last night," said Trevor. "We went to the arcade to get you." The taller boy pointed his arm at Geoff like a spear. "You weren't there."

"Did you ask Mr. Manz?"

"No," Trevor said.

"I spent the whole time stuck in the ion-blasted office," said Geoff. The get-to-class buzzer sounded. The few students remaining in the entry hurried into the school. Geoff reflexively moved as well. The other boys did not.

"The guys there said they never saw you," Trevor said.

"They didn't." Geoff took a second step.

The principal walked out and said, "The bell has gone, gentlemen. You should be in class." That ended the discussion.

Hans, who shared the morning social studies class with Geoff, walked with him.

"You can't just skip out on things," the group's historian said. "You're supposed to be one of us."

"I'm not the only one with a job," objected Geoff. "You guys haven't all always been there."

"We were last night," Hans said. "What're you doing working in the middle of the week anyway?"

"It's only for a couple weeks," said Geoff. "Mr. Manz needs help catching up in the office."

They reached their classroom and suspended the conversation.

It resumed over lunch. They met at their usual table in the crowded cafeteria and talked as they ate. In an attempt to deflect the other boys' questions about why he was working during evenings he usually had off, Geoff asked what they had gotten the previous evening.

"Vacuum," answered Trevor. "Ten deliveries and we didn't even get a free pass to a game or anything."

"We're being punished for Tuesday evening," Hans said. "That's got to be it. We're supposed to deliver again tonight. *All of us.*"

"I'm working," said Geoff. He looked at Trevor, expecting some backup.

"Mr. Manz'll give you an hour off," Trevor said. Geoff glared at his closest friend. Trevor knew he was doing something with Chin. He was supposed to cover for him!

"He can't." Geoff didn't know what else to say.

"You're not *that* important," said Rob.

"*You* call him," said Geoff. "I told him I'd work a couple weeks to get that stuff caught up for his audit. I can't just tell him I won't be there."

"This's important," Trevor said. "And you were part of that fiasco on Tuesday. *You* got caught."

"I couldn't help that." Geoff stood up and grabbed his tray. "You think I wanted to get hauled off like that?"

Geoff stalked to the kitchen window at the side of the cafeteria. He dumped the thin bamboo containers into their recycle chute and slid the tray down the counter. A work-experience student caught it and racked it.

"Geoff!"

Geoff ignored Trevor's call and escaped into the hall.

Chapter 28

After school, Geoff trained with Lui in the little room. That evening's session began as usual in the quarter-g dance hall with Chin, but after the warm-up, the room abruptly transformed.

As holograms filled the room, blank walls and mirrors were replaced with rows of cheering people. Seated in tiers as if watching a show or sports event, they surrounded Geoff and Chin on three sides. The fourth wall took on the guise of velvet curtains. They hung in ebony folds of silence.

The only part of the room not filled with three-dimensional images was the dance floor. It remained clear and empty.

Stunned, with his mouth hanging open, Geoff turned in a small circle. It was impossible to take in. The rows of spectators seemed to disappear into the distance. Their noise surrounded him like a living creature, hammering at his eardrums.

"Focus!" snapped Chin.

Geoff looked at him, wide-eyed, and then slowly turned to look around again.

"That's what it'll be like in the competition," Chin said. "Ignore them. When we dance, the only things that exist for you are the music, the floor, and me." As soon as Geoff returned his dazed gaze to Chin, he nodded to Lui.

The preliminary music for the character dance began. The lights over the audience dimmed. Brilliant spotlights illuminated the stage.

"We walk out holding hands." Chin took Geoff's left hand in his right. At center stage, he silently gestured to Geoff, directing him to his mark for the start of the dance. As they took their places, the crowd grew quiet.

To Geoff's surprise, neither Chin nor Lui corrected his mistakes, even though he made several. Occasionally, the holographic audience burst into applause. The noise jarred and upset Geoff.

At the end, during Chin and Geoff's final pose, the crowd cheered and yelled.

"Take a bow," Chin said as Geoff stepped away from him. "Hold hands." He grabbed Geoff's right hand and led him to the front of the stage. Suiting action to words, he said, "Bow from the waist. Hold it for a three count. Rise." They repeated that acknowledgment of the applause.

"Now exit stage left," ordered Chin. He draped his arm over Geoff's shoulders and steered him off the stage.

The hologram of the stage and spectators disappeared. Geoff and Chin stood beside the wall in the practice hall.

"That's what a competition's like," said Chin. "You have to perform flawlessly even with the noise. We'll do that a few times every day. Now...practice."

They practiced. Lui projected the hologram of the stage and audience five more times. By the end of the evening, Geoff learned to concentrate despite the distractions. But although he thought he was doing well, his instructors always found something to correct.

"He's not dead!" exclaimed Barbara when Geoff entered the kitchen Saturday morning. She and Fallah were setting the table. Tony stood at the stove, cooking sausages and blueberry pancakes.

"Hmmmph," Geoff responded. He sat in what was usually Barbara's chair and reached for the pitcher of juice.

"You could at least help," Barbara said.

"What are you doing up so early?" asked Geoff.

"I've got rehearsal." Barbara rose onto the balls of her feet and twirled in the center of the kitchen. "The drama club's meeting this morning."

"Not in here," Tony said as he deftly avoided her circling arms.

"Since when are you in drama?" asked Geoff. "What are you doing? Turning the lights on and off?"

"I'm an actress," Barbara said. She stopped spinning and struck a pose in the center of the kitchen, shoulders back, one hand on her out-thrust hip. "I play Monique. She's a floozy."

"Huh?" Geoff was not sure what that meant.

"You know," said Barbara. "A prostitute."

"I don't believe it," Geoff said. He was going through hell to keep her from becoming a drugged whore and here she was, all excited about pretending to be one in some stupid school play.

"Why? I'm a good actress. That's why I got the tragic heroine part."

"It's tragic, all right," Geoff said. Life was tragic, like a sappy soap opera where nothing ever went right.

"What's that supposed to mean?" Barbara sounded insulted.

Geoff gulped his juice and said, "Nothing." Her news or maybe her cheery excitement about the play depressed him.

"You're just jealous 'cause I'm in a show."

"No." He set down his glass and headed for his room.

"What's wrong?" asked Fallah.

"Forgot something," mumbled Geoff. He made it to his room before his tears escaped onto his cheeks. Geoff grabbed a T-shirt off the floor and tried to dry his face. The tears would not stop.

Hungry and frustrated because he did not dare go to eat while crying, Geoff stripped his bed. He piled the bedding in front of his door and then began picking clothes up off the floor. If they looked dirty enough to wash, he used them to wipe his face and threw them on the sheets. If they seemed clean, he put them away.

The activity helped. As he put his energy into cleaning his room, his tears abated.

Fallah knocked on Geoff's door and asked, "Are you okay?"

"Yeah," replied Geoff.

"What are you doing? Come have breakfast."

"Coming." Geoff grabbed his mound of laundry. Holding it high against his chest so it hid his face, he slid his door open.

Fallah stepped backward toward the kitchen.

"That could have waited," she said.

"I'm going to work," Geoff said from behind his shield. He carried it into the bathroom.

As he haphazardly stuffed it into the washer, Fallah called, "Don't wash the bedding. I'll do all the sheets together. In fact, leave it and eat. You don't want to go to work on an empty stomach."

"I know." Geoff shut the bathroom door. He sorted laundry for a minute and then flushed the toilet. Before he returned to the kitchen, he splashed cold water over his eyes. It felt so good that he cupped more in his hands and lowered his face into the rapidly warming pool in his palms. Maybe it would take the redness from his eyes.

"You're sure off orbit lately," Barbara said when Geoff sat down and began piling food on his plate.

"And you're not?" asked Geoff.

"Not like you."

"Hmmm." Geoff stuffed his mouth with syrup-dripping pancake. He said little more. Running late for work gave him a good excuse to keep his mouth full and not have to explain himself.

The recreation center bustled with its usual weekend crowd. Geoff followed a group of overweight, middle-aged women down the corridor. They entered the room before him, joining a crowd of similarly flabby weekend exercisers.

Lui waited for Geoff. His mouth full of strawberry sundae, he pointed with the spoon to the locker room.

Geoff changed and had almost completed his warm-up when Chin strode into the dance hall. Dark eyes glowing, his black hair hanging loosely around his shoulders, he radiated vitality.

"Two down," Chin said. "I'm off for an hour." He pulled off his black sweatshirt and matching pants. Beneath them he wore black bicycle shorts. Bruises and red marks covered his chest, arms, and legs.

The Mad Medic stepped into the doorway and said, "You'd better not plan on spending it in here."

"Just a bit." Chin pulled his dance boots out from under a chair and put them on. "Let's go, kid."

"You get fifteen minutes," the Mad Medic said. "Then you have to slow down and have a shake. I'll get you a sandwich, too." He left.

Lui started the music.

The first part of the character dance went smoothly, but as they moved closer together, Geoff grew uncomfortable. It did not seem right to brush against Chin and slide his hands across his chest and back when he wasn't wearing a shirt. Certain he would get hit if voiced any objections to Chin's lack of clothes, Geoff did his best to pretend the older man was in his usual garb.

"What're you jittery about now?" asked Chin. Without waiting for an answer, he turned to Lui and said, "Let's have a look." Lui played brief clips of the dance, pointing out the places where Chin and Geoff were not perfectly matched in how they performed the steps.

"Again," said Chin.

They did it again. Geoff tried to keep his mind on the dance and Lui's instructions to extend his shoulder or correct the angle of his head, but when they turned and he slid his left hand from

Chin's shoulder blade to the outside of his waist, Geoff collected a palm full of Chin's sweat. He wanted to vomit. His reflexive shaking of his hand scattered droplets of moisture across the floor.

"What the hell was that?" demanded Lui.

Chin bopped Geoff on the head as he turned into the next step.

Geoff knew he was supposed to ignore the blow and do the same, but he couldn't. He stood there, eyes rolling like a cartoon character with stars circling its head.

"I think you broke him," Lui chuckled. "Too much adrenaline."

"I'll break you." Chin advanced on the laughing fat man.

Geoff backed against the wall and watched an amazing exhibition of kung fu through unfocussed eyes.

Chin was an acknowledged master, expected to place at or very near the top of the tournament being held that day and the next. Lui easily countered Chin's blows and landed numerous ones of his own. The impromptu match ended with Lui tripping Chin and knocking him to the floor.

"*That's* a real smart way to stay loose between bouts," the Mad Medic said sarcastically.

"You're not supposed to be back yet." Chin grinned up at the doctor standing in the doorway, kicked backward into a handstand, and then flipped himself upright. "Know my next opponent?"

"No," said Doc. "Got your snack."

Chin looked pointedly at the doctor's empty hands.

"In your office." They left.

Lui looked at Geoff and said, "Back to work, kid. We gotta be done in time for me to see the next fight." He filled the room with the hologram of spectators and turned on the music. As they continued rehearsing the character dance, Lui pointed out every error Geoff made.

"How the hell can you see that?" Geoff muttered after Lui ordered Geoff to raise his left elbow slightly.

Lui, pivoting on Geoff's right side, chuckled and said, "I'm a judge. I see everything. Turn your right leg out a little more."

"I'm never going to get this," Geoff said. "No matter how much I learn, you always have more."

"Not the same things." Lui laughed again. "Haven't you noticed you're down to the tiny details? Keep that hand open!"

Geoff huffed out his breath and partially spread his fingers, carefully to maintain the slight curve in his hand.

"You got less than two weeks to get it perfect," said Lui. "Learn it, or we'll pound it into you."

He said it casually, but Geoff knew he meant it. Dead seriously.

The next day, Geoff slept until noon. He lay in bed, listening to the silence before deciding he was hungry enough to get up. He wandered into the kitchen. The apartment was empty. That was odd. Frowning slightly, Geoff looked for a message on the holoview. It was there, a recording of Fallah saying that they were going to the amusement park and that he could join them there if he wanted to.

Geoff was also invited to go Rollerblading with Trevor and Rob. He didn't want to see them, not after the way they had harassed him for not going out with them. He wanted time to zip by, to be past the weekend of October 10th so the dance competition would be over. He would never see Lui and Chin again.

Geoff made himself two huge sandwiches, picked an orange, and sat down in the living room. He was going to ignore the com and spend the afternoon gaming on the large holoview.

Geoff was still on the couch, snoring softly while his paused game waited with frozen patience, when Tony, Fallah, and Barbara returned.

"Look at the lazy lump!" exclaimed Barbara. As Geoff stirred, she reached over the back of the sofa and tickled his ribs.

Geoff stiffened. He raised his arms as if to push her away but stopped the movement half-completed. His eyes popped open.

"Blast off!" said Geoff.

"None of that in here," Fallah scolded.

"Sorry," said Geoff automatically.

Barbara's wriggling fingers were still dancing over his ribs and belly. It didn't tickle. Chin had knocked Geoff's tickles out of orbit. Now Geoff's initial feeling was a flash of panic that he was out of step. He forced himself to relax, lowered his partially raised arms, and swatted at Barbara's hands.

"You're no fun." She kept tickling. "Though you did go as stiff as a frozen mummy."

"Mummies are dried," said Geoff, "not frozen." He grabbed her by a shoulder and the waistband of her jeans and tossed her up to the ceiling. She hit it with a thump and began to drift back down.

"Hey!" Barbara protested. "That almost hurt!"

"Don't dent the walls," cautioned Tony.

"Didn't," Geoff said to both of them. He pushed himself off the couch. Thinking it would keep Barbara from starting a wrestling match, he picked up his empty glass and plate.

"You got your game saved?" Tony asked.

"Yeah, you can close it." Geoff hopped over the table. He made it to the kitchen before Barbara reached the floor.

Fallah turned from the refrigerator and said, "You look like a day off did you good."

"I'm fine," Geoff said. "What time's supper?"

"All you do is eat and sleep," needled Barbara.

Geoff ignored her and said to his mother, "I'm going to the gym for a bit." If he did not stretch properly at least once today, Chin would flatten him.

"You've got a couple hours," replied Fallah. "We won't eat till nineteen. Is Trevor coming? We haven't seen him in a couple of weeks."

"I haven't seen much of him either." Geoff went to his room and grabbed his gym bag.

On his way out, Barbara asked, "When's your competition?"

"Competition?" asked Geoff. How could she know? *What* did she know?

"In gymnastics." Barbara spoke as if addressing an idiot. "When do you compete?"

"Oh." Geoff drew a deep breath to try to calm his panic. "I'm not competing in gymnastics." At least he didn't have to lie about that.

"Then why do it?"

"Fun. Exercise."

Barbara pursed her lips and said, "How do we know that's really where you are?"

"I said so." Geoff stopped by the door and turned to face her. Did she suspect something? "Where else would I go?"

"I heard Trevor and that creepy Hans got caught shoplifting."

"Did they?" Fallah sounded alarmed. She looked questioningly at Geoff.

"Yeah." The one good thing Chin had done for Geoff was keep his name out of that gossip. "Like I said, I haven't seen too much of him lately."

"Is that why you've been so moody?" asked Fallah.

Geoff shrugged. "Guess so." They'd noticed he wasn't himself. He'd better be more careful.

"It'll get better." Fallah walked over and gave him a one-armed hug.

"Yeah." She had no idea.

"So where're you going?" asked Barbara.

"The gym." Geoff swung his right foot up, planted it against the door higher than his head, turned to Barbara, and said, "I can do the splits again." He left before she could ask anything else. The next two weeks were going to last forever.

Monday afternoon, Geoff felt like the next hour would last forever. Chin showed up battered and bruised and in a foul mood because he had placed second in the tournament. Geoff had the character dance almost perfect, but Chin and Lui continuously badgered him about tiny details.

"Every little movement has a purpose," declared Chin. "You can't leave them out, and you can't change them. Each time we do this, it has to look exactly the same."

Geoff nodded, afraid saying anything would earn him a bruise. When their time was up, he escaped to the office in the arcade for a break. He ate supper at his desk and returned to the recreation center at 2030.

"Get changed in the office," Lui ordered. "We're going to work on details till his class is done. Technique has to be perfect by the end of this week. We'll spend next week polishing."

During the twenty minutes following Geoff's warm-up, they rehearsed the traditional dance. At 2100, when they joined Chin in the quarter-*g* dance hall, they switched to the character one.

Half an hour later, Geoff sat down to drink his juice, feeling like he might make it to the freedom on the other side of the competition without getting beaten up again. His instructors were finding fewer things to correct. He leaned against the wall, closed his eyes, and eavesdropped on Chin and Lui.

"We might get there yet," Lui said.

"Stay on him," said Chin. "We won't place in the top money if we're not perfect."

Lui snorted and said, "I *know* you're not doing this for the money. Besides, there's always next time. It's going to take more than one prize to cover what we've invested in him anyway."

Next time! The two words replayed themselves in Geoff's mind, seeming to grow louder and louder.

The cool room, which always felt too warm to Geoff once the practice was underway, suddenly seemed freezing cold. He struggled for breath as if the vents had been shunted to the vacuum outside the station.

"First place is fifteen thousand," Chin said. "That'll cover it."

Lui snorted.

"You know as well as I do no judge is going to give higher than third to a dancer they've never seen before," he said. "And third is only ten thousand. That'll pay out of pocket costs but not our time and trouble."

"Yeah," agreed Chin. "Maybe we can stage a fight show next time."

Geoff tried to think of a way to say he was not doing this for another competition, a way that would not get him beat up or let Chin and Lui know he could overhear them.

As Geoff considered the problem, he began to wonder if Chin had ever said this training was for only one event. Geoff could not remember for certain. He knew Chin had specifically referred to the competition in October when he told Geoff about this arrangement. He did not recall if the wily Chin had left his statement open, phrased it in such a way that Geoff would assume it was the only one when in reality it was not. Chin might expect to have Geoff under his heel forever!

Geoff shivered convulsively, a head-to-toe shudder.

"What's the matter with you?" asked Chin.

Geoff opened his eyes. Chin walked toward him, more than half the distance between Lui and Geoff.

"I'm cold," said Geoff.

Chin scowled and said, "It's warm in here today."

Geoff shivered again.

"Get those stretches done," Chin ordered. "We've got a lot to do yet."

The familiar movements helped Geoff regain his mental balance. He decided to concentrate on what he had to do for the next half hour and worry about Chin's plans later when he was alone.

That was quite a bit later. Cheri joined Geoff in the shower room and even made him forget his latest dilemma, at least for a few minutes.

He gave it all his concentration as he walked from the recreation center to the transit stop. He could see no way out of the trap he was in. As long as he had a family and friends and cared for Cheri, Chin controlled him.

As Geoff boarded the car, he had a new idea. Maybe the way out of this was to make it so he was of no use to Chin. No, if Chin suspected Geoff deliberately crippled himself, he would make someone Geoff cared about suffer. Maybe the only way out was for Geoff to take himself out of the equation, but how? He didn't have the money to pay someone to smuggle him to Mars or the Belt. And while he could hurt himself in the recreation facilities, it was pretty unlikely he could die there.

Staring at the flashy advertising without seeing it, Geoff shivered. He didn't want to die. He didn't want to be Chin's slave for the rest of his life either. How long would it take for him to become like Cheri, with all the spirit and resistance beaten or drugged out of him? Would dying be better?

Chapter 29

Noisy passengers entering the transit car disturbed Geoff's introspection. He glanced up at four college-age men apparently celebrating a win at whatever sport they had played. Behind them walked a couple dressed for a night out.

Geoff's gazed lingered on the husky man, his broad shoulders and very short haircut. He was looking at everyone in the car as if gauging their potential for trouble. A cop. Geoff turned partly sideways and pretended to watch an advertising video as he kept tabs on the cop. The officer guided his wife to the seat right behind the exit. Everyone getting off the transit would have to walk right in front of them.

"Hope they get off before me," Geoff muttered. He watched from the corners of his eyes as several other passengers reached their stops and exited the car. The cop ignored them, apparently occupied with talking to his wife.

Geoff's stop neared, so he got up and walked to the exit. As he stepped towards the doors, he automatically slid his hand along the rail between the exit and the front of the cop's seat. The cop's hand rested there. When Geoff glanced down, the cop flicked his fingers, and a card appeared, standing vertically between the man's thick fingers.

Geoff risked a glance at the cop, and he was surprised at the urgent expression in his dark eyes. Impulsively, Geoff took the offered card as he walked past and out of the transit car.

Tucked between the inside of Geoff's wrist and the cuff of his sweatshirt, the mystery cop's card felt burning hot. Geoff left it there as he strode home.

Public areas like the station corridors were monitored. If Chin could tap into that system—and Geoff had no reason to believe there was anything Chin could not do—Geoff did not want to be seen looking at a cop's business card. He had enough trouble. He didn't need messages from cops. The guy was probably just hassling him, anyway. Once they got your picture on file, the rule-bound jerks went looking for you. He should have dropped it on the floor of the transit car.

When Geoff stepped into his family's apartment, he shifted the card from his sleeve to a pocket in his jeans. He did not want his parents seeing it any more than he wanted Chin to know about it.

After a quick snack with his parents in front of the holoview, Geoff said good-night. In the privacy of his room, he pulled out the card and examined it.

The cop was a detective named Denis Jenn. Why would he give Geoff his card? Puzzled, Geoff twirled it between his fingers as he considered the question. Wait. There was writing on the back.

Bold block letters spelled out "I can help" and a phone number.

Help? He didn't even know what the problem was! Geoff threw the card onto his desk and got ready for bed. As he brushed his teeth and changed, a new thought occurred to him. Why did the cop think he needed help? Surely, he didn't go handing out his card to every kid taking the transit by himself.

Geoff stared into the mirror. Did he look like someone in trouble? Was that man a mind reader who picked up on Geoff's suicidal thoughts? Or did Geoff look as desperate as he felt?

Picking up the card again, Geoff looked at the numbers. The one on the back was different from the office number. It must be the detective's personal one. Did that mean he did not expect Geoff to go through official channels to get help? Or did he figure Geoff was more likely to call if he did not have to phone a police station? Or maybe he heard about last Tuesday and figured now that Geoff had a record, he could put the squeeze on him.

Geoff extended his hand with the card toward the recycle chute and then hesitated. He was desperate enough to consider killing himself. Maybe he was desperate enough to think about calling the cop. Geoff tossed the card back onto his desk. He could deal with it in the morning. Right now, he was too tired.

Even so, Geoff did not get to sleep easily or rest well. His mind vainly searched for a way to get free of Chin and Lui without going to the cops.

Calling Detective Jenn opened up a whole new list of problems—like where to call from. Geoff did not dare use his own phone. Chin might have tapped it. He couldn't call from anywhere he might be overheard by anyone, especially his friends or family. And if he did call, what would he say? He was dancing against his will? It sounded too stupid.

Geoff got up the next morning as tired as he had been when he had gone to bed. He felt nauseated. He couldn't look at breakfast, so he turned around to go back to his room.

"What's wrong?" asked Fallah. "Not feeling well?" She came over to him and felt his forehead.

"You're not fevered." She looked closely at his face. "Trouble with your friends? Honey, people develop different interests and grow apart. You'll find new friends."

"I know. I'm okay." Geoff tried to look alert.

Geoff spent half his time during morning classes trying to figure out how to safely call Detective Jenn. He could use a school phone if he came up with a good excuse. He was not sure when he had decided to call, but it seemed like the only thing to do. After all, even if the cop was out to hassle him, things couldn't get any worse.

At lunch, Trevor and Hans caught up to Geoff as he strolled down the hall, his mind more on cajoling a private call out of the office secretary than on meeting his friends for lunch.

"So you *are* here," said Trevor.

"We thought Mr. Manz chained you to that desk," Hans said.

"Huh?" asked Geoff.

"We had another job last night," Trevor explained. "We went to the arcade to get you, and Manz wouldn't even let us say hi."

"He said we could talk to you when you weren't working," added Hans. "He wasn't paying you to visit."

"When did he get so mean?" asked Trevor. "He didn't used to mind."

"Probably's stress from trying to get ready for that audit," Geoff said. "It'll be done by the end of next week." Twelve days to the dance competition. Maybe the cop could work some magic and get Geoff out of this mess before then. He couldn't if Geoff didn't call him. Somehow.

"Well, you're lucky," Trevor said. He nudged Geoff with his shoulder, bumping him toward the cafeteria entrance. "Word is we got another job today. They're really making us pay for last Tuesday."

"I wonder what they'll make you do," said Hans. "Since you aren't coming out with us."

"I don't want to think about it," Geoff said. He took a bowl of noodle soup and a clubhouse sandwich.

"What? No dessert?" asked Rob when Geoff sat down beside him.

"Not that hungry." Geoff's stomach was filled with cold rocks.

He couldn't get away from the gang throughout lunch and the rest of the school day. When the last bell rang, he waited for the initial rush of students to leave and then took the long way around to the office.

"Excuse me." Geoff waited for the secretary closest to the counter to look up. Then he lowered his voice and continued, "My com isn't working and—" He looked down, pretending to be embarrassed before he continued, "I can't remember if I have an appointment with my psych today. Can I call from here?" He glanced around the crowded office and added, "Uh, privately?"

"Yes." The middle-aged man who did most of the office interaction with students glanced into the small meeting room off the large office and added, "You can go in there. Don't be long."

"Thank you." Geoff barely breathed the words. Faced with the immediate prospect of voluntarily talking to a cop, his lungs were refusing to work.

The little room held a small table with a chair on each side of it. The holoview was a palm-sized square set into one corner of the table. When activated, it projected a blank holocube slightly smaller than Geoff's gym bag.

Geoff quickly read the cop's personal number off the card. As soon as he finished speaking, the holoview filled with the station service logo. Geoff bit his lower lip to keep himself from canceling the call. He had no one else to turn to.

It seemed to take an eternity before the cop's head and shoulders appeared in the holoview. Geoff stared into the man's brown eyes, unable to think of anything to say.

"I'm glad you called," Detective Jenn said. "I was worried. You okay?"

Geoff nodded and said, "I can't be long."

"Why don't we meet and have a lunch?"

"Be seen with a cop?" If the man was that dumb, Geoff wasn't having anything to do with him.

"No." Detective Jenn smiled at Geoff. "I'm not an idiot. Here's an address. Tell me when you can be there." A street address flashed into the holoview: 72J78 Cypress Hall. Horizontally, it was not far from the school. Vertically, it was way up on a light deck in a residential area Geoff had never been to.

"I got half an hour now," Geoff said. "Otherwise not till tomorrow."

"The door'll be open. I'll be right there." The holoview went blank.

Geoff shut it off and left. He called a quick "thank you" and "good-bye" to the secretary before he darted out the side door and down the corridor. He went deeper into the school, the opposite way from where he expected his friends to be. From there, he headed to the transit stops on the far side of the school complex.

The elevator car was crowded with students, unfamiliar faces going to homes filled with families and people who loved them. A handful exited on deck forty-seven with Geoff. As they walked or ran directly to their transport station, Geoff paused to see which cross-deck car to catch to section J. A pair of youngsters around seven and ten strolled together to the same car.

Geoff boarded, holding his breath, afraid he would see someone he knew. He looked down the rows of seats. The faces that bothered to glance up all belonged to strangers. Sighing with relief, Geoff dropped into the rear seat. The changing addresses displayed above the exit let him know his was the second stop.

Another unfamiliar hallway. Built the same as all station residential corridors, its walls were a slightly different blue than Geoff's home corridor; the bushes and shrubs spreading in front of them showed different greens, different flowers, and different fruits.

As Geoff walked down Cypress Hall, he met only one person, a pregnant young woman. She smiled and kept walking. He did the same.

There it was—apartment seventy-eight. Suddenly uncertain, afraid he had impulsively jumped into even more trouble, Geoff decided to walk right past. Two steps later, as he drew even with the entrance, he thought that would look suspicious.

He tried the door. It swooshed easily and silently into the wall. Geoff stepped inside and slid it shut. Breathing quickly and shallowly, he stood still and looked around.

It was a small, sparsely furnished studio suite. Whoever folded the bed into a couch had left some of the blankets hanging out. Fallah would have made them remake it. Viney plants formed a cascade of green from the door to the corner at Geoff's right and completely over the adjoining wall.

The opposite wall had open doors leading to the kitchen and bathroom. Closed closet doors filled the spaces between them. Mirrored doors lined the wall to Geoff's left.

Geoff tentatively took a couple of steps farther into the apartment. There were enough furnishings and stuff lying around that it seemed like someone lived there, yet the place had an empty feel. Maybe this was where crooked cops shook down their victims. Ready to leave, he turned back to the door.

It vanished into the wall. Detective Jenn's wide shoulders filled the doorframe.

Chapter 30

"Glad to see you." Jenn smiled and stepped forward, quickly closing the door behind himself. "I'm Denis Jenn." He held out his right hand. When Geoff hesitated to shake hands, Jenn added, "You can trust me. I know that's easier said than done, but I am one of the good guys." He held up the bag in his left hand as if that would confirm his statement.

Geoff stared into the cop's brown eyes for another half a breath and then took his hand. It was warm and large, like the thick-lipped smile surrounding his big white teeth.

"Come siddown." Jenn walked past Geoff. "This place belongs to a pilot, has a run between here and Luna City, so she's gone half the time."

Geoff followed him to the tiny kitchen.

"Here." Jenn pulled a bottle of chocolate milk out of his bag and handed it to Geoff. He sat down at the table and took out another chocolate milk, two submarine sandwiches as long as his forearm, and a half of a dozen cookies.

"I got two different kinds, so hopefully you'll like one." Jenn unwrapped the sandwiches as he spoke. "Take your pick."

Geoff perched warily on the edge of the second chair. He expected to be bombarded with questions, but Jenn acted like there was nothing more important than lunch. Geoff looked at the sandwiches. One held three meats, three cheeses, and lettuce, the other bulged with chunks of chicken and vegetables. He pulled the first one a little closer to himself.

"I missed lunch." Jenn bit into the chicken sandwich and raised his eyebrows at Geoff. "Wanna tell me your name?"

So the questions *were* coming.

"Geoff Anders."

"Thank you." Jenn took another bite. "I looked you up, found your picture in our system, along with a note Chin Hon arranged for that store to drop charges last week. How can I help?"

Geoff shook his head. His situation was beyond fixing.

"Okay." Jenn lowered his sandwich to the table. "If I could wave a magic wand and change one thing in your life, what would you want it to be?"

"Get Chin and Lui out of it," Geoff said immediately.

"Chin Hon and Lui Ko?"

Geoff nodded.

"Do you mind if I record this?" asked Jenn. "It'll make my follow-up easier, or you can tell me to erase it before I go."

"Okay." Geoff did not believe any police officer would erase something just because he was asked to. At this point, it didn't matter. "As long as *they* never see it."

"They won't." Jenn removed his wrist com and clipped it to his shoulder facing Geoff. "If I leave it on my arm, the picture'll bounce around as I eat. It's probably easier to get you away from them than get them away from you. Prosecuting—"

"If it was just me, I wouldn't have a problem!" Geoff surprised himself with the force in that outburst. "I got a sister...and parents, and friends—"

"It wouldn't be the first time we put a whole family in protective custody. If they've endangered you, we have something to charge them with. How quickly do we need to act?"

"Huh?" Geoff couldn't adjust that rapidly to the idea of being freed from Chin's domination.

"Are you in immediate danger?" asked Jenn. "Being beat up? Raped? Drugged?"

"No." Geoff shook his head, but he felt his face redden.

"I'm a street cop," Detective Jenn said gently. "You can't shock me, and you can't embarrass me. What are they doing to you?"

"Nothing." Was giving him free use of a whore a chargeable offense? "Not now." Well, maybe being hit when he didn't get things right could be considered assault.

"But they did." Jenn made it a statement. "And they're blackmailing you? Threatening your family if you don't cooperate?"

Geoff nodded.

"That's extortion, chargeable offense." Jenn bit into his sandwich again. "To do what?"

"Dance." It sounded ridiculous. Geoff blushed again.

"Where?" Detective Jenn seemed to find nothing odd about Geoff's answer. "Stripping? Exotic dance? Lap dance?"

"No." Two breaths. "Simba." There. He'd said it.

"Hmmmm. For the fall competition?"

Geoff nodded again.

"Eat, Geoff." Jenn's sandwich was half gone. "How did you become his partner? Were you in his class?"

"No. It started as a control thing, punishment. They thought I was being rebellious, so they called me in and said Barbie, my sister, would be their next junkie whore if I didn't dance." Once Geoff started, the words poured out of him. "Then they sent Trev and Rob on a bad job, so I'd work at it. Then they figured out I was good enough to compete. After that, I didn't get beat up as much. Can I get out of this before then? How do you know about it?"

"Chin and Lui are two people we try to keep informed about." Detective Jenn gulped most of his remaining milk. "What date's the competition?"

"October 10th. I thought it would end then. Last night, I heard them talk—they don't know I can hear them—about the next one. It won't. It won't ever end." Geoff felt a return of the despair he had suffered the previous evening. He sipped chocolate milk to hide the tears gathering in his eyes.

"It will," Jenn said. "It just won't be simple. It's never easy to outmaneuver the families, and those two are smart. Chin has degrees in recreation and psychology. Lui has a master's in commerce."

"Yeah." Geoff suddenly felt better. He picked up his sandwich and crammed the end into his mouth.

"We'll work on it." Jenn finished his drink. "Let's plan another meeting. We can't do this too often in case they track you, so it would be helpful if you record activities, places, and names of everyone you're in contact with...or heard about in relation to the Lung families, anything you can think of to tell me."

Geoff stopped chewing and stared up at Jenn.

"What?" asked the detective.

"Everyone?" Geoff didn't want to make trouble for his friends or for Mr. Manz.

"You can't choose who to name and who to leave out," said Jenn. "It's like putting together a giant puzzle. Everything and everyone's connected. If a detail's omitted, it leaves a hole."

"My friends—" Geoff did not know how to explain his fears.

"We're going after the big fish," Jenn said. "Not the kids who make deliveries. The adults who profit from them—Chin and Lui, the family leaders if we can get to them. But when we're in court, the judge expects the truth, the whole truth, and nothing but the truth." Geoff nodded his understanding and checked the time—1645.

He jumped up and said, "I've got to be on the bottom deck for seventeen."

"Take your lunch."

"Thanks." Geoff picked it up and then said, "You want something to work on, they're shipping up another load of people the middle of next month."

"What?" Jenn coughed, as if to ward off choking. "You know this? Chin and Lui are involved?"

Geoff nodded and said, "I heard them talk."

"*That's* something we can use to put them away for a *long* time." Jenn smiled, a toothy, humorless grin. "Can you meet me here after school the day after tomorrow?"

Geoff nodded and circled the table, heading for the door.

"Okay, Geoff." Jenn stood up and clapped him on the shoulder. "We'll get these guys off your back. Be careful." He bent down so his eyes were on a level with Geoff's. "Don't let anyone know I'm helping you, not your closest buddy or your family. You'll find yourself stuffed out an air lock or down a garbage chute with your face burnt off."

"I'm not stupid," said Geoff. "I know what they do to traitors."

"You're doing the right thing."

"Not how they see it."

"True, but don't worry," Jenn said. "I'll get you out of this. That's a promise from me to you." Using the monitor by the door, Jenn checked the passersby in the hallway before he nodded to Geoff that it was all right to leave.

"See you Thursday," he said as Geoff sauntered out the door.

"Yeah."

Geoff devoured his sandwich on the transit, feeling better than he had in three months. He wasn't alone in this mess. Detective Jenn was going to get him out of it. At least, he would if no one in the Lung Organization found out how Geoff had spent the last ten minutes.

Although he felt as if the weight of the station had been lifted from his shoulders, Geoff did not cross the station any faster than usual. He just made it to the dance hall for 1700.

It was as cool as always, but that afternoon, the chill in the large room did not make Geoff shiver. He changed quickly, popped in his contacts, and went to stretch.

Chin was not there. Lui watched and criticized Geoff.

"Keep on him," Chin ordered when he arrived. Dressed in a sparkling yellow Simba suit that showed off every bulge of muscle in his arms and torso, he finished braiding his hair as he crossed the room to Geoff. "Finish stretching in the elevator. I've got a class at eighteen."

They started with the character dance, as usual. Feeling a little like a secret agent and buoyed by the thought that Detective Jenn would intervene before the competition, Geoff performed well. For the first two rounds, there were no sounds but the music and the click of boot taps.

"You're finally getting it right," Lui said.

His comment distracted Geoff, and he missed his hand position during the third circle.

"Concentrate," growled Chin.

At the same time, Lui called out, "Fix your right hand!"

Geoff made a few more errors, but by the end, it was still his best performance ever.

Lui then ran the hologram of a stage and spectators. Geoff surprised himself by continuing to remember most of the picky details. It did not go unnoticed.

"It's about time you started getting it," said Chin. "You've only got a few days to be perfect."

"Whatever you did, do it more," Lui added. "I'm tired of yelling."

Geoff refrained from telling the large man he could stop yelling any time. That would only get him hit.

During the ride back to the heavy deck, Geoff figured out his improved performance was due to Detective Jenn's promise to get him out of this horrible situation. While there had been no immediate change in his circumstances, he no longer felt alone and overwhelmed. Catching himself on the verge of smiling, Geoff quickly frowned. It would be a disaster for anyone to start wondering why he was in good spirits. He didn't have an excuse for looking happy.

Holding that thought in mind, Geoff kept his expression serious as he stretched. It would be great if Lui and Chin gave up some details about the shipment they had mentioned earlier.

They didn't, not that day or the next.

Thursday after school, Geoff had no new information when he hurried back to the little studio apartment to meet Detective Jenn. The cop was there, waiting.

"They never said anything," Geoff reported before he even said hello.

"That's all right. We don't really expect they will," said Jenn. His dark eyes examined Geoff carefully. "How are you holding up? Anyone figure out you're talking to me?"

"No!" Geoff took a deep breath and added more calmly, "If they did, I'd be dead."

"Well, let's try to avoid that," Detective Jenn said. "We've got ten minutes. You want to talk first or listen first?"

Geoff looked at the pizza on the table. His stomach rumbled. Saliva filled his mouth.

"Listen." Geoff downed two slices while Detective Jenn summarized what he had done on Geoff's behalf and with the information Geoff had given him.

"We've got people on Terra quietly following up on your October transport tip," said Jenn. "And we're working on arrangements to make you and your family disappear at the same time as we arrest Chin and Lui and everyone we can connect them to. You'll be stashed in a safe place. The big question is this: Are you going to testify to put these guys in prison, or are we going to have to let them go right away?"

"Yes. Testify." Geoff smiled at the thought of sending his tormentors to jail. "But that takes years. What'll Mom and Dad do?" He couldn't see his family hiding in a little apartment for as long as it took to hold a trial. A new thought struck him: What if his family refused to go into protective custody? Would Geoff have to stay Chin's slave?

Detective Jenn pulled Geoff's mind back to their conversation by saying, "There's a couple ways to go. Lying low for years is one. If you choose that, your family will be relocated somewhere, and you'll meet up with them when it's all over."

Geoff made a face and asked, "And the other?"

"You claim victim's choice. In a nutshell, you stay in the safe house only as long as it takes for a hearing review. A team of lawyers ask you every question they can think of, try to get all the pertinent information you have onto a court record for the judge, the jury, too, if there ends up being one. It can be tough to go through, but you're done in weeks, a few months if things are complicated. Your family can stay with you. Or they can settle in at their new place with their new names, and you join them when you're done. You'll have time to decide that all when we've bagged these two and pulled you out of their reach."

"Uh-huh," Geoff said, but he wondered if there really was a place beyond Chin's influence.

Chapter 31

When Geoff walked into the dance hall Saturday morning, Lui handed him a hanger bag with a new Simba suit.

"It's a week to the competition," said Lui. "Dress rehearsal today. Hurry it up."

"Yeah." Geoff went to change. Inside the bag, he found a Simba suit with matching gloves, made in two shades of purple. The darker purple matched Geoff's purple contacts. The tights were the lighter purple. There was also a blond wig with long, straight hair. He put on the tights and suit. Before he could try to figure out how the wig went, Lui entered the shower room.

"I'll do that," he said. "Put your boot covers on."

"My what?" asked Geoff.

"Check the bag."

Geoff shook it. Two shiny, dark purple pieces fell out. He couldn't see how they fit on boots.

"Like this." Lui stretched one of the covers over Geoff's left boot. It covered everything but the sole. "Do the other one."

As Geoff struggled with it, Lui opened a case filled with makeup, small tubes of cream, and other items. Lui straddled the bench and set the case down in front of himself.

"Sit facing me," he ordered. He pointed to the bench on the other side of the case. "Don't move."

"Why?"

"I said so." Lui dug in his case. "I think we'll leave your pretty little mouth, just add a bit of a pout."

Geoff tried to see into the case.

"Hold still," snapped Lui. "You mess this up, and I'll knock you through the deck." Lui spread light purple paint on Geoff's face and neck down to the wide, flat collar of his suit. He brushed Geoff's eyebrows with dark purple mascara, glued on matching eyelashes, and painted his lips the same color.

Geoff shifted restlessly.

"Freeze!" Lui growled. He took three little dark purple triangles, each one about the size of his thumbnail, and glued them onto Geoff's face. They made a diagonal line from the side of his chin up his left cheek.

Chin came in, dressed in the same dark purple with light inserts as Geoff wore. Blond hair floated around his face and shoulders. The left side of his face was made up to match Geoff's. The right side was monotone skin color, his eyebrows, eyelashes, and lips all the same smooth tone as his cheeks and forehead. He wore the same colored contacts as Geoff. Chin carefully examined Lui's work and nodded.

"Close your eyes and hold your breath," Lui said. "Keep your mouth shut. I've got to spray this."

Geoff scrunched his eyelids together and sealed his lips. Lui coated his face with cold, wet spray. It dried instantly. Geoff's face felt as if it were covered in a thin layer of plastic.

Lui tapped Geoff's right cheek.

"This is waterproof," he said. "You won't even sweat through it." He snapped his case shut. "Where's that wig?"

Geoff looked around, not sure where he had left it.

Chin picked it off the bench behind Geoff and tossed it to Lui.

"Turn here," said Lui.

Geoff turned toward him again.

Lui arranged the blond strands over Geoff's dark curls.

Geoff turned to the mirror. A painted stranger looked back at him. Relief that he really was unrecognizable washed over him, making him sag from released tension.

"Let's go," Chin said. After the usual warm-up, they practiced performing before the holographic crowd. Chin insisted they start with the low-gravity, gliding walk onto the stage, perform the dance, and finish with a proper bow to the judges and the audience. They did the dance once and exited the stage.

Chin let go of Geoff and looked at Lui. The fat man grinned and gave a double thumbs-up.

"Costumes look good," Lui said. "We're in the money if the kid doesn't blow it."

"He won't." Chin cuffed Geoff on the shoulder, not hard enough to knock him off balance but hard enough to hurt. They repeated the dance, alternating between practice in the dance hall and performing before the virtual crowd.

By the end of their hour-and-a-half rehearsal, Geoff's face itched. Some spots burned. In the elevator down to the heavy deck, Geoff rubbed his stinging face. It had no effect on his discomfort. His eyes teared.

"Clean that off," ordered Chin.

Geoff walked toward the shower room, wondering how to wash off waterproof makeup.

Lui followed him and said, "Use this." He held a spritz bottle and a large jar of white cream.

Geoff sat with his eyes closed as Lui pulled off the little triangles and sprayed acrid liquid over the purple makeup.

"Wipe." Lui gave Geoff a handful of paper towels.

Geoff obediently ran them over his face, thankful the paper towels in this ritzy recreation center were soft, not like the cheap, scratchy ones at school. He tossed them in the recycle chute and looked in the mirror over the sinks. Light and dark purple streaks covered his face.

"Quit admiring yourself," growled Lui. "Take the rest off with this." He handed Geoff the jar of cream.

Geoff dipped one finger in it and carefully spread a stripe of cool whiteness over one cheek.

Lui gave an impatient grunt. He grabbed the jar back, scooped out a handful of cream, and slathered it across Geoff's face.

Geoff quickly closed his eyes and held his breath.

"Rub it in good and wash it off," ordered Lui.

Geoff rubbed and then waved his hands in the sink to activate the water. Next time, he'd wash it off in the shower.

That evening in the one-gravity recreation center, the Simba suit waiting for Geoff was a dark blue that shimmered with the same silver as his contacts.

Lui painted Geoff's face and neck silver. With dark blue, he drew a small star on the corner of Geoff's left jaw, a larger one on his left cheek, and an even larger one around his right eye. The same dark blue went on his lips, eyelashes, and eyebrows. It matched the wig that framed his face and hung in a styled mane between his shoulder blades.

Chin wore an identical costume, including his wig and contacts. Once again, he had painted half his face to match Geoff's.

This rehearsal also involved a lot of time in front of the virtual audience. Geoff found that tiring, even though he knew the crowd was not real. Spectators seemed to demand more in his performance—more perfection, more expression, more emotion. He stumbled to the shower, thankful it was Saturday. He wouldn't have to see Chin or Lui tomorrow.

Cheri surprised Geoff by joining him. She rarely came Saturday nights.

When she held out Geoff's towel, he pulled her close and murmured, "When I get away from Chin, I'll take you with me."

She stiffened and jerked away from him, her eyes wide with panic.

"Don't even think like that," she whispered. "It's impossible."

Surprised and hurt, he said, "I won't leave you here. That's something to look forward to."

"No." Cheri clapped her hands over her ears. "Don't say that. Hope kills you from the inside."

"Cheri—"

"Promise you won't say that," she insisted.

"Okay, I won't." He would save her whether or not she believed he could.

Geoff arrived home before 2300, exhausted and starved. He cleaned up half a bowl of salad while he watched the leftover sausages and macaroni with cheese warm up.

Barbara entered the kitchen and asked, "You hungry or something?"

"I didn't have enough supper," Geoff answered around his mouthful of lettuce and peppers. That was often the case when he worked. Having to rehearse for three hours on the same day made him really feel it.

"I think Mom wanted that for lunch tomorrow," Barbara said. "You should ask before you eat everything in sight."

Geoff swallowed and called, "Mom, is it okay if I have this salad?"

"Yes," Fallah answered from the living room.

Geoff made a face at Barbara and stuffed another forkful into his mouth. She left but returned when he took his hot meal from the cooker. He suspiciously watched her go to the lab for a glass of juice.

"Smells good," Barbara said.

"No," said Geoff. "You had yours." He knew she liked sausage as much as he did. He speared one of the sausages with his fork and held his plate close to guard the other.

She smiled and stepped closer to him.

"You could share," suggested Barbara. She took another step.

Geoff braced the small of his back against the counter and lifted his right foot. He held it at chest height in front of Barbara as he ate.

"For a shorty, you sure have big feet," Barbara said. She undid his shoe and pulled it off.

Geoff's muscles were beginning to protest, so he lowered his leg. Before his sister could take advantage of that and move in to steal his supper, he swung his left foot up to ward her off.

She laughed and pulled off his other shoe and then wriggled her fingertips along the bottom of his foot.

The slight tickle was not enough to make him drop his leg. He smiled and continued eating.

"Hey!" Barbara exclaimed. "Why isn't that working?"

"I've outgrown being ticklish," said Geoff.

"You don't outgrow tickles," declared Barbara. She held on to his foot and peeled off his sock.

Her tickling his bare skin made him grin but did not interfere with his meal.

"Oh, yeah?" asked Geoff. His feet had always been less sensitive than his ribs, and because Chin had knocked him around for giggling, neither made him laugh. He crammed the last bit of sausage into his mouth and put his plate on the counter. He jerked his foot from Barbara's hands as he lunged forward and down.

Geoff grabbed Barbara's ankles.

She shrieked and kicked.

He kept his hold. Using his greater strength and taking advantage of the half gravity, he knocked her to the floor. With Barbara on her back, Geoff sat on her lower legs and wedged his knee beneath the cupboard so she couldn't throw him off.

After she failed to toss him, she sat up and tickled his sides and ribs.

He swallowed his mouthful and grinned.

"I gotcha," Geoff said. He leaned forward, shifting his hands closer to the bottoms of her feet.

She shrieked and pulled at his shirt. Geoff gripped her legs more firmly with his own and released an ankle so he could tickle her.

Laughing, Barbara threw her arms around Geoff's middle and tried to pull him off her feet. She tugged him free of the cupboard, but he kept his hold on her legs, so they rolled backward into the center of the kitchen.

"Let...go!" demanded Barbara between gasps. She changed her hold to around his shoulders and heaved again.

Geoff chuckled and kept on tickling. It felt good to be the person in control for once.

"Please!" Barbara caught Geoff's upper left arm in both hands and gave a terrific wrench.

Geoff stopped tickling long enough to twist his arm free.

Sobs interspersed Barbara's laughs. She kicked weakly and hammered her fists on his back.

The fun went out of the tussle. Geoff let go of Barbara and stood up.

She wiped her eyes and glared up at him.

"Sorry," Geoff said very quietly. He hadn't meant to make her cry.

She nodded acceptance of his apology, and he went to his room. Its familiar furnishings and comfortable mess did not make him feel any better. The dance competition was less than a week away. If he was going to miss it, sometime in the next five days, his family had to leave most of their stuff and all their friends to go into witness protection with him. Because of him. If they would do that for him. He was just beginning to realize what an enormous move that was going to be.

It had better be worth it. For putting his family through that, he'd better have enough on Chin and Lui to jail them for a long time—longer than what the court would give for blackmailing him into dancing. He would tell Detective Jenn not to do anything until Chin and Lui said something more specific about smuggling people, even if it meant Geoff had to dance in the competition next weekend.

Chapter 32

Monday after school Geoff went to the arcade with Trevor and Rob. He kept a close eye on the time.

"Here," Geoff said to Trevor when the taller boy's gladiator got swallowed by a tiger. "Take over this one." He moved aside so Trevor could take the controls to Geoff's barbarian fighter.

"Why?" asked Trevor.

"I've got to go." Geoff lifted his hands from the game and stepped back. It was almost 1545.

Trevor took over controlling Geoff's character and asked, "Where?"

"To work," replied Geoff. "I gotta run." He could just make it to Chin's recreation center.

"It takes thirty seconds to walk across the room and sign in. You've got fifteen minutes."

Geoff was not listening. He hurried out of the arcade.

Trevor left the game and chased after him.

"What the hell's going on?" Trevor grabbed Geoff and spun him around.

"You know." Geoff jerked free and continued his brisk walk to the transit. "You think I'm really at work all the time?"

"What?" Trevor scowled and kept pace with Geoff. "What do I know?"

Geoff whispered, "Chin's project."

"Still?" Trevor looked skeptically at Geoff.

"Yeah. We're not done yet."

"Where're you going?" Rob called from the arcade entrance.

"Tell him I'm hungry or something," Geoff whispered. He ran to the opening transit doors.

Geoff wished he had not mentioned hunger. Saying the word triggered complaints from his stomach, as if his after-school snack hadn't existed. In the depths of his gym bag, Geoff discovered a battered energy bar rolling around with the Haynes Heet and deodorant stick. He opened it carefully so that he could catch every loose crumb, and then he licked them up.

Ugh. His hand tasted like sweaty game controls. Stars knew what was on it.

Geoff heard nothing of interest that evening. He went home disappointed about having nothing to tell Detective Jenn.

Tuesday, Geoff showed up at the studio apartment determined to follow through on his decision to stick with the dance until he heard firm details about the suspect shipment from Terra. Detective Jenn again waited with a snack.

"You don't have to feed me or try to bribe me with food," Geoff said.

"I know," said Jenn. "But I remember how hungry school makes a guy. Besides, I like the chance to sit and eat, and if you want to think of it as payment for information, what you've given us is well worth it."

"Really?" Geoff did not think the mundane details he'd spoken of, ranging from meanings in tattoos to how deliveries were arranged to which stores were untouchable for shoplifting, were big news.

"Yeah," said Jenn. "Have a burger and tell me how you're holding up."

"Fine." Geoff held his burger—a two-patty affair stuffed with bacon, cheese, tomato, and lettuce—with one hand while he dug a data card out of his pocket with the other. He slid it across the table and said, "I finished the list of every place I remember making deliveries to and added some I only heard about." Geoff paused, holding on to the card as if changing his mind about giving it to Jenn.

"I put on everything I know about Cheri, which isn't much, and how kids are chosen and recruited, too." He still was not sure he should have done that. After he had stayed up half the night and fretted about it and recorded all the information, he had almost fallen asleep in school that afternoon.

"Thank you." Jenn tucked it into a shirt pocket. "This could wait till you're in the safe house. Speaking of which—"

"I'm not going yet," Geoff interrupted. "This can't wait because if they find out about you, I won't live to get there, and I'm not going till I hear something for sure about that shipment, even if it's not till after it gets here." There. He'd said it. He couldn't change his mind now.

Detective Jenn contemplated Geoff's determined face for a moment and then asked, "Why? That means you might, or most likely will, have to go to the dance competition. It's only a few days away."

"Yeah." Geoff bit the inside of his lip. "If I'm going to turn everyone's life upside down, I want to make sure it's worth it, that those two really pay."

"I understand." Jenn nodded. "You realize your safety is my primary concern? I won't let you unnecessarily risk yourself."

"You can't stop me," Geoff pointed out. "If you take me away before I say to, I won't cooperate anymore. Besides, it's not like I can get into anything worse than I'm already in."

"Don't kid yourself, Geoff," said Jenn. "Those are two very dangerous, very powerful men."

"I know," Geoff said seriously. "But I don't think they'll do anything to me as long as I keep dancing. I'm worth a lot of money to them."

"Let's keep it that way." Jenn flattened his takeout container in preparation for tossing it down the recycle chute. "I'll be here again on Thursday. Come if you can. Don't if you think that's best. You can pop in here any time you need to. If things go bad, come here, call me to get your family, and then stay put. They can't track you if you're not moving."

───────────────

Geoff arrived at the evening rehearsal yawning. The dance hall felt freezing cold, so cold he still shivered fifteen minutes into the training session.

"Look alive," Chin growled when Geoff turned his arm the wrong way twice in the same round. "Put some oxygen in your brain."

Geoff tried, but he was so tired that his mistakes multiplied. Because Geoff did not get into his precise position when Chin did his turning Russian splits, his kick brushed by Geoff's head.

By the mid-practice break, Chin's patience was at its limit. He stalked out and slammed the door. Lui munched on his snack as if no one else existed. Geoff sat by the wall and wished he could go home.

"Stretch," ordered Lui.

Geoff worked through the whole series of leg and arm extensions before Chin returned to begin rehearsing the traditional dance. The first time Geoff lay across Chin's shoulders, he did not balance correctly and awkwardly slid off. When they did the dance again, Geoff made it to the third round without a major error. It wasn't easy though. The music seemed to play faster than usual. Partway through the third round, as Geoff swung in front of Chin and swayed right, his heel clicked on the floor a shade late. He hadn't done that in weeks!

Chin whirled and slapped Geoff across the face.

Pain streaked through Geoff's nose and into his head. He staggered backward and sideways, fell down, and lay with his burning face against the cold floor. A warm pool of blood spread around it.

Chin stomped off the dance floor.

"That's real good," said Lui. "Break his nose three days before the comp."

"It's not broken." Chin kicked a chair. It smashed against the wall and crashed onto the floor in a mangled tangle.

"*He* might be." In one of his deceptively fast moves, Lui got between Chin and the door. "You been dancing twenty-five years, and he's the only one you've found who can keep step with you—"

"*You* can," Chin interjected.

Lui continued as if he did not hear, "You need him. Why the hell'd you knock him out of orbit? He's obviously too tired to put his shoes on the right feet." He paused and then added, "I don't count. Go pick him up."

"Blast off." Chin pushed past Lui and left.

Lui looked across the room and huffed an exasperated breath out through his nostrils.

Geoff did not move until Lui pulled him up and pressed something soft against his face.

"Hold this," ordered Lui.

Geoff held the material, pinching his nose to stop the bleeding. He warily looked around for Chin.

"He's gone to vent his temper on something more durable than your face," Lui said.

Geoff nodded, relieved, and turned the cloth to find a dry spot.

"This's my shirt!" exclaimed Geoff.

"Yeah."

"It's wrecked." He'd have to throw it away.

"Nah," Lui said. "Just rinse it in cold water."

"Cold?"

"Yeah. Hot water cooks the blood onto the fabric." Lui pulled Goff's hands from his face and then pushed them back. "Put more pressure on."

"Can't," Geoff said. His face hurt. He stayed on the floor holding his stained shirt over his nose.

Lui grabbed Geoff by the armpits and half carried, half dragged him into the locker room. He sat Geoff on the bench with an ungentle bump.

"Use this," said Lui as he grabbed a handful of paper towels. He threw Geoff's shirt, which was now more red than blue, into a shower stall. "If that doesn't stop, you might need a doctor." He turned the cold water on Geoff's shirt and left.

Geoff pressed the reddening towels against his aching face and prayed his nosebleed would end quickly. He did not want to be subjected to the attentions of the Mad Medic.

The red flow from Geoff's nostrils had diminished to a trickle when Lui returned to the locker room.

The fat man peeked beneath Geoff's paper towel and said, "Maybe you'll live."

"I get to say that," a new voice said. The Mad Medic walked up to Geoff and set his doctor's bag on the bench.

"It's stopped," Geoff said. "I don't need you."

"Not your choice," said the medic. He put on surgical gloves, took out his medical scanner, and straddled the bench facing Geoff. "Drop your hands."

Geoff reluctantly did as ordered.

The doctor held his little machine a few centimeters in front of Geoff's face and watched its screen.

"You should have had a cold pack on your face, too," he said. He reached back and fished a U-shaped pack out of his bag. "Put this over your forehead and down each side of your face," he ordered as he activated it. "Keep it there ten minutes and then get out of here."

As the Mad Medic left with Lui, Geoff heard him say, "No serious damage. He might get nosebleeds easily for a while."

Geoff sat there, listening to the gentle spray of water on his shirt and feeling the pain spread from his face through his entire head. When he figured ten minutes were up, he showered and dressed.

He retrieved his shirt, amazed to see it was clean. The little bit of remaining blood ran out when he squeezed out the water. He wrapped it in his towel and stuffed it into his bag. He'd go home in his T-shirt...and freeze. He should have brought a jacket for the evening temperature drop.

Geoff slept so soundly that he did not wake up when his nosebleed began again. It was not until blood ran into his throat and he choked that he woke and realized his pillow was half red.

Swearing, Geoff grabbed a T-shirt off the floor. He held it against his nose as he tried to staunch the red flow. When it slowed, he took his pillow and T-shirt across the hall to the bathroom. He threw them both into the shower stall, peeled off the T-shirt he slept in, and tossed it in with them. Then he turned the shower on cold.

Geoff closed the toilet lid and sat on it. He held a cold, wet towel against his face and a fistful of tissue over his nose. The nighttime coolness made him shiver.

The door, which he had only halfway closed, slid fully open.

"Are you all right?" asked Fallah.

"Yeah," Geoff replied from under his towel.

"Let me see." She inspected his nose and added, "Looks like it's pretty well stopped. What's in the shower?"

"My pillow."

"I hope that's not hot water," said Fallah. She squeezed past Geoff to check.

"No," Geoff said as she opened the shower and turned the spray off.

"Why didn't you just put them in the washer to rinse?" asked his mother. "That uses less water."

"Didn't think of it." Geoff shivered again. He should have gotten his housecoat.

"What's up?" asked Tony from the doorway.

"Just a nosebleed," said Geoff. Didn't anybody here sleep at night? All he needed now was for Barbara to show up.

"I'll wash this stuff," said Fallah. "You get him another pillow."

In short order, Geoff was back in bed, and his parents were in their own room to resume their interrupted sleep. Geoff lay on his fresh pillow, looking at the odd shadows cast by his dimmed ceiling light and wondering if he dared go back to sleep. Would he die from blood loss if his nosebleed started up again? How long would that take? It would sure serve Chin right, wouldn't it?

With a smile at how perfectly ironic that would be, Geoff fell asleep. He did not stir until his music blared in the morning.

Geoff worried about the possibility of having a nosebleed at school for the first part of the day. During lunch, he found something new to fret about.

"You coming paintballing with us?" Trevor asked when Geoff sat at their cafeteria table.

"Where?" asked Geoff. "When?"

"Friday," answered Trevor. "We're taking the girls, those of us with girlfriends, and we'll all split into two teams. Losers buy the movie tickets."

Geoff shook his head and said, "You know I work Fridays." Not this Friday, though. Ice collected on his diaphragm as he realized that this Friday, in just fifty-four hours, he would be dancing in a Simba competition with Chin. That was much too soon, but he couldn't wait to be done.

"You always get at least one off a month," said Hans. "If we team up with Rob, we're sure to win."

"I should get next weekend off," Geoff said. "Mr. Manz is almost caught up." Next week, he would be free of the nightly practices.

That exhilarating thought buoyed Geoff's spirits for the rest of the day. Two nights of rehearsal left. Chin would kill him if he didn't get both dances perfect today.

As Geoff walked through the recreation center, he mentally reviewed the reasons he had to perform the best he could. If he danced well, Chin wouldn't knock his head off or touch Barbara or hurt Cheri or force one of Geoff's friends into a bad deal. If Chin was in a good mood, he might talk to Lui about the suspicious shipment coming from Terra next week. If that happened, Geoff could send the two of them to prison.

Mentally bolstered, Geoff strode to Chin's office to change. It was locked.

Lui stepped into the doorway of the dance hall and said, "He canceled his classes the rest of the week. Your stuff's in the locker room."

Geoff followed Lui into the dance hall. Chin was there, dancing by himself in a bright-blue Simba suit. Beads of sweat dotted his face. Geoff found a matching blue suit and tights in the locker room. He changed and went to warm up.

Lui turned on the virtual stage and audience. He had played it longer each rehearsal, and Geoff was now so accustomed to the noisy crowd he hardly noticed it. He finished stretching and looked at Chin for a sign they were going up to the quarter-gravity deck.

Chin nodded and tossed the hooded robe to Geoff.

On the light deck, they paused at the side of the stage, and Chin said, "It's showtime. Get it right."

"Yeah." Geoff took a deep breath and let it out slowly. He could do this. He wasn't too tired today. He *had* to do this. Nervousness made him tense, but he started the character dance on the beat. He blew the first simple side sway, but as far as he could tell, everything else went well.

When it ended and they bowed and walked offstage together, Chin said, "Fix the beginning. Do it again." They did it over… and over…and over.

When they finally returned to the heavy deck, Geoff flopped onto the floor for a rest. He closed his eyes and wiped his face with his towel, and then he did a few stretches to keep Lui from yelling at him. The click of taps alerted Geoff to Chin's approach.

Geoff opened his eyes and turned his head so he could look up. Chin had better not say anything about expecting a better performance. Geoff had it nearly perfect—the steps and the body language, down to the little finger movements and head tosses, the eyelash bats and shoulder rolls, the flounces and stomps and struts.

"You did pretty good today," Chin said. "Keep it up and you'll earn—" Chin broke off and whirled around to face Lui.

Curious, Geoff looked at the fat man as well. He stood beside the chairs, whistling as he packed the wrappers from his snack into his bag.

Chin spun back to Geoff, his face creased in a fierce scowl.

"Why didn't you say anything?" he demanded.

"About what?" asked Geoff.

"Is that why you sit here?" Chin leaned forward over Geoff. "So you can eavesdrop?"

Chapter 33

"Huh?" Geoff couldn't think of anything to say to keep Chin from killing him.

"I know how loud that isn't," said Chin, pointing to Lui. "He can't whistle above a whisper. You've been listening to us."

Geoff surprised himself by getting more angry than frightened at Chin's accusation.

"That's not my fault." Geoff jumped to his feet and glared up at Chin. "This is *your* ion-blasted dance room. You should know its acoustics."

Chin looked surprised. He said, "If this place isn't full of kids, it's empty. It's either noisy or silent, never quiet." He frowned again. "Some of what we say is private family business. You been talking?"

"No." Geoff put Detective Jenn out of his mind, thought determinedly about his silence among his friends, and stared into Chin's black eyes. "I'm sure you'd've heard if I did." He held the older man's eyes long enough to see belief and then turned away and reached down for his juice.

"Yeah," said Chin. "I would've. Let's go." He strode to the center of the holographic stage.

Geoff felt like fainting. Would Chin really let it drop there? Or was he waiting to think up something really terrible to do to Geoff?

Or maybe he wouldn't do anything until after this weekend's show. Stars, was it too late to try to get out of dancing in the competition? There was no hope Chin or Lui would say anything incriminating now. Maybe Geoff should call Detective Jenn and ask if his family could move into the safe house tonight.

"Move it," ordered Chin.

Geoff joined him at the side of the stage.

As Lui played the preliminary bars, they walked out and took their starting positions for the traditional dance. They stood pressed close together, hands on each other's backs. Geoff no longer noticed how erotically close they were. He only paid attention to his stance, the details of his position, and his expression.

As they had done with the character piece, they rehearsed the entire performance without stopping. Lui occasionally called out a comment between the cheers and applause of the virtual audience, but it was not until after Chin and Geoff took their curtain call that he ran clips of the performance to point out places he thought needed improvement.

It was demanding work. Geoff went through his cool-down exercises wishing he did not have to hurry off to work at the arcade between rehearsals. He had wished that every day since Chin had ordered the double practices. It gave him no time to relax or eat a decent supper.

As if he could read Geoff's mind, Chin said, "Don't bother going to work the rest of this week. Manz doesn't expect you back there till next Saturday. You got two hours."

Geoff went to shower, wishing he could go home and wondering where he could eat supper without risking meeting someone who thought he was working in the back office of the arcade. The hot water felt so good that he considered just lying down on the tiles and not going anywhere.

"You've got bubbles in your curls," Cheri said. She reached into the shower stall and pushed Geoff's head into the stream of water.

He splashed water at her and said, "You shouldn't sneak up on people."

"Don't get me wet," Cheri squealed. "Or you wouldn't get supper till everything dries."

"Supper? Where?"

"Here, of course," answered Cheri.

Geoff looked around the locker room.

Cheri slapped his wet chest and said, "In the center, silly. The restaurant. You get supper and a massage, and then we'll go to the hot tub—"

"No massage," said Geoff. He wasn't having any stranger's hands all over him.

"Whatever you want."

When Cheri guided Geoff back to the dance hall shortly before 2030, he felt relaxed and rested. An evening with her was more fun than going out with the guys. He changed into the waiting lime-green Simba suit and entered the dance hall.

Lui sat sprawled across his chairs. As Geoff began stretching, Chin walked in wearing sun-bright yellow.

"Do called," Lui said. He glanced at Geoff and raised his eyebrows questioningly.

Chin made a come-on motion with his hand.

"The product from Shanks is good," reported Lui.

"Going out?" Chin asked.

"Starting tonight."

Chin nodded and joined Geoff in warming up. He worked the evening practice the same as the earlier one. They ended early, with Geoff being sent to the shower ten minutes before 2200. He made it home in record time.

"Well, for once, you're not late," Barbara said.

"Mr. Manz let me off a little early," said Geoff. "We're almost caught up." He got himself a plate of leftover casserole and went to his room. He could do homework while he ate.

Geoff thought about calling Detective Jenn to tell him Do's message about the drugs from Shanks. He did not dare call from his own phone, though. He would have to deliver the information in person when he met the detective at that little apartment tomorrow after school.

A good plan, but it did not work out. Geoff's English teacher held him up at the end of the day and gave him a lecture on completing assignments on time. When Geoff finally got out of there, he found Trevor, Hans, and Rob waiting in the hall.

"We're going blading," Rob announced with his hint of drawl.

"So what are you doing here?" asked Geoff.

"Take a walk," retorted long-haired Hans. "*Without* a suit."

"First, we're going to the mall for lunch," Trevor said. He wore silver chains in his ears and around his neck to highlight the silver stitching on his a burgundy shirt. "You could come with us before you go to work."

"Right," said Geoff. In other words, they wanted their hand to help acquire lunch, and he couldn't refuse without creating hard feelings, having to explain why, and possibly getting into a fight. "Let's blow jets then."

The food court was crowded enough to make Geoff's job easy. He quickly lifted an assortment of snacks, burgers, and treats.

"I get that double-cheese one," Geoff said as he joined the other boys at their table. He wolfed it down and left.

When Geoff went to the locker room off the dance hall to change, he found his costume for the character dance. He dressed in the purple suit and contacts but hesitated to put on the blonde wig without knowing if Lui intended to do the face makeup.

As Geoff indecisively stood there, Lui came in carrying his large kit and said, "Sit." He straddled the bench, facing Geoff, and set the case between them.

Lui picked up the tube of purple paint, frowned, and put it back. He dug through his case and found what he wanted beneath a tray holding false eyelashes and fingernails. It looked like a fat screen stylus.

"Don't move," Lui ordered. He lifted the strange instrument toward Geoff's face.

Not knowing what Lui was up to, Geoff leaned back.

"I said hold still." Lui grabbed a fistful of Geoff's curls with his left hand and touched the tip of his tool to Geoff's right eyebrow. It felt hot.

"What are you doing?" asked Geoff. Lui held Geoff's hair so tightly the pain made his eyes water.

"Just trimming a little," said Lui. "You got enough eyebrows for two guys." He did Geoff's other eyebrow and let go of his hair.

Geoff lifted his hands to rub at the heat above his eyes.

"Don't touch," warned Lui. He took a tiny vial of bright-blue oil and smeared a little beside Geoff's eyebrows. "Gonna be fun making the paint stick to that," he muttered.

As Lui retrieved the tube of purple paint, Geoff rubbed his scalp. It felt like most of his hair had been halfway pulled out.

"How'm I supposed to explain an eyebrow job?" asked Geoff, turning toward the mirrors. He got a glimpse of truncated eyebrows that made his eyes seem even larger and farther apart before Lui's hand landed on the side of his face and turned it forward again.

"Tell'em your girlfriend wanted you to have two eyebrows," Lui said indifferently. "Or you lost a bet or did it on a dare or something. Hold still." He quickly finished Geoff's makeup and sent him to warm up.

Chin was there, also dressed in costume.

As they rode the elevator to the light deck, Chin said, "Watch."

Barbara appeared in his wrist com's holoview. She sat beside Nadine on the transit, chatting and oblivious to everyone else. They were probably on their way home.

Beneath his makeup, Geoff went white.

"For the next three days, someone's going to be real close to her," said Chin. "You don't perform as well as I know you can, and she'll feel it before you get out of the center. You'd better not off orbit the show."

Geoff did not say anything. He had clenched his jaw so tightly he couldn't speak.

"Got it?" asked Chin.

"Yeah," Geoff breathed through a forced exhalation.

"Okay, let's do it for real." Chin inspected Geoff's makeup and clothing. He touched one of the little triangles on Geoff's face.

"This one's loose," he said. "If it falls off, for that matter, if anything ever happens to your costume during a performance, ignore it and keep dancing. Act like you don't even realize something's wrong."

"What do you mean for real?" asked Geoff.

"Follow me." Chin led the way into the dance hall. "Entrance." Chin held out his right hand.

Geoff clasped it with his left.

Chin opened the door and stepped out. If he had not kept a firm grip on Geoff, he would have gone alone.

Geoff gasped and only moved when Chin pulled on his arm.

Thirty chairs faced the dance floor, and each one held a person. Their presence felt real and immediate, more intimidating than the holographic audience Geoff had become accustomed to. Fear rolled through his insides and collected in a cold lump beneath his lungs. He was scared to perform in front of all these people. He was even more terrified of what would happen if he did not dance well.

"Take a deep breath," ordered Chin. He squeezed Geoff's hand.

The pain spurred Geoff to move his diaphragm. As Geoff filled his lungs a second time, the preliminary music began.

"Think only about what you have to do," Chin instructed. "Nothing exists but the floor, the music, and me." With his free hand, he grabbed Geoff's chin and turned his face up.

Geoff had no choice but to nod acceptance of the larger man's directions. They walked onto the dance floor together, but they were looking in opposite directions. Chin smiled at the crowd. Geoff looked for the taped X on the floor that marked his starting point. He positioned his feet and gazed at the wall to his left. For the first part of the dance, he had to pretend to be unaware of Chin. He would do the same with everyone else in the room.

Acutely conscious that someone shadowed Barbara, Geoff made sure he counted the beats to begin precisely on the mark. To his surprise, Chin counted just loud enough for him to hear. Once the dance started, Geoff's nervousness receded slightly. He found the gasps, laughter, and applause intimidating, but he could sense Chin's pleasure at the audience's reaction.

Geoff got through his first show in front of a live audience with just one minor mistake. He heaved a sigh of relief as he stepped out of the final pose.

"Don't forget how to exit," Chin muttered below the applause and whistles.

"Didn't," said Geoff just as quietly. He had not forgotten. He just hadn't been sure if Chin wanted to do the exit they had practiced.

As they walked to the front of the stage and bowed, Geoff realized he knew two of the people there. The Mad Medic sat in the front row. Cheri sat two rows back. Beneath his purple paint, Geoff blushed. Thank the stars no one from his real life would ever see him do this.

The performance finished. Chin basked in the praise of his friends. Geoff stood against the far wall, sipped his juice, and hoped the noisy crowd would keep Chin occupied for a long time.

It was not long enough. In five minutes, everyone was gone, and Chin blasted Geoff for his mistake. They went through the character dance a couple of more times and then returned to the heavy deck. Chin ordered Geoff into the shower room to change. They would have a performance for the traditional dance, too.

Lui followed Geoff. He pulled the little triangles off Geoff's face. None were loose. He sprayed the smelly stuff that dissolved the paint and left.

Geoff finished cleaning up and looked at his eyebrows.

They were half gone! Geoff set two fingers on his forehead, filling the space between his brows. That space used to be narrower than his baby finger. Geoff scowled at his eyebrows, now as much thinner as they were shorter. Lui had made what was left of them finer, arched, and with a slightly winged outside edge. Girls' eyebrows!

"Ion-blasted, down-orbit mutant bait!" Geoff slammed both fists onto the counter between the sinks. He hurt his hands, and his eyebrows did not regrow. He stomped around the locker room a few times and then peeled off the purple suit.

The dark blue, shimmery silver one lay on the bench. When he had it on over his tights, he left the top gathered around his waist and searched in his bag for a snack. It was after suppertime, and his stomach was letting him know it.

"What the hell?" demanded Lui when he returned a minute later. "You're not even dressed!"

"I'm hungry," Geoff said around his mouthful of candy bar.

"Sit." Lui pointed to the bench beside his makeup case. He touched his wrist phone and said, "Bring me a high-calorie strawberry protein shake."

Geoff popped the rest of his snack into his mouth and sat to get his face painted for the second dance.

"How'm I supposed to do this while you're chewing?" grumbled Lui. Despite his complaint, he quickly covered Geoff's face and shoulders in silver, drew on the dark stars, and applied lipstick and mascara.

When they entered the dance hall, Lui pointed to the plastic milk shake container on one of the chairs and said, "Drink that."

"What?" asked Chin from beside the mirrors.

"Kid's starving," answered Lui.

Chin grunted and said, "Hurry it up."

Geoff tentatively sucked on the wide straw. The shake was creamy and thick but liquid enough to pour. He took the lid off and gulped. As he did, he noticed this dance hall was now filled with empty chairs. He burped as he walked over to the dance area.

"That's not allowed during the performance," said Chin. "Let's go."

The music began. They stepped close together, legs and chests touching. Geoff tilted his head back to look into Chin's eyes—silver contacts hiding humorless, dark windows to an evil soul. Geoff shivered.

Chin called a break when spectators began coming in.

Geoff hid in the locker room. Now that he knew what to expect, nervousness made him tremble. He did not want anyone to see him dance, but he knew he had to do it. The only positive Geoff could think of was the complete face paint Lui had done meant no one who didn't already know Geoff was Chin's partner would be able to figure out it was him. Still, Geoff stumbled when Chin ordered him back into the dance hall.

"Get it together," growled Chin. He draped his arm across Geoff's shoulders.

Knowing Chin considered their entrance part of the show, Geoff wrapped his left arm around Chin's waist. It looked friendly, but it didn't feel that way. As always, Chin radiated heat. The thin material of his costume exuded sweaty dampness. Geoff knew his own was the same.

The first strains of music pulled Geoff's attention to the dance. In a conditioned response to the heavy beat, Geoff's heart sped up. His mind called up the opening movements of the traditional dance.

His eyes glued to Chin's silver gaze, his hands apparently magnetically stuck to Chin's body, Geoff performed the dance as if his life depended on it. Barbara's did.

The audience loved it. After the final bow, they mobbed Chin with congratulations.

Geoff escaped to the shower room. Temporarily safe in that tiled quiet, he slumped onto the bench and shook.

He was almost done with this. Two more nights, and he only had to do one dance each evening. It would be a snap. He could do it in his sleep. He *did* do it in his sleep just about every night.

Cheri burst into the shower room and exclaimed, "Wow! Was that ever wonderful! You should be in the money for sure."

Geoff's face reddened beneath the silver paint.

"I don't want to talk about it," he said.

"Whatever you want," agreed Cheri. "I'm supposed to help you get that off and take you to supper. We have to be back here in an hour and a half." She picked up the jar of cold cream and held it out to Geoff.

"Not that." He picked up the little spray bottle of smelly stuff. "This goes on first. Just spray a little." He gave it to her, grabbed a couple of the soft paper towels, and closed his eyes.

When his face was clean, Geoff leaned toward the mirrors over the sinks and examined his eyebrows. He ran his fingers over the unfamiliar arches.

"How long will it take for these to grow back?" he asked.

"Depends how you shaped them," replied Cheri. "If you just shaved them, a few days. If you lased them off, three or four weeks."

"I don't know what he did," Geoff said

"Well, what did he use?"

"A fat pen." Geoff looked in Lui's makeup case and pulled out the round instrument.

"That?" Cheri took it for a closer look. "It's permanent."

Chapter 34

"Permanent!" Anger burned through Geoff in a hot rush. "I've got permanent girly eyebrows?"

"That's a guys' style," Cheri said. "A girl would make them finer and more arched. They look nice. That winged end is the latest in eyebrow sculpting. Real trendy." She touched her forefinger to the space between his brows. "It makes your beautiful baby browns look even bigger."

Geoff pushed her away.

"I don't want to be trendy," he muttered as he took off his suit. "I want my own eyebrows."

"You can always reshape them," said Cheri. "You've still got lots to work with."

"They'd get even smaller," objected Geoff. He did not care what she said at that point. He was mad at Lui for doing this to him, and he wanted to stay mad.

Not that taking it out on Cheri would do him any good, he realized as he showered. He had to testify in court to get back at Lui and Chin.

"I'm sorry," Geoff said when he got out of the water and into a towel. "I shouldn't be mad at you for something he did."

They had supper in the dimly lit, quiet side of the recreation center's restaurant and then splashed in the hot tub until Geoff had to return to the dance hall.

Chin wanted to practice the dances only a couple of more times. After that, they spent three-quarters of an hour doing an exercise routine similar to the stretches Geoff had been ordered to do every day.

"That's it," Chin said when they finished. "Be here tomorrow at seventeen."

Geoff nodded and went to change. He'd make it home tonight at his usual Thursday evening time. Maybe he'd be lucky, and no one would notice his eyebrows.

He was not lucky.

"What did you do to yourself?" Barbara squealed when Geoff walked into the apartment. "They're *pretty.*"

"I lost a bet," said Geoff. "They are not." The last thing he needed was to be called pretty. He resisted the urge to hold his hands over his face. That would only make things worse.

Tony turned from the holoview, and Fallah came out of the kitchen to look at Geoff. He reddened. Too bad he had to go past everyone to get to his room.

"Wondered when you'd do something about them," Tony said. He turned back to his show.

"They look good on you," said Fallah.

"What did you bet?" Barbara asked before Geoff could answer their mother.

"That my sister could keep her mouth shut for five minutes," answered Geoff.

Barbara looked stunned, and then she said, "You did not. It was probably on sports."

Geoff escaped to his room. He had homework to do. Maybe it would keep him from thinking about the competition. Tomorrow.

He got his school assignments done, sort of, but did not manage to stop worrying about everything that could go wrong with the show. After he lay in bed for an hour, watching the numbers change on his clock, Geoff decided the only way to get some sleep so that he *didn't* blow his performance was to concentrate on something positive. By thinking about what Detective Jenn had told him about moving the whole family to a new place and the possibility he might be able to get Cheri rescued, Geoff finally got to sleep. The Simba followed, and he woke in the morning as tangled in his bedcovers as if he had been dancing in them.

School that day alternately dragged and flew past. By the end of the Geoff's last class, his sense of time felt totally out of kilter.

"You're sure off orbit," said Trevor as they strolled down the hall.

"Nervous," Geoff whispered. He glanced around. The corridor was busy but not crowded. None of their friends were near. He lowered his voice even more and added, "That project goes soon."

"Good luck," Trevor whispered back.

"Thanks." Geoff did not look at Trevor. He remembered Detective Jenn's warning about not being able to protect friends from the law, and Trevor would be incriminated when Geoff told of some of the things he'd been drawn into.

Orbiting meteors gathered in Geoff's belly as he rode across the station to Chin's recreation center. Once past its double doors, Geoff was surprised at the number of kids there. He felt like the place should be empty, with everyone distracted by the competition.

Unsure of where to go, he stopped at Chin's office. Lui waited inside. He handed Geoff the purple tights that went with his costume for the character dance and a green practice suit.

Lui said, "Change and warm up in here," and left.

Geoff did his stretches, but he was so tense his muscles would not extend properly. When Geoff had been there for fifteen minutes, Chin walked in.

"We're onstage at 1935," he said. "We have to sign in an hour before that, so we've got half an hour to get ready. Follow me."

They went to an empty meeting room to finish warming up and rehearse the character dance. Chin kept Geoff so busy he did not have time to worry about anything but performing properly.

When they went back to the office, Lui handed Chin and Geoff each a sandwich and a drink.

Geoff did not want to eat. His stomach felt tied in knots. He sipped and recognized the taste of a protein shake.

"Eat," ordered Chin. "You're not fainting from hunger later."

"You've got to finish that in five minutes," Lui said. "Get that suit off and put your clothes on while you chew. Keep your tights on if you don't want to be bare-assed in the dressing room." He waited impatiently while Geoff self-consciously put his clothes on over his tights.

"Sit there." Lui pointed to one of the chairs beside the desk. "I got to make you up." He paused and then asked, "Unless you want your own face broadcast across the system?"

"No," said Geoff. He sat where Lui wanted him.

The fat man applied tiny dabs of clear gel at the outsides of Geoff's eyes, just below the corners of his mouth, and at the sides of his face. As it dried, it shrank, tightening Geoff's skin and reshaping his features. He wrinkled his face at the uncomfortable sensation.

"Hold still," ordered Lui. He quickly smoothed a pale foundation over Geoff's face, making it several shades lighter. "Close your eyes." A spatter of fine droplets felt cold at first but quickly warmed and dried. Lui finished off Geoff's disguise with a brush of reddish-orange mascara over his eyebrows and lashes and a matching wig.

Geoff shifted sideways, trying to see himself in the mirror on the wall behind Lui. The tiny drops made freckles across his face.

"Undo your shirt and drop it off your shoulders," Lui instructed. Chin handed Lui a roll of duct tape. He ripped off an arm's length of it and said, "Slouch forward."

When Geoff hunched forward, Lui stuck the tape across Geoff's upper chest and over the outside of his shoulders.

"What's that for?" asked Geoff.

"Keep anyone from recognizing the way you walk. Get your shirt on."

As Geoff awkwardly—the tape hampered his movements—pulled it back into place, the desk holoview lit. It expanded, filling a quarter of the room with a close-up image of Barbara and Nadine eating popcorn. The message was clear: someone was close enough to harm Barbara if Geoff did not perform adequately.

Geoff fumbled with the seal strip on the front of his shirt. His fingers felt too fat and clumsy to control properly.

"Your name's Robin," Chin said. "Since you're underage, you don't have to give a last name. Let's go." He handed Geoff a costume bag and picked up a second one.

Lui took his makeup case. They escorted Geoff up in the private elevator, through the quarter-g recreation complex, and out an unfamiliar exit.

In the transit, Geoff sat against the wall with Chin beside him. Lui overflowed the seat in front of them. Geoff stared at the advertising holograms and listened to the two men talk about unfamiliar people, paired names Geoff deduced were teams in the dance competition. He absently rubbed at the irritation on his face.

Chin slapped his hand.

"Leave it," he said.

The ride seemed endless, but in less than fifteen minutes, Chin led Lui and Geoff into a performing arts theater. He and Lui waved at the camera crew recording teams of dancers entering the lobby.

The woman at the registration desk obviously knew Chin and Lui.

They exchanged friendly greetings before Lui pulled Geoff forward and said, "This is Robin. I'll sign him in."

"You're under twenty-one?" the woman asked Geoff.

He nodded.

"You know you are here under Lui Ko's sponsorship, and he is responsible for your actions and your safety?"

Geoff nodded again. What kind of a question was that?

"Good luck, gentlemen." The woman smiled and turned to the next team waiting to register.

"This way." Chin went down a wide flight of stairs. They ended in a dim hallway lined with curtained windows and intersections with several narrower corridors. Chin strode down one of them with three doors labeled dressing rooms. He opened the second one and walked into the room. Lui pushed Geoff in behind Chin.

Given a choice, Geoff would have stayed in the hall or turned around and run. The room was no larger than the shower room beside Chin's dance classroom. Two walls held counters with mirrors. One of the counters had three sinks in it. The other two walls and a half wall that bisected the area were covered in bars holding clothes hangers full of costumes and clothing and shelves crammed with more of the same plus a variety of bags. It took Geoff a minute to assimilate those inanimate aspects of his surroundings. The first sixty seconds, he saw nothing but a crowd of male bodies in various stages of dress, undress, costume, and makeup.

Geoff's keepers elbowed their way to the corner with no mirrors. They shoved Geoff into the tiny space against the walls. Lui stood between him and the rest of the dancers.

"Get your suit on." Lui handed the purple costume to Geoff.

Thankful he already wore his tights, Geoff took off his shirt, aware that Chin, like many of the others, was stripping and pulling on his tights as he chatted. It made Geoff think about his being given the chance to arrive partly dressed. Nice did not describe Chin or Lui in any way. Maybe they were trying to keep him from being too overwhelmed to dance.

Lui grabbed one end of the tape and jerked it off Geoff's chest.

"Blast off," Geoff gasped. Good thing he hadn't had much hair on his chest. He had even less now.

"No cussing the instructor," Lui said. He let Geoff get his costume halfway up his torso before he ordered him to stand still and get his makeup done. In short order, Lui stripped off Robin's face and covered Geoff's in purple. He took his time completing the rest, gossiping as he worked.

Once Geoff and Chin were in costume, the three of them went to a large, five-sided practice hall. At the far end, costumed dancers took turns performing to their music, having a final rehearsal before they went onstage. Scattered throughout the rest of the hall, dancers stretched or practiced segments of their routines.

The variety of costumes was as great as the variations in music, yet both shared fundamental commonality with all the others. Each song was based on the original Simba tune. Every costume consisted of a stretchy suit, tight over the torso and loose in the legs, but some had drifting pieces attached. Others were printed with pictures or patterns to create specific images. One couple wore black imprinted with white skeletons. Another portrayed a hunter and a large cat. Others were covered in tiny patterns that were impossible to look at with sober eyes.

When Chin and Lui walked in, half of the performers stopped to stare at them. The remainder stopped to see who everyone else was looking at. Chin smiled and pointed to a small space at one side of the hall.

"Over there," he said to Geoff. He called hello to people he knew as Geoff self-consciously followed him to his chosen spot. They began working through their usual warm-up and stretching routine.

Geoff quickly became aware that Chin was making sure they moved in unison...and that he loved the attention of the other performers. When someone asked if Chin wanted a turn on the rehearsal floor, he said no. The others obviously wanted a preview of Chin and his new partner's show, and their frustration at not getting one showed. Chin seemed to enjoy their disappointment. He continued the slow exercises until it was time to go backstage.

Another narrow hallway, one crowded with twenty men and their coaches, led to the dim rear and wings of the stage where the noise from the audience overpowered conversation. The crowd of dancers sorted itself according to the order they were listed in the program. Then the duos and their coaches gathered in the wings from which they would enter the stage.

Sandwiched between Chin's muscled solidness and Lui's soft bulk, Geoff grew more and more nervous. He was not the only one. Some of the performers chattered to relieve the tension. One young man threw up. Geoff turned away, holding his breath and hoping he would not do the same.

"Don't even think it," Chin whispered without taking his eyes off the show onstage.

Geoff shifted sideways a little, trying to see past the edge of the curtain and get a look at the stage. He managed to see a brief portion of the dance, part of round six from the music. To his surprise, he easily spotted several errors in execution of the steps.

Lui leaned down and said in Geoff's ear, "That is what you'd better not do."

Geoff nodded. He could perform the complicated choreography Chin and Lui had dreamed up. The question was, could he do it here? In this place packed with real dancers who would critique every move? In front of a panel of judges doing the same? Before a noisy audience creating a wild, feverish atmosphere? What insane idea made him think he could do this? He should have told Detective Jenn to get him away earlier, even if it meant Chin and Lui avoided prison.

As Geoff told himself that, he changed his mind. Those two had to pay for what they had done to him and threatened to do to Barbara. He was going to make them pay, and if he had to do it by putting on the performance of his life in front of thousands of people, billions if you counted the ones at home watching the holoview, he would do it. Geoff concentrated on his anger, drawing strength and passion from it.

Too quickly, a familiar, lighthearted version of the Simba filled the theater. Chin took Geoff's hand. They walked onstage together. A new stage, charged with emotion radiated by thousands of spectators. It was like walking into a wall of expectation.

At Geoff's mark, Chin released him and went the additional two steps to his own starting position. Safely anonymous behind his face paint, Geoff gazed into the darkness hiding the audience and waited for the preliminary music to end.

It did. The dance music replaced it. Count along with Chin's barely audible count—seven, eight, begin.

He'd done it right. Chin wouldn't kill him onstage. Concentrate. He had to do the whole dance correctly—through the laughter at his flouncing, the chuckles generated by his flirty eyelash batting, and the cheers for the tricky turns. They froze in place on the final drumbeat.

Automatically, because Chin and Lui had made him practice it, Geoff held the final pose until he felt Chin move. Then, holding hands, they walked to the front of the stage to bow.

"This's the greatest feeling in the world, kid," Chin murmured. "Thousands of people saying they love you, what you did."

Because he knew Chin expected it, Geoff nodded, but he actually felt more threatened than adored. It was a relief to get offstage and into the relative quiet of the group of dancers behind the backstage door. Their backslapping congratulations for an excellent show drew expansive acceptance from Chin and mumbled thanks from Geoff.

"Hey, Robin." A tall, slender man dressed as an orange-skinned alien punched Geoff's shoulder. "You shy or something?"

Geoff looked up at him and frowned but did not say anything.

Chin chuckled. The next pair of dancers began their routine. Most of the ones in the room, all of whom had finished their dances, turned to watch the holoview mounted against one wall.

"You coming to the party?" asked a squarely built man dressed in silver and black and holding a curly black wig.

"Not tonight," replied Chin. He turned from the holoview, apparently satisfied the duo shown there was not a threat to his standing, and said, "*We're* on again tomorrow."

"You're sure of that?" asked someone else. Derisive comments made it plain everyone in the room was certain of that.

"Definitely," Lui said from the doorway. "We're in first place right now. Will probably finish third or fourth. We're in the finals." He made a "come here" gesture to Geoff.

"You don't gotta go yet," said the orange alien as Geoff walked to Lui.

Geoff ignored him.

Chin said, "Blast off."

Geoff followed Lui's wide back through the maze of corridors to the dressing room. With so many dancers in the practice gym and by the stage, he expected it to be empty. If anything, it was even more crowded than before.

"How many—" Geoff did not finish the question, but Lui answered.

"There are fifty-seven teams in this class," he said. "So twice that many dancers plus their instructors, trainers, and managers." Lui pushed his way to the corner. He shoved Geoff against the walls and then turned to where his makeup case rested on a shelf of the half wall. It was locked in place by an internally generated force field that released only after it registered voice and handprints.

"Handy trick," said a man dressing beside the row of hanging clothes and costumes.

"Worth what it cost," Lui said. He turned back to Geoff.

Geoff pulled a triangle off his face and handed it to the fat man. He quickly removed the other two and looked for paper towels to wipe the paint off his face.

"Here." Lui handed Geoff a soft towel. "Close your eyes." In short order, he removed the costume makeup and replaced it with Robin's freckled visage.

Lui then escorted Geoff out of the theater and onto a transit car.

"I'm sure I can find my own way back," Geoff said.

"You don't have access to Chin's office." Lui plopped his wide backside onto a seat. "And Robin has to disappear where no one else can see."

"Everyone in the dressing room saw," said Geoff.

"Not all of them," answered Lui. "And it's like any locker room. Phones and cameras don't work in there. They'd have a hard time trying to find you."

They rode back to the recreation center without speaking further. Geoff wore his own face again before 2100.

"Go home," Lui ordered as he repacked his kit. "Be here tomorrow at 1730. We do it again."

Chapter 35

The next morning, Geoff slept until nine. He lay in bed and tried to doze off again but could not relax. Nervousness about the dance competition that evening kept him awake. Frustrated, Geoff threw back his covers and got up. He might as well stretch.

Unwilling to put up with the difficulties of trying to exercise in his room, Geoff went to the recreation center beside his school. He felt like he had snuck away from home, even though that had not been his intention. Having one parent in the shower and not running into the other on his way out had been a happy coincidence.

Tony and Fallah were both tending the garden when Geoff returned.

"Where were you so early?" asked Tony.

"The gym," replied Geoff, stopping beside them.

Fallah eyed Geoff's flushed, sweat-damp face and nodded.

"That's odd," she said. "You're not usually that ambitious on the weekend."

Geoff shrugged and said, "I couldn't get back to sleep. What's for breakfast?"

"Whatever you fix for yourself," answered Fallah. She returned to her careful pruning of a cherry tomato bush.

Geoff looked at the miniature orange tree. It still held a few sweet fruits. He ate one as he got himself a large bowl of Comet Crunch and milk. Then he parked on the couch in front of the morning cartoons. He might as well enjoy what he could of the day.

"You work today?" Tony asked.

Geoff almost answered no but then remembered work was his cover while he danced.

"Yeah." Geoff swallowed his mouthful of cereal and added, "At seventeen."

"You'll have time to clean your room," said Fallah. "After you help your father seed a new batch of carrots."

"Peas, too?" asked Geoff. He remembered as he spoke that he and his family would not be there to see the new plants sprout. Almost certainly, by next weekend, they would be hidden wherever families in witness protection were kept. If they agreed to go with him.

"We can fit a few in," Tony said. "It'll be a couple of weeks till we can plant a whole patch."

"It can wait," said Geoff. He looked in his bowl to see what was wrong with his cereal. It had no taste.

Breakfast done, Geoff unrolled a meter-long germination strip for the carrots. It looked like masking tape, paper thin and as wide as his baby finger, but when he gently brushed the inside, short fibers stood up to create a fuzzy seedbed. He positioned the tiny seeds with tweezers, carefully depositing them two centimeters apart.

"What's her name?" asked Tony.

"Huh?" Geoff looked up and blushed.

Tony smiled and said, "You're so distracted lately, there's got to be a girl."

Geoff blushed harder. He had to answer something, and he couldn't explain the dance competition.

"Cheri."

"When do we get to meet her?" asked Fallah.

"Uh, don't know." Geoff looked back down. He couldn't imagine introducing Cheri to his family.

"What kind are you planting?" Tony asked, still smiling.

"Nantes Coreless," answered Geoff. Bright orange, juicy, and sweet, they were his favorite. Maybe the family moving in here next would like them, too.

Barbara walked in and said, "What are *you* doing up? It's not even noon."

"I'm usually up," Geoff said.

"Only when you work early," argued Barbara. "And you're not at work."

"Doing more than you." Geoff sealed the container of seed. He rolled the germination strip into a loose coil, like a floppy cinnamon roll, and tucked it into a starter dish. The opaque container would provide a moist, dark environment until the seeds sprouted and the strip could be moved into the garden. Geoff poured a small amount of water into the dish. The strip swelled as it absorbed the liquid.

"Done?" asked Tony.

"Yeah." Geoff handed the container to his father and turned back to Barbara. "What are you doing today?"

"Not much," she replied. "Why?"

"Just wondering. You home this evening?" He hoped so. It would be one less thing for him to worry about.

"We're going to the temperate park. Me and Nadine and a couple of others."

Geoff grunted. He wouldn't sway her from those plans very easily. And if he tried, how could he explain? She wasn't likely to sit at home alone without a really good reason. If he asked her to, everyone would wonder what he was up to. They might even keep him here and make him late.

The time 1630 arrived before Geoff came up with a good way to keep his sister from going out. He said good-bye and left.

The transit car, as usual, rolled through the residential area with only a few passengers. Slouched down in his seat, his mind churning with nervousness about the competition and excitement at the thought of being free of Chin and Lui, Geoff ignored the people boarding.

Geoff's introspection ended when a skinny, rat-faced man sprawled on the seat in front of him.

The man sat sideways, left foot on the floor, right leg extended along the seat. His rumpled clothing emanated an unpleasant odor. He propped his right elbow on the back of his seat and noisily crunched a yellow apple. A spray of saliva and apple juice spattered Geoff. Rat Face's hard, dark brown eyes met Geoff's, held them with their urgent expression.

"Jenn sent me," the man said, barely intelligibly through his mouthful of fruit. "You okay?"

"Yeah." Geoff looked at the man long enough to see he believed that answer and then glanced away. They ignored each other for the remaining five minutes of Geoff's ride to the recreation center by his school.

He went to the gym and tried to loosen up, prepare for the upcoming competition. He now knew that was as much mental as physical. He hoped he could hold on to the anger against Chin and Lui that he had used so effectively yesterday. They had acted like Geoff had only done what was expected of him, but he knew they'd been pleased at the quality of his performance. And if they were pleased, Barbara was safe. He had to do it again.

As ordered, Geoff went to the private recreation club at 1730. Preparation went the same as the previous day, with a warm-up and practice of the dance. Then the makeup was used to turn Geoff into Robin. Geoff winced as Lui slapped the tape across his chest. His skin was tender from having the tape ripped off twice the day before.

"You should put a little lotion on first," Lui said. "That way it'd only really stick to the outside of your shoulders."

Geoff nodded.

"We're in solid third place," said Chin. "If we put on a good show tonight, we'll crowd the guys in second. That'll set us up for a win in April."

Geoff nodded again. Any other response he could think of would get him or Barbara a beating. Did Chin really think he would meekly submit to this humiliation and grueling schedule again without trying to get out of it? Or did that wily bastard have something else up his sleeve?

An hour before their scheduled performance time, Geoff and his extortionists arrived at the heavy deck's theater. He expected it to be quieter, less crowded, because only the top fifteen duos, the ones who would win cash, danced in the final. The hallways and dressing rooms were just as crowded as they had been on Friday. From overheard bits of conversation, Geoff quickly surmised that was because finals for several different classes and levels of dance were being held.

Chin selected the third of the four change rooms. From the corner where Lui performed his makeup magic, Geoff saw the room was laid out the same as yesterday's change room. The men inside it, for the most part, wore more subdued costumes. Many were a single color or followed a subtle pattern like Geoff and Chin's dark blue with silver overcast.

"Finals are usually traditional or classic," Lui said as he spread silver paint on Geoff's face. "Hold still."

Geoff remained motionless while Lui drew the navy stars and applied mascara and eyeliner. He did not look at or try to answer when other dancers came over to say hello.

"Quit trying to mess with the kid," growled Lui.

"Who's messing?" asked a stocky man in a scarlet Simba suit. He reached over Lui's shoulder and ruffled Geoff's dark wig.

As Geoff knocked the unwelcome hand away, Lui swung an elbow back, hitting the man in the stomach and folding him over with a gasp.

"You his mommy?" asked another onlooker.

Lui snorted.

Chin, in costume but with his face not made up yet, pushed his way to the corner and said, "I am." He shoved the others away from Lui and Geoff. "Quit trying to distract my partner."

"If he's old enough to be here, he's old enough to speak for himself," said the stocky man in scarlet. "What'd ya say, kid?"

"Blast off," answered Geoff.

The group around them laughed.

"You been told," chuckled one man.

"Next time, try recruiting *after* the show," said another.

His words caught Geoff's attention. Recruiting? As in getting Geoff to change partners?

"Don't even think about dancing with anyone else," Lui breathed as he touched up the dark star around Geoff's right eye. "You're ours." In a normal tone, he added, "Don't talk. I've got to do your pretty little mouth."

Jaw clenched, Geoff silently endured the application of the remainder of his makeup. In the time it took Lui to finish that, Chin completed his own split-face makeup.

The rest of the time before going backstage was again spent doing stretching routines in the rehearsal hall. Geoff felt nervous and shaky. He tried to capture the anger that had worked so well for him the previous day, but it kept getting overwhelmed by the emotional atmosphere surrounding the performers.

He followed Chin backstage, terrified he would forget the choreography or lose his balance and fall out of the lift or do any number of other mistakes to ruin the show. Panic flipped Geoff's stomach over. He looked for the vomit bags he had seen yesterday.

"Forget it." Chin grabbed Geoff's shoulder and slapped his face.

Geoff shook his head and looked up. Chin's sliver contacts hid whatever expression his dark eyes had.

"Breathe," ordered Chin. "You are going to do this…and do it right. You need some incentive?" He caught Lui's left arm and held his wrist phone in front of Geoff's face.

Geoff shook his head. The last thing he needed was a picture of Barbara and her friends being watched as they innocently enjoyed a walk in the park. He pushed Lui's arm aside and stared down at his navy-covered boot tops.

"Give me those," Lui said, pointing at Chin's eyes.

The taller man nodded and removed his contacts. He caught Geoff's head between his hands and forced him to look up.

"You're messing with my outfit," Chin said. "Make it worth it." Chin seemed to have no trouble seeing through Geoff's silver contacts. His black eyes burned into Geoff's soul.

Geoff nodded, his movement restricted by Chin's hold.

"Okay." Chin released Geoff and led the way to the rear of stage right.

Chin stood with one hand on Geoff's shoulder and watched the performers onstage.

Geoff stared at a bright pink spot, shiny like nail polish, at shoulder level on the wall. He thought about the rat-faced man on the transit and Detective Jenn, how the policeman's huge hands had dwarfed the sandwiches and juice he usually carried and how his physical strength seemed matched by his sharp mind and empathic kindness. Geoff's thoughts moved on to his sister dancing with her friends in the half gravity of their apartment and making fun out of baking. They were so different from Cheri. He wanted to keep it that way. The memory of Chin's horrid little movie showing an assault on Barbara replayed in Geoff's mind. He was not going to allow that to happen.

"We're next," said Chin.

Geoff looked around, realizing again how the noise and emotion and energy of the crowd surged at the stage like a palpable wave. Out there, under the lights, the fourth-place team was beginning their performance. They looked good, well matched, skillful, and smooth.

"Put your contacts in," Geoff said to Chin. He would give Chin the best dance he'd ever had, and then—Geoff smiled a little at this thought—he would call Detective Denis Jenn and give Chin his just desserts.

Chin retrieved his contact lenses from Lui.

Geoff remained in the wings, one hand clenched around the edge of the velvet curtain. He breathed deeply, trying to make himself more angry than scared. The crowd's raucous response to everything the dancers did terrified him.

"Don't hyperventilate," ordered Chin. He grinned and stretched out his arms, as if drawing energy from the thousands of screaming spectators.

Too soon, it seemed to Geoff, the duo on stage took their final bow. The heavy beat of the music Chin had chosen for the traditional dance filled the theater.

Arms around each other, Chin and Geoff stepped into the brilliant lights onstage. They took their starting position, too close together to stand without holding on to each other.

To Geoff, staring up at Chin's sliver eyes, the wait for the preliminary music to finish seemed endless. What was Lui doing? There. Finally. A break in the music.

"Ready?" Chin whispered.

"Yeah." Geoff breathed back.

Their music began. Chin counted without moving his lips. They swayed together.

As he had learned to do during rehearsals, Geoff mentally blocked most of the crowd's noise. His perceptions focused only on the music and Chin. Count to four, turn, slide one hand down Chin's muscular back, don't forget to spread the fingers of the other hand, break eye contact just long enough to turn, brush shoulders.

In that curious limbo where time did not run properly, Geoff repeated the dance he had done hundreds of times before. He flopped backward across Chin's shoulders, barely heard the collective gasp of the audience, slid gently to his feet, swung one boot up to the taller man's shoulder, and turned doing vertical splits. Geoff lowered his head against Chin's chest in their final pose, wishing, as always, he could drop it forward to relieve the neck kink the continuous looking up always gave him.

The music ended. Noise crashed against Geoff's senses. Applause, cheers, shouts, and whistles assaulted his ears and drenched his body in a tsunami of sound. Geoff staggered.

Chin held Geoff up and kept an arm around his shoulders to guide him the three steps to the front edge of the stage.

Geoff bowed by rote, because they had practiced it over and over. He was too stunned by the crowd to do anything of his own volition.

Laughing in triumph, Chin guided Geoff out of the spotlights and through the curtained wings of stage left.

"What d'you think they'll do with that?" Chin asked Lui.

"They'll mark you low," replied the fat man. As he walked with Chin and Geoff to a small spectator box beside the stage, he raised his voice to be heard over the crowd. "Because it's not likely either of the other teams will top that."

Chin turned Geoff to face the judges, a bank of cameras, and a small holoview. It showed the three of them in the box plus their standing in the competition. Each dance was scored out of fifty, and the two were added together for the overall result.

The judges' scores for the just-finished performance appeared. The numbers were high enough to place them ahead of everyone else who had already performed. They were assured of nothing lower than third place, yet there was ample room for the two remaining teams to score higher even if they did not present perfect shows.

The spectators reacted to the scores with boos and jeers. Chants of "Robin" and "Chin" filled the theater. Chin smiled and waved before he went to the backstage waiting area.

"There's going to be a riot," one of the fourth-place dancers said. "You should have shown up for qualifications. That way, they'd give you first place now."

"We'll get it in April," Lui said. He turned to the holoview to watch the second-ranked duo dance.

Many of the spectators continued to chant and boo the judges. Chin laughed.

Geoff backed out of the cluster of people staring at the holoview and leaned against the wall. He wasn't interested in how the competition ended. He wanted to go home.

A dancer wearing tawny yellow, with matching face paint and wig, left the group and walked over to Geoff.

"So how'd you hook up with Chin?" he asked. "You one of his students?"

Geoff folded his arms on his chest and asked, "What's it to you?"

A second man, this one dressed in matte black, came over and said, "Expect a few offers. Kid who can put on a show like you can write his own contract."

"Expect some other offers, too," said the man in yellow. "A few of these guys might want to go out with you."

Geoff pushed himself off the wall, shoved his way between his questioners, and left the room. He thought he remembered the way back to the change room. If he got lost, he'd follow one of the other dancers. There were always some going back and forth.

He did not get lost, but when he turned into the main corridor leading to the dressing rooms, he stopped and looked around to make sure he was in the right place. The hall was filled with people. None of them were dressed for the stage or carried the ubiquitous bag with boots, makeup, and costume.

"Robin!" someone yelled. The throng of people surged toward Geoff.

He stepped back, but before he could turn and run, they surrounded him. What felt like a dozen hands grabbed him and lifted him to the shoulders of two burly men. As they began parading along, Geoff flipped himself off. He landed on his feet behind them.

Geoff did not have a chance to even establish his balance before he was caught in a bear hug that crushed his silver-painted face against a broad chest. As he squirmed to free himself, the crowd mobbed him. Some patted his back and shoulders. Others squeezed his arms and legs and groped his genitals.

Chapter 36

Geoff jabbed his thumbs into his captor's armpits. As the bear hug loosened, Geoff pushed himself free. In a panicked frenzy of headbutts, elbows, punches, and stomps, he forced himself to the edge of the mob. It did not improve his situation. There was not even a doorway to try to brace himself in.

"Come with us, kid," said a woman. She reached for Geoff's arm. "We're protesting what those blind judges did to you."

Geoff eluded her hand and said, "New dancers never get higher than third." Even Chin and Lui accepted that as a fact of life.

His simple statement generated a growl of anger from the moving stream of people. Cries of "We'll change that!" and "Fair scoring!" counterpointed a rising chant of "Robin. Robin."

Captured by the rampaging spectators, Geoff fought to free himself again. It was hopeless. As soon as he knocked one person's hold loose, another grabbed him. He was quickly pulled off his feet. Lifted up and carried with the throng, his world shrank to arms and torsos, boozy breath, and gusts of recreational drugs. Between the people who wanted to carry him above their heads and the ones who wanted to feel him up, he was quickly battered. Geoff's punches were losing strength when the impetus of the mob slowed.

"Let him go," ordered Lui. His trainer badge prominently displayed on his massive chest, hands on his hips, he blocked more than half the corridor. Beside him, Chin barred the rest. As people hesitated in their charge, a muscular arm grabbed Geoff and squeezed his head against a heaving torso.

Chin and Lui glared at the people holding Geoff. Most released him. The man with a headlock on Geoff and the woman latched onto his right arm did not.

"We're celebrating," said the man. "He's with us."

"Blast off," said Chin. He stepped forward with Lui. Chin put his hands on Geoff's waist. He lifted him up and away as Lui slammed his fist into the man's face.

Lui turned toward the woman still holding Geoff's arm. She let go.

Chin carried Geoff into a narrow side hall. Lui planted himself in the end of it, blocking Chin and Geoff from sight of the mob. No one challenged him.

The horde moved on. With no knowledge of Geoff's presence, the people from farther back in the crowd paid no attention to the fat man in the intersecting hall.

When Chin set Geoff on his feet, Geoff swayed and collapsed. Relief and reaction made him shake in quivering spasms. He trembled from his boots to his wig. Sobs threatened to burst from his fear-swollen throat. Tears floated the glittered contacts around his eyes.

"What possessed your bitty brain to wander off without us?" asked Chin.

Determined to not let them see how shaken he felt, Geoff propped himself up against the wall and said, "I was going to change." At least his voice sounded close to normal. "You never said not to."

Geoff tried to take stock of his condition. He felt like one big bruise. There didn't seem to be any part of him untouched by the grasping, pinching mob. He wished he had some Lormal, but it was in his gym bag in Chin's office. All he had here was the bag with his boots and costume.

"Didn't think we had to," Lui growled.

"Even if those vacuum-brains hadn't got past security, you've got to stay with one of us," added Chin.

Lui glanced down the main corridor, where the rioters had thinned to a trickle of people looking more curious than angry, and said, "That's going to look real good on the evening news."

"It will." Chin smiled and added, "Let's go."

Geoff slowly rolled to his knees as he absorbed Lui's last statement. News? Would his struggle with the mob really be broadcast across the station? Or solar system? He didn't want to know. He held on to the wall as he got to his feet.

Lui waited in the center of the wide corridor. Still holding the wall for support, Geoff walked toward him with tiny, painful steps.

"Do I have to carry you out of here?" asked Chin.

"No." Geoff's slow hobble gave lie to his answer.

Chin scooped Geoff up in his arms.

"Ahhh!" At Geoff's wordless cry of pain, Chin loosened his hold. His arm still felt like a hot band against the bruises on Geoff's back. Geoff tried to roll free.

Chin tightened his grip and ordered, "Hold still."

"The media's still out here," said Lui. "Make it look good."

"This'll play better than you hobbling," Chin said. "Rest your face against my shoulder." Carrying Geoff as if he were weightless, Chin strode alongside Lui to the change room. Once inside, he dropped his arm from beneath Geoff's knees and stood him on his feet.

At the counter in the busy dressing room, Geoff was surprised to see the plastic film covering his makeup was still almost intact. A small patch on the right side of his face had been scraped off. A bite-shaped area was missing from the silver at the base of his neck just above his right collarbone. Blue teeth marks showed under his skin.

"Looks like someone wanted a chunk of you," Lui chuckled. "Situations like that, they either pick you up and parade around with you on their shoulders, or they rape you. Hold still." He removed Geoff's wig and sprayed his makeup.

Geoff had on Robin's freckled face before he changed out of his dance costume. When he pulled his arms free of the dark blue Simba suit and pushed it down to his waist, Lui whistled.

"They really had a fight over you," he said. Bruises, some clearly shaped like handprints, covered Geoff's arms and torso.

"You should get some bruise patches from the doctor here," said the man changing beside Geoff.

Geoff shook his head and put his shirt on.

"He'll see our doc," Chin said, "as soon as he gets his pants on."

Feeling as if everyone in the room was watching, Geoff quickly pulled his jeans over his tights and slipped his shoes on. Chin and Lui escorted Geoff out of the dressing room. They left walking three abreast.

"That was stupid," Chin said. "You're worth too much to risk yourself like that." The words were typical Chin, but his tone was almost friendly. He punched Lui's shoulder and added, "That riot in the hall's playing on every news service. We'll get a thousand times the exposure from it."

Geoff hoped Chin's good mood would keep him from delivering a beating for an impertinent question.

He asked, "If I'm so valuable, why couldn't I just finish the show and get out of here?"

"Thinks he can get cocky," said Chin. He ruffled Geoff's red wig and then squeezed his head in an armlock. "You're lucky there are cameras all over, or I'd bruise your butt."

"It probably already is," Lui laughed. "Doc meeting us here?" When Chin nodded, Lui added, "I'll hand him over, and we can party."

"Okay." Chin released Geoff.

Unbalanced, he staggered into Lui.

Lui caught Geoff by the shoulders. Geoff gasped in pain. The fat man released his hold and let Geoff lean against his chest until he regained his footing.

"Hmmm," said Chin. "Good thing you've got the week off."

Lui and Chin waved to a media crew in the foyer, and then Chin stopped to speak with them as Lui hustled Geoff away. They met the Mad Medic at the exit.

The Mad Medic walked with Geoff to the transit. It had the most uncomfortable seats Geoff had ever forced himself to sit on. He shifted restlessly in an attempt to ease his aches. When they finally reached the private recreation club, Geoff limped off the car with relief.

Once in Chin's office the Mad Medic helped Geoff remove Robin's face and then said, "Take your shirt off. Let's have a look."

As the doctor opened his bag, Geoff undid his shirt. He winced as he shrugged it off his shoulders.

"You really got hammered," said the Mad Medic. "Take some Blisso? Lormal?"

Geoff shook his head.

"You want pills or a patch?"

"Patch," answered Geoff. Even the inside of his stomach hurt. If he ate anything, he would probably throw up.

"Sit down," the doc ordered.

Geoff dubiously eyed the hard chair the Mad Medic pointed to. He wasn't sure he *could* sit on that.

"What's the matter?" asked Doc. "Your ass hurt?"

Geoff nodded. Everything hurt.

"Well, take all your clothes off." The doctor took two squares of pain reliever from his bag on the other chair as Geoff removed his shoes and jeans. "Don't know if you've got an unbruised spot to put these. Get those tights off."

Geoff tried to remove the tights without sitting or falling down. He got them down to his lower thighs and then had to hang on to the chair while he tried with one hand to pull the stretchy material below his knees.

Doc opened a wall panel and removed a neatly folded navy towel from a hidden cupboard.

"Wrap up in this," he said, shaking it out and throwing it around Geoff.

It was a huge bath sheet, thick and soft and warm. It immediately made Geoff feel better. He clutched it around himself like a blanket, ignoring the tangle around his lower legs.

"Oh, hell," the Mad Medic said. "Pick up your feet." He knelt down and pulled Geoff's tights off. Then he spread a second large towel on the carpeted part of the floor.

"Lie down," he ordered, pointing to it.

Geoff lay on his stomach. He could feel the individual fibers of the material beneath his face, a thin cushion of comfort on top of the soft carpet.

"You're spacy," said the doctor. He pulled at the towel Geoff wore, rearranging it into a covering blanket. He stuck the two pain relief patches on the backs of Geoff's knees. Then, starting at the top of Geoff's head, he examined him by touch, sight, and scanner.

"The skin's scraped here," he said when he got to the bite on Geoff's neck. "Not really broken, but I'm going to disinfect it and rub on the regeneration gel. If it gets red or swollen, let me know right away. The human mouth carries some nasty germs."

He slowly worked his way down Geoff's arms and back, gently applying ointment and covering it with spray-on bandages. The skinlike material dried instantly, and he replaced the towel over each spot before he bared a new portion of skin. When he bunched aside the center of the towel to expose Geoff's right hip and buttock, he whistled.

"No wonder you can't sit," he said. "You've got a bite here the size of my palm. There must have been a gorilla in that mob." He smeared on bruise treatment gel.

Geoff did not move.

"You pass out?"

"No," Geoff mumbled. He was awake, but everything seemed distant and foggy.

"Am I gonna have to find someone to walk you home?"

"No." Geoff roused himself, lifted his head to look at the Mad Medic. "I'm okay."

"I see you're really hyped on the thrill of victory," the man chuckled. "It'll take a week for Chin to unwind."

Geoff closed his eyes. He didn't want to think about Chin. He was going to call Detective Jenn and never have to see Chin again.

As it turned out, Geoff did not have to call the police officer. Fifteen minutes later, Detective Jenn boarded the elevator car Geoff was taking up to his residential deck. From his corner at the back of the car, Geoff watched the large officer make his apparently inebriated way past the dozen other passengers to the empty seat in front of Geoff. He sat sideways like the rat-faced undercover policeman had. Jenn leaned his head back against the wall of the car and glanced at Geoff.

"You okay?" he whispered.

"Yeah," Geoff replied.

"Got some bruise patches?"

"Yeah," Geoff said again.

"You've done enough," Jenn said. "Almost too much. We got a line on that shipment. We'll have the protection team at your home tomorrow morning at nine."

Geoff breathed deeply. This was it. How was he going to have his family up and ready to leave at nine on a Sunday? On second thought, that was the perfect time. They would all be home, probably having breakfast. Had the cops planned on that? He couldn't ask here.

"After that mob," Jenn said, "we'll slap them with child endangerment, too." Detective Jenn exited at the next stop.

Geoff rode the rest of the way in silence, wondering how to convince his parents to abandon their work and friends, feeling his fear grow as his weight decreased. He fretted over the question he had refused to seriously think about before now. What if his family refused to go into witness protection?

With that turmoil in his mind, Geoff could not face his parents. He showered to remove the Mad Medic's treatments. If Detective

Jenn wanted to charge Chin and Lui with child endangerment, Geoff would save his bruises for evidence.

He hid in his room, stuck on a fresh Blisso patch, and went to bed. Although Geoff did not think he would sleep, the stress of the last two days and the physical damage he had sustained that evening combined to push him toward unconsciousness as soon as he lay down. He did not stir when his father knocked and entered his room.

"I guess he was tired," Tony said to Fallah. She watched as Tony bent over the roll of blankets cocooning Geoff. Only his dark curls were visible. His slow breathing was the only sound. Tony and Fallah left Geoff's room and closed the door.

"It's not even twenty-three on a Saturday night," Fallah said. "I'm afraid we shouldn't have let him do all that extra work."

"He's finished now," said Tony. "And he's got a week off before he goes back to his usual couple of shifts a week. If you're worried, we can talk to him in the morning."

Chapter 37

Sunday morning, Geoff's alarm roused him at 0845. He lay in bed for a while, wishing he could stop time. But the numbers on his clock kept changing, and the pain from his bruises grew worse, so he got up.

What do you wear to tell your family you're turning their lives upside down?

Something with a high collar and long sleeves to hide the bruises.

Seven minutes before 0900, Geoff left his room.

He sat at the table across from Tony and Fallah and asked, "Where's Barbie?" What if she had spent the night at a friend's place and wasn't home?

"Right behind you, sleepy," said Barbara. "Why?"

"I need to talk," Geoff said. He tried to think what to say next. His mind remained blank.

Barbara took her chair at the table. Everyone stared at Geoff.

"Well?" asked Barbara.

Geoff extended his left arm over the table and pushed his sleeve up to reveal the tattoo on the inside of his forearm.

"This isn't just a picture of a snaky dragon," he said, hoping everyone would focus on the picture instead of the blue marks covering his arm. "It's a Lung dragon, a gang symbol."

Tony's coffee cup thumped onto the table. Fallah dropped her fork onto her plate. It clattered beside her half-eaten pancake.

"What?" cried Barbara. "Are you—"

"I joined them three years ago, just before I turned fourteen," Geoff said without looking up. He pulled his sleeve back down. That should distract them from asking about bruises. He was not letting them know about the Simba.

"Why?" asked Fallah. She turned to Tony.

To Geoff, the look they exchanged seemed more upset and guilty than angry.

"Why did you do that?" Tony asked.

"Where did we go wrong?" wondered Fallah.

"You didn't," said Barbara. "He's just—"

"Stop!" Geoff held one hand out, palm flattened toward his sister.

"It's not your fault," he said to his parents. "I didn't just decide to join a gang. They search out kids with skills they want and recruit them. They don't give up."

"Why are you telling us now?" asked Tony.

"A while ago, I learned something really bad about them. I want to testify in court, put at least a couple of the family guys in jail."

Geoff looked around the table. His family looked stunned. Even Barbara stayed quiet.

"I can't do that unless we all go into witness protection," Geoff continued. "It means moving and getting new names, and I don't know what else." He paused and then added, "I need to know if you'd do that."

Tony and Fallah looked at each other again.

Geoff held his breath. Would they go for it? Or would he be Chin's slave forever?

Barbara asked, "Leave all our friends and everything?"

Geoff bit his lower lip and nodded.

"No! You're not ruining my life because you got in trouble."

"What's so important that we should do that?" asked Tony. "Let someone else do it."

"No one else will," replied Geoff. "No one else *can*."

"You're not that important," said Barbara. "I bet there's all kinds of people who can."

"They won't," Geoff repeated.

Barbara stood up and yelled, "You're so selfish! All you ever think about is yourself."

"Why witness protection?" Fallah asked. "For all of us?"

Geoff nodded. He *had* to convince them.

"Remember all those dead people in the shipment at the transfer station? I know who did that. They're going to try again."

Silence filled the kitchen for one long minute.

"Then we have to do it," said Tony.

Geoff breathed deeply. He was going to get free of Chin.

"I'm not going," Barbara declared.

The doorbell rang.

"Don't answer that. We're busy," said Fallah. "When would this happen? How?"

"Now," Geoff said. "That should be the cops."

He checked the monitor. He had to be certain Chin hadn't heard what Geoff planned and sent someone to take care of him and his family. Detective Jenn waited in the hall.

"I hate you forever." Tears streamed down Barbara's face. "You're not my brother anymore."

Biting his lip, Geoff opened the door.

Geoff's story continues in *c-Surfer*.
Watch for it in the near future.

c-Surfer

Chapter One

Private Cory Reddick bolted out of the elevator and down the station corridor.

"ID," the security corporal guarding the door to Room 1132 said as Cory ran up to her.

He held out his left forearm so her scanner could read his implant.

"Retina, too." She lifted her screen for him to look into the lenses embedded in its side.

He tried to stop panting so the unit could focus.

When it beeped, the corporal said, "Go in. You're late."

Cory took a deep breath and stepped through the door at the front of an amphitheater-style lecture hall.

A colonel rose from the stool beside the lectern console and said, "You must be Private Reddick."

"Yes, sir." Cory froze at attention.

"Sit." The colonel pointed to the tiered rows of seats.

"Sir?" Cory looked at the diagnostic scanner clutched in his left hand and back at the senior officer. He was always a little spacey after the nightmares returned, but that order would have made no sense even if he was mentally alert.

"You are not here to fix anything. Take a seat."

"Yes, sir." The tools in Cory's belt pouch clinked as he went up the aisle. He glanced at the crowd, trying to pick out anyone who might have known him by his old name. If anyone here could recognize him as Geoff Anders, he was running out faster than he had come in.

Appendix

The Simba

Traditionally performed by two men, the Simba is a pattern of swaying, steps, and turns repeated through seven rounds. The first sequence is performed to a moderate beat. The speed increases in the second, third, and fourth sequences, and then it slows for the fifth, sixth, and seventh rounds with the last one at the same tempo as the first.

Each round begins with the two dancers standing face-to-face. They sway sideways twice, then stalk in a small circle as if following each other. Next they shift to stand one in front of the other, facing in the same direction, as they sway sideways again. Then they separate, turn, and step aside to face each other while not being directly in line. Two steps forward and they brush shoulders as they pass each other, pivot in opposite directions to stand side-by-side. Then they sway sideways as they take several steps forward, turn twice, and stop face-to-face.

CPSIA information can be obtained at www.ICGtesting.com
Printed in the USA
LVOW082148181012

303486LV00001B/11/P